A DRAGON'S LEGACY

Book Three in the Tsar's Dragons series

The Tsar's Dragons
Princes and Peasants

CATRIN COLLIER

When one has nothing left . . . but memories, one guards and dusts them with especial care.

Saki (H. H. Munro)
The Wolves of Cernogratz

DEDICATION

For the men in my life, John and Ralph

I couldn't function without you

Press article
Nikita and Mrs Khrushchev's ten-day state visit to Britain

April 1956
*Premier and Mrs Khrushchev were guests of honour at a
state banquet in Buckingham Palace yesterday. During the
course of the evening Mr Khrushchev questioned The
Duke of Edinburgh and the Prime Minister, Sir Anthony
Eden as to the history of Welshman, John Hughes, who
founded the town of Hughesovka in the Ukraine where Mr
Khrushchev was born, which has since been renamed
Donetsk.*
*Neither the Duke nor the Prime Minister had heard of
John Hughes. Therefore, they could give Mr Khrushchev
no information regarding the man, or even confirm his
existence.*

PROLOGUE

*Owen Parry's ironworkers' cottage, Broadway, Treforest.
Pontypridd 1956*

*Every morning I wake surprised to find myself still on this
earth. Is it because I have not yet completed the tasks
appointed to me by longevity - or fate? There are so many
papers, letters and photographs to archive, so many years
to record, years that chronicle a history not just of a
people but a town. Or is it two towns?*

*First Hughesovka, the town John Hughes named for
himself and his family. The Russians christened Hughes
"The Iron Tsar", for bringing industry and railways to
their motherland and catapulting it into the modern age.
Then in 1924, in the aftermath of the bloodiest war in
history and the revolution it spawned in Russia, Hughes's
town on the steppe that had evolved into a city was
renamed Stalino. Some say it was for the steel it produced,
not the leader of the state. But either way it will never be
Stalino, not to me. It will always be Hughesovka. My
Hughesovka.*

*Now, when the only new experience that awaits me is
death, I can truthfully say I've had a good life. A long one,
richer in every way than the one of poverty and bondage to
iron and coal I was born into in Pontypridd. I've seen and
done things and travelled to places beyond most people's
imagination. I've lived like royalty in a St Petersburg
Palace and cowered, a hunted animal, in a burrow in the
ground, without a kopek or crust to my name. I've broken
more commandments than I care to think about, including
"Thou shalt not kill". But I feel no remorse. Some men are
evil and deserve death. If that makes me a poor Christian
then so be it.*

—

Perhaps that is why I've lived so long. Ninety-nine years on this earth and still God doesn't want me in his heaven. Possibly He's asked Satan to prepare a place for me but the Devil is also reluctant to extend an invitation. I sense my thoughts meandering into philosophy: the hobby of the ancients, the bane of the young. I'm not so decrepit that I can't recall my irritation when I was on the receiving end of lectures from my elders. I believed I knew everything then, just as my great-grandchildren do now. They sit beside my bed with grave unlined faces, solemn-eyed in the face of my impending death, sure of their knowledge and themselves. They try to fool me, and themselves, that I have a future. That my life isn't coming to an end.

It is, but not yet, not while I can still dream of the past, my last and most precious possession. I've often wondered if memories and emotions, like disease, can be transmitted from one person to another. If so, that would explain why I've always felt so acutely the pleasures and pain of those I've loved.

I pick out his voice above the others in the garden. The language is different, but not the voice. It is his great grandfather's. And while he speaks, my beloved lives again . . .

*I rest my notebook on the frame my great-grandson made so I can work without leaving my bed. There are so many papers, so much history to be preserved for the archives. As I sift through the brittle letters, diaries, maps, plans, age tarnished albums and photographs – Glyn's photographs - scents rise from the long dead flowers pressed between their pages and the perfume of old summers fill the air. They dissolve the mists that shroud the years, evoking memories of **my** Russia more vivid and redolent than those conjured by mere words.*

Where to begin?

I recall Glyn Edwards's photographs of the bare steppe, taken on the site of what was to become John Hughes's city before a single brick of the ironworks had been laid. Before John Hughes imported the Welsh metalworkers and colliers and long before the gamblers and adventurers flocked to colonise the Iron Master's new town. Men and women who saw the possibility of making their own fortunes in the enterprise of Mr Hughes's New Russia Company.

They came, first in their hundreds, then thousands. Salesmen, shopkeepers, hoteliers, priests, whores and whoremongers, murderers, thieves, the moral and downright criminal of every nationality, all crowded into a few square miles. Forced to live next to, if not to respect, their neighbours. Drawn by John Hughes's vision of an industrial town that promised freedom, equality and wealth for all those who had the strength to work and the courage to join him, no matter what their class, creed or lineage.

John Hughes had the vision but he couldn't have realised it alone. It was Glyn Edwards who recruited the people who built the town. I look at Glyn's photographs mounted in albums, and see beyond the images to the first settlers as they were in life.

Glyn, heavily built, over six and a half feet in his stockings, as handsome, swarthy, black haired and eyed as a gypsy. My brother, Richard Parry, with the dark curly hair and pale blue eyes of the Irish; Russian aristocrat Alexei with blond hair and mischievous indigo eyes that belied his angelic features; Nathan Kharber and his sister Ruth, slight, dark with piercing glances sharp enough to penetrate the soul; and myself, Anna Parry, at twelve years old, the youngest, least significant emigrant, taken to Russia as a charity case because I was the subject of salacious gossip in Merthyr.

The women who became closer to me than sisters; Sarah Edwards, healer, mentor, friend, Cossack Praskovia who could have modelled for Titian with her voluptuous figure, red hair and emerald eyes and Sonya who saved us all in the end with her self-sacrificing unconditional love.

Every one of us over-shadowed by John Hughes, who strode the steppe with the air of a medieval king born to govern, command and above all build . . .

Photographs - images that capture a time and place. Like words on paper they can communicate thoughts, even emotion, but to relive the birth of Hughesovka, all I have to do is close my eyes.

We left Wales in the summer of 1869, reaching the almost empty steppe that would become Hughesovka after winter and its attendant snow had arrived. By the summer of 1871 John Hughes's dream was on the way to becoming reality. The ironworks existed, although they were not yet capable of production. But both John Hughes and Glyn Edwards's collieries had begun to produce a steady output of top quality anthracite from their respective pits. Alexei Beletsky went into partnership with my brother Richard and opened the first of many Beletsky and Parry collieries. Alexei celebrated by marrying his childhood sweetheart, Ruth Kharber in the face of fierce opposition from the Christian community and her Jewish family. Alexei's cousin Sonya, attracted the attention of a wealthy Prince, Roman Nadolny and married him. Ignoring the eleven-year age difference between them, thirty-one-year old widow Sarah Edwards married my twenty-year old brother Richard, and I took her place for a few weeks as Matron of the hospital at the tender age of fifteen. Unaware of Richard's marriage to Sarah, Richard's childhood sweetheart, Alice Perkins decided to follow him to Hughesovka with Glyn's wife Betty who had no idea that her husband's housekeeper Praskovia had taken possession of Glyn's bed and heart.

—

I shuffle Glyn's photographs back into the file marked "1870 to 1875". A newspaper clipping falls out, penned by a Moscow journalist who visited Hughesovka during those years . . .

"Hughesovka – all the dregs of mining industry life gather here. Everything dark, evil and criminal – thieves, hooligans, all such, are drawn to this place. You cannot go out at night without risking violent death."

1871 – 1889 My lonely years. Richard was a kind and loving brother, but much as I adored him and his wife Sarah I felt I'd lost something of his loyalty towards me when he married her. Glyn and his Cossack mistress, Praskovia, Alexei and Ruth: even my younger brothers Morgan and Owen, they were thoughtful and caring, but they had one another, while I had no one to love who was solely mine. No one who did not love another more.

Resigned to spinsterhood, I threw myself into my work at the hospital, arriving before my shifts began and remaining until the shift that replaced mine ended. When I wasn't caring for my patients I studied every textbook and copy of "The Lancet" that fell into my hands. I volunteered to help Dr Kharber in surgery whenever he called for assistance because it was preferable to dealing with the solitude that gnawed at me, even - or perhaps especially - when I found myself in a room full of people.

For the first few months after her marriage to Richard, Sarah visited the hospital every day, although as her pregnancy advanced, she rarely remained for a full shift. Gradually, without either of us noticing how or when it happened, I began to assume responsibility for more and more of her matron's duties, the nurses' training, the ordering of medicines and supplies, and the drawing up of staff rotas.

Within a few years the town outgrew the hospital's facilities. John Hughes's solution to the problem was to extend the buildings and hire more doctors, nurses and ward maids. As a result of Sarah's support and mentoring in 1882 at the age of twenty-five I was officially appointed matron.

I was honoured when Sarah and Richard asked me to stand godmother to my nephew Edward, who became "Ted" because that was his first word. I also stood godmother to Glyn and Praskovia's son Pavlo, and Alexei and Ruth's twin daughters, Olga and Catherine, named for Alexei's mother and grandmother, although Catherine was soon shortened to Kitty.

The years brought more babies. Another boy for Glyn and Praskovia, "Tom" and Sarah and Richard's daughter," Maryanna".

The one person who understood that it was possible to feel acutely lonely surrounded by people was Alexei Beletsky's grandmother, Catherine Ignatova who brought up her granddaughter, Kira during those years. I grew to admire, respect and ultimately love her. Catherine saw through the façade of competence I cultivated in the hope of fooling the world. She knew my insecurities and understood how terrified I was of making mistakes, both in my work and socially. She taught me that all men and women, even those with titles, really are equal, and all that really matters is how we live our lives between birth and death and the kindness we show one another.

She sent me invitations to spend my days off at her home with her and Kira, phrasing them so it appeared as though I was the one bestowing the favour in accepting. She sought me out at the parties and social events that became more frequent as the works grew in staff, capacity and output and Mr Hughes and his managers found time for leisure.

Work interspersed with summer carriage rides and picnics on the steppe, boating on the river and reservoir, winter hunting expeditions in horse-drawn sleighs, parties in Catherine Ignatova's ballroom, or watching theatrical productions in the theatre John Hughes built in the New Russia Headquarters in the company of the same small circle of friends made for pleasant, if repetitive memories.

When I assumed the post of matron, Catherine invited me to live with her and Kira permanently, persuading me to accept for "Kira's sake" as a young girl needed the guidance of a modern career minded young woman to counteract that of an aged grandmother.

Fond as I was of Richard and his family, and happy as I had been living with them, I was glad to accept Catherine's invitation. More than flattered to be asked, I felt that I was moving into my own small family because it didn't seem to matter that I wasn't related to Catherine and Kira by blood. Twelve years younger than me, Kira took the place of the sisters I had lost to cholera, and Catherine the grandmother I had never known.

When Praskovia's brother Misha Razin's wife divorced him, he threw himself into his work and concentrated on his career. As the years passed he was promoted from captain, to major, to lieutenant colonel and eventually colonel of the regiment of Cossack soldiers that garrisoned Hughesovka. He occasionally visited his mother Yelena and brother Pyotr who both worked in Glyn's house, but avoided his sister Praskovia. There was speculation in the town as to why he'd never lived with his wife Alice, who owned a ladies' apparel shop. But no one really knows what goes on in a marriage except those directly involved. Widowed Alice, may have arrived in Hughesovka professing undying love for my brother Richard but she'd married Misha within weeks of her arrival, and when Grisha a fellow lodger in Betty's boarding house winked at her, she happily divorced Misha to walk up the aisle with Grisha a third time.

Catherine's orphaned niece Sonya and her husband Roman Nadolny wrote frequently to Catherine and all their friends in Hughesovka. A son, Andrei, was born in London in January 1873. From London, they travelled to Merthyr and Sonya sent us more letters from the Welsh iron town than any other place they visited, principally because I suspected, Roman wouldn't allow her to venture out into the Merthyr streets alone. They stayed with the Crawshays at Cyfarthfa Castle, and for the first time since I'd reached Hughesovka I wished I'd been there, so I could have told my old neighbours, like Maggie Two Suits and Jenny Swine, that I knew a family who'd received an invitation to stay in the castle.

The Nadolnys left Britain for France, Italy, Greece, and Yalta, where Sonya gave birth to a second son, Spartak in the summer of 1874. Roman built a house in Hughesovka and he, Sonya and their sons returned several times over the years for short visits so Roman could oversee his business interests in the town.

Early in 1889 John Hughes received notification that an official government delegation, led by two of the Tsar's brothers, the Grand Dukes' Sergei Alexandrovich, and Alexei Alexandrovich wished to inspect the ironworks. As Grand Duke Sergei was a Major General of the 1st Battalion **Preobrazhensky Life Guard Regiment**, the elite regiment founded by Peter the Great, and Grand Duke Alexei a General Admiral, the visit hinted that both military and naval armaments contracts might be forthcoming.

John Hughes immediately galvanised every employee of the New Russia Company from Glyn Edwards down to the lowliest water carrier and coal hewer, in the hope that at the very least the inspection of the works would stamp legitimacy on the frontier settlement and the town would finally be awarded city status.

But those closest to John Hughes, suspected the visit would attract the attention of John Hughes's enemies who were intent on destroying his life work.

It did.

They brought death, destruction and tragedy. The repercussions of that visit echoed down the years. But the one thing that could not be halted or changed was the progress of John Hughes's dream that grew more tangible and substantial with every passing day – Hughesovka itself, whatever name it bears now.

A shaft of light pierces the darkness. The door opens. My eyes remain closed but I sense him stealing in, wary of disturbing me. It's too dark for me to see his face but I don't need the light. His features are imprinted on my memory. They are those of his great grandfather, alive again. I only have to close my eyes to conjure them.

He moves to the bed, removes the photograph album from my hands and lays his fingers gently on my forehead.

His touch is soft, cool, like the whisper of the spring wind brushing over the Russian Steppe.

CHAPTER ONE

The hospital Hughesovka January 1889

'I can't stand the pain . . . '

'The pain of childbirth is a burden every woman must bear as punishment for Eve's sin in the Garden of Eden, Mrs Grisha.' The young Dutch trainee nurse's lecture inflamed Alice Grisha's temper. Her authoritative "I know better than you" sanctimonious delivery even more.

'I'm in agony and you couldn't give a kopek!'

'Of course I care . . . '

'No, you don't!' Alice gave a blood curdling scream, waved her arms and knocked over the water jug and glass on the trolley next to her bed.

Hearing voices raised in anger followed by a crash, Nurse Yulia and Matron Anna Parry ran into the delivery room. Yulia grabbed the trainee and hauled her out into the corridor. Anna called for a ward maid to clear the mess of spilled water and shards of ceramic and glass before unhooking Mrs Grisha's chart from the foot of the bed and checking it.

'It won't be much longer now, Mrs Grisha?' Anna replaced the chart, wrung a flannel in iced water and wiped Alice's forehead before reaching for her hand and holding it.

'I'm in agony . . . that stupid girl . . . ' Alice glared at the door as she gasped in pain, although Yulia had closed it behind her, '. . . she told me that women have to suffer-' she clenched her teeth as another pain spasm took hold.

Anna wrung out the cloth in iced water again and placed it on Alice Grisha's head. 'I'm sorry, Mrs Grisha, but to some degree the trainee is right. We cannot give women opiates to mitigate the pain of childbirth except in extreme cases as the drug could affect the baby.'

'The baby isn't the one who's suffering! I am!' Alice thrashed around in the bed and threw her arms in the air again.

'Please, Mrs Grisha, this hysteria isn't good for you or your child.' Anna kept her voice, soft, low but Alice wasn't in a mood to be placated.

Alice stared at Anna as she breathed out slowly through narrowed eyes. 'I know you.'

'I expect you do. I live in Hughesovka.'

'I've seen you with Glyn Edwards's mistress. The Cossack ...'

Anna closed out the tirade of invective that flowed from Alice Grisha's mouth. She was used to the curses and anger of women in labour and understood the relief they gained from venting their feelings. But she knew and respected Glyn Edwards and his mistress Praskovia who had lived happily as man and wife for twenty years. She was also aware that Glyn's legal wife Betty Edwards was Alice Grisha's closest friend.

She couldn't understand why Glyn's wife Betty hadn't given him a divorce when he'd made it clear that he would never return to her. Or why Betty kept their daughter, Harriet, from him and least of all why Betty had persisted in living Hughesovka after Glyn had begged her to return to her home town of Merthyr.

Most women in labour shouted and a few (who had the vocabulary) cursed, which was understandable given the pain they suffered but there was a streak of coarseness in Alice's language she seldom heard from a woman and she wondered if Alice's vulgarity was a result of Betty Edward's influence, or Alice's husband.

Gavril Grisha was a legend in Hughesovka. Feared by the workers because he'd set up a union that had established a stranglehold on every job in the town. Tolerated by the managers in the works and collieries because he simplified the process of hiring and firing, Gavril Grisha was a force to be reckoned with.

—

16

No man was appointed to any position in a colliery or ironworks below management level without Grisha's "blessing" and paying his "union dues". The first lesson every newly appointed manager learned was that if men Grisha disapproved of were appointed to lucrative positions, Grisha had no compunction about using his power to organise "accidents" or strikes that would disrupt production and in severe cases halt it and cause closure of the offending colliery or plant.

Anna saw Alice grimace, folded back the sheet and checked the baby's progress. 'Your baby is almost here, Mrs Grisha. Push when I tell you please.'

'You're only saying that so you won't have to give me something for the pain. I can pay for it . . . '

'Push please, Mrs Grisha,' Anna reiterated. 'That's it, just once more . . .'

Alice grunted and pushed. Anna caught the baby as it slid from the birth canal. She smiled as she looked down at the child. No matter what the circumstances or how angry the mother, she never failed to be moved by the miracle of new life entering the world.

'You have a fine son, Mrs Grisha.'

'Send a message to my husband. He'll want to see him.'

Yulia knocked and entered the cubicle. She smiled at the bundle in Anna's hands. 'Congratulations on a fine son, Mrs Grisha.'

'Thank you. I hope you told that girl . . . '

'I've spoken to her, Mrs Grisha,' Yulia broke in.

'I hope you have. Send word to my husband . . . '

'We'll tidy you up first and settle you down in a room with your baby.' Anna tied off and cut the umbilical cord, wrapped the baby in a sheet and carried him over to a basin of water.

'Shall I help you bathe, find you a clean nightgown, brush your hair and add a dab of scent first, Mrs Grisha?' Yulia asked, emulating Anna's calm. 'You'll want to look your best for him.'

17

Alice glared for a moment, considered, then acquiesced. While Yulia saw to the mother, Anna bathed the child, dressed him in a napkin and gown, and wrapped him a cotton blanket before handing him to Alice.

'Have you chosen a name for him, Mrs Grisha?' she asked

'Gavril.' Alice looked down at the child. 'For his father. Gavril Grisha. Gavril means "Worships God" and Grisha means "Watchful".'

'A very apt name as all children are God given,' Anna bundled the soiled linen together. 'I'll send a porter to fetch your husband. Congratulations Mrs Grisha.'

'I don't want anyone here to tell a soul that Gavril Grisha has a son before he sees the child for himself.'

'The staff in this hospital never discuss the patients outside of these walls, Mrs Grisha. We're far too busy to gossip.'

'Your shift ended hours ago, Matron,' Yulia reminded as the ward maid brought in a clean nightgown for Alice.

'So, it did.' Anna smiled at Yulia and the ward maid. 'I'll see you in the morning. Good night, Mrs Grisha, and son, and congratulations again. The best days in this hospital are the ones when babies are born.'

Richard and Sarah Parry's house, Hughesovka January 1889

Anna Parry took the key her brother had insisted she keep when she'd moved out of his house from her handbag, slipped it in the lock and turned it. The door opened and she stepped inside the hall. She muffled the sound by closing her hand over the lock, but Richard had heard her and was standing in the open doorway of his study.

'I wouldn't have called in this late if I hadn't seen the lamp burning in your study,' she apologised.

'Don't tell me.' He held up his hand as though to ward off her excuses. 'You had to work late – again – and on Sarah's birthday?' he reproached.

18

'I'm sorry to have missed Sarah's birthday dinner.' Anna shrugged off her nurses' cloak and hung it in the alcove that held all the family's coats and scarves. She set a package wrapped in blue crepe paper on the hall table. 'We had a glut of babies. Six today. Four boys and two girls.'

'As Sarah is well acquainted with the rigours of your vocation, I've no doubt she'll forgive you.'

'One of the babies is Alf Mahony's. His wife Tonia went into labour this afternoon and an hour later he had a fifth son. They're naming him Dafydd.'

Richard smiled. 'He'll be pleased to finally have a son with a Welsh name.'

'Boris is Welsh and Russian.'

'That's debatable but Bogdan, Anatoly and Artyom, aren't, and I've seen Alf's face when the Welsh boys call Bogdan "Boggy".'

'What's worse is the child answers to it with a smile on his face.' Anna balanced her hat on the hook that held her cloak.

'Are you hungry?'

'No, thank you, I ate in the hospital.'

'I opened a bottle of German wine. Sarah only managed half a glass before she fell asleep sitting in her chair.'

'A glass would go down nicely. I'm surprised to see you still up.' She followed him into his study. 'Last minute arrangements for the Grand Duke's visit tomorrow?'

'As if Mr Hughes would trust me with those?' Richard took a glass from the cupboard behind his desk and filled it for her. 'I've been ordering more wooden pit props from Poland. Alexei and I are extending the shaft in the "Six Bears" pit. You will take tomorrow afternoon off, so you can attend the lunch Mr Hughes has arranged for the Grand Dukes and their royal party in the hotel?'

'Barring an epidemic or catastrophe, I'll be there.'

'Right, I'll warn everyone I meet on my way to the office tomorrow, no epidemics, catastrophes, babies or broken bones allowed until further notice.' He picked up the order forms he'd been working on and closed them into a file. 'Enough for today.'

His eyes narrowed as he gave his sister an appraising look. Like him she had the black curly hair and blue eyes of their Irish mother. But there were dark shadows beneath her eyes, and she was thin, hardly surprising given the hours she worked and the meals she missed. 'You promised me when the new nurses and doctors Mr Hughes engaged for the hospital arrived, you'd cut your shifts down to one a day and five a week. That was three years ago and you're still working around the clock.'

'We're still waiting on two doctors, one Dutch, one German and four Austrian nurses. But you should be having this conversation with your wife as well as me. Do you know the staff call her Matron number two because she calls in almost every day?'

'Only for an hour or two, or so she tells me. Do you mind?'

'What if I told you that I was at loggerheads with Sarah? You'd divorce her?' she teased.

He frowned. 'You know perfectly well I could no more divorce Sarah than I could stop breathing.'

'Just as well, I love her almost as dearly as you, not least because she keeps you, Owen and Morgan in order. But Morgan and Owen are both less troublesome brothers than you were.'

'I'm loathe to admit it but they probably are. Has Morgan or Kira said anything to you about setting the date for their wedding?'

'Other than a vague "this summer" no.'

'They are happy together, aren't they?' he frowned at her.

'You do realise that you are asking a confirmed spinster who has no experience of romance that question?'

20

'Anyone can see that Morgan is very fond of Kira . . . ' Richard faltered when she burst out laughing.

'What is so funny?'

'You,' she smiled. 'For Kira's sake, I hope that Morgan is more than "very fond" of her.'

'You know what I mean,' he snapped,

'I'm not sure that I do, but if you are asking for my opinion, Morgan and Kira appear to be as besotted with one another as you and Sarah.'

'I see.'

'If you do, you see more than me. Whatever's between them, Kira doesn't talk about it. Nor do I expect her to. And to change the subject from our brother's love life, Alice Grisha gave birth today as well as Tonia Mahoney. In between cursing everyone in sight, and me and Praskovia in particular, she asked me not to tell anyone Grisha was a father until he saw the child. Which he should have done by now, so I'm not betraying her request.'

'Why Praskovia?'

'Because she knows I'm Praskovia's friend, and Betty is hers. Betty hates Praskovia and by extension presumably me.'

'I'll never understand why Betty didn't return to Merthyr when she arrived here twenty years ago and found Glyn living with Praskovia.'

'I'll never understand why Betty kept Harriet from Glyn. A father and daughter have the right to know one another.'

'They do,' he agreed.

'In case you need more details to congratulate Grisha when you next see him, Alice told me his son will be named Gavril Grisha after him. His hair is fair like Alice's at the moment, but that might change to Grisha's red.' She took the glass of wine he'd poured for her. 'Thank you.'

'You can be infuriating. Do you know that?'

'So, people tell me, but why in particular at this moment?'

21

'Are you telling me about Grisha's son because you expect me to broadcast the news.'

'That, brother, is entirely up to you.' She sipped the wine. 'Mm this is good.'

'That's my sister. Ask her a question and she'll change the subject.'

'I resent that comment.'

'Truth hurts.' He refilled his own glass.

'What about Owen?'

'What about him?' Anna curled up in the visitor's chair set in front of his desk.

'Do you think if he was sweet on a girl he'd tell me?'

'I think he's twenty-eight years old and that's his business.'

'Like you he lives for work. The metallurgical laboratory sees more of him than we do.'

'According to Kira it sees more of Morgan as well.'

'So, Kira does talk about Morgan?'

'She mentions him now and again when he's promised to take her somewhere and doesn't turn up because he's decided to work late. But to return to Owen, there's a very attractive female chemist working there by the name of Francine.'

'Really . . . '

'Before you ask me any more questions I can't answer, that's all I know. Owen brought her into the hospital with minor chemical burns.'

'But he brought her in?'

'From what I gathered he was with her when a bottle of acid she was holding exploded.'

'It would be nice to see Morgan and Owen settled.'

'So, says the happily married man who wants to pair up the entire world population.'

'Is it so bad for me to want to see everyone in my family happy?'

'Only when you interfere in their personal lives.'

Richard recognised the edge in her voice and changed the subject. 'To quote Varvara,' he referred to their Russian housekeeper, "My eyes are clapping". It's been a long day and tomorrow promises to be even longer. Time for bed.'

'And time I left,' she agreed savouring a last mouthful of wine. 'That really is good. You must give me the name and vintage.'

'Alexei choose it. I've no doubt he presented some to Catherine for her cellar.' He rose to his feet when she left her chair. 'You do have a new, and I hope fashionable expensive dress for tomorrow?'

'You wouldn't know expensive from cheap or fashionable from sackcloth. I thought I'd wear my matron's uniform.'

'Anna . . . '

'Don't worry, Sarah and Catherine picked it out for me because they don't trust me to do my own shopping. Your women won't let you down.' On impulse, she kissed his cheek before fetching her cloak from the hall. 'Sweet dreams until I see you tomorrow.'

'You too, Anna.' He walked her to the carriage Catherine had put at her sole disposal and handed her inside. As usual there were two grooms sitting side by side on the box. Both wore pistols in their belts. He hadn't needed to check if they were armed. Catherine was as cautious with his sister's safety as she was her granddaughters.

Richard spent ten minutes putting his desk and study in order before closing the door and climbing the stairs to his bedroom. Life was good, twenty years after he'd arrived penniless in Hughesovka he and his business partner, Alexei Beletsky had made enough money to consider themselves wealthy, even after they'd reinvested the largest slice of their profits financing the leases of new collieries and extending the shafts of their existing enterprises.

—

23

His house in Hughesovka had been designed by the same German architect John Hughes had commissioned to build his own mansion. He'd finished repaying the low interest loan he'd taken out with the company to pay for it five years ago and, despite Sarah's protests, with money he'd earned, not her first husband's life insurance. He and Alexei had also bought palatial adjoining houses for their families in St Petersburg as well as an office in the business quarter from which they ran the export department of their collieries. John Hughes's New Russia Company bought all the high-grade anthracite coal their pits produced but their collieries also yielded a fair amount of low grade coal that they sold abroad for use in steam engines.

He looked around the wood panelled walls of the study and hall, and sank his slippered feet into the deep pile of the French stair carpet. For all the comfort and luxury his home afforded, acquired with money he'd earned, he felt as though he didn't belong within its walls. The insecurities of the barefoot gutter snipe who'd begun his working life operating the "traps" – air vents - in a Merthyr colliery before his fifth birthday was ingrained in him, along with a sense of inferiority he found difficult to shake, especially in the company of those he regarded his "superiors". Although . . .

He went into his bedroom, closed the door and leaned back against it. All uncertainties, dissipated whenever he looked at his wife.

Blissfully happy, there were still times when he found it difficult to believe that she was actually his. He'd never anticipated anyone like her or their children, Ted and daughter Maryanna in his life, and was simply grateful that they were.

'I didn't expect you to be still awake after falling asleep in your chair earlier.' He shrugged off his jacket and waistcoat and hung them on his valet stand.

24

'As if I could sleep for long without you lying next to me.' Sarah set aside the book she'd been reading and raised her head to receive his kiss. 'I heard Anna come in but I was already in bed. She was late.'

'She asked me to give you her apologies for missing your birthday dinner and left a gift for you. It's on the hall table. There were six births in the hospital today and you know Anna, she thinks the hospital will fall down if she's not there to supervise it, just like the last matron,' he joked.

'She takes her duties seriously . . . '

'As did you, before you put our children's needs before those of the hospital,' he interrupted.

'Until I realised that Anna was even more capable of running the place and keeping the nurses in order than me.'

'My mother used to say Anna was born old. She was the one who kept our family together when our brothers and sisters were taken by cholera in Merthyr in '66. Their deaths broke our mother. She lost the will to live. Anna was only nine but she was the one who made the decision to take in washing to pay the rent and somehow found time to do it in between working shifts in a pub.' He pulled his shirt over his head.

'Why do men do that?' Sarah eyed him quizzically.

'Do what?'

'Lift their arms over their shoulders to grab the back of their shirt between their shoulder blades so they can heave it over their heads without undoing more than the top couple of buttons. Wouldn't it be easier to unbutton your shirt all the way down and slip it off like a jacket?'

'If it was, I'd remove it that way.'

'I can't see that it's more convenient to behave like a contortionist. Think of the poor laundress. Have you any idea what it's like unfasten buttons when a shirt is wet?'

'I've never thought about it,' he replied.

'Which says a lot about how long-suffering Anna was when she did your washing.'

25

'I had no idea you noticed the way I undressed.'

'It's not only men who like to see the opposite sex undressing.'

'And what would you know about men ogling naked women?' he enquired suspiciously.

She winked suggestively. 'I've seen the photographs they collect.'

'I haven't any.'

'None that I've found – as yet.' She raised her eyebrows.

'There are none.'

'And before we married?'

'I'd be lying if I said I never looked at those that fell into my lap.'

'Fell?'

'I never went searching for them. So where did you see them? Your patients. The porters at the hospital . . . '

'Both are too terrified of the nurses to smuggle in salacious postcards. I don't have to go further than your brother Owen's pockets when he forgets to empty them for the laundry. Varvara was shocked when she found them. But then she's never married or had much to do with men – young or old. I told her it was normal for men to be interested in naked ladies and in fact I'd be worried if Morgan and Owen weren't.'

'I'll take a look in their pockets tomorrow to spare Varvara – and your blushes.' He unfastened his belt and unbuttoned his flies.

'Don't, your brothers would be mortified.'

'You didn't tell Owen that you and Varvara had seen them?'

'No. Owen might suspect that we had if he remembered he'd left them in his pocket. I put the ones Varvara found in one of the drawers in his bedroom but he didn't mention them to me and I certainly didn't say anything about them to him.'

'When did you see them?'

'Last week.'

26

'And you waited until now to tell me?'

'I wouldn't have told you now if it hadn't come up in conversation. Your brothers are grown men. We were discussing the way you undress. Please take off your socks before you remove your underclothes.'

'Do you have any particular reason for making that request?' he asked.

'A nude man with socks on looks as odd as a dog in Wellington boots.' She turned down the lamp and settled back on the pillows.

'And how many dogs in Wellington boots have you seen.' He frowned, 'Forget I asked, I'm more interested in the number of nude men with socks on that you've studied.'

'Glanced at in a professional capacity not studied. Probably hundreds if not thousands,' she replied. 'A nurse has no time for modesty – false or otherwise.'

'Sometimes I'd rather not be reminded of the humiliations nurses enjoy inflicting on their male patients.'

'Nurses never set out to humiliate unless their patients are being difficult. Finish undressing and come to bed.'

'Is there any special way you'd like me to finish?'

'Quickly.'

'You're cold?'

'Yes but that's not the only reason.' She crooked her finger. 'I want you.'

'For what?'

'Come here and you'll find out.'

'That sounds as though it could be painful or dangerous.'

'That depends on your definition of danger.'

'Yesterday you found my first grey hair. You want to give me even more?'

'A grey hair isn't life threatening,' she smiled.

'It's a portend of old age that doesn't enhance my good looks.'

'You're handsome enough to overcome it.'

27

He dropped his socks on a chair and folded his underclothes on top. She turned back the bedclothes. He climbed in, stretched out beside her, and melded the full length of his naked body alongside hers before returning the kiss she gave him with interest.

'You could have come to bed an hour ago,' she moved on top him.

'I could have but anticipation is ninety percent of the pleasure.'

'Really?' She gasped as he rolled over and pinned her beneath him.

'Not really. This is,' he whispered as he entered her.

Catherine Ignatova's house Hughesovka January 1889

Anna said goodnight to the night porter who manned Catherine's front door and crept up the stairs to her bedroom. The room was beautiful, originally furnished for Catherine's daughter Olga before her marriage, it had later been used by Catherine's orphaned niece, Sonya before she'd married Roman Nadolny. It had been redecorated for her after she'd accepted Catherine's invitation to live with her and Kira.

Smaller than the state rooms and guest bedrooms in the mansion, it was still large enough to contain everything a young girl or in her case, woman, could possibly want. The furniture was French Empire, enamelled white and ornamented by gilding. A four-poster bed hung with blue and white silk curtains, that matched the bedcover and pillows, dominated the centre of the wall opposite the windows that overlooked the gardens.

French doors opened on to a balcony that encircled the first floor of the house. A desk and chair stood to the left of the French doors, a matching dressing table and chair to the right. A cheval mirror, two bookshelves, bedside cabinets and a Dutch tiled stove completed the furniture.

28

Doors led to a small bathroom fitted with a marble washstand and slipper bath and another door led into a walk-in clothes and linen cupboard.

She turned up the oil lamp on the bedside cabinet and turned down the wicks on the ones on the desk and dressing table before checking her reflection in the mirror. A white ghost stared back at her in the subdued glow. She took the pins from her hair, picked up her hairbrush and tugged it through her waist-length hair before plaiting it, as she did every night. She looked at the amber coloured silk gown and matching silk shoes Catherine's maid had laid out in readiness for the lunch tomorrow. As she'd promised Richard, he wouldn't have cause to reproach her for her dress.

Too tired to do more than wash her hands and face, she undressed quickly, pulled on her nightdress and fell into bed but, exhausted as she was, sleep eluded her.

Every time she saw Richard she took delight in his happy marriage. But occasionally it made her feel – not envious - she could never envy Richard anything that brought him joy, but conscious that something was missing from her life.

She lived in luxury, enjoyed Catherine and Kira's love and the love of her brothers, niece, nephew, Sarah and her godchildren and had found her vocation in nursing. She'd made many real friends in the town, yet whenever she was alone, especially at bedtime and in the early morning, she felt oddly empty.

Richard had Sarah and their children. Morgan and Owen one another and their girlfriends. Praskovia had Glyn Edwards and their children, her closest friend Ruth was happily married to Alexei Beletsky with twin daughters and another child on the way.

She was grateful, but she knew there could be more to her life – if she ever found the courage to overcome the degradation and shame of her past. Could she ever trust a man – any man other than her brothers?

29

John Hughes, Glyn Edwards and his older brother Edward Edwards had never been anything other than kind to her but she still flinched whenever they drew near her. Could she ever bear a man to touch her the way the way the Paskey brothers had when they'd beaten and raped her in Merthyr.

She been twelve years old. Yet twenty years later the woman she'd become still woke in the early hours with the rotting food and ale stench of their breath in her nostrils and the clammy feel of their sweating calloused hands on her bare skin as they'd stripped her clothes from her body.

She shuddered at the memory that was never far from the surface of her mind.

There was little point in thinking of any kind of life beyond the one she had. She'd been defiled. No man would ever want her, so there was no point in wondering if she could bear one to touch her. Better to concentrate on her career, her brother's family and her friends. As long as there were people, there would be a need for nurses. And it was something to be needed if only by strangers.

—

CHAPTER TWO

Beletsky Mansion, Hughesovka January 1889

Count Nicholas Beletsky glanced up as the footman walked into the summer parlour carrying a candelabra.

'Do you want me to draw the drapes, Your Excellency?'

'I do not.'

'Your Excellency.' The man set the candelabra on the sofa table next to Nicholas and left the room, closing the double doors behind him.

The count turned back to the window and continued staring at the narrow view it afforded of the gardens and the tree lined drive that led to the high, wrought iron gates. Levsky had sent word ordering him to set their pre-arranged plans into operation and prepare for his arrival that day.

He loathed living close to the industrial town of Hughesovka, not least because his estranged eldest son Alexei and mother-in-law Catherine Ignatova lived there and approved of John Hughes's enterprise to the extent that they'd both invested in its collieries and iron works. But Levsky had bought up his considerable gambling debts and now owned, due to his defaulting on payments, the Beletsky mansion and the estate around it along with his St Petersburg and Moscow houses and all his country dachas. He would have preferred living in one of the cities, but as Levsky had rented out both of his former city houses to tenants, who unlike him, could afford to pay rent, he had no option but to obey Levsky – sit in the Hughesovka mansion that still bore his name, wait for the man's arrival - and drink.

He refilled his glass after the footman left the room.

Given a choice he would have opted for vintage French Cognac, but the last time Levsky visited he'd ordered his secretary to make an inventory of the contents of the wine cellar, before changing the locks. Levsky had also made a point of taking the keys with him when he returned to Moscow.

The rough peasant distilled liquor burned Beletsky's tongue and throat but it also blurred the edge of his consciousness enough to prevent serious thought, and for the moment that was enough. The French carriage clock struck midnight. Shortly afterwards he heard the crunch of carriage wheels on gravel.

He set aside his glass, rose carefully to his feet and walked to the door. The walls of the room swayed around him and he realised he was drunk. He didn't doubt Levsky would notice, but after the effort he'd put into carrying out instructions he hoped Levsky would make allowances for his self-indulgence. The last thing he could afford to do was irritate his benefactor.

He left the house by the front door. His housekeeper, Maria Chudova, was already waiting beneath one of the columns that supported the portico.

'Can't wait to throw yourself in your lover's arms,' Beletsky slurred, the drink loosening his tongue. He knew Levsky had seduced the woman on his last visit, but he was usually too careful to allude to the fact in front of the servants.

'I am here to pay my respects to the man who pays my wages,' Maria retorted. Believing Beletsky to be wealthy as well as aristocratic she'd left a well-paid position as a cook in a hotel to accept his offer of employment, only to discover his status in the house that bore his family name was that of "charity case" dependent on the crumbs dispensed by his wealthy friend.

One of the footmen stepped down from the back of Levsky's sleigh, opened the door and unfolded the steps. Levsky emerged, extraordinarily large, and immaculately turned out in royal court dress.

—

Beletsky knew from long acquaintance that everything Levsky did, said, and wore, from the tip of his varnished boots to the crown of his silk plumed hats was calculated to endorse the image he cultivated and presented to the world.

His shoes were hand stitched from Spanish leather by master cobblers on his personal lasts. His clothes were bespoke, tailored in London from British woollen broadcloth and tweed by the same Saville Row emporium that served the British Royal family. His carriage horses as well as his mounts were of Arabian stock. His cufflinks, collar studs, pocket watches, and wallets, were crafted in the Faberge workshops patronised by the Romanovs.

Levsky removed his hat and inclined his head towards Maria.

Maria curtseyed. 'Supper is prepared and waiting.'

'I look forward to joining you in the dining room, my dear.' He turned to Nicholas. 'You look sick, Beletsky.'

'Unlike you, Levsky.'

'If I look better than you, it's because I avoid gut rot peasant brewed vodka.'

'I . . . '

'Don't bother to deny it, Beletsky, I can smell it on you from here.'

Nicholas Beletsky stretched out his hand. Levsky ignored it. The Beletsky mansion only bore the count's name because it suited Levsky to keep his ownership of the estate secret. He allowed Beletsky to continue to live in the house, but he had no intention of letting him forget that he would be starving and destitute if it weren't for his benevolence.

'You're devilishly late. I expected you this morning,' Beletsky slurred.

'Why? I gave you no time of arrival.'

Beletsky bristled. 'I'm not your lackey . . . '

Levsky removed his hat and gloves and handed them to the butler while staring coolly at Beletsky. 'Aren't you?'

'No! You might have more money than me . . . '

'Might?' Levsky laughed. Like John Hughes his considerable business interests were rooted in industry, located mainly on the estates he'd inherited that bordered the wastelands of Siberia. He seldom visited them, entrusting the management of his ironworks and collieries as well as his agricultural holdings to managers. His only concern was the profit they generated, which was why he'd been irritated by an uncharacteristic touch of envy as his coachman had driven his carriage through John Hughes's town.

Levsky sensed that Beletsky had retreated into a sulk, but he continued the conversation. 'I heard Hughesovka had grown quickly but I wasn't expecting it to be twice the size it was on my last visit.'

Beletsky shrugged. 'It's said that the town is the most modern and fastest growing in Russia. Some even believe the fire of 1871 worked in John Hughes's favour.'

Beletsky and Levsky knew more than they would have admitted about the origins of that fire, having paid men to set it. Levsky had hoped the conflagration would drive Hughes back to Britain. But instead of surrendering to the setback, John Hughes had used the destruction to plan out his town anew, with wider thoroughfares, and more imposing public buildings. Since then, the brick built hotel, bank and brothel had been extended and the wooden headquarters of The New Russian Company rebuilt in stone. The hospital had benefitted from the addition of three new wings. Most of the shops had been rebuilt in brick, and an imposing theatre and cathedral were close to completion.

'Do you know how much John Hughes is worth?' Levsky led the way into the house.

'No, only that money doesn't appear to be a concern for him.' Beletsky answered.

'Has the Tsar advanced John Hughes roubles as well as tax concessions? Or is John Hughes's wealth down to his personal holdings? Or does he have powerful investors backing him?'

—

34

'How should I know?' Beletsky answered Levsky's question with one of his own. 'The peasants call him the Iron Tsar but I've no idea whether that alludes to his money or his powers. Ignorant and superstitious as they are, the bastards attribute John Hughes's success to a pact with the devil.'

'Hopefully, if there is a pact it will soon be broken. Have you completed the preparations?'

'I have,' Beletsky asserted with a nervous emphasis that aroused Levsky's suspicions.

'So, everything is ready for the morning?'

'It will be. The men are still practising.'

'At this hour!'

'You didn't send confirmation of the Grand Dukes' arrival.' Beletsky protested.

'Confirmation? Why should I? I sent you the itinerary.'

'Grand Dukes set their own timetables,' Beletsky blustered.

'Not when they travel by train, they don't. I travelled with the Royal party from St Petersburg to Hughesovka's station. The Grand Dukes' personal rail carriages have been shunted into sidings there, where they'll stay until the Grand Dukes decide to leave this area. I excused my presence by informing their Excellencies that I had business that necessitated my travelling ahead.' Levsky glanced around the hall when he heard a loud crack. 'Is that a gunshot coming from the back of the house?'

Nicholas nodded. 'The barn.'

'Supper is ready.' Maria signalled to the footman who opened the door to the dining room.

'I will eat later, Maria.' Levsky strode ahead of Beletsky through the house and out on to the covered walkway that led to the stable yard. Lamps burned above the outside of the barn. He pushed open the door.

More oil lamps flickered, illuminating two peasants, Artur and Gleb, wrapped in furs they were lolling on hay bales, drinking vodka and watching Ianto and Mervyn Paskey shoot Colt revolvers at tin plate targets nailed to the back wall. All four men leapt to attention when Levsky entered.

'Go ahead,' Levsky nodded to the Paskeys. He watched Ianto take aim, fire and hit the plate dead centre.

'How many bullets do you have left?' Levsky demanded.

'Four, sir,' Ianto stammered. 'I reloaded just before you came in.'

'It's "Your Excellency" not "sir".'

'Yes, s . . . Your Excellency.'

'Can you hit the target with all four?'

Ianto lifted the gun and fired. Two shots ricocheted off the brick pillars in the wall; two hit the plate, none in the centre.

'Your turn,' Levsky barked at Mervyn.

Mervyn took Ianto's place. Even more nervous under Levsky's gaze than Ianto, he hit the plate only once.

'You need to do better. Gleb, Artur, keep working with them.' Levsky returned to the house.

Beletsky trailed behind him. Levsky went to the drinks tray. He took a flask from his pocket and filled a glass with cognac. Beletsky picked up his half-drunk vodka.

'Is everything ready apart from the Paskeys?' Levsky demanded.

'Yes.'

'The Royal party will travel from the station to the New Russia Company works tomorrow morning by horse drawn vehicles. They are expected to arrive before ten o'clock in the morning. I presume John Hughes has arranged security for the visit?'

'The resident Cossack regiment in Hughesovka will act as escort under the command of Colonel Razin,' Beletsky confirmed.

'The Grand Dukes and their party will be taken by trolley – red baize-covered trolleys that have chairs bolted to the floors, into the centre of the works, where a tented pavilion has been erected to serve the visitors snacks, vodka, and tea.' Beletsky was anxious to reveal the depth of his research into the arrangements that John Hughes had made to entertain his influential guests. 'After refreshments, individual carriages will convey the royal visitors and John Hughes and his senior managers on a guided tour through every stage of metal processing from the coke ovens to the blast furnace. As well as the works, the Grand Dukes will visit a colliery When they've finished the inspection, the party will return to their own sleighs before adjourning to the hotel where John Hughes will host a lunch.'

'Where and when will our diversion take place?' Levsky downed his cognac in one and refilled his glass from his flask.

'On the street outside the hotel when the Grand Dukes and John Hughes arrive for lunch.'

'Why in public?'

'Because there was no way that we could get the Paskeys inside the works. A Mongolian, Gavril Grisha, runs a union that manages the labour force in Hughesovka. No one gets a job in the works or a colliery without his endorsement . . . '

'Did it occur to you to buy the man?'

'The damned barbarian has proved incorruptible.'

'No one is incorruptible,' Levsky sipped and savoured his cognac.

'I don't know what Grisha draws from the union dues the men pay but . . . '

'I'd guess wages, but the men Grisha hires and fires will be prepared to pay him all they own in exchange for a job, tied house and security for their families. And all a man owns can amount to a great deal, Beletsky. A Tsar's ransom and more if he is prepared to sell his wife and daughters. This Grisha does all the hiring and firing?'

'He does, under the authority of the union, for all the managers at the New Russia Company, the Edwards' Brothers' and Beletsky and Parry Collieries . . . '

'Beletsky?' Levsky raised an enquiring eyebrow.

'My son has gone into partnership with a Welshman.'

'Yes, I recall you mentioning it the last time I was here.'

'The managers of every company have briefed Grisha on the Paskeys. Everyone in Hughesovka has been on the lookout for men fitting their description since that nurse was raped and killed.'

'Since the Paskeys killed and raped that nurse,' Levsky corrected.

Beletsky shrugged. 'When it comes to employing men to do the kind of work you want done, Levsky, there isn't a great deal of choice. Grisha checks and double checks the identity of every new man he sends into the works and collieries, because he knows if the Paskeys slip through the net the managers have cast, it would reflect badly on him and he'd lose his influence and position. That's why I've kept the Paskeys hidden here since you sent them here from your eastern estates six months ago. Now that their hair has had time to grow and they've learned enough Russian to pass in a crowd we stand a chance of getting them close to the Royal party, but not into the works. Not with the heightened security John Hughes has imposed.'

'Explain your plan.' Levsky sat in the chair closest to the hearth. As it was summer there was no fire, but he knew the chair had been Beletsky's favourite before he'd acquired the house in lieu of debts.

'This is only the second visit royalty has made to Hughesovka in twenty years. There'll be a crowd . . . '

'Do you expect the Paskeys to mingle unnoticed with Hughes's workers in full sight of Cossack troops, pull out their guns take aim, fire and kill John Hughes and the Grand Dukes before the soldiers shoot them?' Levsky's tone was scathing.

38

'I've left nothing to chance.' Nicholas refilled his glass with vodka. 'The Paskeys will deliver a sleigh load of vodka to the hotel before dawn tomorrow, which they'll unload into the cellar. They'll use the back entrance and the sleigh will be left in the kitchen yard, out of sight of the front of the hotel and the street.'

'They'll just walk in?' Levsky was sceptical.

'I've paid the merchant. He'll allow the Paskeys to haul the goods inside. There will only be the three of them, that's the Paskeys and the merchant. At that time in the morning the kitchen staff will be too busy preparing lunch for the dignitaries to take notice of anyone delivering liquor.'

'Who besides the vodka merchant know that the Paskeys work for you?'

'No one.'

'You're sure of that?' Levsky questioned.

'Yes,' Beletsky bit back, resenting the implication that he'd been careless. 'Once the three of them are alone in the cellar, Ianto will slit the merchant's throat and conceal his body. Both Paskeys will remain in the cellar until the arrival of the royal party with John Hughes. Then they'll leave by the front cellar door, which opens below street level. From there they'll have a clear view of the guests because the crowd will have gathered in the street behind the Royal party. When Grand Dukes and John Hughes alight from their sleighs to walk into the hotel, the Paskeys will step up and shoot them. If they have time to shoot Glyn Edwards and a few of the Grand Dukes aides as well, so much the better.'

'What will happen if the Paskeys miss, which is entirely likely from what I saw of their prowess, or fail to kill the targets with the first bullets?' Levsky took a single cigar from the top pocket of his jacket.

'Gleb and Artur will be outside the hotel carrying gifts of flowers and bottles of the best estate vodka from the grateful town of Hughesovka to the Grand Dukes. I've ordered them to hold back until the Paskeys have fired. They'll be carrying the same size and calibre of revolver. After the Paskeys have emptied their guns Gleb and Artur will kill the Paskeys and wait to be hailed as heroes for gunning down the Grand Dukes' and John Hughes's assassins. I've thought of all eventualities.' Beletsky waited for Levsky's praise along with approval of his plan but it wasn't forthcoming.

Levsky watched Nicholas squirm for a few moments before breaking the silence. 'I suppose it could work.'

'It *will* work,' Beletsky contradicted.

'It won't stand a chance unless you improve the Paskeys' marksmanship.'

'They knew you were watching them. They were nervous . . .'

'And if they're nervous tomorrow?' Levsky interrupted.

'Artur and Gleb will make sure they aren't.'

'How?' Levsky asked. 'Plying them with what you're drinking will only make them more unpredictable.'

'Artur will keep them under control,' Beletsky bit back.

'He'd better.'

'You will join the Grand Duke's party tomorrow?' Beletsky asked.

'As will you. It wasn't difficult to obtain an extra invitation for a local landowner. It's just as well I've kept the change of ownership of the Beletsky estate quiet.' Levsky never allowed an opportunity to remind Beletsky of his poverty to pass without comment. 'I'll be carrying a revolver. I suggest you do as well. The same model and make as the Paskeys, Artur and Gleb. There are several in the gun room.'

'Won't that be construed as incriminating if they're found on us?' Nicholas asked.

'No one will dare search us before the event, and if we find it necessary to use them to silence the Paskeys or Gleb and Artur, we'll be the ones seen as heroes for gunning down the assassins. If something should go wrong it's vital we come out of this as the defenders of mother Russia, not John Hughes and the officers of the New Russia Company. And now, I suggest you return to the barn and monitor the Paskeys progress. I have kept Maria and her supper waiting quite long enough.'

CHAPTER THREE

Hotel Hughesovka January 1889

A frown creased Catherine Ignatova's forehead as she
walked alongside the tables set out in the largest function
room of the hotel. 'I wish John had allowed me to send in
my china and cutlery. The hotel porcelain is serviceable,
its silverware and linen adequate but the place settings
would look so much better set with Meissen and German
silverware.'

'They would,' her granddaughter Kira agreed. 'But as
this is a working lunch not a formal dinner I believe Mr
Hughes wanted to keep the atmosphere low key and
workmanlike.'

Sarah glanced through the archway into the ante-room
where her fifteen-year-old daughter Maryanna and Ruth
and Alexei's sixteen-year-old twins, Olga and Kitty were
arranging flowers that had been grown in one of
Catherine's hothouses under Kira's supervision.

'Other than the girls' floral decorations I don't see what
else we can do to make the table look more attractive . . .'
Ruth Beletsky began.

'You can lay four extra places for a start.' Sonya
walked in and everyone in the room stopped and stared. It
wasn't just her fashionable outfit, although none of them
had seen anything as elegant or striking outside of the
photographic cabinet cards of the Tsarina. Rather it was a
radical change in Sonya herself. She'd always been
attractive, but it was as though her beauty had come of age
in the years that had elapsed since her last visit to
Hughesovka.

Her sons, fifteen and fourteen-year-old Andrei and
Spartak walked beside her. Both were a head taller than
her and both had inherited her husband Roman's
startlingly attractive white blond hair and green oriental
eyes.

42

'Sonya! Why didn't you tell us you were coming?' Catherine rushed to embrace her niece.

'I wrote to tell you that we were arriving with the Grand Dukes' party.' Sonya hugged her aunt and kissed her cheek. She couldn't help but notice there were far more wrinkles on Catherine's face than there had been the last time she'd seen her.

'We thought you and Roman would be visiting the works first.'

'We escaped, because the boys couldn't wait to see their great aunt.' Sonya disentangled herself from Catherine. 'Aunt Catherine, please allow me to present your great nephews?'

'If it wasn't for your resemblance to your father I wouldn't have recognised you. I said goodbye to boys two years ago and two fine young men have returned.'

'It's three years since we were last in Hughesovka, Great Aunt Catherine.' Andrei executed a perfect court bow before kissing the back of Catherine's hand. Spartak followed suit.

'The way time speeds up when you grow older is positively alarming.'

'You look very well, Great Aunt Catherine. Not at all old and extremely elegant,' Andrei complimented.

Catherine smiled, 'I see you've inherited your father's ability to flatter, Andrei.'

'As have I, Great Aunt Catherine.' Spartak added, refusing to allow Andrei to eclipse him.

'I am very pleased, to have such handsome, well-bred great nephews, but you would do me honour if you would address me as aunt, not great aunt, Andrei, Spartak.' 'Of course, Aunt Catherine.'

'One day you two will grace a court.'

'Father wants us to live more useful lives,' Andrei replied.

'That is not polite, Andrei. An insult to every courtier,' Sonya reprimanded.

'There are no courtiers here, are there?' Spartak looked around.

'Whether there are or not, it's still an extremely ill-mannered comment,' Sonya said.

'But it's true. Father did say it,' Andrei protested.

'Did your father specify the direction he'd like these useful lives of yours to take?' Catherine probed.

'He said there'd be time enough to decide that when we've finished our education.' Andrei bowed to Ruth, Praskovia and Sarah before kissing their hands. 'Aunt Ruth, Aunt Praskovia, Aunt Sarah, it is good to see you again.'

'And in such good health.' Spartak followed suit.

Sonya went into the alcove and hugged Kira, Olga, Kitty and Maryanna. 'You make me feel so old. If my sons are young men, you are young ladies. And to think I brought you dolls to play with.'

The girls laughed, knowing Sonya was teasing them.

'You've arranged these flowers beautifully. Could you please teach my boys how to do it?'

'We'd rather teach my cousins and Maryanna to fence and shoot straight, Mama.' Andrei and Spartak joined the girls.

Anxious to be of service, Maryanna poured the boys glasses of lemonade.

Sensing the usual shyness and diffidence between the young people after a long separation, Sonya returned to the dining room to give them privacy to become reacquainted. 'Where's Anna?' She looked around.

'Hopefully preparing to leave the hospital,' Sarah glanced instinctively at the door.

'It's not often the girls are lost for words,' Ruth commented.

'My boys never are,' Sonya said as Alexei's voice momentarily rose, swiftly followed by laughter. 'You look as though that baby you're carrying should have been born yesterday, Ruth.'

44

'According to Sarah, not for another two weeks. I can't wait.'

'My apologies for not being able to predict the arrival sooner,' Sarah slipped her hand around what passed for Ruth's waist.

'The last few weeks are an eternity, aren't they?' Sonya commiserated before noticing tears in Catherine's eyes. 'Aunt, are you feeling well?'

Catherine blotted her eyes with a lavender scented handkerchief. 'Perfectly well, thank you, Sonya. I have absolutely no right to cry when I'm so happy. It's just that I wasn't expecting you. I thought you'd be coming later with the men. I had no time to prepare myself.' She embraced Sonya again. 'I have missed you.'

'And I you, which is why I left Roman at the works. I couldn't wait to see you. All of you.'

'How long are you staying in Hughesovka this time?' Sarah asked.

'Are you moving in with me?' Catherine questioned hopefully.

'Or are you moving into your house? Roman's servants keep it and the garden in perfect order,' Kira added.

'Your clothes will set every tailor in the shtetl reaching for his sketchpad,' Praskovia predicted eyeing Sonya's outfit. 'It's stunning and suits you so well. Did you buy it in Paris, Rome or Yalta?'

Sonya laughed again. 'It is so good to be home, but please, one question at a time.' She pulled a chair out from under the table and sat down. 'Roman promised we'd stay here until the New Year, but I'll try to persuade him to remain until the thaw next spring.'

'What do you think of the table, Sonya?' Kira asked.

'It's perfect, although in my experience the men will be too busy talking to appreciate it or the effort the girls made to arrange the flowers. What will be served?'

'A Russian/Ukrainian menu,' Praskovia took one from the table and handed it to Sonya. 'Starting with borsch.'

'Followed by steamed sturgeon, basturma of beef fillet with stewed mushrooms and potatoes, and vegetable golubtsy, and for dessert cherry kisel, apple kisel, cream and cheesecakes,' Sarah continued. 'If the Grand Dukes eat all of that they won't be able to move.'

'I thought the men would be here by now,' Catherine observed.

Sonya opened the diamond studded watch pinned to her dress. 'I'm sorry to have to be the one to tell you but the Grand Dukes and their party won't be coming to lunch. They have to be back at the station by mid-afternoon to meet the Moscow express train, which is making an unscheduled stop to attach the Grand Dukes' coaches. There won't be another for three days and as both Grand Dukes have pressing engagements in Moscow they couldn't wait any longer.'

'Glyn did say that time would be tight,' Praskovia said philosophically.

'So, ladies, it won't only be Ruth who'll be eating for two,' Catherine joked. 'Either that, or food will be going to waste.'

Hughesovka Ironworks January 1889

'That went well, congratulations,' Roman Nadolny complimented John Hughes as they watched the last of the carriages of the Grand Dukes' party drive away from the ironworks.

John smiled more in relief than triumph. 'It did. Both Grand Dukes said they were impressed.'

'"Miracle" was the word they used,' Glyn said. 'I counted. Grand Duke Sergei used it four times, Grand Duke Alexei five.'

'I'm grateful for your support, Roman. It was an advantage to have a close friend of the Grand Dukes with a thorough knowledge of engineering to hand, and it was good of you to travel up from Yalta for the occasion.'

46

John hailed his driver and the man brought John's sleighs to the gates.

'My pleasure. Sonya and I have been trying to return here for some time, but,' Roman shrugged, 'business dictated otherwise.'

'How has Sonya taken to your gypsy lifestyle, Roman?' John waited while the footman opened the door of the carriage and pulled down the steps

'She's enjoyed seeing all the sights that Europe and the world has to offer. And, if nothing else travelling has broadened the boys' horizons and taught them that not everyone is as privileged as they are, and complaints are best left unspoken if things aren't quite as they'd like them to be.'

'So, you have understanding sons as well as an understanding wife, Roman.' John took the corner seat facing backwards.

'I thank God for them every day.' Roman reached for his extravagantly plumed hat and pushed it down on his head.

'You look like a general, Roman.' Glyn sat opposite him.

'I look ridiculous, but like the Tsar, the Grand Dukes insist that everyone in their entourage wear formal Russian court dress.'

'I would refuse to wear a hat like that, even for a Grand Duke.' Richard sat next to Glyn. Alexei took the seat next to the door. The footman folded the steps, closed the doors and the driver flicked the reins.

'Then it's just as well you don't have to, Richard.' John waved to the crowds that lined the street outside the ironworks.

'Your sons aren't joining us?' Roman asked John.

'They are playing host to my local guests. As they are poised to take over the business it is as well they get some practise running things here as I will be leaving shortly for St Petersburg for various meetings, and from there I intend to travel to Oslo and London.'

—

'I'm looking forward to the day when Andrei and Spartak can take over my business affairs.'

John laughed. 'What will you do with yourself all day when they do?'

'Enjoy life. Maybe take up fishing.' Roman indicated a group of men laden with rods, tackle, bottles of vodka and axes to break holes in the ice that crusted the banks who were walking towards the river.

'I hope their day remains amicable. Too many vodka stalls spring up every holiday for my liking.' John frowned at a group of women who were selling spirit by the ladleful.

'I can smell it from here,' Alexei sniffed theatrically. 'It's what my grandmother calls a "real rust stripper".'

'You can always trust Catherine Ignatova to come up with the perfect description,' John said. 'Remind me to suggest to the managers in the works that they buy some and try it as a metal cleaner.'

'I'm getting drunk on the stench . . . ' Richard was interrupted by shouts from a mob of children.

'Look! A Grand Duke!'

'He's really grand!'

'And HUGE!'

Alexei laughed when he saw the children point to Roman. 'An understandable mistake given your hat. It wouldn't look out of place on stage in an opera, Roman. Don't disappoint the boys. They want to see a Grand Duke. Give them one.'

Roman slipped his hand into his pocket, pulled out a handful of copper polushkas and dengas and threw them to the children before finishing off with a regal wave.

'The ladies will be disappointed to hear that the Grand Duke and his party didn't stay for lunch after all the plans they made to entertain him,' John commented as the sleigh turned the corner and swung past the bank and shops to the hotel entrance.

'We'll have to impose on Roman to continue with his Grand Duke impression.' Alexei opened the door before the coachman stopped the horses and jumped down on to the snow-covered street. He saw Ruth in the doorway of the hotel. 'You should be sitting somewhere warm and quiet.' His words were drowned in the roar of the crowd.

She mouthed, "I can't hear you," and went to meet him.

'I said you should be sitting down,' he shouted close to her ear.

'If you had your way you'd put me in a glass case.'

'That's an idea. At least that way I'd know that you and this little one would be safe.' Alexei guided her towards the door as Glyn, John, Richard and Roman alighted from the sleigh.

A movement to the right of the main door caught Roman's eye. He turned and glimpsed the heads of two men moving upwards from the snow-covered steps that led down to the cellar. They were holding their hands out at arm's length. One was pointing at John Hughes the other at Glyn. Roman had time to register the guns they were holding before twin, high-pitched cracks whistled above the roar of the crowd.

Alexei saw Roman reach into his pocket as he threw himself in front of John Hughes. He pulled out a gun and fired in the direction of the shooter who was aiming at John before crumpling when the bullet intended for John slammed into his body. As Roman fell his assailant jerked, careering back against the wall of the hotel.

Colonel Misha Razin was riding at the head of his men behind John's carriage. He shouted the order to "ready weapons", drew his own gun and shot the second man. The assassin's gun fired as he lurched backwards down the cellar steps and disappeared from view. The shot ricocheted off the hotel wall and hit Misha in the shoulder. Bullets started flying in all directions, from and into the crowd. Blood spurted painted the trampled snow crimson.

Misha clamped his hand over his shoulder, jumped from his horse and shouted to Nicholas Beletsky to stop shooting the assassins who were clearly dead.

Alexei swung round to look at Ruth. She was stretched out on the paving next to Roman. He cried out. A savage bestial sound of pure anguish that echoed even above the crack of gunshots. He fell to his knees on to the snow beside her. Shots flew past his ears but intent on cradling his wife's head he neither knew nor cared what direction they came from.

Oblivious to the fusillade, Anna raced towards the hotel from the hospital. Heedless of her new gown she knelt on the snow covered ground beside Alexei and pressed down on the wound in Ruth's chest in an attempt to staunch the wound, but blood was already bubbling from Ruth's mouth. All Anna could do was watch helplessly as the light blurred then dimmed in her friend's eyes.

She heard screams and shouts of - 'Stretchers!'

Vlad appeared beside her. Behind him were the dark suits and white coats of more porters. She was aware of the blue flashes of nurses' uniforms and Nathan Kharber's presence as he crouched beside her. She looked up at Vlad. There were tears in his eyes but all she could think of was Ruth – and her child.

'Load Mrs Beletskaya on a stretcher. We need to get her into a treatment room. Immediately!'

Anna saw Roman and the rest of the wounded carpeting the street and entrance to the hotel. She could only help one patient at a time and was relieved to see Sarah and Sonya leaning over him.

Nathan laid his hand on his Ruth's swollen uterus looked to Anna then over his shoulder to where Roman was lying. 'I can feel the child moving. You know what you have to do, Anna?'

Anna met Nathan's gaze and nodded. When the doctor moved his hand, she replaced it with hers.

She ran, slipping and sliding alongside the stretcher that held Ruth, conscious that Alexei hadn't relinquished his hold on his wife on the other side of the stretcher.

'What did Nathan mean? "You know what you have to do" Anna?' Alexei asked.

Anna gave him the coward's answer.

Silence.

CHAPTER FOUR

Hospital Hughesovka January 1889

Anna burst through the door of the hospital, shouting for a nurse. She thrust open the door of the treatment room and grabbed a tray and a scalpel. A square built stranger dressed in travelling clothes joined her in the doorway.

'I'm Noah de Vries. . . '

Miriam barged past him.

'Towels,' Anna ordered Miriam.

Miriam stared down at Ruth. 'Is she . . . '

'Towels,' Anna repeated. It wasn't the first Caesarean Anna had performed, but it was the first on a corpse. Without hesitation, she sliced through Ruth's dress.

Alexei made a grab for her hand. She pushed him aside.

'Ruth is dead, Alexei.' She hadn't intended to blurt out the words but there was no time to soften the blow. 'We need to save your child . . . '

Alexei threw himself over Ruth's body.

'The lady is right, sir. Please, this patient is dead. Let us save the child.' Noah de Vries hooked his hands beneath Alexei's arms and lifted him from Ruth's body.

Anna looked for but could not find Ruth's pulse. She cut through skin, a thin layer of fat and finally muscle. She lifted a small bundle from inside Ruth's body. The baby lolled, limp, lifeless. She upended it, cleared its airways, and slapped hard. When that didn't work she administered a second slap.

After what seemed an eternity it cried, a soft pathetic whimper. She handed the child to Miriam.

'You killed Ruth.' Alexei's voice was low, harsh in condemnation.

'Ruth was dead when I removed the child. You and your children were her joy, her world. Think what she would want, Alexei.'

52

'The lady is right. I am a doctor.' Noah offered Alexei his hand. 'I will care for your baby.'

Alexei didn't look at the stranger. He continued to stare at Anna.

'I have to clean Ruth up now, Alexei,' she warned.

'I'm not leaving her.'

'I'm not asking you to.' Faced with Alexei's raw grief Anna struggled to contain her own.

'Don't worry, nurse. I will see to the child.' Noah de Vries followed Miriam and the baby from the room.

Anna pulled up a chair from the side of the room, gently steered Alexei, who hadn't relinquished his grip on Ruth's hand, on to it and began work.

Hotel Hughesovka January 1889

Glyn studied the body slumped in the heap of dirty snow piled at the foot of the hotel's wall. After securing his handkerchief around his gloved fingers, he flicked the corpse's long hair and beard aside. A swarm of lice scurried down over the filthy linen smock that covered the chest.

'Do you recognise him?' Glyn asked Richard in a tone that suggested he had.

'No amount of hair and Russian clothes can disguise a damned Paskey, not from me. That's Ianto. Where do you think he's been hiding himself?'

'Wherever it was, he was well fed, by the look of him.' Glyn covered the dead man's face with his handkerchief and checked his gloves to make certain no lice had stolen into the folds of leather before straightening his back. He beckoned to the hospital porters who'd been waiting for him to finish examining the corpse. They picked up the body, dropped it into the mortuary cart and closed the lid, effectively concealing it from view.

53

By tacit agreement Glyn and Richard walked over to the cellar steps. While Glyn spoke to the hotel doorman who was standing guard over the corpse of the second assailant, Richard kicked the man's beard aside with the toe of his boot.

'Mervyn Paskey,' Richard declared in disgust. 'I can smell him from here.'

'We don't need to examine this body, thank you.' Glyn signalled to the porters with the cart. 'Please take it away.' He glanced around the street. The Fire Brigade responsible for policing the town were dispersing the crowd who seemed reluctant to leave the scene. A squad of their colleagues were lifting the corpses of the onlookers who had been killed into the back of a cart. Cossack soldiers were assisting the walking wounded to the hospital leaving the more severely injured in the care of the porters and nurses. John Hughes was speaking to Colonel Razin who was careful to keep one hand firmly clamped over the bullet wound in his shoulder.

'If either Paskey has left a clue as to where they've been living and who's behind this assassination attempt, the Cossacks will find it,' Glyn said.

Richard watched the porters manoeuvre the mortuary cart over the icy street. When they turned the corner, he drew Glyn aside. 'You don't think the Paskeys were working alone?'

Glyn shook his head. 'Why would they risk trying to kill anyone if not for money? Given the royal party's last-minute change of plans, I believe someone paid them to assassinate the Grand Dukes. When the Grand Dukes didn't turn up I think Mr Hughes and I were afterthoughts, that cost Ruth Beletsky her life . . .'

'She's dead!' Richard suddenly realised he didn't need confirmation. Like Glyn he'd seen enough violent deaths as the result of pit accidents to know that blood bubbling from the mouth was usually a precursor of death. He looked Glyn in the eye. 'I'm sorry I should have realised-'

—

54

'I can't bear the thought of Ruth's death any more than you, Richard. God help Alexei and their girls, but to return to the Paskeys, they've never been more than hired thugs. Any person capable of rational thought in their position would have run as far and as fast from me, you and Hughesovka as possible when we plastered "wanted" posters describing them all over town after they raped and murdered Naomi Rinski eighteen years ago. If either Paskey had dared venture on the streets of Hughesovka since then, we would have heard about it. Someone's been hiding them. Someone who was prepared to wait for the opportunity to kill the royal party – and possibly even planned to kill Mr Hughes at the same time because they knew that without his vision and guidance this town, and the iron works would probably be abandoned.'

'I didn't see all of what happened, it was so fast, but it certainly looked as though the Paskeys were aiming their guns at you and Mr Hughes,' Richard agreed.

'The question is, who put the Paskeys up to it. The problem, there are any number to choose from. This assassination bid could be down to dirty politics by supporters of Alexander III who is doing his damnedest to reverse the progress made by his father. Alexander II, God rest his soul, earned his title of the "modernising tsar". This one is sending Russia hurtling back into the dark ages as if progress is something to be ashamed of. I believe he'd reinstate serfdom if he could.'

'You think so?' Richard wondered if it could happen. Every day men, women and children flooded into Hughesovka in search of paid work. If serfdom was reintroduced they'd be tied to their landlords' estates again as unpaid tenants. Unable to move beyond its confines without the owner's express permission and a passport signed by him. To attempt to travel without authorisation would mean risking imprisonment or exile. Few if any estate proprietors would willingly give up what were in effect unpaid slaves.

'I could be maligning the present Tsar,' Glyn said. 'This attempt could be down to a rival industrialist who hopes to gain Mr Hughes's government contracts once he's out of the way. But whoever's responsible I don't think it's coincidence that the chosen assailants were Welsh. Given the Paskeys' background the assassination attempt could be explained as a feud between fellow countrymen, conveniently deflecting the blame from Russian suspects.'

'Whoever put the Paskeys up to it must have realised that no matter what the outcome, the Paskeys would more than likely be killed by the Cossack soldiers or one of us, which would make them conveniently unavailable for questioning.' Richard's hand went instinctively to his shoulder holster. Like all the managers of the New Russia Company and independent collieries in Hughesovka, he hadn't left his house unarmed since the last assassination attempt on John Hughes almost two decades ago. He replayed the events in his mind. 'Nicholas Beletsky was quick off the mark . . . '

Glyn began talking loudly drowning out the rest of Richard's sentence. 'I told John I'd go to the hospital to check on Roman.'

Richard glanced over his shoulder and saw Beletsky and Levsky standing within earshot.

Grisha approached with Alf Mahoney, a collier who'd travelled from Merthyr to Hughesovka in John Hughes's first party of immigrants along with Glyn and Richard. 'Mr Mahoney said he recognised the assailants as Mervyn and Ianto Paskey, Mr Edwards, Mr Parry.'

'You're right, Alf,' Glyn concurred, shaking Alf's hand.

'I told Mr Hughes who they were, sir. It's good to see them dead.' Alf acknowledged Richard.

'Very, Alf,' Richard agreed. 'Anna and I have to lot to thank you for. Watching over us in Merthyr and here.'

'Not that I did much in either place except watch, sir.'

'It's, Richard, Alf.'

'That wouldn't be right, sir. Not now you are who you are.'

They walked over to where John Hughes was talking to Misha Razin. Despite the blood that trickled down his arm from the wound in his shoulder, Misha Razin stood tall and erect, the consummate Cossack Colonel, revolver in hand, spurs clinking, and sabre rattling in its scabbard at his side every time he moved.

'Colonel Razin has placed twelve men on guard duty around the hotel and ordered the remainder of his platoons to search and patrol the town,' John informed Glyn and Richard.

'You're attempting to discover where the Paskeys have been hiding out, Colonel Razin?' Glyn asked.

'I am, sir.'

'Thank you for your shot, Colonel Razin. From my position, it looked as though it prevented a Paskey firing a second one in my direction. I believe I owe you my life.'

Misha, inclined his head at Glyn's compliment. Glyn was aware Misha despised him for making his sister, Praskovia, his mistress, and fathering her two bastards. It made no difference that it was a situation Glyn would have remedied the moment his wife, Betty granted him a divorce. But Misha took care not to allow his animosity towards Glyn to spill over into his or Glyn's public life lest it affect his standing with his commanding officer, Brigadier Zonov who answered directly to John Hughes and when he wasn't available, Glyn Edwards – John's right hand man.

'It's my responsibility to ensure the safety of this town and its citizens, Mr Edwards.' Misha glanced at Levsky and Beletsky who were too far away to overhear their conversation. 'The man Prince Nadolny fired at might have survived for questioning if . . . '

'Count Beletsky hadn't had other ideas,' Glyn lowered his voice.

'You saw?'

'The three shots that hit the man were all fired by the count,' Glyn confirmed.

'When I questioned Count Beletsky as to why he'd shot to kill, he said he was concerned the man might fire again.'

'Thank you for clarifying my suspicions, Colonel Razin.'

'The Fire Brigade have picked up the corpses of two men who worked on the Beletsky estate. Townspeople have identified them as hard-drinking troublemakers known as Artur and Gleb. They were armed with handguns of the same manufacture as the killers. Do you know them?'

'I've never heard the names,' Glyn said.

'Neither have I,' Richard added.

'You think they were working in conjunction with the Paskeys?' Glyn asked.

'I would have liked to have had the opportunity to question them, but,' Misha screwed his mouth in pain, 'now that is impossible.'

'Shouldn't you be in the hospital?' Glyn suggested to Misha.

'When I get this search underway,' Misha agreed. 'Perhaps we could talk later?'

'Of course,' Glyn answered.

'I've requested reinforcements be sent from the barracks. I'll set up regular patrols over the next few days and ensure that my men remain in the town for as long as they're needed.'

'I'll take Praskovia, Catherine, the girls, Andrei and Spartak to your house, Glyn,' Richard said. 'As soon as I've seen them safe I'll join you at the hospital.'

Glyn nodded agreement.

'Would you like me to post men outside your house, Mr Edwards?' Misha asked.

'You believe it's necessary?' Glyn narrowed his eyes.

'One of the Paskeys aimed his gun at you,' Misha reminded.

—

'An accomplice angered by the death of Paskeys might send someone after you or one of your family to finish what they started.'

Glyn thought of Praskovia and Pavlo and Tom. He didn't hesitate. 'Please do so, colonel.'

'I'll post two men at your back door and two at the front. I'll also order the patrols to call there every ten to fifteen minutes to receive an update from the guards.'

'Thank you.'

'No need to thank me. My mother and brother live with you, as does my sister. And while I may not always see eye to eye with her, or the choices she has made on how she lives her life, Praskovia is my sister.'

'I understand your disapproval of our situation, Colonel Razin and your reasons for it.'

'I will post the guards.' Misha clicked his heels and bowed to Glyn before returning to his men.

Richard emerged from the front door of the hotel with Praskovia, Catherine, the girls and Andrei and Spartak.

Catherine went to Glyn. 'You'll send for me if there's anything I can do for Ruth, Roman, Sarah or Alexei?'

'Of course,' Glyn couldn't bring himself to tell Catherine that Ruth was dead. Not in the public street. 'When there's news I'll bring it to you.'

Catherine took hold of Olga and Kitty's hands.

Richard gripped Maryanna's. 'I'll join you as soon as I've seen everyone settled in your house and talked to the guards, Glyn.'

'No, don't, Richard. Please stay in my house until either I come or send for you. I need to know someone armed and capable is with my family and friends. Glyn instinctively placed his hand on the gun hidden beneath his coat as he strode across the road.

Hospital, Hughesovka January 1889

Nathan left Sarah preparing Roman for surgery.

———

He went into the treatment room to discover that Anna had finished laying out Ruth's corpse. She'd washed the blood from Ruth's face and concealed the bullet wound in her temple by brushing her hair forward. She'd stitched the incision she'd made when she'd removed the child and dressed Ruth in a shroud. Nathan handed her a clean sheet from the linen trolley and helped her to spread it over his sister's body.

While they worked Alexei remained slumped on a chair beside the trolley that held Ruth's body. He held Ruth's hand, gently stroking her fingers, but it was obvious from his pallor and trembling that he was still in shock.

'How is Roman?' Anna asked Nathan after she'd straightened the last fold.

'He has a bullet lodged in his spine and another in his arm. I'll operate as soon as Sarah's finished making the preparations.'

'His injuries are serious?' Anna didn't know why she was asking, when the expression on Nathan's face told her as much.

If he heard Anna, Nathan didn't acknowledge her question. 'My sister's child?'

'The new doctor took her. Miriam went with him.'

'There's a new doctor?'

'He said he was a doctor,' Anna suddenly realised the only proof she had that the man who had taken Ruth's baby was a doctor was his word for it. 'Everything was confused . . . '

'The child was dead?' Nathan broke in.

'Alive and breathing after I removed her from Ruth.'

'Another girl.'

Anna couldn't help feeling that Nathan sounded disappointed. 'I only held her for a moment but she appeared to be healthy.' She turned to Alexei, called his name and touched his shoulder. He turned and stared at her through blank, unseeing eyes. 'I'll be back after I've checked your baby, Alexei.'

Alexei gave no indication he'd heard her.

—

Nathan laid his hand on his brother-in-law's arm. It was a comforting gesture Alexei was clearly unaware of. Anna followed Nathan into the corridor. She closed the door and led the way into a private cubicle off the entrance to the female ward. Miriam had washed the child and dressed her in a baby gown. She was sitting, nursing her.

'She's beautiful, and perfect, Dr Kharber. A gift from God.' Miriam's face was streaked with tears.

Nathan took the child, and unfolded the blanket Miriam had wrapped around her so he could examine the baby. 'You're right, nurse,' he declared after a few moments. 'She appears fit and healthy but given the abrupt way she came into this world, it might be as well to keep her here for a few days. Leave her in isolation, so she doesn't come into contact with any infections and stay with her please. If there's any change in her condition notify me, but as I'll be in the operating theatre for the next few hours, only if it's urgent.'

'Yes, Dr Kharber. Do you know that another doctor has arrived? A Dr de Vries. He checked the baby before being called away to examine Colonel Razin. The colonel's been shot . . . '

'Are there many wounded here?'

'I'm not sure, Dr Kharber. Would you like me to ask in the office?'

'I would like you to remain with the baby, nurse.'

'Yes, doctor.'

'I'll ask one of the other nurses to check on Alexei every ten minutes and give him a sedative if he needs one. If he wants to see the child, you can show her to him but don't leave him alone with her.'

'Yes, Dr Kharber.'

'Do you want my help when you operate on Roman, Dr Kharber?' Anna asked as they left the cubicle.

'Please. It's going to be a difficult procedure and I'd appreciate your assistance as well as Sarah's. I've asked her to administer the anaesthetic.

'Would you delegate Yulia to take over the supervision of nursing duties? Tell her to call in those who are off duty if she needs extra staff. I need to track down this new doctor. I also need to talk to Princess Nadolny and impress on her the seriousness of her husband's injuries to prepare her for the worst.'

Anna took a deep breath. In all the years, she'd worked with Nathan Kharber, she'd never known him to exaggerate the seriousness of a patient's condition. She glanced through the glass panel in the office door and saw Sonya and Glyn sitting in the visitors' chairs. Their heads were close together and Glyn was holding Sonya's hand.

'Sonya will want to see Roman,' Anna warned.

'She can, but only for a minute or two.' Nathan hesitated as he reached for the doorknob. 'Roman Nadolny was unconscious when I examined him and given his injuries I'm not expecting him to come around until after we operate.'

Sonya left her chair when Nathan entered the office. 'Roman's injuries are serious.' It was a statement not a question.

'He's badly injured,' Nathan confirmed, 'and surgery carries a heavy risk. He has a bullet in his arm, which is not serious, but the second shot went into his spine. I suspect it's lodged close to the spinal cord. It may have grazed or even severed it, but I won't know the extent of the damage until I operate.'

Sonya had worked in the office when Mr Hughes had opened the hospital. She knew exactly how dangerous spinal surgery could be.

'And Ruth?' her voice trembled as she asked.

Anna was at the door waiting for Nathan. She saw Nathan struggling to reply so she stepped in. 'Ruth died shortly after she was carried into the hospital. We managed to save her child. It's a girl. A third daughter.'

Sonya steeled herself but she still took a few seconds to find her voice. 'Where's Alexei?'

'In a treatment room with Ruth's body,' Anna answered. 'He's in shock and refusing to leave her.'

'I need to see Roman then I'll go to Alexei.'

Anna glanced at Nathan. He nodded. She offered Sonya her hand. 'I'll take you.'

CHAPTER FIVE

Hospital, Hughesovka January 1889

Anna found Sarah preparing the chloroform apparatus in a side room off the sterile theatre. Roman was lying unconscious on a trolley that had been pushed against the wall.

'Nathan gave Sonya permission to see Roman. Is it all right if we come in?'

Sarah glanced over her shoulder to check that the door to the operating theatre they kept sterile was firmly closed, before beckoning them in. Anna opened the door wider and Sonya crept in, holding her skirts against her legs lest they brush against the equipment.

'Roman hasn't regained consciousness since he was shot,' Sarah said softly. 'Nathan has decided to operate. Roman's lying face down because we're about to try to surgically remove the bullets from his body . . . '

'Nathan told me.' Sonya went to her husband and smoothed his thick white blond hair back from his temples. 'Do you think you'll be able to surgically remove the bullet from his spine?'

Sarah felt as though Sonya was not only testing her veracity, but daring her to repeat one of the platitudes Nathan had advised the staff to resort to when dealing with distraught relatives. Platitudes that Sonya in her capacity as one-time hospital administrator, was all too aware of.

'We're not sure of the damage it's caused. Nathan will try. But . . . '

'All surgery is dangerous and spinal surgery more than most. I should have known better than to ask. My apologies I didn't intend to embarrass either of you.' Sonya stared down at Roman. It was obvious to Anna and Sarah that she was committing his face to memory in case he didn't survive.

—

'You know too much to accept empty assurances, even when they're well meant, Sonya. I won't lie to you,' Anna said.

'Apparently, neither can Nathan. Nor would I want either of you to do so.' Sonya said.

'We'll do our best,' Anna spoke firmly.

'Neither I, nor Roman could ask for more. Would you mind if I stayed in the hospital while you operate?'

'No, but it could take some time . . . '

'I know.' Sonya gripped Roman's hand and kissed it. 'I need to be here. I know I can't do anything to help with Roman's surgery but I'll try to make myself useful and I need to see Alexei – and Ruth.'

'I'll take you to them, while Sarah finishes getting everything ready here,' Anna offered.

'Thank you.'

'You're operating with Nathan, Sarah?' Sonya asked.

'He asked me to administer the chloroform. I'm too out of practice to assist in any other way.'

'You have the steadiest hand I know when it comes to anaesthesia,' Anna said, 'and Nathan and I will need all the help we can get.'

'If you see Nathan tell him I'm almost ready.' Sarah reached for the chloroform bottle and placed it next to the apparatus on the tray.

'You'll need to change out of that silk gown and into a nurses' uniform,' Anna pointed out.

'So, will you.' Sarah shook her head at the dirt and blood stains on Anna's gown.

'Looks like it's past saving, doesn't it,' Anna said regretfully.

'If anyone can save it, it's Yelena. She knows more ways to remove stains than any other woman I know.' Sarah went into the walk-in cupboard where they kept medical supplies, spare uniforms and linen. Anna followed her to give Sonya some privacy with Roman. They'd finished changing when they heard Sonya leaving.

Anna straightened her nurses' hat as she went to the door. 'I'll be back as soon as I've taken Sonya to Alexei.'

'If you have a spare minute to pray along the way, Anna, say one for me. You can tell God I'll pray twice as hard and long to make up for my tardiness as soon as I have time.'

Sonya was standing beside the reassuring bulk of Glyn who was talking to the porters. They'd assembled in the main entrance outside the office and Anna noticed that every one of them shouldered a rifle.

'Are you expecting more trouble?' Anna asked Vlad, the senior porter.

'There are evil forces everywhere in this world, Matron Parry. They assassinated our blessed Tsar Alexander eight years ago, just as they murdered our blessed Ruth Beletskya here today and wounded his excellency Prince Nadolny and Colonel Razin as well as innocents not yet named.' Deeply religious, Vlad made the sign of the cross before continuing. 'Better to be safe than cry more tears for our loved ones. Excuse me, Mr Edwards, Princess Nadolny.' Vlad addressed the porters. 'You've been given your stations and your orders. Go!'

The men filed silently out through the door. Vlad stood back and watched them leave.

'You can assure Mr Hughes and Dr Kharber they need have no concern for the security of the hospital, Mr Edwards.'

'I will, Vlad. Thank you.'

Vlad checked his rifle before taking position in the porters' cubicle opposite the door.

Glyn picked up his hat from the stand. 'I'm going to company headquarters to check on the arrangements that have been made to secure the town.' He knew he should go home and hated himself for procrastinating, but he needed time to absorb the reality of Ruth's death before facing others who'd loved her.

—

66

'I'll be back to check on Vlad's arrangements before I go home to see Catherine and Richard.'

'When you see Catherine, you'll tell her that her new great granddaughter lives. Nathan said she's strong and healthy . . . ' grateful for the touch of Sonya's hand on hers Anna returned the gentle pressure.

Knowing Anna hated to be touched by men, Glyn nodded. 'I'll tell her. You did well to save the little one's life, Anna.'

'I wish I could have done something for Ruth . . . '

'No one can do the impossible, Anna.' Fighting emotion, Glyn strode out of the door.

'Has Alexei seen his new daughter yet?' Sonya asked Anna.

'He was in the room when I took the baby from Ruth, but he didn't look at the child.'

'Could I please see the baby before I see Alexei?'

Anna led Sonya to the cubicle in the women's ward. Miriam was changing the baby.

'Would you allow me to do that please, Miriam?' Sonya asked.

'In all your finery Princess Nadolny?' Miriam cast an envious eye over Sonya's silk costume.

'I was Sonya when I worked here, Miriam, and I'm still Sonya to my friends.' She kissed Miriam's cheek before taking one of the nurse's overalls from a hook on the wall. She tied it over her dress before going to the baby and changing its napkin.'

'A mother's expert touch,' Anna complimented.

'I wouldn't say expert but this little darling doesn't wriggle the way my boys did.' She washed and dried her hands and cuddled the baby before handing her back to Miriam who'd made up a bottle.

'Watered goat's milk?' Sonya asked Miriam.

'It is, but we're looking for a wet nurse for her.'

'I hope you succeed. I'll return after I've seen Alexei. Thank you.' Sonya looked up as the door opened.

Noah de Fries smiled at them. 'I believe I have the honour of addressing the Matron . . . '

'Parry,' Anna finished for him

'Noah de Fries.' He offered Anna his hand. She hesitated. He sensed her reluctance to touch him and withdrew it.

Anna turned to the baby in Miriam's arms. 'Thank you for taking care of the child earlier.'

'Glad I could be of assistance. I have just removed a bullet from a heroic Cossack Colonel, who was so stoical and uncomplaining he passed out rather than alert me to the severity of the pain I was inflicting on him. He's lost a great deal of blood and in my opinion, needs to be admitted. I believe the senior doctor here is Dr Kharber?'

'He is about to carry out spinal surgery.'

Noah's eyes lit up. 'Does he need an assistant?'

'You can ask him. Your patient . . . '

'A nurse is with him and a junior doctor who introduced himself as Moltov. All the brave Cossack needs now is rest and fluids.'

'Do you know the way to the office, Dr de Vries?' Anna questioned.

'It is next to the main entrance?'

'It is. I saw Dr Kharber there a few minutes ago. If you'll excuse me, Dr de Vries, I need to check on someone before I join you there.'

Noah bowed briefly. 'I'll see you later, Matron Parry, Madame.' He gave an extra bow to Sonya before leaving them.

Anna watched him for a moment before going to the door of the treatment room. She hesitated as she reached for the door handle.

Sonya laid her hand on Anna's arm. 'You don't have to come in with me to see Alexei. You have so many other things to do.'

'Alexei needs comforting . . . '

'Alexei and Ruth wrote regularly to Roman and me. They were happy and very much in love. I'm sure Alexei will take more comfort from that knowledge than anything that you or I can say to him at this moment.'

'They are . . . were so very happy,' Anna agreed. Tears burned at the back of her eyes as she corrected herself. 'The only thing Ruth regretted was Alexei's insistence that they leave the huntsman's lodge after the birth of their baby. But even she had to accept that their family was outgrowing the lodge. They intended to move into the wing of Catherine's manor Mr Hughes lived in before he built his house.' Overcome Anna sank her face in her hands.

Sonya wrapped her arm around Anna's shoulders. 'It's all right to weep. You and Ruth were close . . . '

'It's not all right!' Anna wiped her eyes with the back of her hand. 'Not when I'm needed to assist Dr Kharber in surgery. If I cry I won't be able to see what I'm doing, and spinal surgery is delicate.'

'Here.' Sonya handed her a handkerchief but the simple gesture only brought more tears to Anna's eyes.

'I should be comforting you, not the other way around,' Anna protested.

'You can't be strong all the time, Anna . . . '

'I'm not,' Anna protested. 'I'm pathetic.'

'It wasn't a pathetic woman who shot the man who attacked Ruth and saved her life eighteen years ago. It's not a pathetic woman who runs this hospital. I know just how hard you've worked and how indispensable you are, not only to the hospital but the town since we left because when I wasn't here to see it with my own eyes Catherine, Ruth and Sarah wrote to tell me.'

'They are kind.'

'They weren't being kind.' Sonya placed her hand on the door handle. 'Alexei is in here?'

'Yes.'

'I'll stay with him and if he allows me to, I'll introduce him to his daughter.' Sonya kissed Anna's cheek. 'Thank you, I know Roman couldn't be in better hands.'

'Do you think Alexei will understand that I had no choice but to remove Ruth's baby surgically?'

'If he doesn't yet, he will when he's had time to understand exactly what happened and come to terms with the loss of Ruth. No one could have saved her, Anna, but you did save her child. Remember that. If you hadn't been so quick thinking and acting, that baby would be dead. And whatever else, given her father, great grandmother, sisters and cousins, she'll have a good life. A full and happy one despite the loss of her mother. Think on that.'

'I'll try.' Anna squared her shoulders.

Glyn walked down the corridor and joined them. 'If you don't mind, Sonya, I'll go in with you to see Alexei so I can tell Catherine how he is.'

'I'll be glad of the company. See you later, Anna.' Sonya kissed her again.

Anna walked away from them without looking back.

'Poor girl,' Glynn murmured. 'She has taken it upon herself to shoulder the troubles of the world.'

'She's a full-grown woman who holds down a responsible job. She wouldn't thank you for calling her "poor" or a "girl", Glyn.'

'No, she wouldn't. But then I've known her since she was a child. She's very special to me.'

'To all of us.' Sonya opened the door.

Alexei was still crouched over Ruth's body. His eyes were closed, his left arm locked around Ruth's shoulders, the fingers of his right hand entwined in hers. He was so still, so quiet that Glyn wondered he was unconscious until he saw one of his eyelids flicker.

———

Sonya held the door open for the nurse who'd been sitting with Alexei. She left and closed the door behind her. Sonya stepped around Glyn, went to Alexei and rested her hand on his back. After what seemed like an eternity Alexei lifted his head but his eyes were devoid of expression. Without moving her hand away Sonya pulled up a chair next to Alexei's and sank down beside him.

Glyn's thoughts turned to the bleak winter's day shortly after the arrival of the Welsh contingent in Hughesovka when cholera had struck the settlement. His brother Peter had been one of the first to die. Much as he'd loved Peter and sorely missed his presence in his life, he accepted there was a difference between the loss of a beloved brother and the violent death of a wife. He shuddered at the thought of anything happening to Praskovia, his wife in all but name.

If the unthinkable came to pass, he wouldn't want to live . . . but like Alexei, he had children. He hoped Alexei would consider his twins, Olga and Kitty, and the devastation wrought in their young lives by the loss of one parent. Two could well prove unbearable for girls on the brink of womanhood.

He turned his back on Alexei and Sonya, closed the door softly behind him and returned to the office. Yulia was at the secretary's desk, a pile of patients' records in front of her, a pen drooping idly between her fingers. She started nervously when she saw him.

'I'm sorry, Mr Edwards . . . '

'There is no need for apologies, nurse, we are all shocked by the day's events.

Yulia remembered her manners and rose to her feet. 'Would you like tea, Mr Edwards?'

'No, thank you. Please, sit down, I didn't mean to disturb you.'

'Is Sonya with Alexei, Mr Edwards? If not, someone should be with him. If I get another nurse to cover here I'll sit with him,' she volunteered.

71

'Sonya is with him, thank you.' Glyn cast his mind back and recalled Yulia making sheep's eyes at Alexei before he'd married Ruth. He closed his eyes against an image of Sonya bent close to Alexei. Two fair heads together, misery etched in every line of their grief- stricken bodies. He reached for his pocket watch and opened it. Four hours since Mr Hughes's sleigh had drawn to a halt outside the hotel. Only four hours since Ruth Beletskya had been alive, Roman hale and uninjured and his own happy world of Hughesovka intact. Feeling as though he'd been hit by a sledgehammer, he closed his watch.

'I'm going home to tell Catherine Ignatova that her granddaughter-in-law has died, Roman Nadolny is in surgery and my wife that her brother has been injured.'

'Dr de Vries said Colonel Razin's injuries are not serious. He expects him to make a full recovery.'

'Thanks to the staff of the hospital,' Glyn acknowledged. 'When Nathan finishes operating, or Sonya, Alexei, or anyone else needs me, please send a porter to my house. Otherwise I'll return as soon as I can.'

'Yes, sir.' Yulia finally dropped her pen. 'Please give Mrs Ignatova my deepest sympathies on the loss of Ruth and tell her that all the staff in the hospital, will be praying for Ruth's soul and Prince Nadolny's recovery.'

'I will, thank you.' Glyn was beset by a sudden and uncharacteristic envy for the Russian Orthodox certainty in the existence of God and an after-life, finding it preferable to thoughts of absolute nothingness.

A cold shiver ran down his spine bringing an unwelcome awareness of the blood thundering through his veins. Craving fresh air, he left the disinfectant ridden atmosphere of the hospital, strode out of the front door, stood in the snow covered street and breathed in deeply, coughing when the smoke laden air from the furnace hit his lungs.

A few householders, Praskovia, Madame Koshka, and the hotel manager among them, had planted trees in their gardens and he stared at their skeletal branches. It was hard to imagine them as they would be in spring covered in leaves interspersed with cherries, apples and pears burdening their boughs.

He looked across at the hotel. The bloodstained snow had been cleared from the steps and paving in front of the door. Only the Cossack soldiers standing to attention with their rifles remained as a tangible reminder of the tragedy. There were as many pedestrians as usual, testament to the old adage that "life goes on". Women with baskets hooked on their arms were trudging to and from the bakers and butchers in their felt boots; children burdened with school books were walking home from the Russian and English schools and the Jewish Yeshiva. He looked past the buildings to the steppe and glimpsed Father Grigor's one horse troika sleigh in the distance. He wondered if Catherine had sent for him because she'd realised Ruth had died.

He crossed the road, opened his garden gate and walked up the path his servants kept clear of snow. His front door was ajar and Praskovia's brother Pytor, who had the mind of a child locked into a circus strongman's body was standing in the doorway, his plump face streaked with tears, his massive muscled shoulders shuddering in unsuppressed grief.

'I've been waiting and watching for you, Mr Glyn. Do you have news of Miss Ruth and Prince Nadolny?'

Given that Pytor was his brother-in-law in all but name, Glyn had told him many times to drop the "Mr" but to no avail. Glyn handed Pytor his hat and coat

'I have news, Pytor, but I'll tell everyone when we're all together. Are Praskovia, Richard and Catherine in the parlour?'

'Yes, Mr Glyn.'

'Come with me, Pytor.'

73

Pytor took the duties Glyn and Praskovia had given him seriously. 'The door . . '

'If anyone rings, Pytor, you'll hear the bell.'

CHAPTER SIX

Glyn and Praskovia's house, Hughesovka January 1889

Glyn stood in the doorway of his parlour and looked into the room. Catherine was ensconced in the middle of the sofa between Alexei and Ruth's twins, her hands entwined with theirs. Maryanna was perched on one arm of the settee next to them, Kira the other. Richard was on a stool in front of the window that afforded him a view of the street as well as the room. Praskovia was sitting in front of the open doorway that led into the dining room. The drapes over the French doors that opened into the garden had been drawn back and Glyn saw his sons sitting in front of them with Ted and Roman's sons. He could hear the soft echo of their subdued conversation. Hating himself for having to impart the news of a tragedy that would impact on all their lives, he cleared his throat, but in the event, it was Catherine who broke the silence.

'I have sent for Father Grigor.'

Glyn went to the hearth that had been filled with dried flowers for the summer. He faced everyone in the room but looked at Catherine. 'I saw the priest's troika on the steppe. He will be here soon.'

'Alexei?' Catherine asked.

'Is with Ruth. Sonya is with them. You know . . . '

Catherine tensed her lips before speaking. 'I saw Ruth fall.'

Glyn realised everyone present knew Ruth was dead. He was relieved and grateful not to have to break the news. 'Anna saved Ruth's baby. She is healthy and strong.'

'Another girl?' Catherine tried to smile but her voice was heavy with constrained grief.

'Yes.'

'Roman?'

'Nathan Kharber, Anna and Sarah are operating to remove the bullet from his spine now.'

The bell rang shrill at the front door.

'That will be Father Grigor.' Glyn turned to Pytor. 'Show him in please.'

Hospital, Hughesovka January 1876

Conscious of the shadows lengthening in the room Sonya covered Alexei's hand with hers. 'It's time to meet your new daughter, Alexei.'

He looked at her uncomprehendingly.

'I have seen her, Alexei. She is beautiful, perfect, with Ruth's dark hair and your nose and mouth.' Sonya clung to his hand as she rose from her chair.

Alexei shook off Sonya's hand and tightened his grasp on Ruth. Sonya watched the muscles tense in his arms and his fingers harden.

'I could bring the baby here,' she offered.

'No!'

'Alexei, Ruth would want you to be strong for the sake of your daughters. You are the only parent they have left. They need you . . . '

'No!'

Sonya was shocked by the vehemence of Alexei's outburst. He was staring at her, his eyes no longer dark but glittering bright with anguish, his lips white with tension. For the first time in her life she was afraid of the man who'd shared her childhood and been a brother to her in every way that mattered. Afraid, not for herself, but for Alexei and what he might do to himself.

Summoning her courage, she persisted. 'Kitty and Olga and this new little one will never stop missing Ruth, Alexei, and neither will you. But it is your fate to tell this baby about her mother . . . ' Sonya faltered when she realised Alexei wasn't listening to a word she was saying.

'Leave me alone with my wife!'

'Alexei . . . '

'Just go!'

Realising that wherever Alexi was, he was beyond reason, she left the room.

Glyn and Praskovia's house, Hughesovka January 1889

Glyn asked the boys to join them in the drawing room as Father Grigor made his preparations to conduct prayers. When the priest was ready, they stood next to Glyn and Richard at the back of the room behind Catherine, Praskovia and the girls.

Glyn allowed his mind to drift as the priest intoned the age-old words, seeking absolution and forgiveness for Ruth's sins so her immortal soul could ascend swiftly through the waiting period dictated by God, to heaven. He tried to imagine Ruth sinning and failed. He had never met a kinder sweeter gentler soul. Then he remembered Ruth had renounced her Jewish birth-right and religion when she'd married Alexei. That alone "tainted" her in the minds of the more conservative congregation of the Russian Orthodox church.

He'd intended to slip away as soon as Father Grigor finished his prayers for Ruth, but after the priest said his final "Amen" he launched into a prayer for Roman.

'Holy Father, the only true physician of our souls and bodies, who cast down and lift up, accept us as we come in all humility to glorify you and beseech to preserve, by your grace, your servant Roman Nadolny through his operation.

We thank you for blessing the attending physicians and the means employed for his cure, and beg you to restore him safe and sound to his family and Church.

Raise him speedily, we pray you, from the bed of illness on which he lies and return him to his home and peaceful pursuits. Grant that the suffering of his body may avail for the purifying of his soul and may lead him to return, in thanksgiving, to the works of his hands and to Christ Jesus, the Physician of soul and body.

Through the prayers of our Holy Fathers. Lord Jesus Christ have mercy on us and save us. Amen.'

Glyn waited for Praskovia and Catherine to echo the priest's "Amen" before offering Father Grigor his hand.

'Thank you for the comfort you have given everyone in this house, Father, if you will excuse me I must return to the hospital.'

'Of course.' Father Grigor followed Glyn into the hall. Pytor had gone ahead of them and was waiting, Glyn's hat and coat in hand. Richard joined them.

'I wish I could offer you two the same comfort I offer my flock,' Father Grigor looked from Glyn to Richard.

'Being chapel isn't quite the same as being heathen, Father,' Glyn reminded. 'We're not quite pagan savages.'

'You are good men and that is what is important.'

'Will you stay here, Father?' Glyn asked.

'For as long as I'm needed.'

'Thank you, I'd appreciate it if you could try to keep Catherine here. I'm hoping Alexei will return with me. He is close to his grandmother . . . '

'I know how close they are,' Father Grigor broke in. 'You will bring Sonya back here too?'

'If she'll come, but I doubt she'll leave Roman.'

'Not while he needs her. Perhaps when the operation is over and we know the outcome.' The priest faltered as he realised what he'd said.

'Prince Nadolny's life is in God's hands now, Father. We have to trust in him.' Pytor's declaration was as moving as it was unexpected.

'You're quite right, Pytor. We do.' The priest patted Pytor's shoulder.

78

'Keep praying, Pytor, Father Grigor, and I'll pray that God hears you. I believe he stopped taking notice of anything I say when he took my brother Peter seven years ago.' Glyn waited for Pytor to open the door and he and Richard tramped across the snow covered road.

Hospital, Hughesovka January 1889

'Does Vasya know Ruth is dead?' Richard asked Glyn.

Glyn frowned. Ruth was Nathan's sister, but to his shame he hadn't given a single thought to Nathan's wife. 'I should imagine so.'

'I saw Nathan arrive at the hotel with the staff from the hospital to treat the wounded but I didn't see Vasya there.'

'Mr Hughes sent invitations to the lunch to both Kharbers, but as you know they rarely attend any event outside of the Jewish community,' Glyn said.

'Alexei told me he felt as though Ruth's brother and his wife were trying to atone for Ruth's conversion by only accepting invitations from people of their faith. Although they did defy the rabbi by attending Ruth and Alexei's wedding.'

'I remember.'

'Do you think Nathan would have sent a porter to tell Vasya what had happened, even if he didn't go to see her himself?' Richard asked.

'I doubt it. He was too concerned with Ruth and Roman to spare a thought for anyone or anything else,' Glyn stopped outside the office.

'You know Vasya better than me . . . ' Richard began.

'That's debatable. I've only met her a few times.' Glyn knocked and opened the office door. Yulia was inside filing patients' records.

'Is there any news . . . ' Glyn began.

'About Prince Nadolny?' Yulia shook her head. 'They haven't left the operating theatre.'

Glyn opened his pocket watch. 'It's been over two hours.

'Sonya?' Richard asked.

'Is in the kitchen washing dishes. It wasn't our idea, Mr Parry. She said she wanted to keep busy.' Yulia closed the filing cabinet.

'Do you know if anyone has told Mrs Kharber that Ruth has died?' Glyn asked.

Too upset to answer Yulia shook her head.

'I'll go and see her.' Glyn left the office.

'Alexei?' Richard asked.

'Hasn't left the treatment room where Sarah laid out Ruth. He shouted at Sonya when she tried to take him to see his baby, which is why Sonya retreated to the kitchen. I've listened at the door but I haven't heard a sound from him since.'

'If I don't come out in an hour . . . '

'Don't expect me to go in and rescue you after the way he shouted at Sonya,' Yulia warned.

'I was going to say, send in a porter.' Richard looked down the corridor. 'Which treatment room?'

'First on the left.'

Richard braced himself.

Nathan Kharber's house Hughesovka January 1889

Nathan Kharber's house was behind the hospital, the lane in front of it swept free from snow. Glyn tapped on the front door and waited at the foot of the steps. After a minute he heard someone walk over the wooden floor of the hall. The door opened and he looked up at Vasya's father, Levi Goldberg.

'Mr Edwards?'

'Forgive the intrusion Mr Goldberg. I called to see if Vasya needed anything as Dr Kharber is still operating on Prince Nadolny.'

'Did you come to see if Vasya had heard that Ruth Beletskya is dead?' Levi snapped.

Glyn decided there was no point in trying to be tactful. 'I didn't want Mrs Kharber to hear about the death of her sister-in-law through gossip.'

'Your thoughtfulness is to be commended, Mr Edwards, but Ruth Kharber has been dead to her family and community since the day she married Alexei Beletsky and abandoned her people along with her faith.'

Glyn debated whether or not to offer condolences and decided against it. 'Good day to you, Mr Goldberg.'

'Mr Edwards?'

Glyn turned back.

'Do you know the whereabouts of my son-in-law and daughter's nieces?'

'Olga and Kitty are with Alexei's grandmother Catherine Ignatova. Ruth's baby is in the hospital.' Glyn wasn't sure why he hadn't revealed that the girls were in his house, but he was glad he hadn't a few seconds later.

'Ruth gave birth to another child before she died?'

'A daughter.'

'Is she expected to survive?'

Glyn looked Levi in the eye. 'All who knew and loved Ruth and know Alexei are praying for her.'

'As Ruth was Nathan's sister and the children are now orphaned they will be claimed by Nathan and Vasya.'

'They have a father,' Glyn reminded him.

'Girls cannot be brought up by a father. They need a mother's guidance and in the case of Ruth's daughters, to be returned to their mother's faith. Our religion is passed down through the maternal line. You will inform Mrs Ignatova of my daughter and son-in-law's intention to claim the girls?'

'I have urgent business to attend to . . . ' Glyn prevaricated.

'No matter. Vasya and Nathan will call on Mrs Ignatova when Nathan finishes work for the day in the hospital.' Levi Goldberg closed the door leaving Glyn no option but to walk away.

—

'Is Richard with Alexei?' Glyn asked Sonya when he saw her in the kitchen.

'He went in ten minutes ago. We haven't heard any shouting yet, so he must have had more success than I did in talking to Alexei.' Sonya filled two glasses with tea, handed Glyn one, pulled a chair up to the table and sat down. 'You passed the office on the way in. Was there any . . . '

'Yulia told me that no one has left the operating theatre.' Glyn sensed Sonya's ears straining to catch the slightest noise.

'I should go and see Alexei.'

'I'd leave him with Richard for a while. They're closer than most brothers as well business partners.'

'I'm glad to hear it for Alexei's sake. And selfish enough to be grateful to Richard. It's always easier to do nothing than something.'

Glyn glanced out of the window. He saw a movement behind the screening hedge of shrubs in the Kharber's garden. 'I've just spoken to Levi Goldberg. He was in Dr Kharber's house.'

'Did he know about Ruth?'

'Yes.'

'Did you see Vasya?'

'No. Levi asked me to tell Catherine that Vasya and Nathan intend to adopt Alexei and Ruth's girls.'

'That's preposterous!' Sonya exclaimed. 'Nathan and Vasya would never attempt to do anything of the sort. This is the Goldbergs and the Rabbi . . . '

'You may well be right. I didn't argue with Levi. If Vasya was in the house she would have heard him, but she didn't come to the door.'

'Will you tell Catherine of the Goldbergs' intentions?'

'I will warn Catherine and Alexei but I can't see either of them giving Ruth's daughters to Ruth's brother and Vasya, particularly as the twins have been christened into the Russian Orthodox faith and at sixteen, are old enough to know their own mind. Frankly I think they're too old to be adopted and I can't see either of them abandoning their religion in favour of the one their mother renounced. However, Levi Goldberg was right in one respect. It won't be easy for Alexei to bring up the baby alone or see the twins through to womanhood and marriage for that matter.'

'It won't,' Sonya agreed. 'No more than it will be easy for me to guide my boys without Roman's help should the worst happen, but I have no doubt that if it proves necessary God will give us the strength to do exactly that and watch over us and our children.'

'You will have many friends on your side as well as God, Sonya. Will you come with me?'

'Where?'

'To fetch Alexei's new daughter and take her to her father.' Glyn offered her his arm. She took it.

Hospital Hughesovka January 1889

Alexei turned to the door when it opened but he flinched as though it physically pained him to tear his gaze away from Ruth's body.

Richard held out a chair to Sonya. She sat next to Alexei and folded back the blanket she'd wrapped around his daughter before lifting the baby so he could see her.

'Ruth would have loved her, Alexei.' She held out the child in the hope that Alexei would take her.

Alexei was so still he could have been sculpted.

Undeterred Sonya persisted, 'Did you and Ruth pick out a name for her?'

Alexei didn't answer.

She continued. 'She needs her father, Alexei.'

Glyn and Richard held their breath as Alexei finally focused on Sonya. When he spoke, his voice was so hoarse it was barely decipherable.

'You keep her, Sonya. I can't leave Ruth. She needs me.'

'Alexei this beautiful baby . . . '

'Is alive. Her mother isn't.'

'That is not the child's fault, Alexei,' Sonya pleaded. 'There was no choice to be made. It wasn't a case of saving the baby at the expense of the mother but salvaging life from unbearable tragedy.' Sonya looked Alexei in the eye. 'Take her from me, please.'

Alexei continued to stare at Sonya. Glyn and Richard exchanged glances. The door opened. Anna stood in the doorway.

'Sonya . . . Roman is out of theatre . . . '

Sonya thrust the baby at Alexei and rose to her feet. She dived through the door, the click of her high heeled slippers resounding like a drumbeat over the wooden floor as she ran to the recovery room.

Anna followed, her rubber soled nurses' shoes squeaking in her wake.

Time froze as Glyn and Richard continued to watch Alexei. It felt as though hours not minutes passed before Alexei looked down on the sleeping baby in his arms. Slowly, infinitely slowly he moved the child closer to his chest. A wave of relief coursed through Richard's veins when Alexei pushed his finger into the baby's hand.

'They always do that,' Richard murmured.

'What?' Alexei asked.

'Grab the first finger they can. Ted and Maryanna both did it.'

Vlad knocked the door and called out, 'Mr Beletsky.'
Glyn opened it.

'The carpenter is here, sir. He's brought a coffin.'

'A coffin,' Alexei repeated dully.

'Mrs Parry asked Nurse Yulia to order one . . . '

Glyn interrupted Vlad. 'Where's the carpenter now?'

84

'In the office, Your Excellency.'

'I'll see to him, Alexei.' Glyn left with Vlad.

Alexei thrust his daughter at Richard. 'Take care of her. I need to make arrangements to take Ruth home.'

CHAPTER SEVEN

Hospital Hughesovka January 1889

Roman was lying face down on a trolley. It was too short for his six and half feet frame so a long wooden board had been pushed beneath him to support his legs and feet. Sarah was standing next to him, her fingers on the pulse at his neck.

Sonya stopped running and gripped the door post. 'He's . . . '

'Recovering from surgery, Princess Nadolny.' Nathan Kharber was sitting on a stool, his back slumped against the wall behind him. He looked like a man who had used his last ounce of energy. Noah de Vries was standing next to him. He was upright but he appeared to be as exhausted as Nathan.

'Anna . . . '

'Don't blame Anna for my being here, Dr Kharber. As soon as I knew Roman had left the operating theatre, I had to see him . . . will he . . . '

'Survive?' Nathan met Sonya's searching gaze. He'd fallen in love with her before he'd married Vasya and she'd married Roman. It was a feeling he sensed – no *knew* –had been reciprocal and he would have embraced that love wholeheartedly if it hadn't been for his religion. Unlike his sister Ruth he'd lacked the courage to defy the rabbi and entire community, a failing he'd cursed himself for many times. The last time only that morning, when he'd seen Sonya alight from her sleigh and walk into the hotel with her sons.

The years had been kind to Sonya. The girl he'd adored, had become a beautiful woman. Her figure was as slim and girlish as it had been twenty years ago. Her hair as fair and her eyes the same piercing blue . . .

'Will Roman recover?'

Sonya's question shattered his reverie and kindled the professionalism that was never far from the surface. 'It was a long and debilitating surgery. But your husband is strong and was in excellent health. The bullet in his arm presented no problems. It was embedded in his muscle but did little damage. The one in his spine . . . '

'Have you removed it?' Sonya asked urgently.

'It was too close to the spinal cord for us to risk extricating it.'

'Is Roman's paralysed?' From the way Sonya caressed Roman's hand, Nathan could see her concern was for Roman, not herself. He realised she loved her husband, as thoroughly and completely as it was possible for one woman to love a man, and that knowledge pained him more than he would have believed possible.

'We won't know until he recovers from the anaesthetic,' Noah de Vries answered. 'It was a long and complex procedure.'

'It's fortunate that Dr de Vries arrived here today. He is far more experienced than I in spinal surgery,' Nathan said.

'How long will it take for Roman to recover from the anaesthetic?' Sonya asked

'He should start coming around in three or four hours,' Noah answered.

'May I stay with my husband?'

Noah looked to Nathan as senior doctor to give Sonya permission.

'As long as you don't get in the way of medical procedures or inform any of the other patients' relatives that you're receiving special privileges.' Nathan rose from the stool as though all his muscles had turned to stone. 'Tell the porters to move Prince Nadolny to a private room when he wakes. Any change in his condition . . . '

'I'll send for you,' Anna assured him.

'Or Dr de Vries. Welcome to Hughesovka hospital. On our and Prince Nadolny's behalf. We couldn't have managed without you.' Nathan shook Noah's hand. 'Sarah can you stay with our patient for the moment. I need to talk to Anna.'

Nathan waited he and Anna were alone in the corridor before speaking. 'I need to check if my sister's body is still in the hospital. Will you get a sedative ready and a syringe in case Alexei is still with her? I don't want to risk a scene . . .'

He fell silent when the sound of voices raised in anger echoed towards them. They ran down the corridor. Nathan struggled to open the door of the treatment room Anna had used to lay out Ruth. He put his shoulder against it and pushed with all the strength he could muster but failed to open the door more than an inch. From what little he could see, the room appeared to be crammed full of people. His father-in-law, Levi Goldberg flanked his brother Rabbi Goldberg behind the door, facing Alexei who was standing in front of them with Ruth's corpse in his arms. Richard had tried to insinuate himself between the Goldbergs and Alexei but as he was holding the baby he was hardly in a position to protect Alexei should the situation turn ugly. Tucked into the far corner making herself as small and insignificant as possible was the shrivelled figure of his wife, Vasya.

'Silence!' Nathan commanded through the door. 'This is a hospital not a market place. The patients require peace and quiet.' Nathan kept his voice low, even, while trying to glare at the Goldberg brothers who'd been doing most of the shouting, although he could only see the side of their faces. 'Alexei, what are you doing with Ruth?'

'Taking her home. Don't try to stop me.'

'Ruth is your wife. It is your right to take her remains where you will,' Nathan said calmly.

'But surely you don't intend to cross the road carrying Ruth in the open like that. Don't you want a coffin, or at least a porter to help you?'

'I can manage.'

Nathan called for Vlad, the largest and most level headed of the porters. He'd worked for Alexei's family before taking a post at the hospital and had known Alexei since birth. After a murmured conversation between them, Nathan moved back so Vlad could use his superior size and brute strength to push the door open. He succeeded and forced the Goldbergs back against the wall.

Vlad, Anna and Nathan entered the room. Vlad slipped his arm around Alexei's shoulders and guided him, still holding Ruth's corpse out through the door. Richard held out the baby to Anna. She glanced from the Goldbergs to Nathan who was locked in a staring match with the rabbi and his father-in-law. She took the baby and followed Vlad and Alexei out of the room.

Richard joined her. 'I'll fetch more porters.'

'They could exacerbate the situation.'

'Better the Goldbergs fight the porters than Nathan. The hospital needs fit undamaged doctors.'

'Looks like Vlad has been thinking along the same lines as you.' Anna watched four of the largest porters walk down the corridor towards them.

'We need to move out of the firing line.' Richard grasped her arm and guided her from their path.

'I'll take this little one back to the women's ward.' Anna pulled the shawl higher to cover the baby's head.

'Can you spare me half an hour, Anna?' Richard asked.

'After I've seen the baby back to the cubicle and checked Roman is recovering as he should, but only if Sarah agrees to cover my nursing duties.

'It's important.'

'What do you want me to do?'

'I'll tell you after I've arranged it. When you've settled the baby, and asked Sarah to take over, go to the office. I'll wait for you there.'

——

'Why are you here?' Nathan demanded of the Goldbergs. He'd closed the door when the porters Vlad had sent had arrived in the corridor, sealing the three of them into as much privacy as the thin walls of the treatment room would afford.

'We heard – from strangers . . . '

Levi's rebuke wasn't lost on Nathan. He interrupted. 'I've been too busy trying to save lives to make social calls.'

'You were too busy to tell us that that your sister, one of our community had died?'

'When it comes to practising medicine, the treatment of the living takes precedence over deference to the dead.' Nathan crossed his arms across his chest as he faced his father-in-law.

'We came in here to discover that Ruth's corpse had been laid out. No one sent for me, or the Chevra Kadisha, so Ruth could be washed and dressed and prayers said as our religious laws demand.' Rabbi Goldberg's face reddened in anger. 'The requirements of our faith have been ignored, brushed aside . . . '

'They were ignored because they were not relevant to Ruth or her family.'

'You are her family.'

'Her husband and children, are her family. My sister is – was - no longer a Jew.' The blood drained from Nathan's face as the realisation struck anew that his sister really was dead.

'She was of your blood. One of God's chosen people, as you and we all are.'

'Ruth chose a different path. She died a Christian following the faith of her husband.'

'It is not possible for anyone born into our faith to cast it aside like a worn-out coat, or pair of shoes. Our religious laws forbid it.' Rabbi Goldberg declaimed loudly, his voice booming as though he was in the synagogue.

—

90

Nathan knew from experience how anything said in the treatment rooms echoed down the corridor that linked them.

'Please keep your voice down.'

Nathan's polite request only served to inflame the rabbi further. 'As Ruth's brother, it is ordained that you and Vasya should take Ruth's children . . . '

'Ruth's children are Alexei's responsibility,' Nathan spoke softly in sharp contrast to the rabbi.

'Alexei is in no state to look after them. You saw him. Carrying his wife's corpse in his arms instead of burying it swiftly . . . '

'The Christian way is not the Jewish way, Levi,' Nathan interrupted his father-in-law again.

'Alexei can't possibly look after Ruth's children,' Rabbi Goldberg said earnestly.

'There is no one better. He is their father. His blood runs in their veins. He has family and friends to help him and money enough to care for them and pay servants to run his home.'

'Alexei is estranged from his own father, and has no family here except his grandmother who will soon be called from this earth and a sister barely older than his daughters who is soon to be married to a Welshman if the rumours I have heard are true. Ruth told me that Alexei never hears from his five brothers who are all soldiers. Ruth's daughters deserve better, they must be brought up by their uncle and aunt in the faith that was their mother's birth-right, given to Ruth by God to pass on to her offspring.' Vasya's quiet declaration was more powerful than Rabbi Goldberg's shouts.

'And their father's faith?' Nathan questioned.

'Surely, I don't need to remind you that the heritage of our people runs through the maternal line,' Rabbi Goldberg lectured.

'Ruth's daughters need to grow up knowing exactly who their mother was and who they are, while being cared for and guided by a young, religious woman who walks in God's chosen path. Someone who will love and teach them the ways of their faith, and how to pray to He who gives us life and all things. The girls *must* be given to their uncle and aunt.'

'Not a Christian father obsessed by industry who spends more time working than he does with his daughters.' Levi's jaw was set, the expression in his eyes, determined.

Nathan could hear Vasya's opinions behind her father's words. He realised his wife was fighting for the children denied her when she'd suffered a premature menopause before she'd entered her second decade.

He'd given into her pleadings once and allowed her to foster her paternal cousin's three sons and daughter. The experiment had not been a success, probably because all four children were in their second decade when they'd moved in with him and Vasya. Too old to accept discipline meted out by distant unknown relatives, the boys had proved aggressive and unruly, the girl sulky and indifferent to Vasya's gentle kindness. Fortunately, his father-in-law had taken two of the boys into his butchery business, where they'd proved themselves to be reasonable workers, and Alexei and Richard Parry had given the other two positions in their collieries. A husband had been found for the girl, Martha, but only after he'd raided his bank account to give her a substantial dowry.

The experience had scarred him. He was not anxious to repeat it nor was he prepared to challenge his brother-in-law's right to take custody of his own children.

'You want children, Vasya, you will have to find them elsewhere. I will not allow you to take Ruth's and Alexei's and bring them into our house. As the girls' uncle and their only living tie to our faith, my word is final. Please leave the hospital, all of you.'

'Not without Ruth's baby,' Vasya tensed her hands.

92

'The baby has just been born . . . '

'She needs care.'

'The care of a trained nurse in a hospital.' Nathan said harshly. 'Please leave or I will call the porters.'

'You wouldn't dare . . . '

Nathan went to the door and opened it. The porters Vlad had sent down from the office were ranged outside. Nathan looked at the Goldbergs then turned to the porters.

'Please see the rabbi, my father-in-law and my wife out of the hospital,' Nathan said.

The Goldbergs and Vasya glared at him but they filed out of the room.

'Will you be home soon, Nathan?' Vasya murmured as she passed him.

'When all my patients are out of danger and my work is finished for the day, Vasya, not before, and when I do, I will be too tired to discuss this, or any other matter. Don't wait up for me.'

Hospital Hughesovka January 1889

After Anna returned the baby to Miriam she visited Roman. Sarah had done what little was needed until he recovered from the anaesthetic and she promised to monitor him while Anna was away from the hospital. If Sarah knew what Richard was planning she chose not to confide in Anna and Anna didn't ask. As Anna picked up her cloak and hat from outside the office she glanced out of the window. To her surprise she saw Richard's sleigh and his driver waiting at the gate.

'We're driving?' she asked Richard.

'Only a short distance.' Richard took Anna's cloak from her and slipped it around her shoulders.

'I've spoken to Sarah, she's agreed to oversee things here until I return.'

'I know.'

'But I can't stay away for long. Roman could regain consciousness . . . '

93

'We won't be long.' Richard cut her short as he escorted her to the door and helped her into his carriage.

The driver moved off. A few minutes later they reached the Headquarters of the New Russian Company.

'We could have walked here,' Anna demurred when the driver drove into the snow blanketed yard at the back of the building. They halted in front of one of the wooden warehouses that lined the yard. Richard opened the sleight door and jumped down. He unrolled the steps for Anna and offered her his hand. A small door set in one of the large wooden doors that walled the front of the warehouse opened, revealing Glyn and Praskovia.

Anna looked from them to Richard. 'Why are we here?'

'The bodies of the Paskeys are inside, Anna. After what they did to you – to us,' – he corrected himself, 'Glyn and I thought you should see them.'

Anna backed towards the carriage.

Richard took her arm. 'We both need to know that they've finally gone and can't hurt us any more, Anna. I know you have nightmares about them. I lost count of the number of times I heard you cry out in the middle of the night before you left us to move in with Catherine . . . '

'As did you. I wasn't the only one to wake screaming in the early hours . . . '

'It's over, Anna,' he broke in. 'It's finally over. For them and us. It's time to forget what they did to you, me, Mam and our family.' He wrapped his arm around her shoulders.

She stood her ground. 'I'll never forget. Don't try telling me that you will.'

'Perhaps forget is not the right word,' he conceded.

'I'll never forgive them . . . '

'No one is asking you to forget or forgive the Paskeys, Anna.' Glyn walked out to meet her. 'But Richard is right. You need to see their bodies and know that they can't come back to hurt you. Not ever again.'

—

94

'I only have to close my eyes for the Paskeys to hurt me,' Anna said bitterly. 'To see their filthy pockmarked faces. To smell their foul breath. To feel their greasy sweaty hands on my bare skin, pawing, fouling . . . '

Glyn pushed the small door wide and stepped aside.

The coffins were in front of the door. Two unvarnished deal boxes. Roughly sawn lids lay propped against them, their ends ragged with splinters. Feeling as though she were locked in a nightmare Anna found herself moving through the shadowy gloom of the inside of the warehouse towards them. She looked down. Mervyn Paskey's blood spattered corpse was in the one nearest to her. His face was unmarked, his clothes riddled by black powdered bullet holes. Ianto's body had been crammed into the far box. It was too short for his limbs and he lay, knees bent, cramped at an awkward angle.

Glyn lifted an oil lantern down from a hook behind the door and held it above the coffins. It shed a bright yellow light over the grey pinched faces of both men, throwing their features into sharp relief. Anna started nervously and reached for Richard's arm when she saw movement in Mervyn's coffin.

'They're as infested with lice and fleas as they were in life, but the vermin are the only live objects in those boxes, Anna,' Glyn reassured.

'They'll be taken out on to the steppe tonight and buried in unmarked graves without benefit of clergy or prayers,' Richard added.

'That's their punishment?' Anna's eyes were dark pools in the subdued light.

'Their punishment will come when they stand before God, Anna,' Praskovia murmured.

'Our mother collapsed and died when she saw how they'd beaten Richard within an inch of his life. They raped me the day my mother was buried. No punishment God can inflict on those two . . . savages . . . will be enough for what they did to my family. Anna wrenched her arm free from Richard's grasp, pulled her cloak around her, turned on her heel and ran back to the carriage.

CHAPTER EIGHT

Hospital Hughesovka January 1889

Too upset to talk, Anna brushed aside Richard's suggestion that she return to his house. Instead she insisted his driver return her to the hospital. When they reached there, Richard opened the carriage door, unfolded the steps and held out his hand to help her down.

Stifling her tears, she ignored her brother's hand and gentle "good night" and walked into the hospital without a backward glance. She exchanged her outdoor cap for her indoor one, her cloak for her apron and prepared to immerse herself in routine. But an image of the Paskeys' lice infested bodies continued to haunt her.

The porter manning the office told her Nathan Kharber was in his consulting room. She found the doctor stretched out on a sofa he'd salvaged after it had been thrown out by the hotel. He frequently slept on it, using the excuse that patients might need his attention during the night, although all the staff knew that he lingered in the hospital rather than go home to Vasya.

He sat up when she opened the door at his, 'Enter.'

'I'm sorry I didn't mean to disturb you,' she apologised.

'You didn't,' he replied. 'As you see the hospital hasn't fallen down in the half hour since you left. Ruth's baby is fine and feeding well. Vlad and the porters helped Alexei to take Ruth's body home. Sarah has checked on Alexei in his house and administered a sedative. His servants, Lev and Lada are caring for him and Sarah has now returned to her home. The new doctor is monitoring Roman. He's still in the treatment room, as is Sonya who refuses to leave her husband. Misha Razin is incubating a fever, his reward for being idiotic enough to ignore a bullet wound and almost bleeding to death.

97

'The other four patients who were wounded outside the hotel are recovering and barring the onset of infection will be discharged tomorrow. The number of fatalities from the shooting still stands at eight. And to end this bulletin, Matron, your shift ended hours ago, and you should be home in bed.'

'I wouldn't sleep. I'm sorry. I haven't even given you my condolences on Ruth's death.'

Moving slowly and clumsily from sheer weariness, Nathan sat up and ran his hands through his thick black hair. 'There hasn't been time for any of us to do any of the things we should have today.' He looked up at her. 'I can't even imagine living a day without seeing Ruth. I'm so accustomed to catching glimpses of her, out shopping or riding in one of Alexei's carriages with the girls. Her absence will be hard to bear, although we weren't as close as we once were after she married Alexei. And for that, I blame myself.'

'When a woman has children, they eat into her life until they take all her time, leaving very little for anyone or anything else. I've seen it happen with Sarah, Praskovia and Ruth.'

He looked at her as though the thought had never occurred to him.

Embarrassed in case he interpreted her remark as a comment on his childless state, she said, 'Can I get you anything? Tea? A sedative?'

'I like the idea of taking refuge in sleep. The only problem is grief will be waiting to attack me when I wake.'

'It never goes away,' she agreed thinking of her parents, brothers and sisters. 'If there's nothing you want-'

'You've had a long day too, Anna. I've just told you everything is under control here. Go home.'

'I'll stay until Roman comes around.'

'You don't trust us to look after him?'

'I trust you. But like you I don't trust myself to sleep and you're not the only one who craves oblivion after today.'

Even after talking to Nathan Kharber, Anna felt the need to look into the cubicle where Ruth's baby was sleeping peacefully in a crib alongside a junior nurse who was reading a medical textbook in preparation for her next examination. She left them for the wards, checking every patient in the women's, children's and finally the men's.

Misha Razin was asleep, but as Nathan had warned, restless and feverish. After studying his chart, she asked the duty nurse to check his pulse every hour and ensure that he drank at least half a pint of water every time he woke. Making a mental note to look in on him again before she left the hospital, she finally went to the recovery room.

Spartak and Andrei were sitting on the floor, their backs to the wall outside the door. Both leapt to their feet when they saw her.

'Are you going to see my father, Matron . . . '

'It's still Auntie Anna, Andrei,' Anna gave them what she hoped was a reassuring smile although her face felt oddly stiff.

'We'd like to see him, if we can.' Spartak begged.

'I'll check that he's up to seeing visitors.' Anna opened the door just wide enough for her to slide through. Roman was lying on the trolley in the same position she'd left him.

Sonya was sitting next to him holding his hand. She looked up at Anna and mouthed, 'are the boys outside?'

'Yes,' Anna whispered. 'They want to see Roman.'

'I've tried sending them back to Glyn's house. They refused. They insist on waiting until Roman wakes.'

The door to the side room was open. Anna saw Noah de Vries slumped awkwardly on two chairs he'd pushed together.

He opened one grey eye when she approached.

—

'Is there any reason why Roman's sons can't see him?' she asked.

'Not if they're quiet and stay back in the doorway in case they're carrying infection.'

She returned to the corridor. 'If I open the door wide enough for you to see your father, you can look at him, but after one minute you leave for the office where you'll ask one of the porters to give you an escort to Glyn Edwards's house.'

'We don't need an escort . . . '

'You do, Andrei. The Cossack soldiers are still out in the town searching for whoever killed your Aunt Ruth, wounded your father and shot the other bystanders. Think of your poor mother. It's heart breaking enough for her to see your father injured without you two setting out to risk your necks. So, neither of you are to take any unnecessary risks with your own safety, and that is an order. Understand?'

'Yes, Auntie Anna,' they chorused.

'And no further than the door. Your father has an open wound. If any bacteria get into it, it could prove serious.' She opened the door and moved behind them. They looked into the room.

Less than a minute later they stepped back and Andrei closed the door.

'Thank you, Auntie Anna.' He slipped his arm around Spartak's shoulders. The brothers hugged one another for a moment before walking away, backs straight, eyes front, but then Anna thought, she wouldn't have expected any less from Roman and Sonya Nadolny's sons. She returned to the recovery room and checked Roman's pulse.

'Slow and steady and that's good,' she gave Sonya an encouraging smile before going into the ante room where Noah de Vries was still balancing on two chairs.

'You don't look at all comfortable,' she murmured.

'I'm not.' He stretched out his legs and rubbed his knees. 'What time is it?'

She looked at the watch pinned to her uniform. 'Just after midnight. Can I get you something, tea, cake, biscuit?'

'You Russians drink rivers of tea.'

'The Russians drink rivers of vodka,' she corrected. 'We Welsh drink rivers of tea, and Russian tea is good.'

'It is. It's the quantity I object to.'

She sat on the only spare chair in the room. 'My apologies. You were given a rather abrupt introduction to hospital life.'

'There is nothing like seeing what's expected of you right away.' He smiled and it transformed his features, curling the ends of his mouth beneath his sand coloured moustache. His eyes. sparkled in the lamplight, glittering like raindrops.

'I'll stay with the patient and his wife until he regains consciousness. Dr Kharber is in his consulting room and can be here in seconds should he need medical attention beyond my capabilities. So, you can go home and sleep in your bed, Dr de Vries.'

'My name is Noah, as for home and bed, I have no idea of the location of either.' He moved his legs down from the second chair and brushed his thatch of straw coloured hair back from his forehead.

'Haven't you been given one of the doctors' houses behind the hospital?'

'So, I was given to understand when I applied for the position here, but I've yet to see it.'

'Didn't you have any luggage when you arrived?'

'I recall a porter taking it from the driver of the carriage I hired to convey me here from the station and assuring me it would be safe.'

'If one of the porters took it from your sleigh, it will be safe. I'll look for it if you like,' she offered.

'No, please, don't disturb yourself. I don't think our patient . . . I heard someone call him Prince Nadolny. . . '

'He is a prince but not one who stands on ceremony. His name is Roman,' she interrupted.

101

'He won't sleep for much longer. I'll look for my luggage when I'm certain he's recovered from the anaesthetic. If it's lost,' he shrugged, 'it's lost. If it's safe it can survive without me for a while longer.' He gave her another smile.

Given everything that had happened that day she couldn't bring herself to return it.

'I've worked in hospitals in Holland, Vienna and Berlin and all the matrons I've met have been elderly terrifying martinets with voices louder than generals and the manners of an executioner. You on the other hand appear to be a beautiful bright young woman brimming over with kindness.'

'Looks can be deceptive,' she said tartly. Too tartly she realised when she heard her own voice. Noah de Vries was a young man, a stranger in a strange town and simply trying to be polite. The least he deserved was common courtesy. 'I've never met anyone with "the manners of an executioner". How do they behave?'

'They give you a look that says, "disobey me and I'll sever your head from your shoulders and place it on a pole.".'

'I am a martinet when the situation demands it.'

'I've seen no evidence as yet.'

'Stay around and you will,' she replied.

'So, please satisfy my curiosity, and tell me how you reached such an exalted position at such a young age?'

'I'm not that young. I came to Hughesovka with Mr Hughes's party when the hospital was under construction and the town consisted of a few wooden buildings. I trained as a nurse under the last matron – you met her today she administered the anaesthetic . . . '

'Mrs Parry?'

'She's my sister-in-law, married to my brother Richard.'

He offered Anna his hand. 'I look forward to working with you, Matron Parry. You must have been a child when you arrived here.'

'Only in years. I was twelve.'

It was a poor joke but he smiled. 'Which makes you-'

'It makes you ill-mannered to try to work it out.'

'Guilty as charged,' he gave her another winsome smile. 'I'm interested in how long it takes people to study medicine, and from what I've seen working in more than a dozen hospitals it requires as much effort to become a nurse as it does to qualify as a doctor. It's taken me the best part of ten years to become a medical practitioner. That's why I was interested in how you became a matron at . . . ?'

She capitulated. 'Thirty-two but I've been Matron and before that acting Matron for over a decade. You found it difficult to study?'

'No, the difficulty lay in staying alive long enough to study. Unfortunately, due to a pampered childhood I had become accustomed to eating two or three times a day and sleeping under a roof. Albeit beneath my Dutch pig farmer's father's roof. When he and my mother died, I discovered I couldn't study without their support. I devised a plan whereby I would work one year with the intention of saving enough money by living frugally to study the next. It was an excellent plan, unfortunately the living frugally proved difficult, hence the amount of time it took me to qualify. Then, I discovered that even after I'd qualified I needed to gain experience to bring in a decent wage. So here I am, taking up my first senior appointment ten years after I began my training.'

'If you don't mind me saying so you look prosperous now.'

He fingered his moustache and the lapels on his broadcloth suit. 'The expensive barbering – the English suit . . . '

' . . . your top hat, and bespoke leather shoes,' she added.

'Are all down to the generosity of the New Russia Company's advance payment when I signed their contract.'

103

'It isn't easy to attract doctors to the steppe.'

'A situation which proved extremely fortunate for me.' He opened his pocket watch. It was old and worn.

'Your advance, didn't run to a new timepiece?' she asked.

'This was my grandfather's and my father's. The only thing I inherited from them and the one thing of value I could never bring myself to pawn.'

'You're lucky to have something from your parents.' She left her chair. 'it's time I looked at our patient.'

'I think I can just about find my way to the kitchen. I'll ask a nurse to make some of that tea you mentioned. A cup might go some way to keeping me awake.'

Glyn and Praskovia's house, Hughesovka January 1889

Catherine was alone in the parlour when Glyn, Praskovia and Richard returned. Her eyes were dry, but her face was pale, strained by grief.

'Where is Alexei?' she asked.

'At home,' Richard answered. 'We called on him before coming here.'

'Where are the boys?' Glyn asked.

'Andrei and Spartak are at the hospital, they know it's unlikely they'll be allowed to see their father but they wanted to be close to their mother. Ted has driven Olga, Kitty and Maryanna to the church in your second carriage Richard. The girls wanted to say prayers and light candles for Ruth.'

Glyn shrugged off his coat and handed it to Pytor. 'We left Alexei talking to the carpenter. He wants a white coffin for Ruth, and being Alexei has very definite ideas on what it should look like. He also made it clear that when the carpenter leaves he wants to be alone with his wife.'

'He knows where we are should he need us for anything,' Richard added. 'We spoke to Lev and Lada. They promised to look after him.'

'I've no doubt that they will do just that.' Catherine knotted her fingers into the fringe of the shawl Yelena had draped around her shoulders. 'Does Alexei realise that he'll have to make funeral arrangements for Ruth with Father Grigor?'

'He will when he's had time to think about it,' Glyn assured her.

'Is Sarah still at the hospital?' Catherine asked.

'Yes,' Richard answered. 'I'll look in on her and Anna before I go home but I can't see either of them or Nathan Kharber leaving Roman until they're sure he's recovering.'

Glyn saw the priest's Bible and cloak on one of the chairs. 'Is Father Grigor still here?'

'He's in the kitchen comforting Yelena,' Catherine said.

Glyn decided that the sooner he gave Catherine the news, the longer she'd have to consider it – and plan ways to thwart the Goldbergs. 'Rabbi Goldberg wants Vasya and Roman to take Alexei and Ruth's daughters and bring them up in their faith.'

'Has the rabbi spoken to Alexei about this?'

Glyn recalled the numb expression on Alexei's face as he'd carried Ruth's body from the treatment room. 'If he has, Alexei, was too distraught to understand.'

'And Nathan and Vasya? What do they think about this plan of her uncle's?' Catherine demanded.

'You know Nathan, he says very little and nothing contentious in public, but everyone in the hospital heard him ordering the porters to escort Rabbi Goldberg and his brother from the hospital,' Richard said. 'I can't see Nathan or Alexei allowing the rabbi to take the girls.'

'Rabbi Goldberg will never take my granddaughters from their father, me or the one true church, not while I have strength to stop him,' Catherine said vehemently. 'As for the girls. I'd like to see anyone try to tell Olga and Kitty what to do. They have their mother's strength and their father's temper.'

'And your stubborn refusal to concede to tragedy.' Glyn sat beside her. 'Please, Catherine, stay here. At least for tonight. We have Cossack guards outside the door to keep the girls and you safe.'

'I have servants in my house, and guns enough to arm them.'

'If you stay, you'll only be across the road from your new great granddaughter in the hospital. The girls will want to meet their sister and Alexei is next door. He may not want to receive visitors this evening, but he may come here to visit the twins tomorrow.'

Catherine hesitated but only for a moment before asking, 'are you sure I won't be in the way?'

'We're sure,' Praskovia assured her. 'We have plenty of spare rooms, so you can join us or be alone as you prefer. If you make a list of what you'll need, I'll send our coachman to your house. Your maid can pack for you and when she returns with your valises I'll find room for her in our servants' quarters.'

Catherine looked Praskovia in the eye. 'You are sure you want me here, Praskovia.'

'We'd love to have you.'

'Then thank you, both of you. Perhaps I will stay here, but just for tonight.' Preoccupied with thoughts of Alexei, Catherine asked, 'Has Alexei said anything to either of you about where he intends to bury Ruth?'

'No,' Glyn replied. 'I doubt he's even considered it. At the moment, he can't bear to be parted from her.'

'That I can understand.' Catherine gave a sad smile. 'He and Ruth were so happy. They were fortunate to find such love, even if it didn't last a lifetime. If he should say anything to you, would you please suggest that as a Beletsky, Ruth should be buried in our family plot.'

'Of course. Do you think that you could you bring yourself to stay with us until after the funeral, Catherine,' Glyn pleaded.

'Lada said that the twins should visit the house to see their mother's body, but she doesn't think they should return to live there until the ceremonies are over.'

'The house is so small, there won't be anywhere for them to sit where they can't see Ruth's coffin,' Catherine agreed. 'But I can always take the girls home with me.'

'If you and the twins stay with us, it might help Alexei to have you close by. He has many friends but no one is closer to him than you, Catherine.'

Praskovia added her entreaties to Glyn's. 'You've always been such a tower of strength to Alexei, Catherine.'

'I am a shattered and crumbling tower at the moment, Praskovia,' Catherine interrupted, 'but thank you for the invitation, both of you. I'll do as you suggest, Praskovia and write to my maid asking her to bring me some things, but as for staying here until the funeral. I must talk to Alexei first.'

'I'll check on him when the carpenter leaves,' Richard had returned to the chair next to the window so he could monitor Alexei's front door. 'I'll tell him that you want to see him, Catherine.'

'If he will listen to you, suggest that Ruth should be buried beside his mother and sisters.' Catherine's eyes darkened at the memory of her daughter and granddaughters, who like Glyn's brother, Peter, had succumbed to cholera in the epidemic that had ravaged the town in 1869.

'Alexi will need help to organise the funeral,' Praskovia said.

'And time to come to terms with Ruth's loss. If, as people say, the best days are when a child is born, the worst are when someone dies before their allotted span. But it's futile to discuss what can't be changed.' Catherine thought for a moment. 'Do you know if Sonya intends to stay in the hospital overnight?'

'Not even Nathan dared suggest she leave,' Richard answered.

'Then, all we can do is wait.' Catherine fell silent as the sound of Father Grigor's voice intoning a prayer echoed from the kitchen.

'I'm afraid so,' Glyn glanced at Richard who was staring out of the window towards Alexei's gate.

CHAPTER NINE

Beletsky House Hughesovka January 1889

At first glance a casual observer could have mistaken Nicholas Beletsky for a sculpture. A darker shade among the shadows, he hadn't moved as much as a finger since the sun had sunk below the western horizon of the steppe. All warmth had left the air and still he sat, silent, static on the wooden bench in the conservatory that overlooked the neglected rose garden at the side of the house. Night noises echoed in from the wilderness beyond the shrubbery that bordered the estate. The startlingly high human-like screech of a female fox searching for a mate. A wolf's howl carried over the iced plain like a muffled beat on a drum skin. A flurry of wings above his head announced the arrival of an owl on a high branch of a silver birch planted alongside the frozen pond.

He turned his head and looked at the east wing of the house to the left of the conservatory that jutted out from the main house. The drapes on the windows to the ground floor dining room, and a first-floor bedroom were open. The golden glow of lamplight shone out from both before dying in the darkness. He could hear the sound of distant conversation interspersed with the noise of drawers being banged shut and cupboard doors slamming. Annoying as the sounds were, they were infinitely preferable to the gasps, moans and groans of Maria's noisy and theatrical lovemaking with Levsky an hour ago, a performance he was convinced they'd staged with the intention of being overheard by him.

He recognised one of the voices as Levsky's. The second was heavily accented, coarser, but neither spoke loud enough for him to overhear what they were saying.

A sleigh crunched over the ice that coated the stable yard. The front door opened. Footsteps ran up and down the staircase accompanied by the bumping of heavy trunks and boxes. He debated whether or not to make the effort required to move. A pail of vodka and a metal beaker stood on the seat next to him. He picked up the pail and discovered it was pleasantly heavy. He dipped the cup in the spirit and drank. When he emptied the beaker, he refilled it.

Footsteps resounded on the wooden floor of the dining room. He felt warm breath on the back of his neck as someone moved out of the house and close to the bench.

'Beletsky.'

He recognised the voice. 'Levsky.'

'I'm leaving.'

'Hughesovka or the house?'

'Both. I won't be returning to the steppe for some time. If ever.'

'Where are you going?' Beletsky didn't care where Levsky went but he had exactly four roubles in his pocket and no prospect of acquiring more without Levsky's assistance.

'Somewhere that doesn't concern you.'

Beletsky smelled sulphur as Levsky struck a match. The scent of burning tobacco followed. Levsky drew on his cigar. 'Maria is accompanying me.'

'Take the whore with my blessing.'

'My cook doesn't need your permission to leave. I trust you'll vacate the house soon after we've gone.'

'Why should I?' Beletsky demanded belligerently.

'Because Gleb and Artur were both employed here and it can only be a matter of time before the authorities discover the Paskeys were also here.'

'Who's going to tell them the Paskeys were here?'

'Anyone who saw them coming or going, who is prepared to take a fireman, soldier's, or New Russian Company's man's kopecks.'

Levsky sniffed the air as if he'd detected a foul smell. 'I've ordered my steward to sell this place.'

'It's my house . . . '

'Was yours.' Levsky sighed as though he was bored with the conversation. 'Just as your Dachas and Moscow and St Petersburg Houses were yours. I doubt the combined sale of all six properties will cover the IOU's I hold against the advances I gave you.'

'You mean you'll make certain they don't.'

'No need to libel me, Beletsky. I too have creditors. It's time to liquidise the assets you signed over to me and reclaim what percentage I can of my money.'

'I'll be watching the sales.'

'I've no doubt you will. Please consider yourself free to make a bid for any of the properties, that is if you should want one or more to revert back to you.'

'You know my financial situation . . . '

'Better than most,' Levsky interrupted. 'You've proved an expensive liability, Beletsky. Don't come to the front door. Maria doesn't want to say goodbye.' He raised his voice as if he wanted to ensure he could be overheard. 'Make sure you leave within the week.'

'Where do you expect me to go. I have no money . . . '

Levsky opened his wallet and dropped a 10 rouble note on to the bench. It fell into the vodka pail. 'These are the last roubles you'll see from me, Beletsky. Make them last.' Levsky turned on his heel then hesitated. 'Don't take anything from the house with the idea of selling it. I've made an inventory and I won't hesitate to prosecute if you try to steal any more from me.'

'I steal from *you* . . . ' Beletsky could still smell cigar smoke but Levsky had finished talking. The night settled thick, dark and empty around him He turned and knocked the vodka pail from the bench. It splashed to the ground. He rose and fell to his knees.

'Bad luck, Beletsky, you can always lick it from the ground.'

He heard Levsky walk away as he retrieved the pail. It had fallen sideways and there was still vodka in it. He lifted it to his mouth and upended it as he heard the carriage move on down the drive.

He scooped up the banknote and turned towards door that led into the main house. Candles burned in the silver candelabra on the dining room table, illuminating the remains of a cold supper. The table had been set for three. The mysterious third man had been given a place at *his* table in *his* house without his permission. And he hadn't even been asked to sit at the head of the table.

He looked around the room. The house had been a wedding gift from his father-in-law, built to his taste, furnished with pieces he'd chosen - he'd never liked it and now it was Levsky's - or was it?

He took a candle from the stand staggered over to the drapes that hung in front of the window. He held a flame to them. They flared instantly.

He stepped back tripped on the rug and fell to the floor. It was soft, comfortable. He closed his eyes and stretched out.

Tomorrow – he'd think what to do tomorrow.

Hughesovka January 1889

Bone weary, wanting nothing more than to crawl home and into bed with Sarah, Richard said his goodbyes and left Glyn's house shortly after midnight. Yelena waylaid him at the front door and gave him a basket of her baking to drop off at the hospital for the staff. Snow began to fall as he crossed the road. He knocked the glass window in the porch to alert the porter in the cubicle opposite the door. The man rose to his feet and let him in.

'Prince Nadolny still hasn't come around.' Yulia whispered as she beckoned him into the kitchen.

He set the basket on the table. 'You must be exhausted.'

'We all are. But our patients need to be cared for.' The samovar was steaming and Yulia set cups and saucers on trays.

'I have food to go with that tea.'

'Yelena?' she asked.

'Hasn't stopped baking since Father Grigor left Glyn's house. She was making blinys when Pytor closed the door on me. Mr Edwards said it's pointless to try and stop her as it's her way of coping with tragedy.' Richard opened the basket and took out two bowls of savouries and two of cakes.

Yulia set plates of both on the trays. 'I'll take this into Dr Kharber, then look in on Prince Nadolny. Anna, Sonya and the new doctor are sitting with him.'

'Dr Kharber is still here?'

'He never leaves the hospital while he believes a patient might need him. I think he's discovered the secret of living without sleep.' She carried one of the trays into Nathan's consulting room and returned for the second.

'Here let me,' Richard took a tray from her. Yulia opened the door into the recovery room. Anna was filling in a chart. Sonya had moved her chair to the head of the trolley so she could be as close as possible to Roman. Richard set the tray on the windowsill, placed two sugar cubes on a saucer next to one of the glasses of tea Yulia had poured and handed it to Sonya.

'Thank you.' Sonya took it and wrapped her hands around the glass as though she were warming them, although the room was too hot for comfort.

'There's no change in Roman's condition,' Anna said before Richard asked. She took a cup of tea into the side room, and returned with it.

'Did Dr de Vries change his mind about wanting tea?' Sonya asked Anna.

'Dr de Vries is fast asleep.' Anna handed the cup to Richard.

'I'm sorry, this was hardly the homecoming you hoped for, Sonya,' Richard commiserated.

———

'I lived it over and over again in my imagination but I never envisaged a nightmare like this.' Sonya made no effort to drink her tea. 'I should have gone to see the boys in Glyn's house before they went to bed.'

'Apart from being worried about Roman, they're fine. Getting to know Praskovia's boys and Alexei's girls, before Glyn chased them all to their beds. Praskovia has persuaded Catherine to stay with her and Glyn as well.'

'Let Richard escort you to Glyn's house so you can get some rest,' Anna advised.

'If you're going to start bullying Sonya I'm leaving,' Richard warned Anna. 'I'll be in the kitchen if you need me, Sonya.'

'If you see Nathan tell him Roman's pulse is steady and strong, and after you've done that you can go home to your wife.' Anna made a final note on the chart.

'Yes, Miss Bossy boots.'

'It's been a long time since you called me that.' She looked at him and reached for his hand. He knew that gesture was as close as she would get to forgiving him for taking her to see the bodies of the Paskeys.

'Yes, well, even matrons need taking down a peg or two from time to time.'

'Looks like Yelena has been busy,' Anna offered Sonya the plate of savouries after Richard left.

'No thank you.'

'You have to eat,' Anna coaxed.

'I will. Just not yet.'

Anna returned the plate to the tray and picked up her own tea. 'I haven't seen that much of you and Roman since you married, but I have read your – and his - letters. He loves you so much . . . '

'And I him. I can't imagine this world without him. Nor do I want to.'

'He *will* recover from this.' Anna insisted.

'I wish I could be as certain.'

'He has a great deal to recover for,' Anna reminded.

'Roman is always so full of plans, and ideas. Business ideas, family plans. Half the time I scarcely have time to register where I am before he moves us on. He knows people everywhere. Not only important people but ordinary people, workmen, newspaper sellers, beggars, cab drivers, sailors, waiters . . . ' Sonya's voice tailed, and Anna sensed she was lost in memories too personal to share.

'He made many friends in the short time he was here before he married you, and on your trips here since.'

'He has.' Sonya laced her fingers even further into Roman's. 'When I was a young girl I used to imagine what it would be like to be married. I used to look at my cousin Olga – Catherine's daughter - who was totally subsumed by her husband. Physically by his insistence on her endless child bearing, and mentally because whenever she dared to voice an original thought, he dismissed it as worthless. An Arabian slave would have had more freedom than poor Olga. I often wondered if that was to be my fate, or if I'd be even worse off because I didn't have a dowry to attract a man as well educated or placed as Count Beletsky. Marriage to Roman couldn't be more different from my imaginings. He constantly asks my opinion on everything. Politics, purchases, architecture art, literature, and what's more he listens and acts on what I say. I never know when he's going to walk through whatever door we're living behind and shout, "Can you be packed by tomorrow, because we're leaving after breakfast. There's a new country I want to show you and the boys and it will be a wonderful adventure." It always is.'

'You've certainly travelled. Ted and Glyn's boys collect the stamps from your letters,' Anna said.

'The first time Roman gave me twelve hours to pack we were in St Petersburg. We were in Berlin the next night and from there we went to Paris with less thought than Aunt Catherine would have given to travelling from here to Taganrog.

115

'Both cities were wonderful. In fact, anywhere with Roman is wonderful.' There was a wistfulness in Sonya's voice that brought a lump to Anna's throat.

She squeezed Sonya's hand. 'I'm glad you're happy.'

'So am I,' came a muffled voice from the stretcher.

Sonya leaned forward. Roman's eyes were open. She kissed his forehead. 'You're awake, darling.'

'Obviously, but I feel as though a horse has kicked me in the back.'

'Not a horse. A bullet.' Sonya ran her fingers through his hair smoothing it away from his forehead.

'A bullet,' he mumbled. 'Is that all? Are you sure it wasn't a cannon ball?'

Tears blinded Anna's eyes as she went to the side room and shook Noah awake.

Private Cubicle Hospital Hughesovka January 1889

The rays of a weak winter's sun shone through the east-facing window of the treatment room that had been transformed into a private cubicle for Roman. The furnishings were Spartan, the bedstead iron, the air heavy with the acrid stench of disinfectant.

'Can you feel this?' Nathan ran the blunt end of a scalpel along the sole of Roman's foot. 'Don't try to look at what I'm doing,' he snapped when Roman raised his head and peered over his shoulder.

'Just making sure you actually touched my foot.' Exhausted by the effort it had cost him to move, Roman slumped forward and buried his head in the pillow.

'You can take it from me, I did, Prince Nadolny.'

'Given my undignified position face down on this mattress with my posterior in the air, do you think you could bring yourself to call me Roman? It would at least make me feel human. And it's not surprising that I can't feel my foot, or any other part of my body when you take the opiates your nurses have fed me into consideration.'

'You'd prefer to be left in pain – Roman?' Nathan enquired, lack of sleep making him irritable.

'I know I'm alive when I'm suffering, which is more than I say for the way I feel at the moment.'

Anna noticed an ominous sheen of perspiration on Roman's face that she hoped didn't portend fever. She interceded before both men's tempers frayed any further. 'Try moving your toes, Roman.'

Roman frowned in concentration. 'It's pointless when I can't feel my legs.' His voice was weak, but free from self-pity. His question blunt. 'Is this paralysis permanent?'

Nathan walked to the head of the bed and looked down on him. 'It's impossible to say less than twenty-four hours after surgery. We poked around inside you for longer than I would have liked.' He tensed his fists in frustration. 'But when we found the bullet . . . '

'You said you couldn't remove it, because it was embedded in bone close to the spinal cord.'

'You remember what I said when you were asleep?'

'If I'd been asleep I wouldn't have heard what you'd said. I was groggy, but not too groggy to listen to your opinion on the state of my health. It's a subject I have a keen interest in. Is the bullet embedded in one of my vertebrae?'

Nathan looked at him in surprise. 'Pardon?'

'My father and guardian subjected me to a thorough education that included the rudiments of anatomy.'

'The bullet is in your spinal column,' Nathan admitted.

'Too firmly fixed to be removed?' Roman pressed.

'I believe a further attempt to remove it would carry the risk of inflicting permanent damage to your spinal cord.'

'As I can't move my legs, appearances suggest my spinal cord is already damaged,' Roman pointed out.

'One of the side effects of surgery is the swelling of tissue which can cause temporary paralysis. So, it's possible you're simply suffering from the after effects of the operation.

'But even if you aren't, it's too soon to make any predictions as to your final condition.' Noah de Vries walked into the cubicle.

Frustrated by his inability to answer Roman's questions with any precision Nathan was uncharacteristically brusque. 'As I said, the operation took longer than we would have liked. Your muscles are swollen. They could subside and recover in the next few days. If they do, you could regain movement in your legs.'

'You expect me to rely on two "coulds". What if there is no recovery?'

Nathan took a deep breath, but he couldn't bring himself to utter platitudes or lie. Not with Roman's green eyes piercing his. 'Then the paralysis would be permanent.'

'With all the attendant problems of double incontinence and loss of mobility.'

Roman was calm, so detached he could have been talking about the prognosis for a casual acquaintance. Unnerved by Roman's pragmatism Nathan struggled to adopt the same attitude. Noah answered for him parrying Roman's question with one of his own.

'You know a great deal about spinal injuries, Prince Nadolny.'

Roman bit his lip and flinched involuntarily as his back burned suddenly and agonisingly to life. 'A school friend shattered his spine playing rugby. He found it difficult to adapt to the limitations the injury imposed on his body – and his lifestyle.'

'I've heard of rugby but I haven't heard of it being played in Russia.'

'The school was in England. They considered the game character building, although the participants didn't always remain conscious until the referee blew the final whistle. However, it offered an introduction to the savagery frequently found late at night in drinking dens, which has proved a useful skill in some of the social circles I've visited from time to time.'

Roman moved his head sideways on the pillow so he could look up at Noah as well as Nathan. 'If I don't regain the use of my legs in the next week or two, would you consider making another attempt to remove the bullet?'

'No.' Nathan's reply was as definite as it was finite. 'If after weighing up all the risks you decide to opt for further surgical intervention I recommend you consult a specialist in spinal operations.'

'A doctor more . . . ' Roman hesitated for a moment, 'adventurous and prone to taking risks than yourself?'

'A practitioner with more surgical experience of an injury similar to yours,' Nathan amended.

'Dr de Vries? Do you have an opinion? Roman asked.

'We'd need to ensure that your condition was stable and you were strong enough to withstand a second anaesthetic before attempting another procedure. We'd also need to establish that it would be beneficial before we started and that means carrying out a considerable number of tests beforehand.'

'Should you make a second attempt at surgery, what do you think my chances would be of making a full recovery?'

'And regaining the use of your legs?' Noah asked.

'Obviously.'

'Impossible to say because we don't know for certain that you're incapacitated now.'

'Thank you for your honesty.' Roman thought for a moment. 'I need to see Sonya and my stewards.'

'Sonya said she'd return as soon as she'd checked on your sons,' Anna straightened the linen sheet, covering Roman's legs.

'I told her to rest.'

'I heard you, Roman,' Anna adjusted his pillow. 'So did she and I believed her when she said she'd return as soon as she'd seen your sons.'

'In other words, you knew she wouldn't obey me?'

'In my opinion "Obey" is too fierce and forceful a word to describe the relationship between a husband and wife.'

119

'No wonder you're not married.'

'Something I thank God for every day,' Anna said.

'One day you'll meet a man who'll wipe that smug look from your face, young lady. Now there's a challenge for a warrior brave enough to take on the challenge.'

'I haven't found a man with that much courage as yet, and I can hardly be described as young, Roman.' She squeezed his hand briefly to show she harboured no hard feelings, before opening the door to a knock.

Sonya entered dressed in a more serviceable cotton and woollen outfit than the silk ensemble she'd left the hospital in early that morning.

Roman lifted his head and smiled. 'New perfume?'

'It's Praskovia's, as is the gown.' She held out the green and red cotton skirts.

'The rustic look suits you.'

She bent over the bed and kissed Roman lightly on the lips. 'It's good to see you fully conscious.'

'I wasn't my usual self when you left,' Roman admitted. 'How are the boys?'

'Out riding with Pavlo, Tom, Ted and Alexei's girls. Catherine thought the fresh air would do them good and Colonel Razin's lieutenant gave them an escort so they'll be quite safe.'

Roman beckoned Sonya closer. 'Ask Franz and Manfred to visit me this morning,' his voice was weakening.

'I will,' Sonya moved a chair close to Roman's bed.

'Start making preparations to move into our house and have a bed set up in my study next to the window overlooking the river.' Roman looked Nathan in the eye. 'I'll be out of here as soon as it can be arranged.'

Sonya looked at Nathan in surprise. 'Roman can be moved?'

Nathan made a wry face. 'Not in my medical opinion but I wouldn't dare disagree with any decision your husband has made, Princess Nadolny.'

'No, he can't be moved.' Noah added. 'And I am more than happy to disagree with the Prince when it comes to medical decisions that affect his health.'

'See how I'm bullied?' Roman winked at Sonya. 'Call in again after I've spoken to Franz and Manfred.'

Sonya saw the pain in Roman's eyes and realised not all of it was physical. She lifted his hand to her lips and kissed it. 'I'll tell them to visit right away.'

CHAPTER TEN

Private Cubicle Hospital Hughesovka January 1889

'You're in pain, Roman?' Nathan commented as Anna walked Sonya out.

'Some,' Roman conceded.

'You're due another morphine injection.' Noah set Roman's notes aside.

'I'll see to it.' Nathan pulled the trolley that held the syringe closer to him.

'Thank you, Dr Kharber. I'll see how far an uninitiated doctor can get on ward rounds.' Sensing a history between the two men, Noah left the cubicle.

'Are you enjoying this, Dr Kharber?' There was a barb behind the question. Roman hadn't forgotten the way Nathan Kharber had looked at Sonya before they'd married – or the way Sonya had returned that look. He knew that although Sonya loved him now, she would never have married him had Nathan Kharber asked for her hand first.

'No, some doctors may enjoy inflicting pain but I'm not one of them. As for your plans to move out of here,' Nathan took a ball of cotton wool and upended a bottle of antiseptic on to it until it was thoroughly soaked before swabbing the skin on Roman's buttock. 'As Dr de Vries intimated, we would be negligent if we allowed a man to leave a hospital bed the day after surgery. At the very least your surgical scar should be healed enough for the stitches to be removed.'

'How long is that likely to take?'

'Are you a quick healer or a slow one, Roman?'

'Quick. Very quick.' Roman glared up at Nathan daring the doctor to contradict him.

'If that really is the case, I'd estimate two to three weeks provided no infection sets in and you don't succumb to fever.'

——
122

'How long does it take you to train a nurse?'

'Anna is better equipped to deal with that question than me.'

'I would like my valet and steward trained to take care of my physical needs while I remain incapacitated.'

'Not a nurse?'

'The last thing I need is a female fussing around me.'

'Not even your wife?'

'I have no intention of turning Sonya into a drudge.'

'She may have other ideas.' Nathan unlocked a cabinet and removed a phial of liquid morphine.

'None that will override or contradict mine, I assure you.'

'If anyone can train your manservants, it would be Anna.'

'Then I need to talk to her before that,' Nathan eyed the morphine, 'takes effect.' He bit his lip again as he watched Nathan prime the syringe.

Alexei's House Hughesovka February 1889

Lada opened the front door of the wooden huntsman's cottage and stood back so Catherine, Sonya, and Alexei's younger sister, Kira, could enter with Father Grigor. Dressed in mourning Alexei stood at the head of Ruth's open coffin in the living room, Kitty was on his right, Olga his left. Sonya went to her cousin and laid her hand on his shoulder.

'It's time, Alexei. The hearse is at the gate.'

Kitty and Olga laid white roses in their mother's coffin. Catherine and Kira followed suit with the pink roses they'd picked that morning in Catherine's hot house, they took the twins by their hands and led them back towards the door. The undertaker stepped from the corner of the room and lifted the lid of the casket from the floor, as Sonya had remained with Alexei, he hung back as unobtrusively as possible given the limitations of the room.

123

'Are you sure you want to bury Ruth's rosary, crucifix and rings with her, Alexei?' Sonya whispered. 'Your daughters may . . . '

'I bought them for Ruth, they stay with her.' Alexei spoke in a tone that brooked no argument.

It wasn't the first time Sonya had suggested that Alexei keep Ruth's wedding and betrothal rings and the gold diamond and ruby crucifix he'd given her to celebrate her conversion to the Russian Orthodox faith. But impervious to her and Catherine's advice, Alexei had remained adamant that Ruth's crucifix along with her gold and amber rosary and her platinum diamond and sapphire betrothal and wedding rings be buried with her.

Alexei reached for Sonya's hand in atonement for his outburst. She took it and started when he laced his fingers into hers. They were ice cold although the heavily draped room was uncomfortably warm from the stove and the fire that blazed in the hearth.

His voice was rough, hoarse with suppressed emotion. 'My daughters have their mother's most precious legacy. Their memories of her.'

'Not your baby, Alexei,' Sonya reminded. 'She will have no memories of her mother.'

'Olga and Kitty will tell her about Ruth. And when the time comes I will buy my daughters rosaries, crucifixes and jewellery that hold no sorrowful memories.'

Sonya kissed Ruth's forehead and made the sign of the cross before placing a lily she'd brought from her own hothouse at her feet.

Alexei laid the red rose he was holding in Ruth's hand, bent over and kissed his wife's lips for the last time. He took the coffin lid from the undertaker and lifted it into place. The undertaker began to screw it down. Alexei watched every move the man made and Sonya saw him wince as the scrape of metal on wood echoed around the room. She felt that her cousin's pain couldn't have been greater if the screws were being driven into his heart.

She moved back alongside Catherine, Kira and the twins who waited patiently by the door. The last screw sank into place and the undertaker retreated to the shadows.

Sonya stared at the clock on the mantel. She had the oddest feeling that the hands had frozen and nothing and no one was moving in the room. Not even breathing. It was though time had stopped and the room was a still photographic tableau that had captured a moment long past.

The spell broke when Father Grigor stepped in front of the coffin. He swung his incense burner and began the prayer for the dead. Alexei's servants, Lev and Lada opened the front doors and held them open. At a signal from Father Grigor, the bearers, Glyn his brother Edward, Richard, Vlad, Catherine's lawyer, Dmitri and John Hughes, walked in and stationed themselves around the coffin.

Father Grigor took his place at the head of the procession, the bearers shouldered Ruth's casket and walked in his wake. Alexei headed the mourners with Kitty and Olga walking either side of him. Sonya and Kira took Catherine's arms and the three of them fell into step behind them.

Friends and neighbours lined the path from the front door to the garden gate. Outside the snow blanketed street was crowded. Sonya looked for but did not see Nathan, Vasya, or anyone of the Jewish faith apart from Miriam and Yulia who'd trained as nurses alongside Ruth. They'd been her close friends since their shared childhood in the shtetl and had come to pay their respects, even though it meant risking the Rabbi's wrath.

Catherine had ordered her grooms to harness and bring out all her sleighs. Alexei, John Hughes, Glyn, Richard, and the Nadolnys' had added theirs and it was a long cortege that wended its way slowly along the main street and outside the town limits to the snow-covered countryside and burial ground on the Ignatova estate.

'It looks like the whole town has turned out to pay their respects,' Sonya said as she and Kira helped Catherine from her sleigh.

Catherine looked along the ranks of people who stood at a respectful distance. 'Not the entire town,' she commented when she saw a tall, painfully thin, black clad figure standing alone and apart on the fringe of the crowd. Unlike everyone else who carried flowers, his hands were empty. But she recalled that the Jews didn't lay wreaths on their graves. She walked over to him and took his arm.

'You are Ruth's brother and closest living relative from her childhood, Nathan. You must stand with us at her grave.'

'Thank you for your kindness, Catherine, but I cannot. In Father Grigor and his congregation's eyes I am as much an unbeliever as Ruth became to those of our faith when she converted to Russian Orthodox Christianity.'

'Alexei never considered you anything other than Ruth's beloved brother, and Ruth would welcome you if she were here to do so.'

'She would.' He smiled and Catherine sensed he no longer saw his surroundings but his sister as she had been in life. 'However, when I return to the synagogue, as I must on our Sabbath, the Rabbi will chastise me for simply being here. And, as your ceremonies are so very different from ours I would have difficulty interpreting them, so there is little point in my remaining.'

'Yulia and Miriam are here with the other nurses and porters from the hospital, not to take part in the ceremony but to simply show their love for Ruth,' Catherine said.

'They're women who've proved their bravery by defying the Rabbi and our community who ordered them not to work outside of the shtetl when they started training here twenty years ago. If Rabbi Goldberg has learned anything since then, it's not to openly confront them.

'He knows that if he does, they'll plead ignorance, and demand his compassion for their lack of intellect. Given the arguments I had to contend with when Ruth renounced our faith I can hardly claim lack of knowledge.'

'Whatever the laws of your religion – or mine - I believe there is but one God no matter how different our ways of worship.'

'You are a good woman, Catherine, and I thank you for your continued kindness towards me, and the way you welcomed Ruth into your family and treated her as though she was your own. But I have already said my final goodbye to my little sister.' He lifted his right hand and tore the cloth of his coat over his left breast where it covered his heart. 'Now she is truly dead to me.'

'And her daughters?'

'I wish them long and happy lives with their father.' Lowering his eyes, he turned his back and walked away.

Cemetery outside Hughesovka February 1889

'Alexei, people have come here to pay their respects to you and your daughters . . . '

'I need to see my new daughter,' he interrupted his grandmother 'and show her that she has a father who loves her.'

'And Olga and Kitty?'

'Please, bring them home to me tomorrow with Kira, Grandmother.' He kissed his sister's cheek.

Kira embraced him. He returned her hug and kissed Sonya and his daughters before turning back to Catherine.

'I need time to consider how I am going to face the rest of my life without Ruth at my side.'

'It will be hard for you. The girls are old enough to know that the worse thing about losing their mother is the certainty that they will never ever see her again in this life. But knowing that won't stop them from crying for her, sometimes when you least expect them to.'

127

'I need to spend time with them to remind myself that something of Ruth and what we meant to one another lives on. But not now. Today is for my private mourning and my new daughter.'

Catherine gripped his hand tightly and looked him in the eye. 'I understand.'

'Thank you, grandmother. Please tell everyone who came to the funeral I appreciate their condolences but now that Ruth has finally gone from my house and my life,' he raised his eyes to the mound of fresh earth that waited to fill Ruth's grave next to his mother's and sisters' snow dusted headstones, 'I must try to live as best I can for the sake of my children.'

Catherine pursed her lips to stop her tears. Alexei helped Kira, Kitty and Olga into his sleigh. He ordered the driver to take them to Catherine's house and watched them drive away before turning to Sonya and his grandmother. His groom had ridden up to them and was holding his horse Ariston II.

'You planned to leave straight after the ceremony, Alexei?' Catherine asked.

'Yes, Grandmother.'

'Misha Razin came to see me, he wants to talk to you-'

'I saw him this morning.'

'He told you?'

'That Nicholas Beletsky had burned to death in the Beletsky house. Yes, but I told him that as my father had disowned me, I in my turn had disowned him.'

'I asked Father Grigor to bury him.'

'Grandmother . . . '

'Not in the family plot. In the common cemetery. He was my daughter's husband. I couldn't leave him to rot above ground.'

'I could.' Alexei spoke with feeling.

'We don't have to mention him again. Ever. You'll visit me in the morning?'

'No, Grandmother. Please, would you and Kira bring the twins home tomorrow and stay to join us for lunch. You too, Sonya, and your boys if Roman doesn't need you.'

Catherine nodded. 'Thank you for the invitation. We will arrive at one o'clock.'

'I'll ask Lada to cook one of your favourite dishes.' He handed Catherine and Sonya into Catherine's carriage and took his mount's reins. He saw the nurses and porters from the hospital heading towards him, swung up on to Ariston's back and spurred him into a canter.

Hughesovka February 1889

Apart from being led on a rein out of town to the cemetery, Alexei's horse had been cooped up in his stable since the day before the Grand Duke's visit. Alexei gave the stallion his head and didn't rein him in until the buildings on the outskirts of Hughesovka came into view and increased traffic brought the risk of ice beneath the snow. Only then did he slow his pace. He rode through his garden gate and shouted for the stable boy. After giving him instructions to care for his horse he crossed the road and went into the hospital.

To his surprise Anna was in the office. 'I saw you at Ruth's funeral . . . ' he began.

'I went to the cemetery but left with Dr Kharber before the service began. We were concerned about leaving the hospital in charge of the junior doctors and nurses, as Dr de Vries and most of the senior staff are out monitoring an outbreak of typhoid fever in the hole houses. Dr Kharber was so worried about the fever spreading he joined them. I told him I'd stay here until he returns but I will visit Ruth's grave when my shift ends to pay my respects.'

'No one could have cared for Ruth more than you, Anna. I know you saved our child . . . '

'Please . . . don't be kind. I couldn't bear it.' She tensed her fists. 'I wish I could have done something for Ruth -'

129

'No one could have saved her life after that bullet hit her, Anna. She is with God, and those she left must carry on as best we can.' Alexei deliberately changed the subject. 'How is Roman?'

Anna frowned. 'Not good. He's restless and his wound isn't healing as it should.'

'I'm sorry.'

'I thought you'd be at the wake in your Grandmother's house.'

'I need to be home with my new daughter. That's why I'm here. I've come to collect her.'

'Your baby? Have you asked Dr Kharber -'

'No, but when I last spoke to him he said the child was healthy and there were no problems.'

'There aren't but . . . '

'But?' he raised his eyebrows and looked at her.

'You'll need a nurse . . . '

'I thought she was being fed goat's milk.'

'She is, but a baby takes a great deal of care.'

'I know, I helped Ruth as much as she'd let me with Olga and Kitty.'

'That was sixteen years ago and helping isn't the same as looking after a baby full time, Alexei.'

'I realise that, which is why I will take time off work. I've spoken to Richard. He agreed our collieries are so well set up now, they practically run themselves. I promise I won't put too much of a burden on your brother. I'll carry on doing the colliery accounts and wages from home and I'll also see to the invoices and sales sheets. So please, may I take my daughter home?'

Anna couldn't think of a single argument as to why she should refuse his request. She shook the excess ink back into the inkwell from the pen she'd been using to update the drug inventory, set it on the rest and left her chair. She unhooked her apron from the back of the door slipped the loop over her head and tied the ribbons around her waist. 'Have you decided on a name for your daughter?'

130

'Ruth was so sure the child was a boy she wouldn't even discuss girls' names. She wanted to call him Nathan after her brother and father, and Abraham –for the uncle who brought her up after her father died and Alexei . . . '

'After his father?'

'My grandfather. I was named for him. Names are reused through the Christian as well as Jewish communities in Russia.'

'And in Wales. You have no idea what Ruth would have named your daughter?'

'No, but I've decided to call her Ruth, after her mother, Leah after Ruth's aunt who brought her up after her mother died giving birth to her, and Anna, in the hope that the name might entice you into becoming godmother again.'

Anna smiled. 'Ruth Leah Anna Beletskya is quite a mouthful.'

'She'll grow into it.'

'With a father like you to guide her I'm sure she will. I'll put a few things together for you.' Anna made a mental list as she opened the door. 'Little Ruth will need gowns, napkins, blankets, sheets, shawl, bottles, a horn spoon that can be boiled safely without getting too hot to touch . . . Do you have a cot?'

Alexei blanched at Anna's list. Ruth had made caring for the twins so simple. He'd been so certain he could do it. Now he doubted his own capability.

'You do have a cot?' Anna repeated.

'Yes, of course, Ruth had Lev bring down one of the twin's cots from the attic and put it in our room. She also filled one of the cupboards with things she knew the baby would need.'

'Then let's fetch your daughter. After I've looked in on Roman, and made sure I can spare five minutes away from here, I'll go home with you and check what you have. That way we can make sure you're not missing anything vital, or duplicating essentials. If there's anything you need I'll send it over with a porter.'

Anna walked down the corridor to the cubicle off the women's ward. A junior nurse was feeding the baby. Anna looked down at her.

'Here's your Daddy, Ruth. He's come to take you home.'

CHAPTER ELEVEN

Hughesovka Hospital March 1889

Roman sank back against the pillows Anna had plumped up and pushed behind his head and gazed at Sonya. They exchanged smiles. Anna raised her eyebrows.

'You two don't need words, you can say all you want, and more simply by looking at one another.'

'It's a trick old married couples develop,' Roman winked at Sonya.

'Are you still determined to annoy Dr Kharber and Dr de Vries by ignoring their advice?' Anna picked up Roman's empty tea glass and put it on his breakfast tray.

'I do everything they – and you tell me to,' Roman remonstrated.

'You do not,' she retorted. 'You wriggle in that bed worse than an eel when you've been advised to lie face down and still to allow your wound to heal. You insist on seeing all your visitors even when you've been advised to rest . . . '

'How can someone as beautiful as you be so cruel?' he interrupted.

'Flattery will get you nowhere!'

'Put yourself in my position . . . ' '

'If I was in your position I would treat the people caring for me with more respect. The junior nurses tiptoe past this room, heaven only knows why because I'm beginning to wonder if you ever rest, much less sleep.'

'Have you any idea how annoying it is to have people monitoring your every move and breath?'

'If we didn't, you wouldn't be alive to complain.'

'I'm so looking forward to waking in my own time in the morning without being poked, prodded and asked embarrassing questions about the state of my bowels.

'And the thought of having four new walls to stare at after being incarcerated in this cupboard for six weeks makes me positively giddy with excitement. I take it our Hughesovka house is habitable?' Roman asked Sonya.

'Very habitable, and given that you designed every inch of the building, and chose the furniture it feels more like home than any of our other houses. The view over the river from the rooms at the back of the house and the veranda takes my breath away no matter how many times I see it . . . ' She faltered when she realised that she was talking too quickly, too earnestly.

'And my study? The trees in the garden haven't grown too tall to block the vista?'

'No, the gardener has kept them trimmed, just as you ordered. It still has absolutely the best view in the house, as you always said it would, which makes you the entirely selfish one in the family.'

Sonya smiled as she spoke and Anna assumed she'd referred to a private family joke.

'Comes of being an only child,' Roman said without a trace of humour. 'We grow accustomed to expecting, demanding and taking the best. As a breed, we're selfish to the last.'

'I'll second that, especially when it comes to getting your own way,' Nathan Kharber walked in and picked up the chart that was hooked over the metal footboard at the end of Roman's bed. I don't know what the nurses will have to complain about after you've been discharged. One thing is certain. This room and the ward will be quieter.'

'If you're fortunate you may get an even more difficult patient to take my place to torment the nurses,' Roman said.

'I sincerely hope not,' Anna replied before Nathan could. There was always an edge to the banter between the men. 'Try not to allow your temperature to rise to fever level again or we'll be keeping you here another six weeks,' she warned.

'And how would I do that?' Roman demanded.

134

'Keep the window open and think of snow.'

'While watching it melt?' Roman scoffed.

'I'll bring you some iced water. It may help your imagination if nothing else.' Anna left and Nathan followed her.

Roman reached for Sonya's hand. 'You're concerned about something?' he whispered.

'Nothing,' she lied.

'I know you . . . '

She glanced at the door as she lowered her voice. 'It's nothing really . . . '

A patient the other side of the thin partition walls that separated Roman's cubicle from the men's ward started coughing. A loud hacking that brought the realisation that anything they said would be overheard by Roman's fellow patients as well as any staff in the vicinity.

Roman gently squeezed Sonya's hand. 'One good thing about my leaving here will be the prospect of privacy.'

'When I consider how much Andrei and Spartak have missed you I doubt they'll give you a moment's peace.'

He picked up their photograph from his bedside locker. 'I've missed them.'

'They've missed you more. Seeing you here for a few minutes day is not the same as being able to talk to you whenever they want.'

She started nervously as the door swung back on its hinges with a loud bang, before rebounding on its hinges.

Richard caught it and jammed it open with the toe of his boot. 'Your new carriage, sir, built to your exact specifications.' He flourished a formal bow.

Glyn pushed a wheelchair past Richard. They had spent the last few weeks designing it with Roman's help before overseeing its manufacture in John Hughes's workshops.

'As, you see, your excellency.' Richard gave a credible imitation of the French salesman who'd arrived in Hughesovka in the hope of selling tools to the ironworks only to be sent away empty handed by Glyn.

'We adopted your suggestion of using rubber bicycle tyres on the main wheels so they can be pumped up to facilitate a smoother ride. We've also added small castors to the front and back of the chair frame that can be turned in any direction to add extra support for the main wheels, which can be lifted off the ground and out of the way of the castors when you pull up this lever.' Richard demonstrated and the main wheels slid smoothly upwards into the frame of the chair. 'Once they are off the ground the chair can be moved diagonally or sideways as well as straight ahead and backwards.'

'The chair is upright, not sloping as you demanded, so it in no way resembles a bath chair, which as you rightly pointed out, is only suitable for nonagenarians whose back muscles have decayed to the point where they can no longer hold their bodies in a sitting position,' Glyn added. 'The high back is rigid, firm enough to support you, but upholstered for comfort.'

'And, our own invention and improvement is this lap tray that can be hooked into the arm rest to do duty as desk or temporary table. When it's not needed you can lift it out and slot it vertically down beside the right armrest.' Richard slid the tray in and out.

'Do you approve?' Glyn asked Roman.

'You certainly listened to me when I told you what I wanted. I'll give you my verdict when I try it. Wheel it alongside the bed. If it's a comfortable as it looks I'll go home today . . . '

'You will not.' Nathan Kharber growled from the corridor. 'I only gave Richard permission to bring the chair in today so any faults can be rectified before you use it. You'll be discharged when I give my permission and not one minute before.'

'May I ask Dr de Vries for a second opinion?'

Nathan glared at Roman. 'You may not. You have the man completely under your thumb. Besides I think you're forgetting who's the senior doctor here, in years of service if not medical experience.'

'I would never dare question your authority,' Roman managed to keep a straight face which served to infuriate Nathan further.

Glyn attempted to lighten the atmosphere. 'Surely Roman hasn't been giving you any trouble, Dr Kharber?'

'Since the day he was carried in here,' Nathan replied. He attempted to adopt the same jocular tone as Glyn but didn't succeed.

'Shall I fetch Manfred and Franz to help you into the chair, Roman?' Sonya asked.

'No, let them eat their lunch. Anna doesn't give either of them a minute's peace.'

'To good end. You have to admit she has turned them into competent medical attendants,' Nathan commented.

'That was an observation not a criticism, Nathan,' Roman demurred. 'I'm grateful to her for training them.'

Glyn wheeled the chair alongside Roman's bed. Roman gripped the metal bar at the head of his bed and hauled himself upright. Richard joined them and lifted down Roman's legs so they hung over the side of the mattress. Roman hooked his arms around Richard and Glyn's shoulders. They supported his weight. Roman braced himself and nodded to show he was ready. Glyn and Richard moved in a single smooth movement and deposited him in the chair.

'Let's see if we've got it right.' Glyn reached for the leather straps at Roman's waist and chest level. When he went to buckle them, Roman burst out laughing.

'Did you make them this long to accommodate the weight you'd assume I'd put on after lying in bed for six weeks?' Roman brought the ends of the strap and buckle together. There was a two feet gap between the strap and his body. 'Or did you propose to tie Sonya on top of me.

Richard took his penknife from his pocket tightened the strap and made a mark. 'Unfasten it, Glyn and I'll make a new hole.'

'Keep the excess to use as a dog lead or two or three,' Roman suggested.

137

Glyn bent down and lifted Roman's feet on to the footrests before fastening the ankle straps. 'At least we got the length of these right.'

'Is the back too upright?' Sonya tucked a blanket around Roman's waist and covered his legs.

'Better upright than a low slope that would encourage me to slump.' Roman grasped the arm rests with both hands and levered his body to a more comfortable position.

'Will it do?' Richard asked.

'Push me down the corridor and I'll find out. And while you're pushing, see if you two engineers can come up with a way to make the chair self-propelling and add adaptations to turn it into a sleigh for outdoor use.'

'You don't want much. do you?' Richard asked.

'If you could find a surgeon capable of digging the damned bullet out of my spine I'd be grateful.'

Hughesovka Hospital March 1889

Sonya watched Richard and Glyn wheel Roman away. He waved back at her without turning his head.

'Take care not to go too fast,' she called after them. 'Roman hasn't moved in weeks, fresh air alone will make him dizzy.'

'No fear of that,' Richard answered, 'you obviously haven't been outside long enough to notice that the furnaces are in full production so there's not much air, let alone any that's fresh, in Hughesovka.'

The room seemed strangely silent after they left.

'You're worried about Roman's discharge from the hospital?' Nathan asked.

'Are you?' Sonya turned the question back on him.

'Yes.'

'Then don't discharge him,' she pleaded.

'I've run out of excuses to keep him here and he knows it.'

'You said the bullet in his spine could move at any time and cause further damage. Possibly even sever his spinal cord and kill him. Isn't that reason enough for you to insist he stays here where he can be watched day and night.'

'Until when would you suggest we monitor him, Princess Nadolny?'

'You address my husband by his Christian name, you've known me even longer so please, do me the service of addressing me by mine.'

'The bullet could remain wedged in your husband's vertebrae for years without affecting him any more than it already has. Or it could drift one minute from now . . . '

'If Glyn and Richard should jolt the chair over a stone?'

'Not even something as dramatic as that. It could happen if Roman sneezes or coughs vigorously. As your husband's doctor, I would like nothing better than to order him to remain in bed and not move until . . . '

Sonya cut him short mid-sentence. ' . . . another surgeon attempts to remove the bullet, which you refuse to even try to do?'

'As I've said I don't consider myself qualified in spinal surgery. Has Roman told you that we've received a reply from Herr Franz, the German surgeon de Vries suggested we contact?'

'The surgeon Noah de Vries recommended because he worked with him in Vienna. Yes, he told me.'

'Herr Franz asked for Roman's medical records and my notes. After discussing his request with Roman and de Vries I gave him the information he requested.'

'Do you think he will try to remove the bullet from Roman's spine'

'That will be his decision and Roman's.'

'You have no opinion?'

'I made my opinion clear when I operated on Roman. I risked your husband's life by keeping him under anaesthetic for longer than most doctors would recommend. But I explained that to you at the time.'

The sound of laughter drifted in through the open window. Sonya rose from her chair and looked outside. Richard and Glyn had pushed Roman through the front door and on to the covered veranda. They were talking to the porters.

She glanced across the street and saw Alexei standing at the window of his living room. He was holding his baby against his chest patting her back, but from the way Ruth was struggling and pounding Alexei with her small fists, she could see the child was distressed.

'You do realise Roman has no function or feeling whatsoever below the waist?' Nathan asked.

It was the first time he'd broached the subject of Roman's injury in relation to the intimate side of their married life. Sonya wanted to discuss the implication of Roman's situation, but not with Nathan. 'I have spoken to Sarah and Anna about Roman's injuries.'

'I'm glad to hear it. I trust you're not harbouring any unrealistic expectations of your husband's capabilities. But then, you wouldn't be. Sarah knows as much if not more about medical matters that relate to marriage as your average doctor.'

'After seventeen years of marriage, I know Roman too well to anticipate his reactions, with any expectations, unrealistic or otherwise.'

'Roman has adapted better to his injury and disability than I expected any man as active as him to do so. But I have also noticed that he is an intensely private man not given to share his thoughts.'

'He shares them with me.' She turned from the window. 'The chair will help. It was kind of Richard and Glyn to design and make it, especially when I consider how busy they are.'

'Roman is also fortunate to have Hans and Manfred to care for him.'

'Not only to see to his physical needs but his business affairs.' Sonya suddenly found the small cubicle room – and Nathan's presence - claustrophobic.

'If you'll excuse me Dr Kharber I'll must make sure Roman isn't tiring himself.'

'Please, persuade him to return to his bed. Threaten him if necessary. Tell him if he exhausts himself I won't allow him to leave for another six weeks.'

'You'd use force to keep him here?'

He shook his head. 'That threat would be an idle one and he'd know it. If I tried to restrain him he'd find some way to fight me even from a wheelchair.'

'He would.' She went to the door and opened it. 'Thank you, Nathan.'

'What for?'

'Looking after him.'

'It's my job to care for my patients.'

'You do so with more dedication than most.'

She left and Nathan took her place at the window. He watched her join Roman, Richard, Glyn and the porters on the veranda. She waved at Anna who was leaving the hospital before leaning solicitously over Roman and adjusting his cravat.

He'd dreamed of Sonya even before she left Hughesovka, especially when they'd worked together when the hospital had first opened. Since her return, the dreams had become more frequent. It made no difference that she no longer looked at him the way she once had, or that she was obviously completely and utterly in love with her husband.

His feelings hadn't changed since the day he'd returned from studying medicine in Paris and Vienna to discover that the childhood friend of his sister that he'd left on the steppe had grown into a beautiful young girl. It was hardly surprisingly he'd fallen in love with her. It was his misfortune that he'd been unable to forget Sonya, and even more unfortunate for his wife Vasya. Their hastily arranged match had been made with the Goldberg family to assuage the slight Ruth had inflicted when she'd rejected Abraham Goldberg's offer of marriage in favour of Alexei's proposal.

141

Abraham Goldberg had looked for and found love elsewhere. He envied him. His marriage to Vasya was a disaster. Not least because of her continual and overwhelming gratitude to him for rescuing her from a life of spinsterhood, a gratitude that manifested itself in subservience to the point of embarrassment.

She not only held him in awe, but on occasion actually appeared to fear him. As a result, he found Vasya's presence profoundly irritating. He worked longer and longer hours to escape seeing her, and frequently slept on the sofa in his office, even when he didn't have the excuse of a critically ill patient who needed his attention.

He surfaced from his thoughts to see Sonya rest her hand on Roman's shoulder. Her husband reached for and held her fingers before kissing them. A casual gesture, but one that highlighted their intimacy. He turned away from the window before he saw anything more to fan the flames of jealousy that burned within him.

CHAPTER TWELVE

Alexei Beletsky's House Hughesovka April 1889

'Thank Christ you've come, Nurse Parry. The master is going to kill that poor baby with good intentions if someone doesn't stop him.' Lada grabbed Anna's arm and pulled her into Alexei's house. 'I will make tea for you and the master, and while you drink it I would be grateful if you talk some sense into him. It would make Lev's and my life easier if you succeed.'

Anna resisted the temptation to shout "coward" after Lada's retreating figure. She didn't blame Alexei's housekeeper. Given the choice she would have preferred to have followed her into the kitchen rather than face a fraught Alexei and judging by Ruth's wails, an even more hysterical baby.

She hung her cloak on a hook behind the front door and went into the living room. Red-faced, distraught, Alexei was pacing from one end of the small room to the other with Ruth in his arms. Wrapped in several layers of crocheted wool, Ruth's face burned even more crimson than her father's.

Anna blocked Alexei's path and opened her arms. 'Please, give her to me, Alexei.'

He looked at her through desperate eyes. 'I've tried everything. Her napkin is dry, she won't take her bottle, she won't calm down . . . '

'Here,' she snapped, switching to what her brother Richard called her "matron must be obeyed voice", 'hand Ruth over.' She lifted the baby from his arms and unwrapped the shawl from around her. 'Ruth's fingers are caught in the decorative holes in the shawl. There, darling, that's better isn't it?' she murmured, freeing Ruth's hands and massaging the red pressure lines from them.

'Oh God! Is Ruth going to be all right? Have I cut off the circulation . . . '

143

'There's no permanent damage, but in future it might be as well to wrap her in a light cotton sheet, with no fancy stitching to catch tiny fingers.'

'Babies have to be kept warm,' he protested when she dropped the shawl on a chair.

'Warm not broiled alive, Alexei. In case you hadn't noticed we had our Russian spring two days ago. I think it lasted an entire afternoon before were catapulted into the height of summer. This is a wooden house and the temperature in this room is high enough to roast a goose. Please open the windows. Not the ones facing the street,' she warned when he went to them. 'Lada won't thank you for allowing the dust from the road to blow in. Open the ones that overlook the back garden, and prop open the back doors as well while you're at it. This temperature is unhealthy.'

He did as she asked and the sounds of conversation flooded into the room.

'Are Olga and Kitty in the garden?' she asked.

'With Andrei and Spartak. Lada made them an early lunch so they can ride out to the shrine on the steppe with Ted, Maryanna and Glyn's boys, to leave offerings and light candles for Ruth.'

'Let's join them. Ask Lada to bring the tea she's making out there.'

'Isn't too much fresh air and sun bad for babies?'

'Not if the air's warm and the baby is kept in the shade.'

Alexei disappeared into the kitchen and Anna took the opportunity to remove even more layers of woollen clothing from Ruth. When the baby was down to a flannel napkin and thin cotton gown she carried her outside.

Alexei had built a bower against the back fence that bordered the open steppe. Three latticework walls supported a roof of woven willow that provided shade and sheltered it from the occasional shower of rain. It housed a table and two wooden benches padded with upholstered cushions.

144

Anna arranged herself comfortably on the cushions of one of the benches, lay the baby face down across her lap and gently massaged her back. It was cooler in the shade than it had been in the house. Soothed by Anna's gentle touch Ruth stopped crying. Olga and Kitty left the gazebo behind the kitchen and joined her.

'She recognises her sisters,' Anna told them.

'Do you think so, Godmother Anna? Aunt Vasya says babies can't recognise anyone until they are at least a year old.' Olga sat next to Anna. Kitty moved to the other side of her.

'Did she?' Anna frowned. 'When did you see Aunt Vasya?'

'She comes to see us or rather Papa every day every day since we returned home after Mama's funeral. She brings us Pryaniki and Oladyi doughnuts.'

'Because she thinks we're six not sixteen years old,' Kitty wrinkled her nose.

'That's a horrid thing to say, Kitty. Aunt Vasya means to be kind,' Olga remonstrated.

'Lada says too many sweet things are bad for growing girls.'

'Lada is quite right,' Anna made a swift decision not to undermine Alexei's housekeeper who by dint of living in Alexei's house, wielded more influence over the upbringing of Alexei's daughters than any casual visitor possibly could.

Anna allowed Kitty to lift Ruth from her lap. The twins resembled Ruth more than Alexei and their black hair and enormous dark brown eyes, so like their mother's, tore at her heartstrings. She and Ruth had grown close while studying nursing under Sarah's tutelage, forming a friendship that had strengthened after Ruth's marriage and the birth of their twins. It was unsurprising as Alexei and her brother Richard had entered a business partnership that had led to numerous dinner parties and social events involving both families that Sarah and Ruth made sure always included spinster Aunt Anna.

145

The boys and Alexei carried trays of tea, glasses, small bowls and cutlery out of the kitchen door and set them on the table. Lada followed with two large bowls filled to the brim, one with rice, the other stew.

'I smell Lada's special Goulash.' Anna detected the mouth-watering aroma of lamb, tomatoes and onions simmered in bay leaves.

Lada set the bowls on the table. 'It was a good idea of yours to eat lunch in the garden, Nurse Parry. I keep telling the master he needs fresh air.' She wiped her hands on her apron before stroking Ruth's head, which was covered by a fuzz of fine hair. 'That's the happiest I've seen the little one since the master brought her home. Just look at her, sir, I told you it's Nurse Parry you should be listening to, not heathens.'

Alexei took the last tray from Spartak and set it on the table, before sitting opposite Anna.

'If you want anything else, Matron Parry, sir, send one of the children in to tell me. Eat, both of you,' she looked from Anna to Alexei and shook her head dolefully. 'There's no meat on your bones. Either of you!'

'You have your orders.' Alexei handed Anna a bowl.

'Heathens?' Anna raised her eyebrows.

'Vasya,' Alexei mouthed above Kitty's head, 'like most Cossacks, Lada disapproves of Jews. I've caught her sprinkling holy water she begs from Father Grigor, around the house after Vasya leaves.'

'Has she told Father Grigor why she needs it?'

'I've never dared ask her, but I doubt it.'

Andrei approached and bowed to Alexei. 'Do you mind if we leave now, Uncle Alexei? I promise we'll take care of Kitty and Olga.'

'Make sure you do just that. Has Colonel Razin's captain given you an escort?'

'Not that we need one, sir, but he has. Six armed men. We'll return before dark.'

146

'If you don't, you'll answer to Maryanna's father as well as me. And don't forget to take Lada's picnic basket, or I'll never hear the end of it. I'm almost afraid to ask, do you intend moving on after you've visited the shrine?'

'If there's time we'll go to the works' reservoir, sir. Pavlo rode up there this morning and reserved two boats just in case.'

'It's as well he did, a fine day like this, all the idlers will be out to rent one.'

'We're only idle in the holidays, sir.' Andrei bristled.

'I was teasing, Andrei. Forgive me I need to practise my smile so people will know when I'm joking.'

'Hurry up, Andrei,' Spartak called. 'Pavlo and Tom are here with their carriage.'

'Papa, see you later,' Kitty ran up, hat in hand, ribbons flying from her hair and kissed Alexei's cheek then Anna's.

'Don't worry, Papa, we'll be fine.' Olga followed her sister at a more sedate pace.

'Your assurance won't stop me worrying.' Alexei kissed her.

'Thank you for visiting, Godmother Anna, and giving Papa some much needed instructions on how to care for Ruth. I don't know who was crying more before you came, Papa or Ruth.'

'I wasn't crying, and off with you before I change my mind about allowing you to go,' Alexei's smile didn't reach his eyes.

'You were weeping,' Kitty contradicted, 'but I would have been if I'd had my baby sister screeching in my ear.'

'Your girls are beautiful,' Anna murmured a little enviously as they ran across the garden. She couldn't help thinking of the children she'd never have or wondering what they would have looked like.

'And Sonya and Roman's sons are handsome,' he frowned. 'I'll have to watch the girls when they're around them. I remember only too well what I was like at Andrei and Spartak's age.'

147

'You'll be beating boys off with sticks when Olga and Kitty are older.'

Alexei's expression changed.

Anna set down her bowl. 'I'm so sorry . . . '

'It's me, not you. I can't bear thinking of the girls having to grow up without a mother. About all the things they and . . . ' he struggled but failed to say Ruth's name, ' . . . will miss. My grandmother was arranging for them to be presented at court the next time we visited St Petersburg. She and Ruth spent hours looking at dressmakers' catalogues and comparing fabric samples. There's a chest full of scraps of velvets, silks and satins in my grandmother's house. And that's without young suitors coming to call, and planning balls to mark the important events in their lives. Their entrance into society, their engagements and weddings . . . ' he choked on barely supressed emotion. 'I'm bound to make a mess of looking after them. Just look at the baby. I spent all morning trying to placate her without success. You walk through the door and she's fine.'

'She was too warm and her fingers had caught in her shawl that was all. It was soon remedied and you would have noticed in a few minutes,' she assured him.

'But I didn't . . . '

'You would have. Did someone advise you to wrap her up like a pudding ready for boiling?'

'Vasya.'

'She still wants the girls despite Nathan's opposition to adopting them?'

'Maybe I should let her take them.'

'That's exhaustion talking,' she said. 'How long has it been since you've slept?'

'I sleep,' he replied unconvincingly.

'I mean a full night's sleep.'

'I can't remember. But it's not the baby . . . I welcome her waking as it gives me someone to talk to. It's . . . ' He stared bleakly into space, before whispering, 'so hard to continue living without her.'

148

His grief was so intense, so suffocating Anna felt ill equipped to do anything other than turn to the practical. 'Have you discussed Vasya's offer with Kitty and Olga?'

'No.'

'You do know they'll refuse to go. Not least because they're of an age when they consider themselves grown up.'

'When Vasya talks, her suggestions seem to make sense. She and Nathan have a large house, a lot roomier than this one, the girls would have an aunt to turn to as well as an uncle . . . the baby will have a mother to care for her as well as a father . . . '

'Have you any idea of the hours Nathan works?' she asked. 'The hospital is his life. Even if your girls lived with him they'd hardly see him. And consider what it would be like if they did move in with Vasya with you living across the road. Would you want to be their father and see them every day or would you abdicate your responsibilities and become a sort of uncle figure?'

He absent-mindedly spooned goulash into his bowl because it gave him an excuse not to look at what he assumed would be condemnation in her eyes.

'Think about Ruth and what she would have wanted for your daughters,' Anna said earnestly.

'Every time I do, I come to the conclusion that the girls would be better off with almost anyone other than me, and I'm not just saying that to sound pathetic.'

'You're far from pathetic,' she reassured.

'Yes, I am,' he contradicted. 'I'm a hopeless father. You've seen the way Kitty and Olga speak to me . . . '

'Like daughters who love their father and are close enough to him to tease him.'

'Don't be kind, Anna. I can't bear it. The girls are suffering and I don't want you or anyone else to feel sorry for them or me.'

She set the bowl he'd given her on the table and waited for him to continue.

'I haven't a clue how to bring up children, especially girls. I rely . . . relied on Ruth for everything.'

'Catherine would like you to move in with her.'

'She told you that she asked me?'

'She has.'

'If we do it wouldn't be me providing for my family the way a father should, but me relying on my grandmother to pick up the pieces of my life – again. Just as she did when my father disowned me when I started working for Mr Hughes before your brother and I entered into a partnership.'

'Catherine wouldn't mind . . . '

'But I would,' he interrupted. 'I should be shouldering my grandmother's burdens not the other way around. As for moving in with her, the twins are having problems enough adjusting to life without Ruth without moving house – we all are. They need security.'

'And they'd get it if they moved in with Vasya and Nathan?'

'Probably more than I could give them, but you're right they wouldn't go. If only I didn't feel so utterly useless.' He moved his bowl on the table in front of him but made no attempt to eat. 'Just after Ruth became pregnant my grandmother asked us if we would take over the guardianship of Kira if anything happened to her. To everyone who knows her, Kira's an adult in every way but under the terms of the trusts my grandfather set up for all his grandchildren – even the ones that weren't born before he died, no girl in the family can inherit anything until she's thirty-five – or marries a "suitable man" whatever one of those might be.'

'That's harsh on the women in your family.'

'It's unfair,' Alexei said. 'Of course, Ruth and I agreed to look after Kira . . . but now Ruth has gone, how on earth can I ask my grandmother to take in Kitty, Olga and the baby as well as continue to look after Kira.'

'You just said it yourself. Kira's an adult in every way that matters.'

150

If Alexei heard Anna he didn't acknowledge what she'd said. 'No one Catherine's age should be expected to care for their great granddaughters.'

'You're talking as though you wouldn't be with them in your grandmother's house.'

'Physically there maybe, but able to guide them?' He sighed as he turned to her. 'And then there's the question of religion. Vasya believes the girls should be returned to their mother's faith. What do you think?'

Anna set down her spoon. 'I think I'm not the person to talk to about religion.'

'Ruth always admired your bravery – with good reason after you shot the soldier who was attacking her. I can think of no one better to ask for advice.'

'I admire the Jewish faith and its teachings,' Anna began hesitantly. 'To me they seem akin to those of the Christian chapels and churches. Your grandmother told me both religions are based on the same scriptures, the differences are down to how people have interpreted those writings over the centuries. I love Yulia and Miriam but I'm not so blinded that I didn't see the antagonism Ruth faced from her fellow Jews when she converted to Christianity. You and Ruth christened the twins into the Orthodox faith. Ruth wouldn't have done that without giving the matter a great deal of thought. I have no doubt that Ruth would have wanted your baby christened into the Orthodox faith as well if she'd lived.'

'She'd already picked you out as one of the godparents.' Alexei stared down at his goulash and stirred it.

'Do you think Vasya would allow the girls to forget their mother's rejection of the Jewish faith if you allowed her to convert them?' Anna shifted Ruth, who was still sleeping from her lap, and set her face down on the cushion next to her.

'You think that if I gave the girls to Vasya to bring up in the Jewish faith they'd suffer slights and snubs from the Jews because of Ruth's conversion to Christianity?'

151

'I doubt you could "give" the girls to anyone, without their consent. As for your question, not all Jews would snub them. I can't imagine Vasya, Miriam and Yulia being anything but kind. But there are narrow minded bigots in every religion. I admired you and Ruth for ignoring them and their malicious gossip after you married.'

'It seemed the best way to deal with them.'

'I'd say the only way.'

'I tried talking to Richard once about your religion, you call yourself Baptists?'

'We do,' she agreed.

'He didn't say much about your beliefs.'

'They are much the same as all Christian beliefs, including Orthodox. "Do unto others as you would be done by. Pray to God when you need help. Be kind to the afflicted, assist those in need, don't harm any living thing if you can avoid doing so, - which I failed dismally . . . '

'For which Ruth and I blessed you. If you hadn't killed that soldier he would most likely have killed Ruth.'

'I hope God sees it that way when I stand before him on the day of judgement. There is one major difference however, compared to your Orthodox services, ours are very plain and simple.'

'I frequently see Glyn in our church with Praskovia, but apart from weddings, christenings and funerals I've never seen you, Richard or Sarah there so I assumed you hadn't considered joining our congregation.'

'I love your Church, I love the way it's decorated with paintings covering every inch of wall and gleaming gold and silver incense burners and candle-sticks. I love the pageantry of your services and I was very happy when Father Grigor gave me permission to be godmother to Olga and Kitty but . . . '

'But?' he pressed when she faltered.

'The "but" is down to my prejudice. I've discussed it with Richard and Sarah. None of us feel at home in opulent surroundings. The church – or rather chapel we went to in Wales had whitewashed walls, wooden benches and a plain unadorned cross not a crucifix with a figure of Jesus's body on the wall behind the pulpit. That is why Mr Rees, our minister here, is happy to conduct services in the staff dining room of the hotel on Sunday evenings after the kitchens have closed. Like our chapels it has white walls and wooden seats.'

'No altar, no paintings?'

'No and not a trace of gold leaf or a silver chalice anywhere.'

'It sounds as dull as a schoolroom.'

'The idea is to provoke thoughts about our spiritual life, not overwhelm the senses. Richard, Sarah and I are awed whenever we enter the church on your grandmother's estate. It's beautiful, inspirational but small as it is, it . . . '

'Overwhelms the senses,' he repeated her phrase.

'Exactly.' She rested her hand on Ruth's back. The baby's breathing was shallow as she slept.

'Then you must be even more overwhelmed by the one Mr Hughes has almost finished building. It's ten times the size of the one on my grandmother's estate.'

'I am.' She tasted the goulash. 'Lada's a good cook.'

'Better than me,' Alexei agreed.

'Please don't take this as a suggestion that you're doing a poor job of bringing up your daughters, but you employ Lev to look after your house and garden and Lada to cook, clean and do your washing. So why not employ a governess to take care of and educate the girls and a nursemaid to care for Ruth?'

'You want me to hand my daughters over to servants?'

'Nothing of the kind. Olga and Kitty would benefit from the companionship of a trained, educated and qualified governess, who can teach them languages, deportment, literature, music and art.

'And a nursemaid with experience of caring for babies, who could take over from you whenever you are busy, which need not be often, could look after Ruth under the care of Lada. It would be no different to the arrangements Sonya and Roman, Glyn and Praskovia and Richard and Sarah have made for the supervision of their children and it would enable you to return to work . . . '

'Has Richard complained about my absence?'

'Nothing of the kind. He's grateful that you've taken over most of the administrative work, the hiring, firing and wages not to mention the sales and buying of the equipment you need for the collieries.' She ate another spoonful of goulash. 'Don't you miss working with the managers?'

'Yes,' he replied with an honesty that surprised her. 'It would be easier than looking after the girls.'

'I could try and find a nursemaid for you,' she offered. 'More girls than we take on apply for nursing training every day, and some have experience of caring for children. There are even one or two nurses in the hospital who would prefer to work regular daytime hours so they could care for their elderly parents in the evenings and on Sundays.'

'I'll consider it.'

'A little time spent apart every day, might be good for the girls and you.'

'If I did hire anyone, I would need a Russian nursemaid and an English governess?'

'That comment proves you're considering it. But you'd need more than the two existing bedrooms in this house if you did.'

'Did my grandmother ask you to suggest this to me, so you could add your persuasive voice to hers to move into her house?'

'No, but you have to admit it's an idea. Catherine could keep an eye on anyone you employ to look after the girls. But,' she looked across the garden as the kitchen door opened.

'No decisions have to be made in a hurry. However, I think you need to do something about Vasya,' she whispered as Nathan's wife walked into the garden, 'for her sake as well as the twins.'

'Vasya's sake?' he echoed in surprise.

'It's common knowledge in the hospital that she wants a child, Alexei. If you tell her you won't allow her to adopt your girls, she may finally succeed in persuading Nathan to allow her to take a baby from the Jewish orphanage.'

Ruth moved, waving her tiny arms.

'Pass Ruth to me, please, Anna.'

Anna picked up the baby and placed her in Alexei's arms. Ruth settled almost immediately, snuggling into her father's chest.

Vasya walked across the grass towards them. Anna saw Vasya watching Alexei with his daughter and read envy and desolation in her eyes and something else. She hated herself for even thinking it, but it seemed akin to greed. She wondered if she dared to raise the topic of adoption with Nathan, before realising that Sarah would be better placed to do so. And not only because she was closer to Nathan than any of the other nurses.

Sarah had been abandoned in a workhouse shortly after her birth. She knew exactly what it was to grow up unwanted and unloved in an institution.

CHAPTER THIRTEEN

Glyn and Praskovia's House Hughesovka, April 1889

'Miriam may be able to look after Ruth for Alexei a few days a week,' Anna suggested. 'She asked if she could be taken off the night rota so she could help her mother care for her grandmother who's taken to her bed.'

'I've heard,' Praskovia wheeled the tea trolley closer to the table. 'Is she really ill?'

'Not according to Nathan who examined her at the request of Miriam's mother. She's not even that old.'

'She's barely sixty according to my mother who's made it her business to know the age of everyone in Hughesovka,' Praskovia handed plates and napkins to Anna, Sonya and Sarah.

'Miriam told me she's pleaded ill health ever since she can remember. The family believe it's her way of getting everyone to run around doing her bidding.'

'I agree with Nathan.' Praskovia filled glasses with tea from the samovar. 'That Babushka has made it her life's work to bully and irritate everyone around her. The last time I spoke to her at the market, she looked as fit as a flea in a hole house. Two days later I heard she was refusing to rise from her bed. When I spoke to her she complained that Miriam spent more time caring for strangers than her own grandmother.'

'Didn't you remind her that Miriam is a trained nurse and earns her living by caring for patients in the hospital?' Anna asked.

She'd returned to the hospital from her visit to Alexei to find Sarah and Sonya in the office. They'd made a unanimous decision to call on Praskovia because they all felt a need to spend time with a sympathetic friend and partly because Yelena had told Sarah to remind Sonya that it was her baking day and she was making something special to tempt Roman's appetite.

'I didn't dare remind Miriam's grandmother of anything. That would have taken time I didn't have.' Praskovia slipped the full tea glasses into silver holders and distributed them. 'As it was she spent over half an hour describing every one of her aches and pains – down to the faintest twinge.'

'Do you think Alexei will employ a nursemaid and governess to help him bring up his girls?' Sarah asked Anna.

'I honestly don't know.'

'At least he was prepared to discuss the idea with you, Anna. And from what you said he took your advice about swaddling Ruth in layers of wool.' Praskovia finished handing out glasses and picked up a cake knife. 'Every time I've called on him since Ruth's funeral, he couldn't wait to sweep me out of his house.'

'I could talk to Dr Kharber about taking on an extra nurse, which would ensure that one would be available should Alexei need help. The hospital can always find work for an extra pair of hands and Alexei would pay her wages if – and that really is an "if" - he decides he needs a nursemaid for Ruth, but his house is too small to house a nurse and a governess without extending it, so that would mean him employing people who had their own accommodation.' Anna looked to Sarah for advice.

'If it's a question of finding rooms for a nursemaid and governess, we have rooms to spare here,' Praskovia offered. 'This house seems incredibly empty compared to the early days when you, Richard, Sarah, Richard's brothers and Alexei all lived here, Anna. And it would make sense for your boys to spend time either here or in Sarah's house, Sonya, to give Roman peace and quiet to recuperate. The children get on so well together - ' Praskovia made a wry face, 'at the moment.'

'Probably because they haven't spent enough time together to start squabbling. My boys are quite capable of being monsters,' Sonya said.

'They look so angelic.'

'"Look"', Sonya repeated drily. 'Spartak and Andrei have been known to plant beetles in girls' hair and lizards in their pockets.'

'Pavlo used to put spiders down the back of his playmates' shirts,' Praskovia revealed.

'Something he taught Ted to do when he isn't slipping frogs under Maryanna's pillow.' Sarah said.

'Almond or Sandy biscuit, or one of my mother's Krendelki?' Praskovia handed around the cake stands. 'Which reminds me, Sonya, the surprise my mother made for Roman is an outsize Krendel cake.'

'It's not his birthday.'

'My mother decided he needs pampering. I've learned not to argue with her. I advise you to do the same.'

'As we already have a tutor he could give all the children lessons in our house,' Sonya suggested, still thinking of ways they could help Alexei with his daughters.

'You also have Roman returning home tomorrow. The last thing he needs is a mob of noisy young people charging around. We have rooms to spare, and as we're only next door to you it makes sense for your sons to spend some time with us, with or without their tutor.' Sarah helped herself to an almond biscuit. 'Either way I'm looking forward to you moving into your house.'

'I'm not,' Praskovia passed around the sugar bowl. 'I'll miss you and your boys, Sonya.'

'Thank you for putting up with me, Sarah. It was kind of you to allow us to stay so close to the hospital.' Sonya impulsively grabbed Sarah and Praskovia's hands. 'You'll have to put your hand on top, Anna, as I haven't a third hand.'

Anna did as Sonya asked.

'I wouldn't have survived these last weeks without you three.' Sonya said huskily.

'You most certainly would have,' Sarah contradicted. 'But to return to practical considerations, Richard built four self-contained apartments in our house. The one we live in is the largest with six bedrooms, but there are three more each with three bedrooms, living room and kitchen. He had it mind that the boys and Anna might want their own space at some time in the future. Any one of them would make a perfect school. Your tutor is welcome to make use of whichever he chooses.'

'Thank you for the offer, but . . . ' Sonya hesitated.

'It's there if you need it, but you won't be able to make any decisions until Roman has seen the German surgeon?' Sarah guessed.

'Roman is hoping he'll operate.'

'Noah insists he's the best surgeon he knows, and he doesn't praise lightly,' Sarah reassured.

Sonya forced a smile. 'I'm looking forward to, and dreading Roman leaving hospital in equal measure. He says he can't wait to be home with me and the boys, but although he tries, he can't hide the constant pain he's in, especially from me. I doubt he'll be able to rest as much in our house as he does in hospital where's there are nurses to watch over and bully him.'

'I've ordered Manfred and Franz to shout at him, when Roman exhausts himself but they seem reluctant to do so,' Sarah said.

'Employees are always reluctant to give their employer orders.'

'If you like Anna and I could take in turns to come around and reprimand him a few times a day,' Sarah joked. 'Richard says Anna has a better matron's voice than me now I'm out of practice.'

'I may ask both of you to do just that. When Roman's in a mind to do something, no matter how injurious it may be to his health, nothing will stop him.'

'Not even you?' Sarah asked.

'Not even me. He's had his own way for far too long. Given his father's illness and early death he practically brought himself up.' Sonya set her glass down on the trolley. 'But if he had to get shot, I'm glad it was here in Hughesovka, among friends who will care for our boys while we concentrate on his recovery.'

Anna looked at the clock. 'It's time I returned to the hospital.'

'You're looking tired. I hope you're not thinking of working on beyond the end of your shift,' Sarah warned.

'I don't intend to as Catherine's ordered Lyudmila to serve an early dinner.'

'Which will spoil if there's an emergency,' Sarah pointed out.

'They seem to occur with increasing frequency these days, which is hardly surprising given the amount of vodka consumed in this town.' Anna rose from her chair.

'Glyn and Mr Hughes did try to hold back the men's wages on high days and holidays but that didn't work when riots led to even more broken heads and bones.' Praskovia cleared the used plates on to the lower shelf of the trolley.

'Don't move, Praskovia, I'll see myself out.' Anna blew them a kiss as she left.

'Does Anna ever do anything or go anywhere except the hospital, Sarah?' Praskovia asked.

'Not that I've seen. Richard and I have both talked to her about the long hours she puts in, but she insists she's happiest when she's in the hospital. I know Mr Hughes was concerned about the amount of time she and Nathan Kharber spend on duty, which is why he engaged more doctors and nurses. But there are still times when the hospital is short staffed and it's impossible to stop Anna and Nathan from treating people who need medical attention.'

'It's a pity Anna missed the last two music recitals. Glyn mentioned that Mr Hughes has engaged a London theatre company. They'll be here at the beginning of July with a repertoire of six plays and they'll stay until the end of October to give us a chance to see all of them.'

'If they stay any later they'll have the snowed in winter to rehearse another half a dozen. Thank you for the tea and cakes, Praskovia.' Sonya left her chair. 'I want to call in and see Roman before I return to the house to see if he has any last-minute instructions for me.'

'Don't forget his cake.'

'I won't. I'll go out through the kitchen so I can thank Yelena and say goodbye to her.'

'You are welcome to send the boys down here anytime.'

'Thank you, Praskovia, but I doubt the boys will visit anyone for a few days. They have made a banner with WELCOME HOME PAPA across it and hung it in his study. This is the longest he's been separated from them. They've missed him so much.' A frown creased her forehead. 'I hope that they'll understand that he needs rest.'

'I'm sure they will.' Praskovia rose to her feet. 'Let's get that cake. The boys can cut and serve it. It will be a great welcome home present for them to give Roman.'

Catherine's House Hughesovka, April 1889

'More kisel, or cheese, Anna? You haven't eaten enough to keep a fly alive.'

'I've eaten ten times more than I normally do, Catherine.' Anna took her linen napkin from her lap, folded it and replaced it in her silver napkin ring.

'And you, miss,' Catherine smiled at her great granddaughter. 'Was it a very long day helping Father Grigor and the twins at the soup kitchen?'

'Long but worthwhile,' Kira qualified. 'Nine new families arrived from the Urals today, all looking for work. After we fed them Father Grigor managed to find them beds in a dormitory.'

'Will he be able to find them work as well as beds?' Catherine asked.

'He sent for Grisha, who said he'll try to find them positions as coal hewers in one of the collieries. If you'll excuse me, Grandmamma, Anna, I need to get ready. Morgan and Owen are picking me up in half an hour. We're auditioning for the next amateur dramatic production.'

'Is Francine going with you?' Anna asked.

'Yes, how did you know?'

Anna tapped her nose, 'big sisters know all there is to know about their little brothers.'

Kira left the table. 'I'll say goodnight before I leave.'

'Mind you do. Are you likely to be late?' Catherine asked.

'I shouldn't think so but Morgan and Owen will be bringing me home so I'll be quite safe.'

'All Richard's drivers and footmen carry arms,' Anna reminded Catherine.

'I hate the thought that it's necessary.' Catherine watched Kira leave the room. 'I'm not sure whether to thank you for turning my granddaughter into a modern young woman who feels the need to help those less fortunate, or berate you for highlighting the deficiencies in my own life.'

'When it comes to helping those less fortunate, no one has worked harder than you, Catherine. The whole of Hughesovka has a great deal to thank you for.'

'You are kind to an old woman.' Catherine turned to her butler. 'Please serve our coffee and cherry brandy in the drawing room, Boris.'

'Yes, Madam.'

'And thank the cook for me, that was a fine meal.'

'I will, Madam.' Boris opened the door and Catherine walked ahead of Anna into the drawing room. Like all the rooms in the Beletsky house it was beautifully furnished with hand-crafted furniture, damask silk upholstery and hangings, a plethora of books, crystal and bronze ornaments and the inevitable chess set.

One of the first things Anna had discovered about Russian houses, was no matter how opulent or humble, they all contained a chess set. Cobbled together from oddments of paper and cardboard in the "hole houses" that had been dug underground and roofed with turf by the poorest in Hughesovka. Artisan made from wood in the apartments of the supervisors and foremen, the richer families had figures carved by craftsmen in ebony and ivory or cast by amber smiths in dark and light molten amber.

Catherine's was amber, the white pieces light enough to be mistaken for ivory, facing an opposing side of gleaming rich dark brown pieces.

'Would you like coffee with your brandy, Anna?' Catherine picked up the silver pot.

'Please.'

Catherine placed Anna's coffee cup on a side table along with a glass of cherry brandy. 'I've been meaning to thank you for calling in on Alexei as often as you have since Ruth died. It can't be easy for you to find the time given your duties in the hospital.'

'It's only the odd five minutes here and there.'

'But it means a lot to the twins and me to know that you are keeping an eye on him and Ruth.'

Anna sipped her coffee. 'The twins told you?'

'They call here every time they ride out of town, which is most days, and Kira visits Alexei whenever she goes to help Father Grigor. Or to see your brother,' Catherine added wryly.

'So, between the twins, Kira and Lyudmila who calls on Lada every time she goes to the market, you have your spies watching Alexei and your newest great-granddaughter.'

'You could say that,' Catherine frowned. 'Alexei will have to find his own way out of the darkness he's fallen into but your visits are very much appreciated and not only by Alexei and his girls, Anna. I'm grateful to you.'

'He said you'd invited him to move into the wing Mr Hughes lived in.'

'I did and I hoped he'd take me up on my offer but he refused. Did he also tell you that I asked him and Ruth to take on the guardianship of his sister Kira?'

'He did.'

'That was before Ruth died of course.' Catherine's hand shook slightly as she reached for her cherry brandy. 'Not that the guardianship would have been very onerous. As you know Kira may be young but she is quite independent, although not financially. My husband made it clear in his will that no female in the family was to inherit anything until her marriage or 35th birthday. Kira is a sweet girl, she has given me very little trouble and much less heartache than my daughter Olga. I heartily approve of Kira's choice of suitor. Your brother Morgan is a fine young man.'

'They appear to be very much in love.'

'They do, don't they?' Catherine smiled. 'I hope Kira will find the happiness Alexei enjoyed for a while. If she and Morgan marry soon then what I'm about to ask you to do may prove unnecessary. But as Dimitri says it is well to be prepared for all eventualities.' Catherine looked inward to a past Anna could only guess at. 'I wish Olga hadn't been so eager to please her father when it came to selecting a husband. Count Beletsky may have been rich when the match was arranged but his weaknesses were obvious, however . . . that water has long flowed down the Don.'

Catherine changed her tone to brisk and business like as she opened a drawer in the table and removed a leather folder.

'I asked Mr Dmitri to draw up a new will for me. It is already signed, witnessed and notarised, if you disagree with anything it contains I will simply tear it up and ask Dmitri to draft a new one. Am I right in saying that you are fond of Kira?'

'Do you need to ask me? Kira is very lovable'

'Thank you. She is an angel - most of the time - which brings me to the enormous favour I want to ask you. I would like you to become her joint guardian with Dimitri after my death. I know it is a great deal to ask of any woman, particularly one who is married to their career as you are . . . but Alexei will be so busy with his girls that I'm afraid he won't have any time for Kira. And of course, Kira is accustomed . . . '

'To having your undivided attention, as well as that of her maid.'

Catherine smiled. 'You've summed up the situation so well my dear. So, will you care for my Kira for me?'

'If anything should happen to you, of course I will take care of her.'

'You won't have to concern yourself with finances. Dimitri and his law firm will see to that side of things but I would appreciate it if you would advise her on her personal choices whenever you think she needs guidance.'

'Catherine, you don't know everything about me . . . '

'I know all I need to, Anna. You're bright, intelligent capable of running a busy hospital superbly well, managing a large staff and as well as all that, you're a trained nurse who loves my granddaughter. I can't think of anyone better placed or qualified to guide Kira.'

'If you're certain you've made the right choice. . . '

'I'm more certain than I've ever been of anything in my life before.' Catherine lifted her glass and touched it to Anna's. '"Cheers" as they say in England.'

165

Anna reciprocated. 'A Welsh toast to go with your English one, Catherine. "Iechyd Da", which means your very good health.'

'I'm afraid not even a Welsh toast can grant me that.'

Anna's eyes grew wide in apprehension.

Catherine laid her hand on Anna's arm. 'Please, no tears, don't be sad and not a word to anyone. I've had a long life, if not always a happy one. And I have so much to look forward to. Seeing Olga and the rest of my granddaughters again. And my Alexei, unfaithful as he undoubtedly was, he will always be my husband and my first, last and only love. Thank you, Anna, for easing an old woman's mind and making it so easy for me to prepare to depart.'

CHAPTER FOURTEEN

Madame Koshka's Brothel Hughesovka, April 1889

A knock echoed through the door of Koshka's boudoir.

Without looking up from the tapestry she was stitching she called out, 'Enter.'

The door opened and her German manservant, Fritz floated noiselessly into the room, no mean feat for a man of his height and weight. 'A lady has arrived at the kitchen door asking to see you, Madame.'

'Is she looking for employment?'

'She didn't say and I didn't enquire her purpose in calling, Madame. She asked to speak to you. She is heavily veiled but there is only one lady in Hughesovka I know of with her distinctive voice and figure. I believe it to be Princess Nadolny.'

Koshka breathed in sharply. 'Has anyone else seen her?'

'Only the cook, Madame. I asked the lady to wait in the still room after warning the cook not to allow anyone in there until I returned.'

'I'll go down . . . ' she left her chair.

'Would that be wise, Madame?' Fritz asked.

Koshka considered. 'No, you're right, Fritz.' On pain of dismissal, she had sworn every member of her household staff to secrecy, never to reveal the comings, goings or affairs of her employees or clients to anyone, family, close friend or casual acquaintance. After her dire warnings, she was certain that no one in her employ would identify any of her visitors or the business that brought them to her door to anyone outside. But the relationship between herself and Sonya Nadolny was a closely guarded secret known to only four people in Hughesovka, Sonya, Roman, Catherine and herself, and she intended to keep it that way. The last thing she wanted was to spark gossip that would lead to questions better left unasked.

'Show my visitor up the back staircase, Fritz, and make sure she remains veiled until she reaches this room. We're not expecting deliveries at the cellar door today?'

'No, Madame.'

She opened a drawer in her desk and tossed him the keys to the exit she reserved for her "special guests", those who demanded – and received – complete privacy. 'When you escort my visitor out, take her through the basement.'

'Yes, Madame.'

'She shouldn't have come here,' Koshka muttered more to herself than Fritz. 'I'll try to persuade her to leave quickly . . . you'd better send for a cab. Better I pay the driver to wait than keep her in the house a moment longer than necessary. Tell him to take his carriage into the cellar yard and close the high gates while it's there. Don't open the gates again until she's safely in the cab. Make sure the blinds are down and cover all of the carriage windows- ' Uncharacteristically flustered, random thoughts whirled through Koshka's mind like dead leaves in a high wind. Had she covered every eventuality – every avenue that might lead to the discovery of her most closely guarded secret?

Fritz had worked for Koshka for over twenty years and had never seen her so panic-stricken. 'I assure you, Madame, I will arrange everything with discretion.'

She gazed blankly at him and he sensed her struggling to concentrate. 'Of course, you will, Fritz. I trust you implicitly to do just that.' She gave him an apologetic smile. 'Ask the cook to bring up a tray of tea, wine, sandwiches, canapes and cake – no - ask her to make up the tray, and bring it up after you've shown my visitor in here.'

'Yes, Madame.'

Koshka sat back in her chair, only to immediately jump up again and check her reflection in the mirror.

Fritz's voice echoed from the doorway. 'You look perfect, as always, Madame.'

Koshka looked back at him in the glass. 'You always know exactly what to say and when to say it, Fritz.'

He bowed. 'I will escort your visitor here, Madame.' He closed the door behind him.

Koshka moved restlessly around her boudoir after Fritz left. She frequently entertained patrons as well as friends in the room consequently she took care not to leave any personal items, photographs or letters on display. She stood back and tried to look at the room dispassionately, viewing it as a stranger might.

It was adorned with the trappings of wealth, too many and too ornate to be termed "good taste". The sofas, chaise longue and chairs were French Empire, craftsman made with an expensive attention to detail. The gilding was real gold, the upholstery a rich blue silk velvet. Even her bureau and occasional tables were gilded with real gold lacquer. The tables were topped with Italian marble. One in black and white chessboard squares sported carved black and white marble chess figures.

There was an abundance of object d'art and trinkets. Every ornament was a gift from a friend or admirer, all beautifully made, all costly. Amber boxes, marble and bronze busts and statuettes, an ebony cigar humidor inlaid with silver filigree, an ivory desk set, and a silver tray set out as a drinks tray were casually arranged on a sideboard and chest of drawers. A silver samovar and tea glasses filled a table in front of the stove. Crystal decanters, glasses and brandy balloons were displayed in a glass fronted cupboard, yet she knew to a fraction of an inch where everything was placed, and corrected deviations immediately if the maids dared to shift anything out of its allotted place.

A large oil painting, commissioned by a wealthy admirer and set in a frame that would have graced a castle dominated the wall opposite her chaise.

The painter had portrayed her in a cream silk ball gown standing before a mirror, an ostrich feather fan in her hand, a ruby and diamond choker around her throat and a matching tiara crowning her hair. It wasn't the only painting in the room. Watercolours of St Petersburg, pen and ink drawings of herself and her "girls", current and past, and sketches of Hughesovka made by the architect's apprentice who had fallen in love with the most beautiful and talented of her "girls", hung on the other walls.

Fritz's knock on the "secret door" which was indistinguishable from the wall panelling broke through her thoughts and startled her. She returned to the sofa, arranged the folds of her black silk skirt and called out, 'Enter.'

Fritz opened the door and stepped back to allow a woman to walk in ahead of him. Just as her butler had done, Koshka recognised the slim upright figure beneath the enveloping black veils and crepe widow's weeds as the daughter she'd handed over to Catherine Ignatova shortly after her birth.

Sonya was illegitimate, the result of a liaison between Koshka and the first man she'd truly loved, Catherine's stepbrother, Sergei. When Koshka asked Catherine to bring up her daughter, Catherine had agreed and gladly, treating her brother's child no differently from her own daughter. When Sonya was old enough to ask questions about her parents, against her better judgement Catherine complied with Koshka's demands, and related the story Koshka had concocted. That her mother had died giving birth to her and her father had contracted a virulently infectious strain of tuberculosis and was incarcerated in a Moscow sanatorium.

Catherine would have preferred to tell her niece the truth, but Koshka had insisted the lies were necessary to protect Sonya, and her, because the existence of a child would make them both vulnerable to blackmail.

A tuberculosis sanatorium certainly conjured more a sympathetic image than an insane asylum, particularly when the inmate in question was suffering from insanity induced by syphilis as Catherine's stepbrother Sergei was. And a mother who'd died in childbirth was a saintly figure in comparison to a successful – and wealthy - brothel Madam.

It had taken a great deal of persuasion from both Catherine and Roman to persuade Koshka to meet with and acknowledge her daughter shortly before Sonya's wedding, but given Koshka's profession the madam still insisted on keeping their relationship secret.

Sonya lifted her veil. Koshka rose to meet her and they embraced.

'I am sorry for calling on you unexpectedly. . . '

'If you had written we could have met in a suite in the hotel. It would have been safer for both of us.'

'I'm sorry. I didn't think but I didn't know what to do or who to turn to . . . then I thought of you and I hoped you'd see me . . . '

'Please, sit down,' Koshka took Sonya's cloak, shawl and veils and draped them across a chair before ushering her to the sofa. 'Come,' she called out in reply to a second knock.

Fritz entered with a tray that he set on a table between the sofa and Koshka's chair. He went to the door that communicated with the rest of the house and turned the key, locking it.

'You have told the household I am not to be disturbed, Fritz?' Koshka asked.

'Yes, Madame. Would you like me to return in half an hour for the tray?'

'No one saw you bring my visitor here?'

'No Madame.'

'Return in one hour, Fritz, and make sure that a hire carriage has arrived by then and is waiting at the cellar door.'

'Yes, Madame.' Fritz left closing the door softly behind him.

'Wine? Tea?' Koshka asked Sonya.

'Tea please.'

Koshka poured it and handed Sonya a glass and a plate.

'How is your husband?'

'Insistent on being moved into our new home. The tears Sonya had managed to keep in check since Roman had been shot, trickled down her cheeks.

'My dear child.' Koshka left her chair and sat beside Sonya on the sofa. 'What on earth has happened?'

'Nothing – everything . . . ' Sonya's voice faded, choked by silent tears.

Koshka was accustomed to comforting her girls when they lost the patronage of a customer, or someone from their family or past life died. But she lived with her girls, day in day out, talked to them, ate meals with them and cared for them as she would have for a family, as a result she knew exactly how to console them when they needed reassurance. But the only time she'd held her daughter as an adult was on her wedding day.

She reached out, hesitated, then took Sonya's hand and held it between her own.

'Has something just happened?' Koshka ventured when Sonya finally quietened.

'No . . . I'm just so afraid . . . '

'Of what, my darling.'

'Of the bullet in Roman's body suddenly moving and cutting through his spinal cord. Of him bleeding to death. Of him insisting on undergoing another operation and dying under the surgeon's knife on the operating table . . . of losing him and never ever seeing him again . . . '

'My, dear Sonya, the one thing I do know about death is that's impossible to live in fear of it and truly live. If you do, you will ruin your days. Not one single God given moment will be worth the effort it takes to draw breath. The only thing to do when death stares you in the face is dare it to do its worst and ignore it.'

She held Sonya at arms' length so she could look into her eyes. 'But this is more than just the fear of Roman dying, isn't it?'

'He's always been so active, so passionate in everything he does.'

'Including loving you,' Koshka guessed.

'I'm terrified that if the doctors can't help him regain the use of his legs, he'll believe there's nothing left for him that he'll . . . '

Koshka clamped her hand over her mouth. 'You can't really believe that he'll take his own life?'

As Koshka had put her worst fear into words Sonya nodded. 'I can and I do. For all that suicide is a mortal sin that will consign him to burn in hell for eternity. God forgive me but I do.' She met Koshka's steady gaze. 'It's unbearable to watch Roman suffering. After seeing him fight pain for weeks I can understand why he could be driven to kill himself. But for the sake of his soul I have to stop him.'

'You must,' Koshka pleaded.

'I don't know how. But I do know that I must try.'

Koshka reached for the cognac and poured two glasses. 'You're worried he'll try to kill himself when he's at home?'

'People watch him all the time in hospital. The nurses, doctor, porters, ward maids and visitors are in and out of his room at all hours, checking his symptoms and temperature, but he refuses to hire a trained nurse to care for him at home. Sarah Parry has trained his valets Franz and Hans to care for him . . . '

'Surely they would stop Roman from taking his own life?' Catherine interrupted.

'They will carry out Roman's orders. Even if it meant breaking man's law, or God's.'

'Surely you and your sons give Roman enough reason to go on living?' Koshka questioned gently.

'Roman is a proud man, a physical man. If he was permanently crippled he'd see his life as a burden to himself and those around him. He'd believe the boys and I would be better off without him. Manfred let slip that Roman has sent for a cousin he trusts, a wealthy banker. I think Roman wants to make sure his business affairs are in order and that I have someone to turn to . . . after . . . '
Sonya clenched his fists until she regained control. Koshka watched helplessly, wishing she knew her daughter better so she could comfort her.

'Do you know this cousin's name?'

'Erik Romanov but he's not connected in any way to the royal family. At least not for a few centuries. His mother was German.'

Koshka nodded.

'You know him?' Sonya asked.

'I've met him,' Koshka answered guardedly. 'Like Roman he is a man of integrity with a reputation for fairness and honesty. You said the bullet in Roman's back could move without warning. Don't you think that Roman could have sent for Erik simply as a precaution, to ensure that his finances are cared for and his wishes respected if the worst does happen?'

'I would like to believe that.'

'You think Roman sent for him for a more sinister reason?'

'Glyn and Richard have made Roman a wheelchair. Although Roman has said how useful he finds it I know from the way reacts whenever he's lifted into it that he believes it robs him of dignity. I know – just know – that it makes him feel like a helpless child. When he returns home tomorrow I will try to spend every moment I can with him, but . . . '

'It will be impossible for you to watch him every second of the day and night, Sonya. You'll exhaust yourself if you try.'

'When I'm not with him Franz and Manfred will be and-'

'I've heard that Nathan Kharber has contacted a surgeon who might be able to help Roman.'

Sonya was amazed how well informed Koshka was, but she didn't pry as to who had told her the news. 'We'll travel to St Petersburg so Roman can consult with him as soon as Nathan and Noah believe he is strong enough to withstand the journey.'

'Than surely Roman will wait . . . '

Sonya bit her lip. 'I don't quite know how to put my feelings into words. There isn't one definite thing I can point to and say, that is why I'm worried. But whenever I try to discuss the future or his injuries with Roman he changes the subject.'

'Could that be because there's no privacy in hospital?' Koshka suggested.

'It could be but I don't think so.'

Koshka suddenly realised why Sonya was having so much difficulty in translating her fears into words. She wondered if she'd even admitted the root of her concern to herself. 'This is a somewhat indelicate question but do you and Roman enjoy a close physical relationship?'

'Yes.'

'Are you afraid that Roman won't be able to make love to you?'

Sonya swallowed hard. 'Afraid – yes – but for Roman, not for myself.'

'Isn't there more to your relationship than the physical?'

'Of course, a great deal more but . . . ' Sonya hesitated.

'Catherine did a fine job of bringing you up, Sonya. She imbued you with the natural modesty of a wealthy woman of your class, but I hope it didn't prevent you from enjoying married life.'

'It didn't.'

Koshka left the sofa and went to her desk. She opened a drawer and removed a copy of a leather-bound book. Sonya recognised it.

'That book . . . '

'Roman gave you a copy.'

'He did. You gave it to him?'

'Not exactly. I recall, he took it because he said his father had one and he found it invaluable.' Koshka opened it and flicked through the index. 'Pages 80 – 95 should tell you all you need to know about the positions you can use to make love, especially for those who are incapacitated in some way.'

'When I asked Sarah whether or not Roman would be physically able to make love, she said there was no way of knowing until he tried. Some men with similar injuries as his can, some can't . . . '

'Trust me.' Koshka smiled. 'Roman will.'

'You seem very sure of it.'

Koshka suddenly realised how her comment could be misinterpreted. 'My relationship with Roman was one any woman would be delighted to have with the son of a close - very close - old friend. I knew Roman's father well enough for him to choose me to nurse him through his final illness. He suffered a great deal and there were days when he prayed for the end to come swiftly.'

'He talked of killing himself?'

'He admitted to me that he spoke of it to a priest. The priest dissuaded him by reminding him of the burden he would leave behind for his loved ones, so he continued to suffer until God chose a time to call him from this earth.'

'Would you talk to Roman for me, please and tell him exactly what you have just told me . . . '

'Roman has many friends, all closer to him than I am.'

'Friends he wouldn't admit a failing to. Please call on us . . . '

'That is out of the question. Brothel Madams do not call on respectable married women and their husbands.'

'Not even to make the acquaintance of their grandsons?'

'Not even that, no matter how much they yearn to do so.'

She gripped Sonya's hand. 'But there may come a time, not here, but elsewhere when we are all on holiday perhaps . . . but to return to your problem, I will see Roman, if you think my talking to him will accomplish anything.'

'I do.'

'You'll leave the place and the time to me.'

Sonya nodded agreement.

'In the meantime, I trust you to give him reason enough to keep living. That is Fritz's step on the stair. The hour is up and soon I will be greeting tonight's visitors. Please, for all our sakes, don't come here again, Sonya. Send a note with a servant giving me a time and the number of a room in the hotel. I'll meet you there.'

CHAPTER FIFTEEN

Richard Parry's House Hughesovka, April 1889

Anna looked across the hearth to the sofa where Richard and Sarah were sitting side by side.

'Catherine invited me to travel to Petersburg with her and Kira.'

'You said you didn't want to go to St Petersburg with us when we asked you,' Richard reproached. 'You said you couldn't leave the hospital . . . '

'Now that the new staff are here . . . '

'They're working out really well,' Sarah broke in after lifting a warning eyebrow in Richard's direction. One of the few things they differed on was his refusal to accept that his younger sister was a grown woman, and more than capable of making her own decisions. He still expected her to look to him for advice, despite the fact that she ran the hospital with as much precision as he did his collieries.

'Mr Hughes pays well and money attracts the best. I think it helped to have Nathan Kharber overseeing the appointments,' Anna smiled at Sarah, grateful to her for interrupting Richard.

'Have you accepted Catherine's invitation?' Richard steered the conversation back on course.

'I have.' Feeling the need to explain, she added, 'Catherine said she's beginning to feel her age . . . '

'Aren't we all,' Richard interposed.

'Apparently even an old man of thirty-six,' Sarah teased, 'more even than his slip of a youthful wife at forty-seven.'

'After arguing with colliers who see no point in what they call "excessive shoring of pit shafts" all day I feel like a tired old man. If they had their way they'd be buried alive in slag and coal dust.

'And then when I come home, Ted demands I teach him how to wrestle like the Cossack boys, which I might enjoy more if my son understood the term "play" when it comes to wrestling.'

'And, you think that gives you the right to feel older than Catherine?' Sarah asked. 'I've never asked her, but given that her grandson is thirty-eight she must be what, in her seventies?'

'She told me she's over eighty,' Anna revealed.

'She certainly doesn't look it,' Richard reached in his pocket for his pipe. 'I've never given Catherine's age a thought in all the years we've known her. She always looks so elegant and she's so interested in what's going on around her, unlike most of the old people I recall from Merthyr who seemed to give up on life and the world long before they reached sixty.'

'Probably because the Crawshays had worked them to the point where they were no longer capable of feeling anything,' Anna commented. 'Catherine says she has the will to live forever but she concedes that God might have other ideas. She's worried about Kira being left alone if she's taken ill, especially now. With Ruth gone . . . ' she hesitated as tears blurred her eyes as they did every time she spoke of Ruth's death. She swallowed hard and blinked them away. ' . . . all of Alexei's time and attention will be focused on his daughters. He'll have no time to think of Kira.'

'Surely Catherine knows that we'll all take care of Kira if she can't.'

'I'm sure she does, Richard, but she wants to make a more formal arrangement, which is why she asked me to take over joint guardianship of Kira with Mr Dmitri,' Anna said.

'Why is she so concerned about Kira now, just before travelling to St Petersburg? Surely, she wouldn't contemplate travelling if she was unwell,' Richard frowned.

'She knows older people are more susceptible to illness and Kira has had so many invitations to balls, Catherine wants to make sure she has a chaperon and someone to turn to for advice if she is too tired to accompany her.'

'You're an unmarried woman,' Richard said. 'I thought they couldn't be chaperons.'

'I'm an elderly spinster.'

'Hardly elderly,' Sarah demurred. 'But I can understand why Catherine wants you with her. Kira was close to Ruth and she's grown close to you since you moved in with Catherine. She knows both of you are missing Ruth . . . ' she turned Richard. 'With everything that's happened I'd forgotten that Alexei's girls and Maryanna were going to be presented at court. Catherine arranged it but do you think that Alexei and Catherine will want to go ahead now?'

'I think Catherine assumes that the plans stand.' Anna sipped the glass of wine Richard had poured for her. 'I saw you visiting Alexei this afternoon Richard. Do you think he'll want to go to St Petersburg with us? It was all arranged before Ruth . . . '

'I don't know. I honestly don't,' Richard reiterated. 'When I saw Alexei today I had the feeling that he's deliberately shut himself off from the world. Praskovia was leaving as I arrived. She's doing what she can as are Lev and Lada but . . . '

'He needs time,' Anna said. 'I'll go and see him on the way back to Ignatova, and if he has any ideas of not going to St Petersburg I'll try to talk him out of them.'

'What if he refuses to listen to you?'

'I'll remind him that Kitty and Olga wanted to be presented to the Tsar and Catherine's friends at court won't be pleased if she asks them to postpone the girls' introduction.'

'In your best matronly voice,' Richard said. 'And what about the baby?'

'What about the baby?'

———

180

'Will you suggest he takes her to St Petersburg as well?'

'Babies are not made of porcelain, Richard. They can travel.'

'He still has to find a nurse for her.'

'He hasn't found a nurse because he can't bear the thought of handing her over to anyone else's care. Ruth is the sole reason he leaves his bed every morning.'

'You think so?' Sarah asked.

'I know so. Kitty and Olga only pretend they need him and he knows it. I think we should all travel together. I'll remind him that you, Praskovia, me and Sonya if Roman is up to travelling with us, will all help him to care for Ruth.'

'You'll travel in Catherine's railway coach?'

'Yes.'

'So, you can keep an eye on Catherine as well as Kira?' Sarah enquired astutely.

'You're talking as if Catherine really is in failing health,' Richard reproached Sarah.

'The one thing nursing has taught me is that older people seem to possess some sort of premonition when it comes to failing health. But there isn't anything wrong with Catherine is there?' Sarah asked Anna.

'Nothing that makes me think a journey to St Petersburg will have a detrimental effect on her health.' Anna hated lying but she had given Catherine her word that she wouldn't tell anyone about her condition.

'What about Alexei?' Richard asked. 'Has Catherine talked to him about Kira?'

'Not since Ruth died. Catherine was hoping that Alexei would act as guardian to his sister. She asked him and Ruth to formalise the arrangement, but now she thinks Alexei will have enough to contend with just surviving and caring for his girls.'

'She's right. Frankly Alexei's a mess. I wasn't going to say anything but now we're talking about him, you may as well know. When I called on him today he looked as though he hadn't shaved or changed his clothes in days. I tried but . . . ' Richard ran his hands through his hair, something he was prone to do when confronted by a situation he couldn't control.

'Ruth used to complain that if Alexei didn't want to do something, nothing on this earth would persuade him.' Anna understood grief and the debilitating toll it exacted from the living. There had been days – weeks – after her mother, sisters' and brother's deaths when she'd wanted to crawl under the bedclothes and remain there until death came to take her too. But much as she sympathised with and understood Alexei's feelings of wanting to divorce himself from the world and all feeling, she wanted the old teasing Alexei who loved and enjoyed life back for his daughters' sake. Catherine, Lev, and Lada and all of Alexei's friends were keeping an eye on them, but she knew the girls were missing their father's presence in their daily life as much as they were mourning the loss of their mother . . . suddenly aware that Sarah was talking to her, she said, 'sorry I was miles away.'

'I wondered if you've already arranged to take time off from the hospital?'

'Three months.'

'Three months! Richard exclaimed. 'The place will fall down without you.'

'No, it won't, no one is indispensable.'

'I never thought to hear you say that.' Richard said. 'I thought you liked being matron.'

'I do, for the moment. But who knows what the next few years will bring?'

'Business growth beyond my wildest dreams for Beletsky and Parry I hope,' Richard said. 'Mr Hughes intended to extend the New Russia Company's offices in St Petersburg even before the Grand Duke's visit.

'Alexei and agreed to move Beletsky and Parry's export office into the same building, the rent will be higher but we are well in profit and can easily afford it. In fact, our business is so cash rich Alexei and I agreed to look around for investment opportunities in St Petersburg when we move there. But then that of course was before Ruth . . . '

'Move there? You never said anything about leaving Hughesovka to me,' Sarah turned to him in surprise.

'When Alexei and I discussed it, a few months ago the future felt very distant but we agreed it was worth considering.'

'And now it doesn't?' Sarah gripped his hand.

'We can't escape the fact that Hughesovka has become a dangerous place. Glyn and I discussed the future after the shooting. We Welsh – and that includes you my love,' he smiled at Sarah, 'because after marrying two Welsh men you are Welsh whether you consider yourself as such or not, came here because of Mr Hughes. Don't misunderstand me, I'm grateful to Mr Hughes for the opportunities he gave me, but I am and always will be a Welshman, and for that reason I've never thought of Hughesovka as a permanent home. Now after what's happened perhaps we should talk about our next move.'

'You intend to go home?' Anna said unthinkingly.

'There, you've just said it, Anna.' Richard pointed out. 'Home! Maybe not Merthyr but no matter how hard we've worked to make our lives here, Wales will always be home to us.'

'Treforest and Pontypridd,' Anna smiled. 'When Daddy was alive. I remember those Sunday walks along the bank of the Taff and up the Rhondda Valley. The trees and the streams where we used to paddle, jumping up and down the steps of the stone bridge that spanned the river . . . the hills all around, below an endless blue sky in summer,' Anna continued lost in a time and a place Sarah knew nothing of.

183

'Or what you could see of a blue sky beneath the smoke from the ironworks chimneys. Pontypridd wasn't any cleaner than Merthyr, Anna, and you know how much you hated the dirt in that town. And now for all that Hughesovka was clean when we arrived . . . '

'Only because the blast furnaces hadn't been built,' Sarah reminded him.

'I was going to add, it's not clean now. But you haven't said how you feel about Catherine's request that you care for Kira, Anna. It may turn out to be a considerable responsibility.'

'Not after she marries Morgan.'

'Have either of them said anything to you about setting a date?' Sarah fished.

'No.' Anna shook her head.

'I know Mr Hughes has offered Morgan a job in a metallurgical laboratory in his works in Greenwich,' Richard revealed.

'Has Morgan taken it?' Anna questioned.

'Not yet, but he hasn't said no either. I think he wants to talk it over with Kira.'

'Catherine will miss Kira if she moves to London,' Anna mused.

Richard shared the last of the wine in the bottle between their glasses. 'She'll be even more reliant on you for company then, Anna.'

'I think Catherine will be relieved to see Kira married. She told me she approves of Morgan, and with Count Beletsky dead there is no one to challenge her guardianship of Kira except Alexei and his younger brothers, and from what Catherine has said none of them are likely to challenge any decision she's made on Kira's behalf. Catherine asked me to go to Mr Dmitri's office tomorrow to sign the papers that would make me Kira's joint guardian if she was unable to care for her.'

'And how do you feel about that? It's a lot of responsibility to agree to safeguard a young woman's property.'

184

'Thankfully the safeguarding of Kira's finances will be down to Mr Dmitri and his firm. I know and like Kira, and it's not as though she's headstrong. I'm flattered that Catherine believes me up to the task. To be honest I'd welcome the responsibility. It's not as though I ever intend to marry or have any children of my own. And it won't mean that I'll see any the less of you or Ted and Maryanna, unless of course you move to Wales.'

Sarah and Richard glanced at Anna. It was an intensely intimate look that said more than hours of conversation.

'You may even see more of me before then,' Anna added. 'Catherine has made me promise that I'll cut down to five shifts in the hospital a week.'

'If Catherine can hold you to that promise then she's a stronger influence on you than either Richard or I,' Sarah said.

Alexei's House Hughesovka April 1889

'Are you sure I'm not interrupting?' Anna apologised to Lada as she showed her into the living room of Alexei's house.

'You're not interrupting me, Matron Parry, although I have to return to my baking. As for the master now: that's a different matter.' She placed her hands on her hips and glared at Alexei who was working on the accounts with baby Ruth over his shoulder. He could do with interrupting. That's the third lot of balance sheets he'd started on without finishing one in the last hour. I told him no one - man or woman can think, let alone work with a colicky baby in their arms but he won't listen.'

Alexei narrowed his eyes and glared at Lada.

'If you can tear yourself away from your mixing bowl for five minutes you can bring us, cherry juice please, Lada.'

'And some of the savoury lamb cheburekis I've made for supper?'

'Anna will be hungry after her shift.'

185

'I'm fine, thank you, Lada.' Anna lifted Ruth from Alexei's shoulder without asking his permission.

Alexei tossed his pen down on to his blotter and watched the baby curl up in Anna's arms.

'She prefers you to me.'

'She prefers to be held by someone who is giving her undivided attention.'

'How does she know who's holding her when she's looking over a shoulder. One must seem very like another.'

'They probably are, but the owners' of the shoulders must smell very differently and babies can always tell when someone is upset.'

'They can?'

She took Ruth and sat on the sofa opposite him. 'Look at yourself Alexei. You're perspiring which isn't unusual when you consider the temperature in this room. You're frowning as though you have a thumping headache . . . '

'I do.'

'And you look as though you haven't slept for nights, eaten properly for days or bathed in a month.' Anna pretended that she hadn't seen Olga and Kitty peeping through the carved bannisters of the stairs.

Alexei leaned back in his chair. 'You're right.

'I came here to talk to you.'

'To talk to me or lecture me?'

'To talk to you but I can see it's useless. Go to the bath house. I'll ask Lada to prepare a meal for you when you return. Eat it and go to bed. I'll come back tomorrow. Go.'

He stared at her for a moment. 'What about the girls?'

'I'll take all three of them to my brother's house for the evening. Kitty and Olga can spend it with Maryanna and Ted.'

'And Ruth?'

'I'll spend the evening getting to know my Goddaughter. I'll bring all three back before their bedtime and tomorrow morning, I'll return and talk to you.'

'About what?'

'We'll start with your family.'

CHAPTER SIXTEEN

Nadolny's House Hughesovka April 1889

Roman reached for the bar Manfred had screwed above his day bed, and hauled himself upright. 'So, in your medical opinion I should withstand the journey to St Petersburg without suffering any ill effects.'

'That is not what I said, Roman,' Nathan broke in impatiently. 'What I said was, now that we've had a reply from Herr Franz and he's declined to operate because he considers surgical intervention too dangerous, there may be a surgeon in St Petersburg you can consult with. But my professional opinion has not altered. All it would take for that bullet to move is a jolt. The wheel of your chair hitting a stone or a kerb, a sneeze, a cough would be enough . . . '

'I understand,' Roman broke in.

'I don't think you do.'

'Oh, I do,' Roman contradicted. 'I understand that you would like to incarcerate me in this room and on this day bed to ensure that the bullet in back does no further damage.'

'It would be one way of ensuring that your condition remains stable, yes.'

Noah de Vries stifled a smile. Although Nathan had his back turned to the doctor he sensed it and turned just in time to see Noah clamp a handkerchief over his mouth to stifle a theatrical cough.

'Well, I'll test it this evening.'

'You will?'

'I'm going to the hotel for dinner with Glyn and Richard and if they can persuade him to join us, Alexei.'

'I see.'

'As for St Petersburg, Manfred?'

'Sir,' his valet stepped forward.

'Make arrangements for us to travel and alert the butler in my town house. Tell him to prepare for our imminent arrival.'

Manfred smiled, 'I'll see to it right away, Your Excellency.'

Alexei's House Hughesovka April 1889

Lada opened the door to Catherine and curtseyed.

'Is my grandson at home, Lada?' Catherine asked.

'Yes, madam.' Lada took Catherine's shawl and hung it on a hook behind the door. Catherine went into the living room. Alexei was sitting at his desk in the window alcove of the living room. He was staring blankly into space holding a pen, but she noticed the tip was dry and the sheet of paper in front of him blank.

She spoke his name twice before he turned to her. He dropped the pen and rose to his feet. 'I'm sorry, grandmother, I was miles away.'

'So, I see. I came to discuss arrangements for our St Petersburg visit.' She continued to stand in front of him. 'It might be nice to receive an offer of a seat.'

'I'm so sorry, Grandmother, please sit down.' He indicated the most comfortable chair in the room. 'Lada, bring tea please.'

'I'd prefer a glass of wine.'

'Wine please, Lada . . . '

'I heard you, master, the house isn't so big that you have to shout. I know what is due to Madame Ignatova. I will bring refreshments directly I've made up a tray.'

Alexei lifted a small table near the chair he'd indicated.

Catherine sat down. 'When was the last time you bathed and shaved, Alexei?'

'I bathed yesterday.' He narrowed his eyes. 'After Anna visited me, but then she would have told you she called on me.'

'She did. So, I take it, the beard is intentional. You've decided to grow one?'

'No. I've been busy.' He indicated his desk. 'I may stay at home to be with Ruth but I work on the colliery accounts . . . '

'So, I see,' Catherine broke in. 'I spoke to Richard. He said there's no problem with both of you travelling to St Petersburg as you've arranged for your managers to take over your duties in Hughesovka.'

'If arrangements have been made, Richard has made them.'

'He assured me that they have. So, the only question left, is will you travel to St Petersburg with Richard in his railway carriage, or join Anna, Kira and I in mine, or make arrangements to take your own.'

'I was going to write to you . . . '

'Why write when I live on the outskirts of town and come into town at least twice a week.'

'I didn't want to disturb you.'

'You mean you didn't want to face me.'

He lifted his head and forced himself to look into her blue eyes, so like his and so different from those of his daughters.

'That too,' he admitted.

'If you think for one minute that I will take your daughters to St Petersburg and leave you alone in Hughesovka . . . '

'I won't be alone, I'll have Lev and Lada.'

'Servants who are paid to carry out your orders. No, Alexei, I will not leave you here with Lev and Lada. Nor will I take your daughters to St Petersburg . . . '

'The girls need to go. It will give them something other than their mothers' death to think about.'

'I am an old woman . . . '

'Kira and Anna will be with you and Richard, Sarah, Glyn and Praskovia will be travelling there at the same time and staying in the city . . . '

'You expect a woman of my age to accept responsibility for *your* daughters.'

'Not all my daughters. Ruth will stay with me.'

'So, you trust me to take Kitty and Olga to St Petersburg to introduce them at court to escort them to balls and oversee their entrance into polite society, which as you well know is packed with unscrupulous, immoral charlatans and scoundrels on the lookout for rich heiresses . . . ' Catherine reached for the fan in her reticule and waved it vigorously in front of her face.

'The twins are children. They're barely sixteen years old . . . '

'I was married at fifteen,' she reminded him caustically.

'Times were different then. I would never allow them to marry at that age or make a match for them. I want them to marry for love . . . '

'As you and Ruth did,' she said daring to mention his wife. 'Your attitude towards marriage is very modern and commendable, Alexei. But surely you realise that your daughters are every bit as headstrong as you and Ruth were at their age. It's well known that you and I are rich. If either of them should fall in love with a charming, personable man who can lie convincingly enough to make them believe that he loves them not their money, they could elope . . . '

'Are you saying you wouldn't stop them from running off with a man who would marry them for their money?'

'If the girls didn't confide in me, and they made secret plans to elope how would I know?' she demanded. 'I haven't forgotten how secretive you were when you were when you were young, Alexei. You kept your courtship of Ruth from your parents and everyone in your family until the year you married her.'

'I wasn't sixteen when I married her . . . '

'You were fifteen when you started courting her. Alexei. I'm your grandmother, an old woman . . . '

'Not that old.'

'I feel old,' she said quietly.

'At my age a good book, glass of wine and warm hearth is everything and as such I categorically refuse to take on your responsibilities as well as my own. Either you come to St Petersburg with your girls or all of us remain here.'

'You're serious, aren't you? You really would postpone their presentation at court.'

'Not postpone - cancel. And yes, I am serious, Alexei. If that is what it will take for you to start taking responsibility for your own daughters then I will do it.'

Alexei pulled one of the dining chairs out from the table, and sat down. Without even thinking what he was doing, he leaned forward and sunk his head in his hands.

'If you don't know how to begin living again, start by looking at Kitty and Olga, Alexei,' she suggested, 'they are as lost and in as much pain as you.'

'And Ruth?' When he took his hands from his face his cheeks were wet with tears. Catherine saw them but didn't comment. From the expression in his eyes she knew he was unaware he'd been crying.

'Ruth is a baby who needs warmth, love and care. Have you considered Anna's suggestion about employing a nursemaid for her? Or are you still debating whether or not to take Vasya up on her offer of adopting her and the twins.'

'I was incapable of thinking about anything other than losing Ruth when I listened to Vasya, so there is no debate – not anymore and I haven't had time to consider employing a nursemaid for the baby. Not yet.'

'If you are determined to stay in Hughesovka you won't need one, but if you decide to accompany us to St Petersburg you most definitely will. It's some years since I moved in court circles, but I recall it being incredibly time consuming. Entire mornings, afternoons and evenings disappeared, waiting for members of the Tsar's family or various dignitaries to appear.'

Alexei fell silent and Lada who'd been hovering outside the door that led to the kitchen, took the opportunity to carry in a tray of glasses a bottle of wine and cakes.

'Thank you, Lada.' Catherine took a glass.

'Yes, thank you, Lada,' Alexei remarked absently.

Lada bowed and scuttled back to her domain.

'Where are my great granddaughters?' Catherine asked.

'The girls are next door in Glyn's house, being tutored in French and German by the professor Glyn has engaged for Pavlo and Tom.'

'And Ruth?'

'Is in her basket outside the kitchen door. Lada insists she needs fresh air . . . '

'Which she does,' Catherine concurred.

'She's close enough for me to hear her should she cry.'

Catherine left her chair and went out into the garden through the back door. Ruth's basket was in the shade of an apple tree. She looked down and smiled at the sleeping child.'

'She is all right, isn't she?' Alexei began anxiously.

'Perfect. I thought Kitty and Olga were mirror images of Ruth but this one is even more so, Alexei. I'm glad to see that you've finally relaxed enough to allow her out of your sight if not your hearing.'

'Anna convinced me that we both needed a little time apart.'

'Anna is right.' She gripped Alexei's arm. Her fingers closed around his wrist, surprisingly strong. 'You will give St Petersburg some thought?'

'I will.'

'Should you decide to remain in Hughesovka for the summer you can tell the girls they'll have to wait another season or two before they can be presented at court, and they'll have to do their waiting at home with you.'

'You're serious, aren't you?'

193

'I am, Alexei.' She softened her answer with a small smile. 'I love you too much to watch you give up on life at your age.'

Nadolny's House Hughesovka, May 1889

Roman raised his arms and lifted Sonya up and away from him. She curled alongside him in the bed, wrapping the full length of her naked body alongside his. He slid his arm around her shoulders. She rested her head on his chest before looking up and eyeing him.

He saw her watching him and smiled. 'You have the longest eye-lashes.'

'Thank you.'

'It's me who should be thanking you.'

'I'm your wife, you don't have to thank me.'

'Yes, I do, as you're the one who has to make allowances for me.'

'You made many for me when I was pregnant with the boys.'

He moved his arm, and closed his hand over her breast tenderly thumbing her nipple. 'Nathan called in when you were out this morning.'

'And you spoke to him again about travelling to St Petersburg. Do you intend going there soon?'

'You saw him?'

'I didn't need to.' She combed through the white blond hair on his chest with her fingertips. 'I can see how frustrated you are. You would give anything to be the way you were before you were shot.' She longed to say "and you will be again" but she knew exactly how hollow those words would sound. Besides, she heard the tremor in her voice and hated herself for allowing him to see her fear.

'Almost anything,' he qualified. 'I wouldn't sacrifice anything that would harm you and the boys.'

'But you'd risk your own life?'

'It's mine to risk.'

She sat up in the bed, leaning forward so he couldn't see the expression on her face. 'No, it isn't Roman. Your life is not your own to do with as you wish. It belongs as much to me and Andrei and Spartak as it does to you. I had hoped that would give you reason enough not to take any unnecessary risks. If the bullet should become dislodged . . . '

'You saw Nathan after he left here?'

'No. But I was there when Nathan spoke to you in the hospital. He warned that the bullet could move any time and the journey from here to St Petersburg will be a long one. We'll have to drive to the station in the carriage . . . '

He closed his hands over her shoulders and pulled her back down on to his chest. 'I promise you, I will not take any unnecessary risks, but, my darling, don't you see, I don't want to remain a cripple for the rest of my life if there's any chance of my being able to walk again.'

'But you won't be dissuaded from going to St Petersburg?'

'I need to seek out and consult with the best doctors and they are not to be found in Hughesovka.'

'And if the doctors advise you that an operation would be dangerous?'

His eyes narrowed to emerald slits. 'I refuse to pre-empt the advice they chose to give me.' He looked at the French Ormolu clock on the mantelpiece. 'The boys will be back from Glyn's in two hours.'

'And wanting to eat tea with you.'

'I've asked Manfred and Fritz to help me bathe and dress for the evening as Glyn and Richard are so determined to take me out. He leaned back on his pillows and locked his arms behind his head. 'We have at least three quarters of an hour now in which I intend to watch you bathe and dress.'

She reached for her robe. 'Hardly entertainment.'

'It will be for me.' He grabbed her hand after she slipped her robe around her shoulders. He lifted it to his lips and kissed the tips of her fingers.

'You will be careful tonight won't, won't you?'

'I doubt Glyn and Richard will allow me to be anything but.' He frowned at her. 'Why this sudden concern?'

'It's not sudden. It's just that . . . I . . . we . . . almost lost you.'

'You didn't. I'm here.' He smiled.

'Don't you dare laugh at me.'

'I'm not. That was a happy smile because we're together here and now. Nothing more.'

'I love you so much,' she said seriously.

'And I love you and the boys and I always will, wherever I am. Deeply and truly. I want nothing more than to live a long and happy life with you and them, Sonya, but when I was in hospital we talked about how fragile life is, and how some things spiral beyond our control.'

'I haven't forgotten those talks.'

'This isn't just about me and the bullet in my spine, it's something more, isn't it?'

'It's Ruth . . . '

'I know how much you loved her and how much you love Alexei . . . '

'I was talking about Ruth's baby, Roman. We'll all tell her about her mother but it won't be the same because she'll grow up never knowing how beautiful and kind her mother was and . . . '

'And?' He looked at her quizzically.

'I don't want that to happen to our child. The child I'm carrying,' she whispered so there was no chance of him misunderstanding her.

'You're pregnant?'

'I am, and I know you believe me to be strong but I'm not strong enough to bring another of your children into the world, Roman. Not alone. So please don't make me.'

CHAPTER SEVENTEEN

Hotel Hughesovka May 1889

Roman arrived at the hotel in his own carriage, which the shtetl carpenter had adapted to take his wheelchair by the simple expedient of removing half of one of bench seats and installing bolts and chains in the floor to secure the wheels and frame.

Franz and Manfred unfastened the chair with Roman in it and wheeled it down the wooden ramp that was kept clipped to the side of the carriage.

Glyn and Richard stepped out of the hotel to meet them.

'Manfred, Franz, you can go where you will until . . . ' Roman looked expectantly at Glyn.

'Eleven,' Glyn suggested.

'Eleven o'clock,' Roman repeated to Manfred and if you and the driver want to dine here instead of at home, put it on my bill.'

'We had something else in mind, sir,' Manfred said.

'Whatever and wherever the something else is, add it to your expense account.'

'We intended to, sir.' Manfred tipped his hat to Glyn and Richard before helping Franz return the ramp to the straps that secured it to the side of the carriage.

Knowing better than to offer to assist Roman, Richard watched him wheel himself to the foot of the hotel steps. When Roman reached there, he and Glyn stepped forward, tilted the chair back, manoeuvred it up the short flight of steps and set it down in the foyer.

'We've rented a private dining room, second door on the left,' Glyn directed as Roman propelled his chair forward.

'For the three of us?' Roman raised an eyebrow.

'Mr Hughes. Alexei and my brother Edward are joining us. We'll be with you in half an hour. Someone is waiting to talk to you. We thought we'd give you time and privacy to share a conversation.'

Glyn opened the door, Richard moved behind Roman's chair and turned it so Roman could negotiate the doorway.

A dining table set with porcelain and gleaming silverware dominated the centre of the room. Koshka was sitting on a chair that flanked the hearth. A bottle of champagne in an ice bucket and two glasses were laid out on a side table next to her.

'Good evening, Koshka.' Roman propelled his chair to the other side of the hearth, noting that a chair that matched Koshka's had been relegated to a corner, to make way for his wheelchair. 'You are very thoughtful.'

'Not that thoughtful. I've been waiting for you to arrive to open the bottle.'

'I was referring to the space for my wheelchair.' He removed the foil and exerted pressure with his thumb on the side of the cork, easing it slowly from the bottle. 'You could have called the house waiter.'

'And alerted the staff to my presence here? A brothel madam meeting the head of one of the leading aristocratic families in Russia in a hotel? The gossip would rebound around Hughesovka for years.'

'Possibly but neither I nor Sonya would care, and you have yet to meet our sons.'

'And how would you explain me to them? This is Madam Koshka, do go and consult with her when you're old enough to seek out casual female company.'

'No. We'd say, Andrei, Spartak, this is your kind, thoughtful beautiful grandmother.' The cork spurted from the bottle with a soft "pop". Roman filled the glasses, handed one to Koshka and holding his glass in one hand propelled his chair backwards with the other until he faced her across the hearth.

'I will meet them one day.'

'Soon I hope.'

'Perhaps, but not here, in Hughesovka. On neutral territory, where no one knows me.'

'And where would that be?' He enquired. 'I've heard people talk about you in every town in Russia as well as Rome, Paris, London and Berlin. Like it or not you are famous, Koshka.'

'One of your secluded houses out of sight of casual observers might suffice. You inherited your father's palace in Yalta, or so I've heard.'

'I did. It would be my pleasure to welcome you there.'

'As I recall it was close to the Lividia. Do you go there often?'

'I occasionally visit the Tsar in the small palace. The large palace hasn't been used since his father was assassinated eight years ago. They are both set in delightful gardens but the real architectural beauty is the church. Small but exquisite. Have you never been there?'

'I have but not for twenty – no probably nearer thirty years. And then only for an evening party.' She smiled. 'I have fond memories of the time I spent in Yalta at your father's house.'

'I have made some improvements.'

'I have no doubt.'

'They were needed but you're not here to talk about my father's house or Yalta.'

'No.' She sipped her champagne before setting it aside. 'I came to enquire how you are.' She looked directly at him. 'Truthfully,' she added.

He felt as though she was daring him to lie to her. He pulled out the small table Richard had built into his chair and set his champagne glass on it. 'I am as you see, unable to walk at present.'

'You're hoping it will prove to a temporary condition?'

'You know me, Koshka,' he forced a smile, 'ever the optimist.'

'I remember you well enough from when you were a young man to know that you put on a brave front whenever you suffer a setback, and this setback must be devastating to an active man like yourself.'

'I will be travelling to St Petersburg soon. There are surgeons there I wish to consult with. If they fail to suggest a treatment that may improve my condition, there are always the medicinal practitioners in Berlin and Vienna.'

'Nathan Kharber approves of this search?'

'As Nathan Kharber cannot help me, he suggested I look for a second opinion, as did the new doctor in the hospital.'

'I hope you find a surgeon who can help you.'

'I hope I find one who'll be willing to try to remove the bullet now residing in my spine.'

'Nathan and the doctors in the hospital have refused to make a second attempt to remove the bullet?'

'They have.' He chose not to elaborate.

'You appear to have adapted well, or is it a case of needs must . . . '

'"When the devil drives",' he smiled, 'one of my father's favourite expressions. Like him when he faced his last illness I have no choice but to accept the cards fate has dealt.' He shrugged. 'You said you wanted to see how I was. How do you think I am?'

'Treating your misfortune exactly as your father would have done. With jokes, a brave face and courage.'

'You can see beyond the brave face?'

'Enough to ask you not to try to shut your wife or children out of your suffering. They have a right to support you.'

'What makes you think that I have shut them out?' he asked suspiciously.

She left her chair and refilled both their champagne glasses. 'I have no evidence whatsoever other than my knowledge of what your father was like during his last illness. I wanted to remind you.'

200

'Of what?'

'A broken devastated boy who spent a summer quarrelling with his father unaware that his father's short temper was down to the debilitating effects of a terminal illness. A secret his father point blank refused to share with the boy, although everyone who knew he was dying begged him to. I will never forget the guilt on your face when you returned to Russia for his funeral.'

'There is one thing wrong with that comparison between me and my father, Koshka.'

'What is that?'

'I am not dying.'

'You think there is no risk of you dying should you opt to go under the surgeon's knife?'

'That is a risk I will need to discuss with a surgeon – if I find one.'

'Have you talked about possible treatments with Sonya and the boys?'

'I will when the time comes.' He sipped the champagne she'd poured for him.

'You won't treat them the way your father treated you?'

'Not now you've reminded me of it.'

'He didn't talk to you because he believed, really believed that he was sparing you pain. I couldn't make him see that he was only delaying it.'

'And making it ten times worse by keeping his condition from me.' Roman picked up his glass again and studied it as though it was an Object D'arte. 'But then isn't that the aristocratic way? Always behave correctly, especially to social inferiors and younger family members and never – never allow them to see your failings. Etiquette before emotions. Never show anyone how you feel. The English had a term for it when I was in school there. They called it "The stiff upper lip." If you paralyze it, there will never be the slightest tremor, it will never wobble and in theory you'll never blub.'

Koshka opened her watch. 'Our half hour is almost up.'

'So, tell me, Mother-in-law,' Roman murmured conversationally, 'when did you see Sonya?'

'I . . . '

'God will see you if you lie.' His smile broadened. 'And before you ask. Yes, it is that obvious.'

Koshka hesitated but only for a moment. 'A few nights before you left hospital. She was terrified that you were pushing her away to prepare her for your death. It didn't help that she'd heard your father begged the doctors to kill him.'

'Who told her that?'

'Rumour. You know what courtiers are and several came to visit your father that last summer.'

'Yes, they did. Including Beletsky, damn him.'

Koshka crossed herself at the mention of Beletsky's name.

'If there is justice after death I doubt he's in heaven,' Roman said drily.

'I am a poor Christian but I try not to speak ill of the dead.' Koshka's eyes shone mischievously. 'Even if they deserved harsh words.' She rose from her chair and picked up her shawl, veil and reticule from one of the dining chairs. 'I've been meaning to thank you, Roman.'

'What for?'

'Making my daughter so happy. Don't ruin the life you share by taking unnecessary risks, what you and Sonya share is very rare and precious.'

'Sonya has given me a very good reason to be cautious in a search for a remedy for my condition.'

'What is that?'

'We are expecting another child. I haven't told Sonya, but I'm rather hoping for a daughter. And if I should be fortunate enough to have one, I'll ask Sonya if we can name her Elizabeth Catherine.'

Koshka turned her back to him as she draped her shawl around her shoulders and reached for her veil. 'Wish her well from me.'

He thought he heard a tremor in her voice, but the oil lamp was smoking. It was slight but enough to catch at the back of his throat as well as hers.

'I will.'

She kissed his cheek, draped the veil over her head and left the room. He blessed Glyn and Richard's tact for giving him a few minutes grace. He had time enough to reach for a cigar and light it.

Hotel Hughesovka May 1889

'I had a letter from St Petersburg this morning. The lease for the new headquarters is ready for signing so I'll be leaving early next week.'

'And the works?' Glyn asked.

'I have no concerns,' John Hughes stopped talking long enough to fork a portion of his cod and horseradish salad to his mouth. 'My four sons run the place like clockwork. And we've had no trouble from the workers since John and Arthur let the anarchist Ukrainians know what we thought of them the last time they tried to win the support of our employees.'

'They won't try again in a hurry that's for sure,' Richard agreed.

Three men – all miners, two who worked in the Beletsky and Parry collieries had been killed in the riots the anarchists had engineered in their failed attempt to win over the Hughesovka ironworkers and colliers. Richard had no sympathy for any man who sought to engineer change through violence. But he dared not look at Glyn and Edward who were sitting opposite him. Given the poor conditions of the average worker both in Hughesovka and the surrounding area, he knew that like him, Glyn and his brother understood the frustrations of those forced to sell their labour below subsistence level.

After growing up in Merthyr they had first-hand knowledge of how a glut of unemployed men and women who were prepared to do almost anything to put food on the table, could affect the wages and living conditions of desperate families.

'When are you leaving for St Petersburg?' John asked Glyn and Richard.

'The day after tomorrow,' Glyn informed him. 'Edward's volunteered to stay behind and look after the Edwards's Brothers' collieries.'

'And keep half an eye on the Beletsky and Parry collieries, not that we're expecting any problems,' Richard nodded to Alexei who'd hardly said a word all evening.

'Give my regards to your wife, Edward,' John Hughes finished his salad and pushed his plate aside.

'I will, thank you, sir.'

'So, your daughter is to be presented at court, Richard?' John said.

'Along with Alexei's daughters,' Glyn looked across the table at Alexei.

'My grandmother persuaded me to accompany her. I dared not refuse when I saw how much the twins are looking forward to the trip. My wallet however is a different matter,' Alexei joked.

'Daughters can inflict grievous wounds on a father's wallet,' John laughed. 'It will be the tail end of the season in St Petersburg, but no less enjoyable for that. I intend to stay there for a month or two before I have to depart for London on business. Time enough to enjoy your and your families' company as well as Catherine's. It's strange how St Petersburg – and Russia - feels more like home to me these days than London.'

'Not strange at all, sir, when you think of how much time you've spent here in the last thirty years,' Glyn said.

'Just look at what you've accomplished.'

'Thank you, Roman and thank you for not being bitter.'

'Over what? It's hardly your fault that two Welsh anarchists decided to take pot shots at me.'

'Life is dangerous and not only on the steppe. I have a feeling the entire world is changing and not for the better,' Alexei handed his hors-d'oevres plate to the waiter who was clearing the table.

'It's we who changed it, along with everyone who fought for a new industrial world that would bring increased wealth to every nation brave enough to embrace progress. I'm afraid many countries as well as people have been left behind,' John said.

'That's hardly your fault, sir. Russia was positively medieval when we arrived,' Glyn pointed out. 'Most of our workers now earn a fair wage and the company houses are far better than the hole houses,'

'For those fortunate enough to live in one,' John agreed. 'But there aren't enough to go around. And for that I blame myself.'

'Give us another twenty – twenty-five years,' Richard said. 'The rate the town is growing it really will be the ideal town you planned back in 1869, when the new century dawns, sir.'

'You think so?' John looked around the table.

'Progress always takes time. I remember standing with you on the empty steppe, possibly on this very spot, sir. Twenty-five years from now will be 1914. I suggest we meet again then . . . '

'When I'm ninety-nine years of age?' John laughed.

'Wherever you'll be, sir, I'll warrant the world you built will be a better and fairer place.'

'I may not be here to see it, Glyn, but I can depend on my sons to make it so.' John replenished their glasses, rose to his feet and raised his glass. 'A toast, gentlemen, before the waiters bring the next course. To the next 25 years and 1914.'

The toast echoed around the room and as Roman looked up at his friends' faces he shivered. A shiver that had nothing to do with cold, and everything to do with fear.

205

'Are you all right, Roman?' Glyn murmured quietly as he returned to his seat.

'What's that British expression? "I think someone has just walked over my grave."'

Richard caught the end of Roman's sentence and misunderstood what he'd said. 'You intend to be buried on the steppe?'

'Not if I can help it,' Roman demurred, 'but there's a grave waiting for every one of us, and do any of us know where it will be?'

'Not if we're fortunate,' Glyn declared. 'And if we're even more fortunate, not on the steppe.'

CHAPTER EIGHTEEN

Catherine Ignatova's house, Hughesovka, May 1889

'I've overseen the loading of the luggage into the second carriage, my lady,' Catherine's butler Boris entered the dining room where Catherine was breakfasting with Anna and Kira. Catherine knew Boris too well to ask if he was certain nothing had been overlooked.

'Has my grandson arrived with his daughters yet?' Catherine asked.

'Not yet, my lady.'

'He'll be here.' Anna helped herself to another roll and a spoonful of cherry jam.

'You're very sure of that,' Kira commented.

'My brother promised me that he would call on Alexei last night. I know what Richard's like when he's out to persuade someone. He drips arguments like a leaking tap until he succeeds in getting what he wants. Alexei will be here.'

'With all his girls?' Catherine asked.

'He won't leave Ruth behind, not now Yulia has found a wet nurse for her.' An unmarried Cossack girl, had hidden her pregnancy from her family, but she hadn't been able to conceal her labour pains. Her mother had brought Olena into the hospital in time to save her life but not the life of her child. Disowned by her father, she had been grateful for Alexei's offer of employment as Ruth's wet nurse. And even more grateful when she discovered it meant her immediate removal from Hughesovka to St Petersburg.

'I hear a carriage now, Madame.'

'Inform my guests that breakfast is ready, Boris, and remind them that we must leave here within the hour.'

'Yes, Madame.'

Before Boris reached the door, Sarah and Praskovia walked into the dining room followed by Richard and Glyn.

'Alexei?' Catherine mouthed to Glyn.

'Present and correct, Grandmamma,' he smiled at her when Glyn moved so Catherine could see him. I'm travelling in Glyn's coach because Sarah and Praskovia wanted to take turns in cuddling Ruth,' he held up the baby so she could see her. 'The girls are following in my coach with Maryanna, Kira and the boys. And they've just drawn up outside.'

Catherine gave a relieved smile. 'Eat, we have a long journey ahead of us.'

Catherine Ignatova's house St Petersburg June 1889

'And here come the bridesmaids,' Madame Roussard clapped her hands and Olga, Kitty and Maryanna strolled arm in arm into the parlour of Catherine's town house.

They were wearing gowns of the palest pink silk, chosen because the shade complimented Maryanna's fair complexion and brown hair, as well as it did Olga and Kitty's darker more striking olive skin and black hair. The skirts were cut to the latest fashion, narrow in front, sweeping back to a bustle of lace trimmed frills. The lace had been dyed a slightly darker shade of pink than the silk and trimmed the bodice, neck and cuffs as well as the hem and ruffles that layered the skirt.

'Beautiful,' Catherine smiled. 'Just what we wanted, gowns that can be worn to evening parties and balls after the wedding.'

'But not together, Grandmamma, or we'll look like the vanguard of an invasion,' Kitty said.

'A beautiful invasion of Hughesovkians,' Anna quipped.

'And now the bride,' Madame Roussard said proudly.

'Oh, Kira!' Praskovia exclaimed.

'You are an absolute vision. That white silk gleams like silver,' Sarah said. 'And the bridesmaids' gowns perfectly compliment the style. They're cut more simply but echo the same lines.'

'A fairy tale bride.' Anna's smile broadened. 'My brother Morgan is a very fortunate man.'

'As you see, my lady,' Madame Roussard stepped forward to show the gown off to Catherine who'd insisted on paying the dressmakers' bill, not only for the bride and herself but also the bridesmaids. 'All the gowns are cut to the very latest Paris fashions, and the Bruges lace for the bride's veil and on her gown, is the same pattern as that on the bridesmaids' gowns, but in white.'

'You have surpassed yourself, Madame Roussard.'

'Colette, bring Madame Ignatova's gown if you please.' Madame Roussard stood back as Anna, Sarah and Praskovia left their seats to examine Kira's gown at close quarters.

'Perfect,' Catherine smiled. 'Seeing you dressed like that, my child, makes me wish the next month away and us back in Hughesovka. An August wedding will ensure that the sun shines down on you and Morgan.'

Madame Roussard's assistant re-appeared with a violet silk gown over her arm. Cut to the same narrow skirted pattern as the bride's and bridesmaid's dresses it was trimmed with grey lace.

'No one has an eye for colour like you, Madame Roussard.' Catherine fingered the lace when Francine laid the gown over her lap. 'This is the exact same shade of grey as my hair.

'I hope the men are doing as well at the tailor's,' Sarah commented.

'With Glyn and Richard to guide the younger ones I'm sure they will. Although,' Anna qualified, 'I can't see Morgan outshining you on your wedding day, but Sarah and I will take care that there's no chemical stains or burn holes in his shirt.'

'If you manage that, I'll be grateful. I think it will be the first time I will have seen him without any.' Kira turned to the mirror and examined the neck of her gown.

Madame Roussard clapped her hands. 'If you ladies are absolutely certain that no alterations need to be made I will see that these gowns are packed ready for transportation to Hughesovka.'

'Thank you, Madame Rousseau, would you and your staff like some refreshment?' Catherine offered.

'Thank you for the thought, Madame Ignatova, but we have to leave. The end of the season is a busy time for us with our patrons ordering gowns for the winter. We took delivery of the new fabrics yesterday. There are some magnificent velvets in muted shades of magenta that would suit you perfectly, and beautiful autumn colours for the ladies,' the dressmaker looked to Praskovia, Sarah and Anna, 'and of course jewel colours for the younger ladies,' she nodded to the bridesmaids.

'We will call in the very next time we visit Nevsky Prospekt, Madame,' Catherine assured her.

'And when you do we can begin fitting the ball gowns you ordered for the young ladies to see if any last-minute adjustments need to be made before their presentation at court.'

Hotel Angelterre St Petersburg June 1889

'Thank you, gentlemen, I believe we have finished the negotiations. Shall we sign the contracts now?' John ushered the Russian naval and military buyers along with the representatives of the French, German and American companies he'd invited to the private dining room in his suite in the Hotel Angelterre, from the dining table to a desk where his clerks had laid out copies of the papers that required signatures. Richard and Glyn stood back waiting to witness the documents.

When the ink had dried, the waiter poured the champagne and his assistant served it. John raised his glass and waited for everyone else to follow suit.

'To Mother Russia, enterprise, modernisation and prosperity,' he toasted. 'We can now leave it to my clerks to file the paperwork and my works to supply you with first rate pig iron and steel. Good to do business with you gentlemen.'

The waiter held the door open, and after much hand shaking and polite but meaningless exchanges, the buyers filed out.

'That was worthwhile, sir,' Richard gathered the signed contracts he and Alexei had had drawn up for the potential buyers of their low-grade coal and pushed them into a folder marked Beletsky and Parry.

'It certainly was.' Glyn closed the contracts he'd garnered for Edward brothers' collieries into his briefcase.

'Bring more coffee and brandy please, Nicholas,' John ordered the waiter. He opened a humidor. 'Help yourself to cigars, gentlemen, I believe we've all earned one.' He took a cigar for himself, and settled back in a chair set in front of the window that was open to the balcony. The waiter handed John the silver cigar lighter lamp, fashioned like a tall Aladdin oil lamp that accompanied him everywhere he went.

Glyn, Edward, Richard and Alexei sat on the chairs and sofa opposite him.

'Thank you for inviting us to your business breakfast meeting, sir. We've succeeded in offloading all the low-grade steam coal we can produce for the next five years,' Richard said.

'As well as the Edwards' Brothers low grade output.' Glyn leaned back in his chair.

'You can add the New Russia Company's low-grade coal output to that, although it was only five percent of our production last year.'

John savoured his cigar for a moment. 'Just as well I've invested in a permanent office for the company here. This one meeting has generated enough income to cover the cost. I believe it may be advantageous for my eldest son and you to move to St Petersburg permanently, Glyn. Do you think Praskovia would countenance the idea?'

'As long as she could move the entire family here, sir, although I believe she would still want to visit Hughesovka from time to time.'

'I've heard it said that those born on the steppe wither when they try to make a home elsewhere. If that is true it proves that the Ukraine is similar to Wales,' Richard commented. 'Those born among the hills can't leave there for long.'

'Only twenty years or so,' Glyn reminded Richard.

John laughed. 'You are thinking of returning home, Richard?'

'It's gone no further than thinking at present, sir. But as we've,' Richard glanced at Alexei, 'taken care of both our low and high-grade output from our collieries for the next five years, what do we do now? Look for new investments?' he answered his own question before Alexei had an opportunity to do so.

'If you can wait until I return from London I may have a proposition for you,' John looked thoughtfully at his cigar. 'In the meantime, as long as the New Russia Company and the Beletsky and Parry and the Edwards' Brothers' collieries continue to produce anthracite in sufficient quantities for the New Russia Company to manufacture enough pig iron and steel to fulfil my contracts I'll be content. Well, gentlemen that's the business part of this trip over with. I imagine you're off to the tailors now?'

'We're meeting the boys there to see to their and our winter wardrobe,' Glyn confirmed.

'I'll meet you all at Catherine's tonight for dinner and tomorrow I'll see you at the ball she'll be hosting to introduce the young people to society?'

———

212

'All Maryanna can talk about is Catherine's ball,' Richard said.

'And Kitty and Olga.' Unlike Richard, Alexei didn't smile at the prospect and they realised he was thinking of Ruth and how much she would have enjoyed seeing her girls entering a ballroom for the first time.

'What about Pavlo, Tom and Ted?' John asked.

'They're happy enough but not as immersed in balls and parties as the girls,' Glyn revealed. 'A messenger came early this morning from Sonya to give us advance warning that she and Roman and the boys are hoping to arrive in the city today in time to attend Catherine's dinner. They were making plans for an afternoon picnic in the park tomorrow when I left the house.'

'Hughesovka has come to St Petersburg.' John outed his cigar in the ashtray.

'Just some of it.' Glyn rose from his chair and took a vodka bottle from the sideboard when the waiter entered with a trolley of coffee, a bottle of cognac, cups and glasses. 'You've made a fair number of toasts this morning, sir, this toast is on me and it is fitting that we drink it in what the Welsh in Hughesovka have christened, "Russian whisky". Just over twenty years ago, you, Alexei and I stood on the barren steppe above the Donbas river. We were in distinguished company. Several aristocrats, Dukes, Grand Dukes, Princes and Lords were there with us. Not all present believed in you then, but I never doubted you and neither did Alexei. And here we are twenty years later. The town you painted in your imagination is a fact, the New Russia Company has manufactured enough iron rails to cross all the Russias from east to west and north to south several times over. You and you alone with your vision, your sense of purpose and hard work have made your dream a reality. Congratulations, sir. You've dragged this great country into the nineteenth century and set it on course for the twentieth.' He raised his glass higher. 'To John Hughes, a remarkable man, and the best boss I could have hoped for.'

213

John looked up as all the men rose to their feet and raised their glasses. 'Thank you for your accolade, Glyn, but I am but a man. One who has to go to the new office and ensure it is being set up correctly.'

'We'll see you later at Catherine Ignatova's, sir.' Glyn set down his empty vodka glass.

'Give me a moment to get my hat and coat I will walk down to the square with you.' John went into his bedroom.

'It's certainly a beautiful morning, sir.' Glyn commented as he looked out of the open window.

'Beautiful enough to walk down to the river on my way to the new offices.' John reappeared wearing his hat. 'Shall we gentlemen?'

St Isaac's Square St Petersburg June 1889

Alexei breathed in deeply as they left the hotel foyer. 'Fresh air smells intoxicating when it's not polluted by furnace smoke.'

Richard glanced at his watch. 'We should have met the boys in the tailor's an hour ago. I dread to think what Ted will be ordering.'

'The same unserviceable fashionable garb as Pavlo and Tom,' Glyn prophesised gloomily.

'You go on ahead,' Alexei said as Richard climbed into the cab after Glyn. 'I have enough clothes and no sons to buy for. Unfortunately for me as outfitting boys appears to be a good deal cheaper than outfitting girls. And I have an appointment at Faberge's.'

'To buy the twins a little something to mark their social debut?' Richard asked.

'And my sister a wedding present. Regrettably I have a suspicion that the "little" won't apply to the price tag on any of the items.'

'Would you care to walk down as far as the river with me?' John asked Alexei.

'I would, sir.'

214

'I'm glad that you decided to bring your girls and join your grandmother in St Petersburg,' John said as they headed into St Isaac's Square. 'Catherine has been making plans to introduce them to society for some time. Especially since Kira became engaged to Morgan Parry last Christmas.'

'I trust it will be a while before the twins need my grandmother's matchmaking skills, sir.'

'The years will pass quickly. Too quickly for any father's liking and I'm speaking from personal experience. When I wake first thing in the morning I find it difficult to believe that my eldest son and daughter are both over forty years of age, and my other children too old need a father's guidance. So, take an old man's advice, and enjoy being part of your daughters' lives while they still need a father.'

They reached the promenade that ran alongside the river. John leaned on the parapet of the wall and looked out towards the island that housed the fortress of St Peter and Paul.

'Peter the Great knew what he was doing when he planned this city.'

'He did, sir,' Alexei agreed, 'although I'm not sure my ancestors appreciated being press ganged to assist him by hauling stones on to this marsh to build it.'

'The end result justifies the demands he made on his subjects. This city truly is golden in every sense of the word. Much more than any other I've visited and that includes, Rome, Paris and London.' John felt in his pockets and pulled out a small leather case. He opened it and offered Alexei one of the cigars it contained. 'I lost my wife nine years ago along with my youngest son so I know something of your suffering, Alexei. I doubt you need to hear anything I have to say but I promised your grandmother I would speak to you.'

Unsure how to respond Alexei remained silent.

'Would you like me to stop talking right now,' John struck a match and lit first Alexei's cigar then his own.

'No. My grandmother is right. I would undoubtedly benefit from hearing the experiences of someone who has suffered a similar loss to mine.' He turned to John. 'Tell me truthfully. Does the pain ever go away?' His question was calm, controlled and all the more heartrending for being softly spoken.

'Truthfully?' John met Alexei's steady gaze. 'I won't lie and tell you that you will feel the loss of Ruth any the less in the future, or that you will ever become accustomed to her absence. The pain I felt when I lost Elizabeth is as raw today as it was nine years ago when I heard she'd drawn her last breath. All time has brought me is the acceptance that this is my life now, and loneliness is my lot. I've learned to take pleasure in the children and grandchildren Elizabeth left to me. I hope that one day you will be as fortunate and take the same pleasure from your children and in the future grandchildren.'

'Thank you, sir.'

'For what, Alexei?'

'Not giving me platitudes about time being a healer. I don't even mind the pain.' He grimaced. 'When I feel it, I know I am still alive.'

John looked across the river. Sunlight streamed down and danced on the waters turning the river the same shade of cerulean blue as the sky. 'This is a day when it is good just to be alive. The kind of day to savour all that you ever really own. Your memories.' He smiled at Alexei. 'Elizabeth and I built a library of them to choose from. I will enjoy debating which one to relive as I walk to the new offices.'

CHAPTER SEVENTEEN

Catherine Ignatova's house St Petersburg June 1889

'That was the doorbell and I don't think you can squeeze another person inside this house,' Glyn murmured to Richard and Alexei as he looked around the crowded reception room. Catherine had ordered Boris to open the doors between her dining room and parlour so people could move freely between the two and the winter garden at the back of the house where Catherine had ordered her servants to set up refreshment tables. So many people had accepted Catherine's "Four o'clock at Home" pre-ball invitation that it was no longer possible to walk between rooms without asking some of her guests to move.

A footman appeared in the doorway and signalled to Boris. Catherine's butler glided through the throng and he and the footman disappeared into the hall. Boris reappeared a few moments later, stood on tip toe and looked around the room. He couldn't see Catherine but as she was still tired from the journey, he suspected that she'd have found a seat which would place her below the sea of heads. He saw Richard, Glyn and Alexei standing in a knot of men in front of the hearth. Kitty, Olga and Maryanna were talking to the boys from Hughesovka in front of the door that opened into the winter garden. But there was no sign of Sarah, Anna or Praskovia. Boris headed for the hearth.

'Excuse me, sir.'

'Of course, Boris.' Glyn turned to him and froze. He'd known Boris for over twenty years and during all that time never known the man to lose his equanimity. The butler looked as though he was about to break down, but when he spoke his voice was steady.

'May I have a word please, in the privacy of the small evening parlour, sir.'

Glyn followed the butler out of the room and into Catherine's private domain. It was the first time he had been in the room, and as he looked around he realised it mirrored her personality.

A display of family photographs hung above the mahogany desk that had been placed against a wall. Several featured Olga Beletsky and her daughters who had died in the cholera outbreak. In prominent position were more recent studio portraits of Sonya, Roman and their sons; Alexei, Ruth and their twins and a few of the amateur dramatic group that included Catherine, Kira and Anna as well as him Richard and their wives. The bookcase next to the desk was filled with leather bound volumes. A silver framed photograph on the desk contained a portrait of a man in old fashioned clothes who bore a strong physical resemblance to Alexei.

A round table and four leather upholstered chairs filled the window alcove. A low sideboard, small sofa and chaise covered in the same blue leather as the chairs completed the furniture. The air was redolent with the scent of roses that filled the bowl on the table.

'It's Mr Hughes, Mr Edwards,' Boris began when he closed the door on them.

'John Hughes?' Glyn didn't know what he'd been expecting, but it hadn't been a mention of John. 'Has he sent a message . . . '

A tear welled in Boris's eye and rolled down his cheek but his face remained impassive. 'An officer just called. He brought the news that Mr Hughes has died. He didn't stay because he was on his way to the New Russia Company to find someone who could identify Mr Hughes's body.'

Glyn stared at Boris in disbelief. 'Was he certain? We breakfasted with John Hughes this morning . . . '

'The officer knew that Mr Hughes and Mrs Ignatova were friends, sir. He said Mr Hughes's body has already been taken to the mortuary.'

'How . . . where . . . '

———

'The officer told me that Mr Hughes had collapsed near the Winter Palace.'

'When we left him, he said he intended to walk to the new offices. Alexei walked part way with him . . . ' Glyn stared at the drinks tray on the sideboard.

Butler first, man second, Boris asked, 'would you like a brandy, sir?'

'No . . . no thank you, Boris. Could you ask one of the footmen to fetch Alexei and Richard. And someone will have to tell Catherine. Kira, and Anna and my wife and-'

'I'll send a footman to fetch Mr Beletsky and Parry, sir. And perhaps I should tell the guests . . . '

'Nothing until Catherine has been told, Boris. I'll find her and bring her here.'

Catherine Ignatova's house St Petersburg June 1889

Catherine ordered Boris to announce the news of John Hughes's death to her guests along with notice of the cancellation of her evening ball. All but her family and closest friends filed silently out of the house. Sonya, Roman and their sons arrived just as Praskovia and Sarah were taking the younger people back to Glyn and Praskovia's house.

After a hurried consultation, Glyn and Richard left Alexei, Kira, Sonya and Roman with Catherine. They visited the headquarters of the New Russia Company and returned late in the evening to find Catherine and the others sitting next to an untouched buffet in the winter garden.

Catherine's eyes were dark with misery when she looked at Glyn and Richard.

Glyn thought he'd never seen anyone age so much in the space of an afternoon. 'The company clerk had telegraphed Hughesovka before we reached the office. John's sons are already on their way here. Apparently, John left instructions. He wants – wanted to be buried next to his wife in London.'

'We thought he might want to be buried in the town he founded,' Richard said.

'It would have been fitting,' Alexei commented.

'It's fitting that his sons will be accompanying him home to Britain to lie next to his wife,' Catherine whispered.

'I'm sorry, Catherine,' Glyn pulled a chair close to Catherine's and clasped her hands 'We all lost a good friend today.'

'He left a giant legacy,' Roman wheeled his chair close to a side table and handed out the "shot" glasses he'd filled with vodka. 'Not many men can say they founded an iron works and a town and single handedly carried an empire into the industrial age. And he did it while providing the best housing, hospitals and wages in Russia for his workers.' He raised his glass. 'To John Hughes, friend, mentor, and inspiration to us all. And to the embodiment of John's life's work. May Hughesovka thrive into the next century and beyond.'

Richard drained his glass and threw it into the hearth built into a stone wall of the winter garden where it shattered into shards. 'So that no lesser toast can ever be drunk from that glass. Not many men would have countenanced travelling half way across the world to land on the steppe in the middle of a Russian winter to build an ironworks. John Hughes did, and he succeeded.' He smiled as he recalled the expedition he had been proud to be a part of.

'Every day of that long cold journey back breaking journey, John Hughes used to say we were making history. He was right,' Glyn threw his glass on top of Richard's where it splintered into as many pieces.

'We'll not see his like again.' Roman finished his vodka and followed suit. Catherine rose to her feet and threw hers. Alexei's glass was the last on the pile. He stood and stared at the debris for what seemed like a long time before ordering his carriage.

Catherine's house fell strangely silent after the last of her visitors left. Kira, Anna and Catherine continued to sit in the Winter Garden until sunset simply because they couldn't summon the energy or the will to move.

'Do you think there will be a memorial service for Mr Hughes in St Petersburg before his sons take him to Britain?' Anna asked. The shadows had lengthened and Boris entered to light the lamps.

'Both in St Petersburg and Hughesovka I should think,' Catherine answered, 'he was an important man who touched many lives and changed them for the better. But whatever happens, Kira, I don't think you and Morgan should change your plans to marry because of his death. Mr Hughes was keen for Morgan to set up the new laboratory in London. If he were here, he would tell both of you to go ahead with your wedding and journey to London exactly as planned.'

'Do you think so?' Kira asked doubtfully. 'I'll talk to Morgan about it, but you know he absolutely hero worshipped, Mr Hughes. And with good reason. He and Owen would never have received the education they had if Mr Hughes hadn't opened the training programme for the metallurgy laboratory.'

'Think about, Kira, Mr Hughes is no longer with us. What possible good would postponing your wedding achieve? Nothing will bring Mr Hughes back and as for a mark of respect, the best Morgan can do for Mr Hughes now, is to set up the new laboratory he wanted,'

'My head tells you that you right, Grandmamma.'

'But your heart weeps for Mr Hughes?' Catherine guessed.

'I feel as though we have lost the head of our family.'

'We have, Kira,' Catherine said sadly. 'The head not only of our family but the town of Hughesovka.'

Eyes brimming with tears too choked to speak Kira bent her head to Catherine's and kissed her cheek.

221

Catherine patted her granddaughter's hand. 'Try and get some rest, sweetheart. I'll come and say goodnight to you.'

Kira nodded and almost ran out of the door.

'I can't imagine returning to a Hughesovka that will never see Mr Hughes again,' Anna steeled herself in an effort to control her emotions. 'He often made trips away but he always returned and even when he wasn't in Russia he sent telegraphs and letters with instructions and plans not only for the hospital but improvements for the town.'

'His sons have been taking over the works and the town for a while. I don't think much will change, at least not at first, but you're right, Anna. We may be able to fool ourselves for a while that he will be returning but sooner or later realisation will dawn and with it the knowledge that he has left us for good. That is the worst thing about death, its absolute finality. The closing of a door that can never be reopened.' Catherine squeezed Anna's hand lightly. 'Do you think you will be able to sleep?'

'Probably not,' Anna replied. 'But I would welcome the opportunity to lie in bed and remember Mr Hughes. All his many kindnesses to me and Richard and later when they joined us Owen and Morgan. Did I ever tell you that he gave me my first job when we sailed here through the Mediterranean?'

'No.'

'He paid me to write to his youngest son, Owen Tudor. He was a year younger than me and away at school. Like me, Owen felt lost and lonely in a strange place surrounded by strange people. I was happy to write to him but Mr Hughes insisted on paying me. He said I needed to earn my own living.'

'Which you did when you reached Hughesovka, as a ward maid in the hospital.'

'If I'd stayed in Merthyr I would have probably ended up skivvying in a pub kitchen and taking in washing for the rest of my life. I never dreamed that someone like me could become a nurse. Much less a matron, but Mr Hughes, Sarah and first Dr Edwards then Dr Kharber believed in me and made it possible.'

'If Sarah were here, she would tell you that you, not she and the doctors, made it possible, Anna, you passed your nursing examinations, not Sarah, and you were chosen from several candidates to become matron of the hospital when Sarah retired,' Catherine reminded her. 'Which only goes to prove what I've always said, that it doesn't matter where someone was born, or what class they were born into. The only person responsible for shaping your destiny is yourself. And you can see no better example of that than Mr Hughes himself. From what you told me, he, like you, Richard, Morgan and Owen, was born the child of a labourer in the Merthyr ironworks.'

'We were.'

'And look how far you and your brothers have come,' Catherine said.

'More than just the country and miles,' Anna said. 'I never thought I'd set foot in a palace like this or a country mansion like yours in Hughesovka, except perhaps as a scullery maid hired to scrub the floors.'

'Houses are just places to live, Anna. In the end, we all live in no more than two or three rooms no matter how many we have. A bedroom, kitchen and living room is all that's necessary and we could probably manage without the living room, although a garden, especially a winter garden, she looked around at the lilies that had just come into bloom, is a luxury and feast for the eyes.

'I love the way you seem to have surrounded yourself with flowers.'

223

'That is thanks to my mother. She adored them. One of her favourite sayings was "a life without flowers is like eating meat without salt." You'd survive but there'd be no taste or excitement. I suddenly feel very tired. Can I prevail on you to give me your arm to lean on? I think that like you, I would like to go to bed and indulge myself in remembering some of the conversations I shared with Mr Hughes. He was such an intelligent man. Roman was right, we'll never see his like again.'

Catherine Ignatova's house St Petersburg June 1889

Anna escorted Catherine to her room. Before she left Catherine whispered, 'promise me something?''

'If it's within my capabilities, anything,' Anna answered solemnly.

'Take care of Alexei and his girls when Kira leaves for England with Morgan.'

'I will, but he appreciates your advice more than mine, Catherine.'

'The trouble with grandmothers is their advice can be discounted as old fashioned.'

'Not yours, Catherine. Never yours.'

Anna helped Catherine into bed, before walking along the corridor to her own room. She opened the drapes and the door that led on to the balcony and stepped outside. The moon hung low, an enormous orb over the river sending silvery shadows dancing over the blue-black waves. The outlines of the palaces that lined the banks were silhouetted against the night sky, the lamps in the windows gleaming like the multiple eyes of huge monstrous beasts.

She was in the centre of the city but felt as though it was only a stone variation of the forests that had been the first dwelling of the people who'd lived in this land. "All the Russias" - would she ever feel truly at home here?

She leaned on the balustrade and looked out over the garden. A dog barked in the distance, a cat yowled, its cry joined by those of others. The tramp of booted feet echoed over the pavement and half a dozen soldiers marched up the street heading away from the river into the centre of town.

They were laughing and joking amongst themselves and it suddenly seemed so wrong that life was continuing while John Hughes, a man who had loved St Petersburg, Russia, the world and all it had to offer, who had given so much to so many people lay dead and cold in the mortuary.

Catherine Ignatova's house St Petersburg June 1889

Anna woke with a start when she heard a light tap on her bedroom door. Confused, her mind whirling with disjointed dreamlike images, she sat up and saw that she'd fallen asleep on the high window seat to the side of the balcony door. She looked down and realised she hadn't even undressed.

The tap came again, louder and more urgent. She jumped to the floor and went to the door. Boris stood on the galleried landing outside with Catherine's maid.

'Boris . . . '

'It's the mistress, Miss Anna . . . '

Anna ran out into the corridor and was halfway to Catherine's room when she heard Boris say, 'God has taken her and by the look on her face I believe He blessed her by taking her peacefully while she was asleep, Miss Anna.'

CHAPTER TWENTY

St Petersburg and Hughesovka June 1889

The days after the deaths of John Hughes and Catherine Ignatova were bleak, and not only for Anna. She found herself surrounded by grim eyed, solemn faces that mirrored her own sense of loss and pain. Minutes blurred into hours that blended into days and nights during which dreams and nightmares merged. There were times when she couldn't have said with any certainty whether she was awake or asleep.

Boris ordered the drapes in Catherine's St Petersburg palace to be left closed day and night. The absence of natural light darkened the atmosphere, transforming the familiar into sinister. She found herself stumbling over the furniture as she constantly looked over her shoulder half expecting to see someone standing behind her.

She moved from place to place, room to room without sense, or purpose. She spoke to people without listening to what they were saying. Merely going through the motions of life, like a puppet on a marionette stage.

Trapped in Catherine's palace, all she could do was wait. For arrangements to be made to ship Mr Hughes's body back to England – for preparations to be finalised for Catherine Ignatova's last journey to the estate outside Hughesovka where she had lived most of her life. She sat with cohorts of distant relatives, friends and acquaintances of Catherine who called on Kira, Alexei, the twins and Sonya to offer their condolences. The only time she left Catherine's house was to visit Richard and Glyn, who'd taken it upon themselves to lighten the load on John Hughes's sons by fielding the sympathy visits John Hughes's business connections felt obligated to pay. So, even there she found herself surrounded by mourners.

She took delivery of the gowns she'd ordered from Madame Roussard and packed them away together with all her St Petersburg clothes except her black crepe mourning gowns. She made an effort to immerse herself in mindless domestic tasks, but no matter what she did, she found herself yearning for Hughesovka and her life in the hospital. Whenever she thought about it, she deliberately tried not to picture herself back in Catherine's house, for without Catherine's presence and invitation she felt that she could no longer consider the place home.

She couldn't have said with any certainty how much time elapsed between the morning Boris knocked her door to tell her that Catherine had died, and the day she stood next to her brothers, Sarah, Roman and Sonya, Glyn, Kira and Praskovia on the Admiralty Quayside in St Petersburg watching as John Hughes's coffin was carried by the Tsar's personal guard on board the ship that would convey his body back to England. They stood for what seemed like hours before John's sons and their families took leave of them and followed John's remains on to the vessel. The final image she retained from that day was the ship weighing anchor and sailing majestically out of the harbour on the first leg of John Hughes's final journey back to England.

A brass band had assembled and was playing on the quayside when they arrived and it still played as they left. She was aware of the music, it was regal, solemn and fitting for the occasion, but afterwards she couldn't recall a single tune. All she remembered was the heaviness in her heart and the sting of the salt laden air as it blew in cold and misty from the sea. Had there really been a mist? Or had her memory been tainted by a surfeit of emotion, or the eye searing, biting Baltic wind? If it was the wind the effects lasted until they left the port.

The last goodbye was said by Alexei. 'Poor Mother Russia. She will not see the like of John Hughes or his vision and drive again.'

227

A day later Anna stood in line with her brothers and friends on a railway platform in St Petersburg watching the surprisingly small black ebony coffin that held Catherine's earthly remains being loaded on to one of Catherine's private carriages at the end of the train that would take them back to Hughesovka.

The coffin was highly polished. She could see her reflection in the surface. The black patina was offset by wrought silver coffin furniture, handles and plate. She couldn't help but admire the craftsmanship, but neither could she close out the image that intruded unbidden into her mind of Catherine's body lying cold and solitary inside the fine linen and lace folds that lined the box.

She had a bizarre thought. That everything that had gone into the manufacture of the coffin had existed when Catherine had been alive. The wood had been stored and seasoned before being sawn into planks and polished. The silver smelted before finding its way to the silversmith who had cast, polished and engraved the plate with Catherine's name and dates.

Once she'd pictured the items waiting for the coffin maker to begin work on Catherine's casket, her mind turned to the materials for her own coffin. It was a concept she found herself returning to time and again as she wondered how long it would be before a carpenter began work on her final bed.

Her brothers, Roman, Sonya, Glyn, Sarah, Praskovia, Kira and Alexei were all kind, sympathetic and supported her in every way they could, yet she couldn't bear to talk about Catherine or John Hughes's death with any of them.

She journeyed to Hughesovka from St Petersburg, entered and left carriages, horse drawn and rail, looked out through windows at passing towns, villages, hamlets and countryside, all the while fighting the trance-like state that had fallen over her in St Petersburg.

228

Nothing registered on her consciousness for any length of time, nothing was real, and time lost all meaning. She was consumed by a uniform greyness that even blotted out the sun.

The only comfort she could draw on during those dreadful numbing days, was the thought that one day she too would be dead. She didn't allow herself to think as far as what lay beyond death, only a vague hope that she would be reunited with Catherine, her parents, brother and sisters – and if it should turn out to be nothingness, she would at least have company.

When they reached Hughesovka Kira insisted she return with her to Catherine's house. Realising that Kira didn't want to be left alone any more than she did, and conceding that she had to pack anyway, she acquiesced. Dr Nathan Kharber and Noah de Vries were among their first visitors on their return. Both insisted she should continue her sabbatical from the hospital and she agreed simply because it was easier to drift aimlessly than make any decisions before Catherine's funeral.

Hughesovka 1889

Father Grigor led the procession of mourners that left Catherine's house after private family prayers, for the service in the flower decked church that Catherine's husband Alexei had built for her as a wedding gift. The pews were crammed with Catherine's close and distant family and wealthy influential friends. The standing space behind them filled with peasants, iron workers, colliers and Cossacks. So many had gathered to pay their respects to the woman they regarded as their mistress and benefactress, they overflowed out of the doors, filling the churchyard and the steppe outside the walls. Visibly moved by the size of the congregation, Father Grigor left the church doors open so those outside could hear the prayers and hymns.

Anna spent the entire service staring at Catherine's coffin while wishing that she could freeze time because she wasn't ready to say goodbye. When Father Grigor intoned the final "Amen" he waited for the bearers Alexei had chosen to lift the coffin before leading the procession out of the church. They were all Cossacks whose families had been in the service of Catherine's family for generations, Praskovia's brother Misha among them. Kira, Sonya and Alexei followed with Alexei's daughters, Sonya's boys and Roman, and at Alexei's invitation, Anna walked with them.

None of Alexei and Kira's brothers had been given leave to travel to Hughesovka for the funeral. Like Alexei all five had been sent to the military academy in Allenstein at the age of ten and after finishing their education they had accepted commissions. Three served as officers in the Russian army, one in the Prussian and one in the Austrian. Alexei doubted he would have recognised them if they had turned up. He hadn't seen any of them for over twenty years and Kira had never met them. Proof, as if any were needed, that their family had splintered irrevocably when their mother had died.

It was a sombre procession that made its way from the church to the Ignatova family graveyard where Catherine was laid to rest alongside her husband, daughter and granddaughters. The mourners who were wealthy enough to own or hire carriages, headed for the Ignatova house for the "pominki" the funeral meal laid on for those who'd attended the internment. The poor walked.

Anna glanced back at the Ignatova family plot as she climbed into Richard's carriage. Alexei alone lingered at the graveside. She saw him take a flower from his pocket. A white rose she'd watched him cut that morning in one of Catherine's beloved greenhouses. He placed it on Ruth's headstone, bowed his head and gripped the top with both hands. Feeling like a voyeur she dropped her veil and sat alongside Sarah who clasped her hand in sympathy.

Boris and Dmitri had carried out the instructions Catherine had detailed in her will. A generous buffet of traditional funeral foods, blinis, fish pies, the wheat and fruit dish Kolyva, accompanied by bread, stuffed eggs, cheese, biscuits and herring and sauerkraut salads, with unlimited supplies of the low alcohol Kvass "bread beer" to wash down the food, had been laid out in the barn for the Cossacks and peasants.

A more elaborate buffet of cold meats, vegetables, salads, cakes, pastries, wine and vodka had been laid out for Catherine's family and friends in the dining room. Unequal to making small talk Anna found a secluded table shielded by a row of orange trees in the winter garden. She gazed at the path that led to Catherine's hot houses and recalled all the times she and Catherine had walked along it. She'd just risen to her feet with the intention of slipping away to her bedroom when Mr Dmitri approached her.

'Matron Parry, may I have a word, please?'

'Of course, Mr Dimitri.' Without thinking she repeated the phrase she had repeated constantly since leaving the church. 'It was a beautiful service.'

'It was, Matron Parry. If you could make your way to Mrs Ignatova's study I will be along shortly with the others.'

'The others.' She looked at him blankly.

'It's time to read Mrs Ignatova's will, and all the beneficiaries have to be there.'

'But I'm not a beneficiary . . . '

'You are, Matron Parry.'

Kira saw Anna's confusion and crossed the room. She took Anna's arm. 'We'll go together.'

Catherine Ignatova's House Hughesovka 1889

Mr Dmitri's voice trembled slightly as he read.

'To my grandson Alexei Beletsky, a quarter share of all my investments, to my granddaughter, Kira Beletsky, a quarter share of my investments, to my niece Sonya Nadolny a quarter share of my investments, and my close friend Anna Parry likewise a quarter share of my investments, to sell or retain as they wish.

'To my granddaughter Kira Beletsky my niece Sonya Nadolny and my great granddaughters Olga, Kitty and Ruth Beletsky the jewellery I have itemised and listed in the appendix to this will. To my close friend and confidante for the past twenty years, Anna Parry, the amber jewellery in the red morocco leather case that my husband Alexei Ignatova gave me on our wedding night.

'To Alexei and Kira, I leave each a half share in my St Petersburg home to sell or use as they wish, the only stipulation being that should it be sold it must be a decision that they both agreed to.

'To my close friend Anna Parry, I leave my main house, and all its contents in Hughesovka and an annuity sufficient to cover her expenses and the upkeep of the house. She is free to live in or sell the house and estate as she wishes and should she decide to do so, I trust that she will do so without any tears or sentiment thoughts. Given the way that the town of Hughesovka has grown I suspect the land of the estate will in time become a great deal more valuable than the house or its contents. I attach no conditions to this bequest other than the wish that she continue to care for the welfare of the workers who live on the estate as I have done.

To my grandson Alexei I leave the self-contained wing of my house in Hughesovka and all the furnishings it contains in the hope that he will see sense and move into it with his daughters. Girls need space to breathe away from their father, Alexei.'

Anna took a deep breath, Mr Dmitri had spoken the words, but the voice was Catherine's.

'Knowing Anna Parry as I do, I can imagine her trying to refuse this inheritance, which is why I enclose letters from my grandson Alexei, granddaughter Kira and niece Sonya stating that all three are aware of this shared bequest and approve. It is made with recognition of the special relationship based on love and friendship that lasted between Anna Parry and myself for over twenty years.

'To John Hughes, I leave the amber casket that he has so often admired. To my friends, I beg them to choose any book they wish from my library that they might remember me when they read it. To Father Grigor I leave an annuity for him and his successors in the post of priest in Hughesovka, to distribute among the poor of the area as they see fit.

'I thank my family and my friends for their love and support and for tolerating the idiosyncrasies of an old woman. I trust that their lives will be as long and happy as mine.'

Mr Dimitri turned to the desk behind him and picked up several envelopes. 'Here are details of the bequests you have been left.'

'Grandmamma thought of everything,' Kira murmured. Her eyes were dry, burning and Anna, Sonya and Alexei knew that her grief, like theirs, cut too deep for tears,

'These,' Mr Dmitri held up a box that contained several more letters, 'refer to minor bequests, principally mementoes and keepsakes to be distributed among a few close friends, tenants and servants on the estate.'

'Did you approve my grandmother's will, Mr Dmitri?' Alexei asked.

'I did, Mr Beletsky,' he confirmed.

'Then as my grandmother drafted it and you endorsed it I am certain it is in order.'

Anna stared at Alexei. Sonya and Kira in disbelief. 'I can't take this house . . . '

Alexei smiled for the first time since Catherine had died. 'Didn't you hear what Mr Dmitri said. It's yours. To refuse it would be to deny my grandmother her wishes. She wanted you to have the house, Anna. Sonya has a house here, Morgan has an apartment in Richard's house that is more than adequate for any holidays he and Kira will find time to take when they visit Hughesovka after they've moved to Britain, and I have my house in town as well as a wing of this one. So,' he beamed at her, 'it's perfectly fitting that you inherit this house and all my grandmother's possessions along with her responsibilities. To refuse would be to shirk them.'

'Don't you see,' Kira took Anna's hand. 'Alexei's right, all you've been given is a heavy work load, my aunt through friendship and when I marry Morgan, sister-in-law.'

'Along with a beautiful house full of artefacts that belong to your family,' Anna protested.

'Take it with our blessing, Anna. My grandmother thought of you as a daughter. So, welcome to the family,' Sonya kissed her.

Anna didn't find time to open the letters Mr Dmitri had given her until she went to her room late that night. She left the letters on her desk, opened the window and looked out over the gardens towards the church and the family graveyard. The last stragglers were walking down the drive. Beyond the walls she saw lights flickering close to the Ignatova family graves and wondered who was paying their respects so late.

She sat at her desk, reached for her letter opener - an amber and ivory gift from Catherine - and began reading. Three of the letters were as Dmitri had said, testimonies from Alexei, Kira and Sonya on how they grateful they were that Catherine had decided to leave her the house.

Sonya pointed out that she had more than enough to do caring for Roman's numerous residences. Kira reminded her that she would shortly be married to Morgan and living permanently in England, and Alexei, that as no one else wanted the house, he was extremely grateful that she had taken it over and he was certain she would care for it as Catherine would have if she'd lived.

There was one more envelope, addressed to her in Catherine's firm sloping hand and distinctive navy-blue ink.

She opened it and removed the pages it contained.

Hughesovka,
May 1889

She read the date and started in surprise. Catherine had written it only a few weeks ago.

My dear Anna,
You have only just left me and it seems strange to be sitting at my desk writing to you when you are upstairs, and most probably not yet asleep.
As I intimidated to you, I know that I am not much longer for this earth, but coward that I am I could not bring myself to mention the subject again as I know it will bring tears to your eyes and I beg you, Anna, do not cry for me.
Already I see my beloved dead clearer than I see my beloved living but that is not why I am writing to you. I want to write to you about Alexei. I know that Ruth is embedded in his heart and mind and will be for the remainder of his life. But it is possible to love again after death has robbed you of those you hold most dear, I am living proof of that, and I hope and pray that given sufficient time Alexei's heart will thaw enough for him to love his daughters as they deserve to be loved.

I beg you, persuade Alexei to move into the half of the house I have left him and stay close to my great granddaughters. They deserve every happiness they can claw from life after losing their mother, especially baby Ruth who will have no memories of her mother's love. There is no one I trust more to advise my granddaughters and bring an occasional smile back to Alexei's face.

I would love to leave this appeal for a year or two but I sense that I don't have much time left to me and the older I grow the more I find myself relying on my instincts. They have never let me down.

I know why you can never love any man and why you trust only your brothers and men you have known for a long time like Glyn Edwards and Mr Hughes. But please, Anna, I beg of you, don't allow your fear to close out the greatest love that can be experienced in life. That between a man and a woman.

I have a dream for you, Anna, one in which you find the happiness you so richly deserve.

Set this letter aside and look at it again in a year or two. I can imagine it bringing a smile to your face then. I only hope that I am right.

I love you like a daughter Anna, or is it granddaughter?
My Love, as always, Anna,
Your friend, Catherine.

CHAPTER TWENTY-ONE

Catherine Ignatova's House Hughesovka 1889

Anna looked up from the estate's account book at the knock on the study door.

'Come in,' she called.

Boris opened the door. 'Dr Kharber is here and asking if you can see him, Madame.'

Anna glanced at the clock on the mantelpiece. 'Mid-afternoon is a strange time to pay a social call, Boris. Is there an emergency at the hospital?'

'Not that he mentioned, Madame. He appears calm and composed.'

'Do you think you could bring yourself to call me Anna? Miss Anna if you must, Boris, but please not "Madame." Every time I hear you say it,' she tried to keep her voice steady, 'I expect to see Mrs Ignatova.'

'It would be disrespectful of me to refer to you as "Anna" or "Miss Anna" as you are now mistress of this house, Madame.'

Anna sighed as she set down her pen. One of the most difficult things she had found in her transition from guest to mistress of the Ignatova estate was the acceptance of all the staff of the house along with the outside workers and tenants as Catherine's heir and successor when she felt so unsuited to the role. 'I'm sorry, Boris, but you will have to find a name other than Madame to call me.'

'Mistress?' he suggested.

Anna recalled Alice Grisha spitting out the word in relation to Praskovia. It conjured an image of an extravagantly dressed woman lounging on a chaise longue awaiting her lover.

'Mistress it is, Boris, until we can think of something better,' she answered, aware that Nathan was waiting in the hall. At least there was a fire there but she had given orders that the fire in the parlour was only to be lit when she expected company.

'Show Dr Kharber in here please, Boris, and give my apologies to Lyudmila for disturbing her routine and ask her to set up a refreshment tray for us.'

'Yes, ma . . . mistress,' Boris corrected himself.

Anna closed the ledger, tidied her desk and cleared away the books and papers that littered the side tables.

Boris opened the door. 'Dr Kharber, mada . . . mistress.'

Anna smiled as he stumbled over the word a second time.

Nathan walked in. 'My apologies for disturbing you.'

She rose to meet Nathan and held out her hand. He shook it.

'No need to apologise, Dr Kharber. It's lovely to see you. I've been wrestling with figures and welcome an interruption. Thank you,' she smiled at the footman who wheeled in a trolley that held a samovar, tea glasses, plates and trays that held selections of sweet and savoury snacks. 'Please sit down. The two most comfortable chairs are next to the hearth. The best place for them now that the first snow has arrived. Would you like tea, or vodka, sherry or wine?'

'Thank you for agreeing to see me without an appointment and I would welcome a cup of tea please.' Nathan sat on one of the chairs she'd indicated.

'I'll pour it, thank you, Boris.'

The butler wheeled the trolley closer to the chairs, waved the footman out of the parlour, followed him and closed the doors behind them.

Anna filled two tea glasses. 'How are things at the hospital?'

'Busier than ever.'

'Even with the new staff?'

'That's why I'm here.'

'Problems?' she asked tactfully.

'Not as such. When it comes to dealing with everyday ailments they are all, doctors and nurses, more than competent.'

'I sense a "but",' she picked up a tray of sandwiches and held them out to him.

He took two absently without even checking the filling. 'The nurses are excellent, all well trained for ward duty, but none have any surgical experience. I talked to Sarah about training them, but she pointed out that you've had far more experience than her. And because you've kept up with your studies and reading, you are more conversant with the latest techniques.'

'So, you want me to come back?'

'I'd love to have you return as matron but Catherine left you quite a legacy here,' he said wryly.

'She did. I had no idea how much she did to help people in the town, or how many sought her advice on a daily basis until I attempted to take over from her. It's overwhelming. Lady of the manor – or rather Ignatova estate - is not a position I'm suited to fill.'

'Given your organisational skills, I'm sure you're being modest.' He set the plate of sandwiches aside, took a lump of sugar and placed it in the saucer of his tea glass.

'On the contrary. Catherine was born here, she knew the people, their families the differences between the Cossack community and the peasants . . . '

'And you know the Welsh colliers and ironworkers who travelled here with you and your brother. And through your work in the hospital you are acquainted with the Russians, Cossacks and Jews who live here as well as the other nationalities who have come to this town with the intention of making it their home. I've no doubt they'll all come knocking at your door sooner or later.'

'Word has already spread. The newcomers certainly aren't shy when it comes to visiting Catherine's house to ask for help.'

'Your house now. And people will always knock on a door where they can be sure of receiving food when they're hungry and blankets when they're cold.' He finished his tea and set down his glass.

She picked it up and refilled it without asking if he wanted more. Given how few times she'd actually seen him eat, she wondered if he lived on tea. It would explain his emaciated frame. 'Catherine has been helping those who've come to Hughesovka looking for work since the very first arrived here just after Mr Hughes.'

'She was a special woman, as are you, and no, I'm not asking you to return as matron full time to the hospital. Given what you are doing here that would be too heavy a workload for any one person, but if you could spare one or two afternoons a week to help me and the other doctors with the more complicated surgery and train a few of the nurses while you do so, it would help. The sooner you start the sooner we will have a pool of experienced surgical nurses to draw on.'

'I know your requests, Dr Kharber. "One or two afternoons".' she repeated. 'Are you asking me to spare you two afternoons a week?'

'Three would be better.'

She smiled. 'You have them.'

'Everyone misses you at the hospital.'

'I miss them.'

'Then this could be a good compromise for you too?'

'It could,' she said thoughtfully. 'After looking at Catherine's legacy I've begun to think about my own.'

'You're not even thirty . . . '

'Thirty-two,' she corrected.

'I'm more than a decade and a half older and I haven't considered my legacy yet.'

She thrust a tray of cakes at him. 'Don't you know that your legacy is the hospital, Nathan?'

'I suppose it is,' he said as though the thought hadn't occurred to him.

'And you have your family . . . '

'Vasya raised them because I was always working. If there is credit due to anyone in bringing up our foster children it is her. The boys rarely visit us. Two of them work for my father-in-law in his butchery business, but all four room with him and my mother-in-law. Martha makes time to visit Vasya once a week, although she's married to the carpenter's son, Isak Kaplan.'

Nathan's comments coupled with what Anna knew of the estrangement between Nathan and the orphaned children of the Goldbergs' cousin he'd been forced to adopt by his wife's family, didn't invite a continuance of the conversation.

As if he realised he hadn't said enough, he added. 'They are all leading useful lives. My father-in-law has turned two of the boys into competent butchers, and the two who work in Alexei and Richard's colliery seem to be keeping out of trouble. Martha knows how to run a house.' He shook his head when Anna offered him a plate of cakes. 'Have you heard from Prince and Princess Nadolny?'

'I received a letter from Sonya yesterday. Roman has seen seven surgeons but only one of them is prepared to go ahead with the operation. As you can well imagine he gives no guarantees as to the outcome. From what Sonya wrote, I believe he's outlined all the risks in detail to both Roman and Sonya.'

'Prince Nadolny strikes me a man who would risk his life to regain his full strength and health.'

'I believe he would.' She looked at his plate of untouched sandwiches. 'Would you do me a favour in return for my agreeing to return to the hospital.'

'If I can,' he answered.

'There is no need to sound worried, It's not anything illegal or immoral. Just eat one or two of Lyudmila's chicken sandwiches or a few of her cakes. If you don't, she'll berate me for my failure as a hostess and your omission an insult to her skills as a cook.'

He picked up his plate and bit into one of the sandwiches. 'You can tell her the sandwiches are delicious.' He leaned back in the chair and stretched his legs out towards the fire. 'I think I've forgotten the comfort a well-furnished home can offer. This is a lovely room.'

Anna had visited Nathan's house. It wasn't furnished expensively but it was comfortable, and she suspected that if he'd forgotten what a home had to offer it was because he spent so little time in his, and so much in the hospital.

'This is very much Catherine's room and I intend for it to remain that way. The only changes I've made is to add a few framed photographs of my brothers, Sarah and my niece and nephew to the collection on the desk.'

'I miss our late evening conversations in the hospital.' He sounded almost wistful.

'As, do I,' she admitted.

'I also miss your diagnostic ability. No other nurse has your capacity for spotting potential infections and fevers before a patient shows the most obvious symptoms.'

'There's no magic involved, just simple observation,' she said.

'That's not what the junior nurses you've trained tell me.'

'Then they need to look at their patients more closely.' She glanced across at him and realised his boots were wet and his trousers sodden to the knee. 'How did you get here?'

'I walked.'

'In this snow?'

'It's not that deep and I felt like some fresh air.'

'Along with pneumonia?'

'This fire is excellent. Why are you ringing the bell?'

'To ask Boris to find you a pair of dry trousers, socks and shoes.'

'Please don't trouble yourself . . . '

'I have no intention of being troubled, which is exactly why I won't continue this conversation until you've changed into dry clothes. And when you have, we'll continue talking over an early dinner. And when we've finished our discussion you will travel back to the hospital with Dr de Vries and Acting Matron Yulia who have kindly accepted an invitation to dine with me tonight.'

He stared at her for a moment. 'You've just reminded me why you made such a good matron.'

Anna Parry's House Hughesovka 1889

The dinner was, as Anna had expected given Lyudmila's skills a good and ample one, which was just as well as Miriam, and Noah's orderly Paul, had accompanied Noah and Yulia. They all retired to the parlour after dinner and Anna found herself sharing a sofa with Noah de Vries while the others became engrossed in a game of Halma.

'It's the latest craze to sweep the hospital,' Noah explained. 'All you can hear in the kitchen at meal breaks is the clack of wooden dolls being pounded on boards.

'You don't play?' Anna asked.

'Only when I'm coerced. Nathan is right about one thing.' He took a cigar from the humidor she offered him. 'We do miss you. It will be good to have you back a few afternoons a week.'

'Not that you'll see much of me, as I'll be in surgery training surgical nurses.'

'I hope you'll be able to spare a little more time, even if it's only long enough to drink a cup of tea.'

'I think I'll be able to manage that. You and Paul have settled into the hospital?'

'We both have especially now Paul has finished hanging curtains and pictures, transforming my tied house into a home. Every doctor should live with a capable orderly who enjoys creating order out of chaos. His efforts are heroic considering we've only been here seven months. I can't believe we'll be celebrating Christmas next week.'

'You and Paul will be coming to my Christmas party.'

'We wouldn't miss it. From what I've heard, the Ignatova Christmas parties are the talk of Hughesovka.'

'They used to be.' Anna agreed, 'but given the losses we've suffered this year I doubt anyone will feel much like celebrating Christmas or the turning of a New Year. Everyone's thoughts will be with Mr Hughes's family and Catherine's. We're not expecting any of Mr Hughes's family to return before the summer, and the Nadolnys' won't leave St Petersburg until after Roman has had his operation. Alexei is staying with Roman and Sonya to support them, although he did say that the twins have some idea of attending the Christmas celebrations in the city with Andrei and Spartak.'

'It might be months before Roman is well enough to travel,' Noah warned.

'I hope our company at Christmas won't be too depleted.'

'We'll all do our best to make it look as though we're more people than we actually are.'

'I can't believe you said that with a straight face.'

'The staff who'll be on duty over Christmas are dreading the holiday.'

Anna didn't have to ask why. 'The last time I spoke to my brother he mentioned that the managers of the works and collieries had discussed holding back a proportion of the workers' wages again, but they decided it wasn't worth trying after what happened last time.'

'Vlad told me there were riots.'

'Five deaths from violence, twelve from alcohol poisoning and we lost count of the number of broken limbs and heads. Glyn asked the manager in accounts to work out roughly what percentage of the wage the average Hughesovka worker receives, is spent in the vodka and beer shops.'

'Fifty percent?' Noah guessed.

'The companies withdraw fifteen thousand roubles from the banks in the town to pay out in wages every week. Twelve thousand are banked in bar takings. I'll leave the percentages for you to work out.'

'Do the workers eat – or pay their landlords for the roof over the heads?' Noah asked.

'Not much if those figures are anywhere near accurate.'

Boris knocked the door. 'Apologies, Dr de Vries, sir, but your coachman is concerned about the weather.'

Noah left his seat, brushed the curtain aside and looked out of the window. Anna joined him. She loved the view over the garden when it snowed. The stone statues of Gorynych the Dragon, Nightingale Robber, White Duck, the Bog Hag and Ivan the Fool that Catherine's father had commissioned when he built the house, were transformed into magical ice encrusted figures.

'It is snowing heavily,' Noah agreed.

'I have taken the liberty of ordering the footmen to bring your coats, sir,' Boris informed him.

'I'm sorry you have to go. Come again soon,' Anna kissed and hugged Yulia and Miriam and after a moment's hesitation, Noah and Paul, but she shook Nathan's hand. 'Please give my guests a flask of brandy for the journey, Boris.'

'I have prepared one, mistress.' Boris opened to the door that led to the hall, revealing the footmen who waited with her guests' coats. Anna stood in the doorway while Boris and Noah's driver spread fur cloaks over Miriam and Yulia. As soon as the bustle of leave taking was over, Noah's driver cracked his whip alongside the ponies and the troika sped along the drive leaving twin tracks like plough furrows. They were covered by fresh snow before the troika turned on to the main drive that led to the gate.

'It's cold, Mistress.' Boris held out Anna's cloak.

'Not that cold, Boris, it never is when snow falls. The cold comes before and later.' She watched the troika diminish in size as it approached the gates.

245

She wished she was inside the sleigh with her friends and colleagues heading to Hughesovka and the hospital. Instead she turned, handed the fur cape Boris had draped around her shoulders back to him and walked inside.

Her footsteps echoed over the marble floor and despite the servants she was suddenly acutely aware of the empty rooms that surrounded her. She had never felt so alone in her life.

CHAPTER TWENTY-TWO

Hughesovka 1889

Nathan Kharber helped Yulia and Miriam from the troika and said goodnight to the driver Noah had hired before heading for the front door.

Noah waylaid him, gripping Nathan's arm through his wolf skin coat before he reached the entrance. 'I saw the new staff rota this afternoon. Barring a catastrophe, earthquake or outbreak of disease, you're not on duty until the day after tomorrow, Dr Kharber.'

'I thought I'd just check . . . '

'The staff will never assume responsibility if you don't give them free rein. If a situation arises they can't cope with, they'll send for you.'

'Force of habit,' Nathan muttered.

'Take a leaf out of Matron Parry's book. Go home, pour yourself a glass of tea, sit in front of a crackling fire and . . . '

Nathan looked at Noah as he hesitated. 'And?' he reiterated.

'Read a medical text book or journal, or even - ' Noah suddenly recalled that Nathan didn't drink alcohol, 'an exciting novel. If you can read Dutch or German I can lend you one, if you don't have any.' He slapped Nathan's back. 'Go, enjoy a rare night off at home with your wife. I'll make sure the hospital doesn't fall down.'

Nathan felt redundant and to his surprise resentful. It proved what he had long suspected and was reluctant to admit, even to himself. He had nothing in his life beyond his work and his patients.

Feeling he had no option but to follow Noah's advice he walked along the path that led around the side of the hospital buildings to the row of staff accommodation behind it. He hesitated when he reached the lane that ran in front of the houses.

Vasya hadn't closed the drapes or shutters in their house, probably so she could watch the snow fall. She took immense pleasure in the simple things. The change of seasons, a flower breaking into bloom in their garden, the rise of a full moon . . . possibly because she also had very little in her life other than the work generated by their house and garden now that their foster children had left.

She was standing at the table in the kitchen, kneading dough. He watched her drop the dough onto a bowl, cover it with a cloth and set it on the shelf to the side of the stove. Every night she made bread and set it to rise, leaving her bed before dawn to bake it so there'd be fresh rolls for breakfast. Nathan was beset by a pang of conscience when he recalled all the times he'd walked out of the house as soon as he'd dressed, insisting he didn't have time to eat. Half the time he couldn't even bring himself to glance at the breakfast table, that Vasya always set with fresh flowers when they were in season, and candles when they weren't.

His guilt didn't subside until he considered what would happen if he entered his house.

The moment he turned his key in the lock Vasya would run and wash her hands. Drying them in her apron to save time, she would rush out and pick up his slippers from the basket in the hall, and continue to fuss over him as stepped inside. She'd help him off with his coat and scarf and while he removed his hat, she would brush down his coat and hang it in the hall cupboard before kneeling to unfasten his boots. After helping him on with his slippers she would usher him to the most comfortable chair in the house, the large one next to the hearth in the living room, while offering him food and drink. And when he refused, she would itemise every single thing she had stored on the shelves of her kitchen cupboards and pantry, taking it as a slight on her housekeeping prowess when he continued to refuse the results of her baking marathons.

He'd tried everything he could think of to stop his wife from fawning over him. The sterner and more abrupt he was, the more subservient she became. He knew she would insist on plying him with food until he'd told her he'd dined in Anna Parry's house and then – Rabbi's niece that she was - she'd demand a list of every morsel that had passed his lips to determine whether or not they were kosher so she could check that he hadn't infringed any of the laws on food with her uncle.

He simply couldn't bear the thought of hearing Vasya's voice or meeting Vasya's reproachful looks after the free and easy atmosphere of Anna Parry's house. He stepped back into the shadows that shrouded the back of the hospital.

There was somewhere he could go even at that hour. Somewhere where he would be assured of a warm welcome and congenial feminine company. If not exactly friends, at least the women wouldn't stutter, stammer and tremble around him.

Glyn's House Hughesovka 1889

'It's strange to see the front of Alexei's house in darkness.' Praskovia carried her mending basket into Glyn's study. Whenever their boys went out for the evening, and Glyn retreated to work on the Edwards's Brothers' collieries' books, Praskovia usually moved her mending basket or embroidery frame into his room so they could sit in comfort together while they worked.

He set down his pen. 'The house seems unnaturally quiet.' Are the boys still at Richard and Sarah's?'

'They are. Richard sent his stable boy to ask if they could stay the night. Ted's tutor offered to give them a lesson on astronomy and Richard's house has more balconies with clearer views than ours.'

'I won't argue with that last observation, Richard and Roman knew what they were doing when they built their houses more than a mile from the works.'

'But they had to wait for their houses to be finished while you simply moved into this one the day you arrived here.'

'And this house has the advantage of being closer to the works, even if the air around it is polluted. Is Ted missing Alexei's twins and Maryanna as much as Pavlo and Tom?'

'If not more. Sarah said he even admitted that he misses Maryanna, but he did add, like toothache. But as Sarah said, as much as he and Maryanna quarrel they're used to one another. If you think about it, our children have more or less been brought up together. Other than the time they spend studying they're either with us or Richard and Sarah or Alexei . . . '

'And Ruth. We can say her name, Praskovia,' Glyn prompted gently when she fell silent.

'It's just that I wish I didn't cry every time I think of, or mention her.'

Glyn hesitated. He wanted to offer Praskovia comfort but he felt all that could be said about Ruth had been. She was gone and her loss would burn with all of them for the rest of their lives. There were no words he could say that would mitigate or soften the blow. 'It's good that the children generally get on well together,' he continued. 'And please note, I did say generally. Our two fight as much as Ted and Maryanna but you heard Pavlo at breakfast bemoaning the loss of Andrei and Spartak as well as the twins and Maryanna.'

'Hopefully Roman and Sonya will return here from St Petersburg early in the summer.' Praskovia tossed Glyn's sock that she'd finished darning back into the basket. 'I wish there was something more I could do to help Roman and Sarah other than pray for successful surgery.'

'We all do.' Glyn picked up his pen again. He dropped it when he heard voices and a shuffling in the passage.

'That will be Misha. He arrived just before I joined you in here. He stayed in the kitchen to talk to Pytor and Yelena and asked if he could see you. I said you could probably spare him a few minutes. But if you're busy . . . '

250

'I'm not.' Glyn reached for his humidor. He needed all the help he could get to ease the strained relationship between him and Praskovia's brother and Misha was partial to a good cigar. 'If anyone knows exactly what's going on in this town it's Misha.'

Praskovia left her chair when she heard a shuffling outside the door. 'Wait, I'll open it.'

Misha carried in the supper tray Yelena had prepared. Glyn cleared a space on his desk so his brother-in-law could set it down.

'Vodka?' Glyn held up a bottle.

'Need you ask?' Misha replied.

'I was being polite. One day you may amaze me.'

'That won't be amazing that will be a miracle.' Praskovia took a plate from the tray and handed it to Glyn.

'Anything happening in town?' Glyn's question was casual, the look he gave Misha anything but.

'People are restless, and drunk.'

'So, nothing new,' Praskovia gave Glyn and her brother knives, forks and linen napkins.

'Any sign of serious trouble?' Glyn pressed Misha, suspecting he was holding something back.

'That depends on what you mean by "sign". The anarchists are unusually quiet, they're drinking in the back room of the Dronov tavern with the railway workers, but if they're intent on stirring them into riot and mayhem they didn't try in front of my spies.'

'How long have the anarchists been drinking in the Dronov?' Glyn speared a slice of smoked salmon and lifted it on to a piece of rye bread.

'A few days, no more. As they were behaving themselves my men let them be. They've all been warned not to look for trouble. I know the anarchists usually drink in Divshitzer tavern. It's unlikely but possible they just want a change of scenery.'

'As you said unlikely, but I'm happier with them fermenting unrest among the railway workers than my colliers.' Glyn bit into the sandwich he'd made.

251

'There were two stabbings in Perevich's tavern south of the river before eight o'clock tonight.'

'Anyone I know?' Glyn asked.

'Grisha's men collecting unpaid "commissions" from coal hewers for their jobs. You know what's they're like when the men refuse to pay "their cut". Grisha has everyone working on a percentage of what they collect, so money, no pay. Yulia stitched and bandaged the victims. Neither man was seriously injured. But Grisha usually sends out a dozen warnings starting with gentle hints and ending with hard fists before conveniently "disappearing" his target. From the state of them, I'd say the coal hewers were less than half way through Grisha's punishment scale.'

'Were the injured men working for Edwards's Brothers or Beletsky and Parry?'

'They're on the books of Beletsky and Parry's Four Bears' pit. I'll ask Richard to have a word with his managers. If the colliers want to continue breathing, they'd better tip Grisha his commission.'

'Anything else happening?' Glyn filled two vodka glasses and pushed one towards Misha.

'A mass brawl that started inside, but spread outside the Zhivopinsk tavern.'

'Between?' Glyn raised an eyebrow.

'Cossacks and Mongols.'

'They don't usually fight.' Glyn thought for a moment. 'Do they?'

'They do when the Mongols accuse the Cossacks of fixing a horse race.'

'Did they?'

'Of course. Cheating is in our blood. I confiscated both horses to prevent a rerun of the race and negotiated a somewhat fragile truce between the warring factions but I've cancelled all leave until the second week of the New Year.'

'That's a bit harsh on your soldiers and more especially their wives and children,' Praskovia admonished.

'I put all the unmarried men on patrol duty to free the married men to attend mass with their families, if they want to go. Aside from church they can celebrate Christmas and the New Year with their families a little later than most. It won't be the first time.'

Praskovia had learned from experience there was no such things as a short argument with her brother, capitulating, she turned to her husband. 'I promised my mother I'd go through the menus for next week. If you want me, I'll be in the kitchen.'

Knowing that Yelena would have kept a selection of sandwiches and cakes in the kitchen for the servants' supper, Praskovia picked up her empty plate and left.

'You are expecting trouble over the holy days?' Glyn questioned Misha after she closed the door. It wasn't a question.

'There are grumblings to be heard in every corner of the town. You and your brother employ two of the Goldberg boys Nathan Kharber adopted, don't you?'

'Ifim and Naum. What of it?'

'Have they caused you any problems?'

'Alf Mahoney has mentioned that Naum has a big mouth and enjoys an argument.' He didn't elaborate. 'Knowing Alf, I assume that meant he was keeping the boy in check. Are they anarchists?'

'They are both among the ringleaders.'

'I thought most of the anarchists were anti-Semitic Russians and Cossacks. Naum and Ifim are Jews. Why would the anarchists let them join?'

'Men of all persuasions hate the Tsar. And war makes strange bedfellows. Even rats from warring tribes can sink their differences when it comes to killing mice.' Misha downed his vodka and took the bottle from Glyn who offered it to him.

'You have ears in rat holes?' Glyn questioned.

'I have men undercover in all areas of the town, especially the drinking dens.'

253

'And no one has recognised them as soldiers?' Glyn was incredulous.

'The idea came to me when I was in the hospital with nothing better to do other than stare at the ceiling. I wondered if we would have picked up any gossip before the assassination attempt if I'd had men posted in the beer shops. I asked two of my captains to go to the barracks in St Petersburg and pick out twenty recruits who possessed intelligence but looked like peasants. They found nineteen. We trained them in St Petersburg and briefed them on the situation in Hughesovka during the months it took them to grow their hair. As soon as we considered them up the task we let them loose in the town.'

'Does anyone know their identity?'

'Other than all nineteen of them, me and three of my senior officers, no.'

'Why three?'

'I try to make sure that at least one of the four of us is on duty in case one of them hits trouble.'

'Do I know them?'

Misha smiled. 'You've probably seen them around. They're not only in the taverns. We have five working in the Edwards' Brothers collieries, another four in the Beletsky and Parry pits, four in the iron works and the remainder, as I said, in taverns and vodka shops.'

'What happens if they're caught up in something illegal and arrested and the fire brigade refuse to send a message to the barracks?'

'That's one of the reasons I'm here.' Misha unbuttoned his pocket and pulled out two sealed envelopes. 'May I impose on you and Richard Parry and ask you not to open either of these, but to keep them safe until such time as you receive a message from someone requiring identification.'

'You may.' Glyn took the envelopes. 'I have a safe here and Richard has one in his house. I can vouch for his security as well as mine.'

'I'll sleep easier knowing that.'

'Another vodka?' Glyn offered.

'No, thank you, I'm on duty tonight.'

'The hot-headed young captain really has reformed into a middle-aged colonel?' Glyn raised his eyebrows.

'I can't ask my men to obey rules I break. But I will eat some more of that salmon.'

'Help yourself. You said the delivery of these,' Glyn held up the envelopes, 'was one of the reasons you're here. You have another?'

'I do.'

Glyn waited while Misha swallowed the salmon in his mouth.

'It must be serious, you look as though you're about to choke.'

When Misha began speaking he talked quickly. Almost too quickly for Glyn to follow what he was saying. 'It's about your daughter.'

'Harriet Maud?' Glyn had no idea why he'd repeated her name. He had only one daughter born to him and his estranged wife Betty after she'd insisted on remaining in Merthyr in 1869, when he left for Hughesovka. He'd wanted to be a part of Harriet Maud's life but Betty had categorically refused to allow him to see her, not even telling him of Harriet's existence until she had turned up in Hughesovka three years after their parting on Merthyr station.

'What about her?' Glyn demanded.

'You know she's employed as a teacher in the barracks' school for soldiers' children?'

'I do,' Glyn had made it his business to watch over Harriet as much as he could from a distance, despite her mother's antagonism towards him. Furious when he'd refused to leave his Russian mistress Praskovia or their child, Betty had remained in Hughesovka and opened a boarding house. Determined to make Glyn's life as difficult as she could, Betty refused to speak to or acknowledge Glyn, or allow any contact between father and daughter while Glyn continued to live with Praskovia.

255

Glyn had dealt with the situation the only way open to him, by ignoring it, while relishing the few chance glimpses he caught of the dark haired and eyed daughter Betty had refused to allow him to own as his.

'Harriet Maud and I have come to know one another well . . . ' Misha began.

'How well?' Glyn growled.

'I have always behaved honourably towards Harriet. I know that you and I haven't always seen eye to eye and-' Misha hesitated as he searched for the right words.

'Spit it out,' Glyn snapped.

Opting for honesty, Misha blurted, 'I'm in love with Harriet and have asked her to marry me.'

'What did Harriet – and her mother say to your offer?'

'Harriet agreed but her mother barred me from her house, which made little difference as Harriet hasn't lived with her mother for two years. Not since she took the teaching post in the barracks' school.'

'I see.' Glyn's mouth twitched. Misha couldn't tell whether it was in disapproval or humour. 'I don't find Betty's reaction surprising if half the rumours I've heard about the way you treated Alice Perkins before she divorced you are true.'

'I admit I treated Alice badly and I take full blame for the breakdown of my marriage.'

'That's noble of you. Do you intend to treat Harriet any better?'

'I'm not the man I was twenty years ago, sir. I've spent the last fifteen years building my career. I am now a respectable colonel with an excellent salary, a healthy bank account and a good pension which will enable me to keep my wife in style. I also have a rent-free house, staffed by a cook, groom and servants within the confines of the barracks, and enough money to buy a similar if not better house when I retire. Harriet Maud will want for nothing-'

'I believe you.'

'Then you give us your blessing?'

'How can I give you and Harriet Maud and you my blessing to marry when I have never met her?'

'You could if I brought her here to meet you.'

'She wants to meet me?'

'She does.'

'And her mother?'

'Hasn't a good word to say about you, so I doubt she'd be pleased at the thought of you meeting Harriet. But then Harriet doesn't visit her mother often. It's not surprising they aren't close, Harriet is more like you than Betty. When she says something, it is the truth, and when she gives her word she means it.'

Seeing past the flattery, Glyn said, 'Have you asked Betty for permission to marry Harriet Maud?'

'Yes.'

'And?'

'She threw me out of the house, and threatened to set Grisha's men on me.'

'I know Grisha lodges with her, are they so close he allows her to give his men orders?'

'Alice is Betty's best friend as well as Grisha's wife.'

'You say Harriet has accepted your proposal?'

'She has. I offered to marry her in the Russian Orthodox church or Welsh chapel whichever she prefers.'

'Ignoring Betty's objections?'

'Harriet's mother not only refuses to allow me into her house, she refuses to talk to me. But Harriet knows why I came here. She asked me to give you this.' He slipped his hand inside his pocket again and removed another envelope.

Glyn turned it over. 'Do you know what's in here?'

'I do, because Harriet asked me to read it.'

Glyn opened the letter. The writing was clear with beautifully formed letters that reminded him of his mother's hand.

Dear Father,

It seems very strange to write those words when we have never spoken to one another, although I have seen you often and I know who you are. I hope you don't mind me calling you "Father". Misha told me that you are a kind man, a good father to your sons and very much in love with his sister.
He believes you will agree to meet me. I hope he is right. There are so many things I would like to ask you and with your permission, I would also like to meet my half-brothers.
Your daughter,
Harriet Maud Edwards.

'Will you see her, sir?' Misha had to repeat his question twice before Glyn replied and when he did his voice shook.

'Tell I would be honoured.'

CHAPTER TWENTY-THREE

Koshka's Hughesovka 1889

'I'm sorry you had to wait, Nathan.' Adele apologised as she joined him in one of the "general rooms" that were kept for use when the maids changed beds and cleaned the "ladies" personal rooms between clients.

'It's me who should apologise. I made no appointment.'

'You could have seen one of the others . . . '

'I wanted to see you.'

Koshka had asked Nathan Kharber to examine her girls on a weekly basis when John Hughes appointed him chief doctor at the hospital. In addition to his fee, it was suggested by Koshka's "ladies" that he avail himself of the "complimentary benefits" of the house. It took a great deal of coaxing before he accepted the offer, but he'd only ever availed himself of Adele's services, and only then after he'd treated her for a dislocated jaw. The result of an altercation with one of her rougher clients.

'I'm here now,' she gave him a professional smiled and caressed his cheek with the palm of her hand. 'Would you like a drink – something to eat – '

'I've just eaten.' He checked she'd locked the door before removing his jacket and hanging it on the valet stand.

She went to the bed and turned down the cover to display pristine starched sheets. 'I'm glad you came tonight. I've been meaning to talk to you.'

'You have a medical problem?'

'Only old age, I've decided to retire.'

'You're leaving Hughesovka?' He felt as though his heart had leapt from his ribcage into his mouth.

'No. I'm staying in Hughesovka to help Koshka run the house but I will no longer be entertaining clients.'

'But why . . . '

'I'm nearly fifty years old, Nathan. There comes a time in every whore's life when she wants to sleep, not work, in her bed.'

'Please, won't you make an exception and keep seeing me? I can pay . . .'

'This isn't about money, Nathan. In fact, I've just bought one of the apartments in the block that's been built behind the garden here. It's a quiet spot and the building is spacious and well-constructed. My self-contained unit has five rooms, a kitchen and bathroom, and two fine balconies overlooking the gardens.'

'If you're talking about the house Koshka has had built, it looks finished.'

'It is. I'll be moving in next week but the owner of the apartments is supposed to be a secret.'

'Few secrets are kept in Hughesovka, even Koshka's.'

'That's a depressing thought.' She considered for a moment while undressing. Thanks to Koshka's innovated design of a gown fastened by a single button worn over a chemise, stockings and garters and nothing else, it didn't take her long. She untied the ribbon at the neck of her chemise, stepped out of it and laid it over a chair. Naked, she looked across the room at him.

He returned her gaze as he continued to unbutton his shirt.

She looked down at her body. 'You could do a lot better than me, Nathan. We have very beautiful younger girls in the house, with firm muscles, upturned breasts and trim waistlines . . .'

'I've examined them,' he reminded her.

'I thought that was professionally in your capacity as a doctor.'

'It was, but doctors are allowed to admire feminine beauty.'

It was difficult to determine given his sallow skin but she thought he'd blushed.

'It's you I want,' he said simply.

'Only because you're accustomed to me. You would soon become used to a replacement in your bed.'

'It's far more than what we do in bed,' he insisted. 'I can talk to you about almost anything.'

'All the girls are trained to be good listeners.'

'I . . . like you.' He stammered. 'I thought you liked me.'

'I do, very much.' Adele knew something of Nathan's life from the glimpses he'd given her during the conversations they'd shared over the years. She knew he filled his days and nights with work to stave off feelings of isolation and loneliness.

He'd been visiting her bed on an almost weekly basis for nearly two decades but it had taken her five years to coax him to confide his sexual preferences, which were more adventurous than she'd given him credit for when she'd first met him, and another five before he'd said anything remotely personal. The one subject he never discussed was his relationship with his wife, but he didn't need to. The way he touched and kissed her said more about that than any words.

Modest to the point of prudery, self-effacing, hidebound by the innumerable, and to her, incomprehensible rules of his religion, she knew he'd prefer to remain silent rather than risk upsetting her by voicing opinions she might find distasteful.

He walked to the side of the bed climbed in and divested himself of his underwear under cover of the blankets. She stepped in, rolled alongside his naked body, wrapped her arms around him and entwined her legs into his.

'You're cold.' She ran her hands down from his nipples to his thighs, slipping her fingers between his legs.

He gripped her wrists, immobilising her hands. 'Will you continue to see me?' he questioned.

'I've always been honest with you, Nathan.'

'You have.'

———

261

'As I said, you wouldn't be my only client. I have already agreed to continue to see one other regular . . . '

'Who?' His voice sharpened.

'I told you that discretion is essential for a whore?'

'I wish you wouldn't call yourself that.'

'Your friendship can't make me anything else, Nathan. It's what I am.'

He relaxed his hold on her hands and she continued to move her fingers lightly tantalizingly.

'Will you continue to see me?'

'If you make an appointment I will make every effort to be available.'

'Every Monday afternoon after I examine the rest of the ladies?'

'If that is your preferred time, I will ensure that I am free.'

He moved closer to her under the covers and lifted her on top of him. He gripped her buttocks hard, and pulled her down.

She drew her breath in, gasping as he entered her.

'Thank . . . ' Anticipating what he was about to say, she silenced him by the simple expedient of placing her mouth over his.

'I'm only alive in the time I spend with you,' he murmured, when he could speak again.

She was half asleep, one of his hands on her breast, the other between her thighs when he asked, 'may I stay the night?'

'Yes.'

'We'll talk again over breakfast before I have to leave for the hospital.'

Nadolny's Palace, St Petersburg December 1889

Sonya stood at the window and watched Manfred and Franz fix the ramp into the slots the carpenter had made at the side of the carriage.

Once they secured it, Manfred stepped inside the carriage and eased Roman's chair out of the vehicle and down on to the paved portico.

Sonya remained where she was. Roman had become more vociferous in his protests against what he referred to as "fussing" whenever anyone tried to help him. She didn't have long to wait. The butler tapped the door, opened it and Roman wheeled himself into their drawing room.

She smiled. A smile he returned with interest.

'Doctor Grunwasser has fixed a date for your operation, and soon,' she said.

'Franz and Manfred are behind me, so how do you know?'

'Your smile. Will it be before Christmas?'

'No.' He wheeled himself to the drinks tray and picked up a bottle of cognac. He held it up to her. She nodded. 'It will be in the New Year.'

She bit her lip to stop it from trembling. She knew precisely why he'd set the date for the New Year. He wanted to enjoy what might well turn out to be his last Christmas with her and the boys.

'January?' she asked hoarsely as he filled two glasses.

'I thought I'd wait until after the baby is born. You said she will be here by the end of the month at the latest.' He kissed his fingertips and touched her baby bump.

Not trusting herself to speak, she buried her hands in his hair and stroked his head.

'I will survive the operation, Sonya,' he said.

'The surgeon told you that you will?'

'He's certain I'll survive but he'll give me no guarantee that I'll walk again. He lectured me at length, ignoring my protests that I had heard all the arguments against my proceeding several times.'

'What if he's wrong and you don't survive?' She felt the slow crawl of a tear trickling down her face and lifted her hand to brush it away.

———

263

'If there's the slightest chance that I can regain the use of my legs, I will take it. Anything has to be better than this half-life.'

'You have me and the boys and whatever this little one turns out to be. You don't have to lie in bed. You can travel, talk, think and work from your chair. Is your life so unbearable that you'll risk losing it in the hope of recovering the ability to walk?'

'No.' He handed her one of the glasses he'd poured. Grasping her free hand with his, he pulled her down on to his lap. 'If this was all the life I had left, I'd take it and be glad, sweetheart.'

'Then why risk the operation?'

'Because the surgeon studied Nathan Kharber's and Noah de Vries's notes. The one thing he is certain of after examining me, is that the bullet is moving. A fraction the wrong way could sever my spinal cord or a blood vessel.'

Her hand flew to her mouth.

'I don't want to leave you sweetheart and I don't want to die. You and my children are my world. I'll take this risk, just to have a while longer with you, and who knows, it may be longer than a while and you'll end up being sick of me.' He wrapped his arms around her and kissed her lips.

'I could never be sick of you. Not if God gave you and me another thousand years.'

He laughed. 'I wouldn't look very pretty after a thousand years and although I hate to admit it, I don't think you would either.'

'I wouldn't care how you looked as long as you were with me.' She locked her hands around his neck and returned his kiss.

'So, you understand why I have to go ahead with the operation?'

'I do.' Sonya climbed off his lap at a knock on the door. The butler walked in and announced Alexei.

Roman reached for the cognac bottle and fresh glass.

Sonya went to Alexei and kissed his cheek. 'This is a lovely surprise, Alexei.'

'You find your house unbearably quiet as the twins and Maryanna have gone ice skating with Andrei and Spartak?' Roman handed him the cognac he'd poured.

'Peaceful rather than empty,' Alexei said. 'I had a letter from Kira. I thought you'd like to read it Sonya.' He took it from his pocket and handed it to her.

Sonya opened it and began reading. 'She seems happy with Morgan.'

'I thought so.' Alexei agreed.

'And there's not a single word of regret for the elaborate wedding that Catherine planned and she and Morgan decided to cancel in order to observe mourning for Catherine and Mr Hughes.'

'There isn't,' Alexei sat on the sofa opposite Roman. 'But after all it's the marriage itself that's important, not the pomp, ceremony or even the prayers.'

Sonya finished reading the letter and handed it to Roman. 'Kira told me that she couldn't have gone ahead with the ceremony in Ignatova church because she would have felt that she and Morgan were looking at Catherine's coffin.'

'It was fitting for the first wedding ceremony in Hughesovka's church to be between a Russian bride and a Welshman.' Alexei sipped his cognac and set his glass on a sofa table. 'Even if I hadn't received the letter I would have visited to hear the doctor's verdict.' He looked expectantly at Roman.

'I've decided to allow Dr Grunwasser to operate.'

As Alexei couldn't think of anything to say, he nodded.

'To quote the doctor, "the bullet is not stable." It has moved since Dr Kharber operated on me and could move again at any time.'

'And sever the spinal cord?'

'Or a blood vessel,' Roman added.

'When will Dr Grunwasser operate?'

'After our daughter is born,' Roman laid his hand on Sonya's stomach.

'And until then Roman will live quietly and do as he is told,' Sonya added.

'Really?' Alexei raised a sceptical eyebrow in Roman's direction.

'Of course.' Roman winked at him.

'I told the boys to bring the girls back here. You'll join us for dinner?' Sonya asked.

'Thank you, I will, but I'd better send my groom to warn the cook we won't be in tonight.'

Encouraged by her unexpected success, Sonya continued, 'Have you thought about your Christmas and New Year celebrations yet?'

Despite all her offers and pleading, she had yet to elicit an acceptance from Alexei that he, the twins and Maryanna would be their guests over the holidays.

'That is one of the reasons I've come here. I was hoping you'd invite the girls and Maryanna to stay with you over the holidays because they are so looking forward to the Christmas and New Year balls and parties.'

'We'd love to have Maryanna and the twins and even their grumpy father although he retires to the card room at every ball he attends and doesn't emerge until the orchestra packs up.'

Roman eyed Alexei. 'You won't be attending any balls, even in the card room. You want to go home, don't you?' he asked intuitively

'I do,' Alexei admitted.

'Home? You mean Hughesovka?' Sonya was surprised.

'Yes.'

'Why, Alexei. With your twins here, and Catherine gone there's nothing for you there.'

'I know.'

'It's Christmas Eve tomorrow. Surely it would be better to spend it here with Kitty, Olga and baby Ruth . . . '

'I've wrapped their and Maryanna's and your family's presents and I was hoping you'd allow me to put them under your tree. Baby Ruth and wet nurse Olena will be travelling with me.'

'You can't travel with a baby this time of year. . . '

'I'll see she's well wrapped up. There's a train leaving early tomorrow morning that will take me to Moscow, from there I'll get a train to Kharkov . . . '

'But you'll be stuck all alone in some dreadful hotel in Moscow . . . '

'I won't be alone, I'll have Ruth and Olena . . . '

'There are good hotels in Moscow,' Roman reminded Sonya mildly.

'Not at Christmas when everyone is with their family. And after Kharkov. What then? Who knows what trains will be running where. You could get stuck in some horrid way station . . . '

'Very possibly, but if I do, I'll have no one to blame but myself.'

Sonya realised she was losing the argument and turned to Roman. 'Talk some sense into him, please.'

'You want to be with Ruth that much?' Roman asked.
'Yes.'

'I understand why, but the snow is heavier than it's been for years. And as Sonya said you might well get stuck if you try travelling while it's falling and that won't be fun with a baby.'

'Ruth is resilient. I'll make sure that she and Olena won't freeze. As for myself, it doesn't matter.'

'Because you'll be on your way to your wife?'
'Exactly.'

The front door opened and the sound of the girl's laughter and Andrei and Spartak's voices drifted from the hall.

'You'll stay to dinner tonight?'

'Yes. And I'll take the girls home so they can pack. I'll bring them back tomorrow morning on my way to the station.'

267

Sonya went to the door. 'I'll order the housekeeper to prepare rooms for them.'

'Thank you, Sonya.' Alexei turned to Roman. 'And thank you, both of you for your understanding.'

CHAPTER TWENTY-FOUR

Ignatova Estate early hours of January 1ˢᵗ 1890

As the last fireworks burnt out in a glittering shower of blue and white sparks, there were deafening shouts of, 'Blwyddyn Newydd Dda, Happy New Year! Novy God! S Novim Godom! Frohes neues Jahr! Bonne Annee!' in a babble of Welsh, English, Russian, Ukrainian, Dutch, German, and French . . . and those were only the languages Anna recognised.

The cries echoed up to the sky from the carriage halt in front of the portico of the Ignatova mansion before dying into the deep dark velvet, snow laden night.

Glyn Edwards stepped forward and looked down the drive. He cupped his hands around his mouth and shouted, 'where is Ded Moroz, with his granddaughter Snegurochka?'

On cue a beautifully decorated wooden horse drawn sleigh rounded the corner that led out of the stable yard at the back of the house. The jingle of dozens of small silver bells woven into the branches of greenery and ropes of ivy that festooned the vehicle added a ghostly music box background. Vlad, dressed for the occasion in old fashioned blue Ignatova livery, drove the sleigh, Glyn's brother Edward sat in the back, his features obscured by an enormous false beard and moustache. He wore the white fur trimmed blue velvet long coat and trousers of Ded Moroz - Grandfather Frost, the Russian Father Christmas. Next to him was Lyudmila's ten-year-old granddaughter Dina, dressed in a blue velvet, white fur trimmed gown, in the guise of Ded Moroz's granddaughter, Snegurochka, the snow maiden. Wedged between them were sacks of toys, books and carved wooden figures.

269

The horses made painstakingly slow progress through the avenue of burning torches, as parents held back children eager to run to and touch Ded Moroz and Snegurochka.

'Wait for the sleigh to stop,' Boris shouted as the children of the estate workers surged forward. Anna was relieved when Vlad, anticipating the rush, managed to draw the ponies to a halt before a child ended up under the wheels.

'We have set a chair for you next to the Christmas tree in the hall, Ded Moroz,' Anna shouted loud enough for all the children to hear.

'I will carry one of your sacks for you, Ded Moroz,' Glyn stepped forward and swung one on to his back while Vlad lifted the others from the sleigh and handed them out to Pavlo, Tom and Ted.

'Looks like I'm just in time to help.' Alexei took a sack from Vlad.

'Alexei!' Sarah and Praskovia ran forward and hugged him. He dropped the sack and hugged them in turn before Lyudmila grabbed him.

'Where are Olga, Kitty and Maryanna?' she demanded.

'Kitty, is she here?' Pavlo looked around expecting to see her behind her father.

'I can't see the girls,' Tom complained.

'That's because they're in St Petersburg, too far away to see even with a telescope,' Alexei answered. 'They send you, Tom and Ted their love.'

'When are they coming home?'

'They're having such a good time in St Petersburg I'm not expecting them until the end of the winter season. Summer at the earliest.'

Pavlo's face fell and Alexei wondered if there was more than friendship between him and Kitty.

'It's good to see you, Alexei.' Anna joined him as he watched the tide of estate children surge towards Ded Moroz and Snegurochka. 'Have you been home?'

'Yes, I left Ruth and her wet nurse with Lada, who was complaining she'd had no time to prepare for my arrival. The baby posed no problem because she and the nurse can sleep in the girls' room. But apparently Lada had ordered Lev to take my bedroom apart as, according to her, "it needs a thorough cleaning which will take at least another two days". Lada was making so much noise I rousted the stable boy and asked him to saddle Ariston. So here I stand before you, a homeless beggar soliciting hospitality because his servants have thrown him out of his own house.'

'The homeless beggar is more than welcome to stay as long as he likes. I'll tell Boris to have your old room prepared for you.'

'No need to upset the entire house, a blanket and sofa will do.'

'Catherine would turn in her grave if she thought her grandson would be reduced to sleeping on a sofa in his ancestral home. 'You'll have your old room and a properly made up bed.'

'Yes, matron.' He removed his hat and rugged his forelock in mock subservience, 'and thank you, matron.'

'Idiot.' Anna glanced down at Alexei's boots and trousers. They were sodden. He'd obviously been kneeling in the snow and didn't take much thought to realise exactly where. 'I'm sorry . . . '

'Don't be.' He saw her glance in the direction of the churchyard. 'I confess, I'm here because I couldn't stay away from Ruth, and as Lada gave me the perfect excuse to ride here. I spent the last hour with my dead watching the fireworks from their resting place and sending Ruth, my mother, grandmother and sisters, Christmas and New Year greetings.'

'I understand.'

He looked into her eyes 'If anyone does it's you, Anna. You've never said much about your parents or the brothers and sisters you lost but it's not hard to see how much you and Richard miss them.'

271

'We carry our dead with us wherever we go, Alexei.'

'I'd like to believe that, but when I look for a sign from Ruth, I feel as though she's fallen into an abyss where I can't hear, see or reach her. And when I try to remember her, it's as if that same abyss has consumed even my memories of her and every moment we spent together.'

'It can take years for memories to return especially the happy ones.'

'How do you survive those years?'

Moved by the depth of misery in Alexei's eyes, Anna gave him the only answer she could. 'One minute, one hour, one day at a time. And while you're trying to survive you dare not allow yourself to look to the future.'

'That requires a strength and patience I don't possess.'

'Your daughters will help you, Alexei, if you ask them.' She heard a noise and turned. Vlad was driving the empty sleigh back to the stables. Everyone had gone into the house leaving her and Alexei alone outside.

Alexei walked to the edge of the balustrade and looked beyond the limits of the estate to the church and graveyard. Lights flickered in the windows of the church and smaller candles burned among the gravestones, a reminder to both the dead and the living that those buried there were remembered. Even at a distance the white marble Beletsky memorial gleamed with reflected light and Anna wondered just how many candles Alexei had lit and placed around the grave.

'The flame of a candle shines bright on a dark winter's night,' she said.

'Even inside a church. Father Grigor is welcoming the New Year into God's house.'

'He is holding a mass in the New Church in town tomorrow.'

'It's finished?' he asked.

'No, but that won't stop Father Grigor.'

He gave a short mirthless laugh. 'No, it won't. Not a determined man of faith like him. When God is with you, no roof is needed.'

272

'May I ask you to escort me?'

'To an Orthodox Mass? It will be long – very long - and without the interest of a baptism, wedding or funeral.'

'I know, but I feel that by going I would in some small way be remembering Catherine.'

Without giving a thought to Anna's aversion to men, Alexei slipped his arm around her shoulders. 'My grandmother loved you like a daughter, Anna. It would be my privilege to escort you.'

Anna's muscles tensed. She'd known Alexei for over twenty years. She couldn't hurt his feelings by shrinking from him. Not when he was mourning Ruth.

Too late Alexei recalled that Anna didn't like being touched. By then they were entering the house. As she hadn't shrugged off his arm, he left it draped around her shoulders. They pushed their way through the throng in the hall where Edward and Dina were enjoying themselves, doling out gifts to the estate children.

'Welcome home, Alexei.' Richard pushed a glass of vodka into his hand. 'We've missed you.'

'I've missed you too.' Alexei looked around the crowded hall and realised he meant it. These were his people, this was his town, his place. With Sonya caring for the girls he had nothing to worry about but baby Ruth and business. As for his arm, it was still around Anna's shoulders. He made no effort to move it. Somehow it seemed to belong there

CHAPTER TWENTY-FIVE

Ignatova Estate May 1892

Anna enjoyed the troika ride back from the hospital in all seasons, especially when the warmth of the sun melted the snows and early summer touched the steppe. The scent of blossom from the fruit trees and birdsong filled the air and if she looked carefully she occasionally spotted rabbits at play among the burgeoning grass, and behind them, stalking foxes.

The three afternoons she'd initially volunteered to assist at the hospital had become four full days within a month of her starting the training sessions for nurses. But the women and men she trained were bright and intelligent and after a year she managed to cut the time she spent at the hospital down to two days a week. Now she was well into her second year she was confident that she could reduce the time to one day a week by the end of the summer.

She saw Alexei's horse Ariston tethered to the railings of the graveyard and asked the groom who was driving her to stop. She knew Alexei visited Ruth's grave every day, but she'd also noticed that the amount of time he spent there had gradually diminished over two years that had elapsed since Ruth had been killed.

Alexei saw her leave the troika and went to meet her at the gate. 'I was hoping to catch you driving home.'

'Come to dinner?' she invited. 'Lyudmila and Boris would love to see you.'

'Do they like feeding beggars?'

'You're hardly a beggar.'

She watched him untie Ariston's reins. 'I called in to see Ruth between operations today.'

'Lada and Olena told me. Did you call as a nurse or her godmother?'

'Her godmother but I couldn't resist checking her over. She's blooming, Alexei. A beautiful child in perfect health, and her English is as good as her Russian.'

'I wish I could take credit, but it's all down to Olena who speaks excellent English. In fact, that's one of the things I was hoping to have a word with you about.'

'One of the things – you have a list?'

'I do.'

'So, this meeting really wasn't accidental?'

'Knowing your generosity, I confess was expecting an invitation to dinner. Lada's a good cook, but not as good as Lyudmila. And if you tell Lada I said that, I'll say you made it up.'

'There's no need to issue threats to keep my silence. Your secret is safe with me, and Lyudmila is a good cook.'

He looked up at the sky. 'As my grandmother used to say at this time of year, "the trees are blossoming to blot out the memory of the winter snows". It's a fine evening, shall we walk to the house.' He offered her his arm.

'Yes, but it's unfair to keep the groom waiting. I'll send him on ahead.'

'I'll tie my horse to the back so the boys in the stable can unsaddle and feed him.

After she'd spoken to the groom and Alexei had given the man orders to care for Ariston, Anna slipped her hand into the crook of Alexei's elbow. He closed his fingers over hers.

'That feels good.'

'It does?' Her voice trembled but she kept her grip on his elbow.

'To have a woman's hand on my arm. I've been missing the twins but what chance does a mere father have of competing with White Night Balls in St Petersburg? I just hope they're behaving themselves for Sonya.'

'They are and they're having the time of their lives.'

'I knew it. Admit it. They do write to you?'

'They do.'

275

'And tell you things they wouldn't dare tell their father?'

'I am their godmother.' She smiled as she reminded him.

'Just answer me one question. Do I have anything to worry about?'

'Not immediately.'

'I don't find that reply in the least reassuring.' He stood back and took a deep breath when they reached the gates of the mansion. 'Living in Hughesovka I've forgotten what fresh air smells like.'

The gatekeeper's wife waved to them and they waved back.

'This is your home much more than mine, Alexei. The east wing looks very sad shuttered up. Do you intend to leave it empty to moulder in damp and decay?'

'You want me to rent it out?'

'That would depend on who you intend to rent it to.'

'That's one of the things I wanted to talk to you about.' He gave her a sideways look. 'Have you been writing to the girls about moving here?'

'No.'

'Not exerting the slightest pressure about there being enough space for all three of them to have their own rooms?'

Her mouth twitched. 'You must admit, Alexei, there is more room for them here, and the twins are eighteen on their next birthday. That is an age when girls appreciate privacy, even from their twin.'

'They've always done everything together . . . '

'Which is wonderful when they both want company. But they're no longer children. What happens if one of them wants privacy – to think – to dream – to sneak a glass of vodka, or a cigarette without anyone – especially her father, or even her twin knowing?

'Much as I adore Richard who's the best possible older brother I could have, there have been times when his interference in my life has been unwelcome. Especially when he tries to behave more like an overbearing father than brother.'

'I know what you mean. There have been occasions when I've had to curb myself when he starts lecturing me on mine safety. A subject he's an expert and I'm a novice on. But that doesn't make it any the more fascinating for me to listen to. Have the girls written to you about the governess Sonya has hired to look after them.'

'Countess Cernograza? Yes, they have. They appear to adore her.'

'So, I understand. Sonya has written to tell me that she trusts her implicitly to chaperon the girls to balls and parties, although from what she and the girls have written Andrei and Spartak take care of them and Maryanna, as well, if not better than any doting father or guard dog.'

'A great deal better from what they've written to me and probably better than they would like. Maryanna said it's just as well there are only two Nadolny brothers, otherwise she and the twins would never have an opportunity to dance with any other young men.'

Alexi stopped before they turned from the drive on to the carriage halt. 'I'd forgotten how beautiful it is here. Or perhaps I never took the time needed to look around when I lived here with my grandmother after my father threw me out.'

'Do the young ever take time to stop and look around?'

'If someone heard you say that and couldn't see you, they might be forgiven for believing you were ninety.'

'Sometimes I feel as though I'm ninety-three not thirty-three.' She hadn't intended to put so much feeling into her reply, but the words were out before she could retract them.

'Tough day?' Alexei greeted the doorman and gave him his coat as they walked into the house.

'We lost a patient,' she admitted.

'Anyone I know?'

'A three-year-old girl tumbled from a ladder trying to climb out of one of the hole houses. She landed face down on a wooden box, and fractured her skull. Nathan and Noah did their best but there was simply too much damage to her brain.'

'Those houses are a disgrace.'

'The problem is people keep flooding into Hughesovka even though they know competition for jobs is fierce, simply because the wages and conditions for those who are lucky enough to find work are better than anywhere else in Russia. More than double for some trades according to Glyn.'

'The people should be turned back.'

'From where?' she asked.

'The outskirts of town. No one should travel here without guarantee of lodgings and work.'

'Noah and I talked to her family. They arrived here a week ago from an estate east of St Petersburg. They'd heard Hughesovka was a town where no one went hungry or lacked a roof over their head. The owner of their estate hadn't visited it since serfdom was abolished thirty years ago. Most of the peasants there were hungry and destitute. Rather than wait for death they walked here carrying their only possessions – their children. The father said they would have starved on arrival if it wasn't for Father Grigor's soup kitchen. I sent him to Beletsky and Parry's offices and told him to put his name down on the list of men looking for work.'

'The last time I looked we could paper the offices twice over with those lists,' Alexi said. 'But if you have his name, give it to me and I'll see what I can do.'

'You'll move him to the top of the list?' she asked hopefully.

'If I did that I'd cause a riot, not to mention make an enemy of Grisha for appointing people without his approval, and I can't afford to do either.'

'Sometimes, I think that man wields more power than anyone else in Hughesovka.'

'He does.'

Alexei followed her into the small parlour that overlooked the orchards at the side of the house. Boris appeared.

'Can I get you anything, Mistress?'

'Mr Beletsky is staying to dine, Boris. Rather than use the dining room we'll eat in here, that's if you have no objection Alexei?'

'That sounds good to me.'

'Do you wish me to convey any choices for the meal to Lyudmila, Mistress?'

'Any preference, Alexei.'

'Only for Lyudmila's cooking, Boris.'

'We'll eat at the usual time, thank you, Boris.' Anna said as he helped her off with her coat.

Boris folded it over his arm. 'Would you like me to pour you a drink, Mistress?'

'I'll do it, Boris.' Alexei looked at the drinks tray. He held up a bottle he recognised as Lyudmila's brewing. 'Cherry cordial?'

'Sounds lovely,' Anna replied. 'There should be ice in the bucket.'

'There is, mistress,' Boris took Alexei's coat, hat and scarf, and placed them on top of Anna's coat.

'I didn't doubt it, Boris. Thank you.' Anna curled up in one of the enormous thickly upholstered chairs that had been angled to get the best view from the window. She took the glass of cordial Alexei handed her and sipped it. 'Mm Nectar.'

'No one makes cordial like Lyudmila.'

'So, from our conversation earlier I take it the girls want you to move into your half of the house.'

'You know full well they do.'

'And?'

'Do you have any objections?'

'None whatsoever. If you should need more room I could always move out . . . '

'More room? We'll be coming from a two-bedroomed cottage to a ten-bedroomed self-contained wing and that's without the rooms downstairs. And to be honest you are part of the attraction.'

Anna felt the blood draining from her face. Had Alexei read more into their friendship than she'd intended. 'I . . . '

'Sonya's been marvellous,' he continued quickly as if he'd read her mind, 'but I can't rely on her to look after the girls every time they want to go to St Petersburg. Not when she has the baby as well as Roman to care for.'

'Have you heard anything recently . . . '

'Not since Sonya's last letter. She wrote that the surgeon confirmed that Roman had recovered well from his last operation. Roman accepts that the damage to his spine is permanent, but as the surgeon managed to remove the bullet they didn't have to worry about it causing further problems.'

'I hope Roman can come to terms with not being to walk.'

'He has no choice in the matter and from what Sonya wrote, little Tatiana is now walking, has him wrapped around her little finger and is keeping him too busy to mope.' He refilled their cordial glasses. 'Fathers and daughters! Frankly my girls can't come home quickly enough for me. I've imposed on Sonya's good nature long enough. I can't expect her to continue to put the twins before the needs of her own family. And as Sarah and Praskovia have their own children to worry about, you are the ideal person for me to impose on.'

'Because I have no children or husband?'

'Because you'll be next door.'

'So, you are moving in to your half of the house?'

'Of course. What did you think we've been talking about?'

'I wasn't sure,' she said.

'I try to help Olga and Kitty as much as they'll let me but it would ease the strain considerably if they were able to consult their godmother on all the things young girls don't want to discuss with their father. Do you want me to enumerate them?'

'I'll spare your blushes.'

'And then there's Ruth. Although she no longer needs wet nursing she's close to Olena. Vasya says too close, and already Ruth thinks of Olena as her mother.'

'Ruth knows her father because you spend time with her every day.'

'As you suggested I give her tea, and put her to bed every night.'

'Then she knows exactly who her father is.' Anna frowned. 'Are you sure that Vasya isn't the reason you want to move here?'

'She's part of it,' he admitted. 'But more than anything it's security. This house and the estate is safer than anywhere in town.' He took his glass of cordial and walked to the window. 'Hughesovka grows more violent by the day. The girls have spent so much time with Sonya the last two years I doubt they'll recognise it. Besides, I don't want them returning to the town where their mother was murdered.'

'I can understand that.'

'I sense you're not entirely happy. If you don't want me to move in, Anna, just say the word . . . '

'It's not you and the girls, Alexei, it's me. There are things about me that you don't know.'

'That you can't stand men because you were attacked before you came to Russia?' he suggested bluntly.

'Richard told you?'

He shook his head. 'He didn't have to. I've seen you tremble every time a man draws close to you. Ruth told me what you said when you killed the soldier who was doing his damnedest to rape her.' He turned from the window and met her gaze. '"I'm not sorry. I'll never be sorry."'

281

'I was raped when I was twelve years old by both Paskeys.'

'Little wonder you don't like men.'

'So, I'll understand if you don't want me near your daughters . . . '

'I can think of no one I trust more to care for them or give them sound advice on boys, men and how to cope with the world. Ruth and I had twenty wonderful years together that we wouldn't have shared if you hadn't saved her life that day.'

'It's kind of you to say so. But you don't know what they did to me . . . '

'I don't want to,' he interrupted. 'Whatever those evil men did to you, isn't a part of you, Anna. You are an intelligent, strong admirable woman. A nurse who isn't afraid to do whatever is necessary to heal someone who is sick. Your common sense is tempered with large doses of compassion and kindness I am proud to call you my friend.'

Tears started in her eye.

'If I thought I wouldn't hurt you I'd hug you. This is by nature of an apology.' He handed her a fine linen handkerchief.

'Alexei . . . '

'I think we should have another drink before dinner. Something stronger this time perhaps?'

Unable to speak she nodded agreement.

CHAPTER TWENTY-SIX

Glyn Edwards' house Hughesovka July 1892

Glyn returned from his office at the end of the day to find Misha ensconced in his kitchen with Yelena and Praskovia. That all three were sitting quietly without hint of argument suggested there was a problem.

'How lovely. You're home on time for once.' Praskovia kissed his cheek. 'Tea?'

'Please. Is this a private kitchen party or can anyone join?' He pulled up a chair and sat at the table.

Praskovia picked up a glass and filled a glass with tea for Glyn. She passed it to him along with the sugar bowl.

'If you want dinner to be served on time this evening, you should all leave this "kitchen party" now so I can get started,' Yelena snapped.

'We'll go into the parlour.' Glyn rose and pushed his chair back under the table. He was too well acquainted with Yelena's temper to try to remain.

'Why don't you take Misha into your study,' Praskovia suggested. 'The boys will be home from Richard and Sarah's soon with their homework and you won't be disturbed in there.'

Glyn led the way through the door and Misha followed him.

'I take it you want to talk to me,' Glyn closed the door behind them. He turned to see a young woman sitting in a chair next to the fire. She rose to her feet and looked at him.

'You told Misha . . . ' she faltered and Glyn finished her sentence for her.

'That I'd like to see you, yes.'

'I'm not what you expected, even after seeing me from a distance?'

He realised he'd been staring at her. 'No, it's just that you look like Tom . . . '

'My half-brother with dark hair and eyes. Yes, I think I look like him too.'

Glyn couldn't stop looking at her.

'May I call you father?'

'You can call me Father or Dad or Daddy or anything you like. We have a lot of lost time to make up, daughter.' He opened his arms to her. After a moment's hesitation, she fell into them.

Alexei's house Hughesovka July 1890

'The Nadolnys are back in Hughesovka.' Lada was waiting to give Alexei the news as he walked through the front door of his house.

'When did they arrive?' He stopped unbuttoning his coat and pulled his hat back on his head.

'They drove down the street half an hour ago. I thought the twins would come straight here . . . Master . . . '

Alexei went to the cupboard beneath the stairs that did duty as his wine cellar, removed three bottles and packed them into a leather satchel.

'See you later, Lada.'

She went to the door and called after him. 'Will you want to eat when you return?'

'I've eaten, but thank you for asking, Lada.'

'That boy gets worse as he gets older.' Lada shook her head at Lev as she closed the front door and threw the bolt across it.

'That boy is heading for forty and has two grown daughters and a baby,' Lev reminded her.

'He'll always be a boy to me because like all men, no matter how old or young, they never grow up.'

Nadolny's house Hughesovka July 1892

Alexei pulled the bell next to the Nadolny's front door and waited impatiently for the butler to answer.

To his surprise Sonya opened the door. She hugged him so hard he protested.

'Are you trying to crack my ribs?'

'No, but what are doing standing there, come inside.' She pulled him through the porch into the hall.

'You've only just arrived. I didn't expect to be invited in . . . '

'You thought I'd leave my cousin standing on the doorstep?' Sonya sidestepped past the butler who ran down the stairs.

'I was carrying the luggage upstairs when I heard the bell, Madame. I would have answered it in a few minutes,' he reproached.

'I was already in the hall, Yuri, and it's only my cousin.' Sonya stood back from Alexei and looked him in the eye. 'You've lost weight.'

'No, I haven't.' Alexei glanced up the stairs. 'Is that your daughter I hear?'

'It is. Tatiana Ruth Catherine Nadolny, it's long past her bedtime but she doesn't wish to be put down in her cot and she has exceptional lungs.'

'So, I hear.'

'She'll soon quieten down because she has doting parents and an exceptional nanny.' She guided him into the parlour.

'Lada told me that she saw you and Roman arrive over an hour ago. Where are the girls?'

'They'll be here in two days. They wanted to stay for the last "White Nights" Imperial Ball of the season in the Winter Palace. This year's will mark the end of the social season as well as twenty-four-hour daylight in St Petersburg. They have more stamina than me. I had enough of White Night balls weeks ago. Frankly it's a relief to arrive at a place that has sunset and nightfall.'

'You won't be saying that if you try to travel around the streets of Hughesovka in the dark.'

285

'I'll take Roman's duelling pistols with me.'

'You'll need more than those to protect yourself. I suggest a couple of Cossack soldiers armed with primed rifles and plenty of shot. Who are the girls travelling with?' he asked.

'Roman hired a small army so neither he, nor Richard nor you needed to worry,' she reassured. 'And before you ask, Roman and I tried to persuade the twins and Maryanna to travel with us but all three had bought new gowns from Madam Roussard. There was no talking them out of staying in St Petersburg so they could show them off. As well as the army, Countess Cernograza and my sons will be watching over them and all three are fiercer than wolves when it comes to protecting the girls. But as I said, Roman has armed a dozen servants. All men with military experience. He won't allow the children to travel any distance without them.'

'A sad indictment of Russia and the times we live in.' Roman propelled himself out of his study into the parlour and shook Alexei's hand. 'From what I saw of the streets when we drove in the girls may need them. Hughesovka hasn't changed for the better. There are even more drunken layabouts cluttering up the gutters than there were the last time I was here.'

'Unfortunately, you're right. Here.' Alexei rummaged in the satchel. 'Cognac and vodka for you,' he handed the bottles to Roman. 'And wine and Lyudmila's cordial for you, Sonya. And now I must run . . . '

'No, you don't. We haven't seen you since you left St Petersburg before Christmas. You will dine with us and give us all the news. I'll check on the baby to make sure she's sleeping and ask the butler to lay an extra place setting.'

'You'd better obey, Alexei. She's become unbearably autocratic lately.'

'I heard that, Roman,' Sonya called back as she began to climb the stairs.

'I hoped I'd pitched it loud enough.' Roman winked at Alexei as he studied the bottle of cognac. 'Very nice and very old. Time it was liberated from its glass prison. Shall we try it?'

'If your doctor agrees.'

'He agrees. This,' Roman held out his arms, 'is me from now on.'

'I was devastated when I read your letter. I'm sorry.'

'Don't be. It's something to know for certain that nothing can be done other than come to terms with the limitations imposed by my condition. It could be a lot worse. I am married to the love of my life and have two strapping sons eager to carry out my every wish because they know that if they don't it will affect their allowance and a beautiful daughter who brings me more pleasure than I thought possible.' He wheeled himself to the table and prised the cork from the bottle.

Alexei fetched brandy balloons and watched Roman fill them.

'Do you want to know more about my condition?'

'Not unless you want to tell me.' Alexei raised his glass. 'To Tatiana Ruth Catherine Nadolny's lungs, she appears to enjoy exercising them.'

'To Tatiana's lungs. Remind me to ask the butler to close all the doors between here and her nursery' Roman savoured the brandy. 'That is excellent cognac thank you for bringing it. To answer the questions most people are too polite to ask but still want to know the answer to, my legs are paralysed and there's nothing that can be done to remedy the situation. However, in all . . . and I stress "all" other respects I am what I was before I was shot, as Sonya can and does attest to every time someone is ill mannered enough to ask about our private lives.

'However, I admit I find confinement to a wheelchair irksome and there are days when I would give . . . ' he hesitated and thought for a moment.

' . . . If not my right arm, then possibly my left, to be able to walk into my stables and shout for my horse to be saddled instead of being hauled into my carriage in this chair.'

'So, you're almost, but not quite resigned to your injuries?' Alexei suggested.

'I doubt I'll ever be resigned. Particularly when I'm asleep. In my dreams, I do everything I was once capable of. Run, ride, hunt, dance – even though I was never over fond of that last pastime, but one thing I can do even when I'm awake is work, which is why we've travelled ahead of our sons and the girls. I have a meeting with the New Russia Company's chief accountant first thing in the morning before he leaves for London. I asked him to delay for a few days but apparently John's sons need him urgently to oversee a consultation with the company's shareholders.'

'You have a problem with the company?' Alexei asked.

'None, but I've decided to sell my shares and thought it only fair to offer the majority shareholding the first option to buy me out.'

'Any reason?' Alexei's thoughts immediately turned to his own investment in the company.

'I'm streamlining my business interests . . . '

'To cut down on the hours he works and free up more time for his family.' Sonya walked in, picked up Roman's brandy glass and sniffed it. 'Excellent cognac, thank you cousin.'

'Want one?' Alexei picked up Sonya's hint.

'Please.'

Alexei left his chair and took a clean glass from the cupboard. Sonya grasped Roman's shoulder. He reached for her hand and held it.

'We discussed the future, our family's future,' she qualified, 'in light of Roman's injuries, and the outcome of his last surgery, and decided to reorganise our life.

288

We'll spend most of every winter in St Petersburg, and the summers in Yalta, while taking occasional trips to Moscow, Paris, Rome and Berlin, where we will "all" including my husband, take the time to enjoy a holiday.' Sonya dropped a kiss on Roman's forehead.

'That sounds like a plan,' Alexei agreed.

'You should consider it. The girls are of an age when they adore balls and there's no better city to enjoy them in than St Petersburg. And our house in Yalta is large enough to accommodate your family and our friends.'

'We're leaving here for Yalta as soon as I've settled my business affairs. We'd love to have you and the girls accompany us.' Roman added his persuasive voice to Sonya's.

'Between sea bathing, yachting and garden parties – not to mention the inevitable balls, the girls could continue the social life they enjoyed so much in St Petersburg,' Sonya continued. 'The Tsar has just bought the Massandra Palace from the Vorontsovs. It's larger than the Lividia Palace where he's been spending his summers and it's rumoured he acquired it with the intention of providing balls and entertainments there.'

'If you divide your time between your Yalta and St Petersburg houses . . . '

'Roman has other houses in almost every capital of Europe,' Sonya reminded Alexei.

'Will you have time to visit this house as well?' Alexei asked.

'We've decided to sell it,' Roman revealed.

'Which explains why you've decided to offload your shares.'

'Much as I respect John Hughes's sons, John's death ended my personal connection with the New Russia Company. It's thriving and no longer needs my input or rather the input of my connections. The business is safe in the hands of John's heirs, and it feels like the right time for me to bow out.'

'So, this may well be your last visit to Hughesovka.'

'Possibly.' A tear rolled down Sonya's cheek. Roman saw it and squeezed her hand.

'Given what happened here I can understand you wanting to break your ties to the town,' Alexei said when he and Sonya had settled on the sofa with their cognacs, and Roman had wheeled his chair opposite them. 'I've decided to move out of my house and into the wing of Catherine's house that she left me, for many reasons, not just lack of space. But I admit my main concern is the state of the town, especially the areas around the vodka and beer shops, I'd never allow the girls to go out alone, even in daylight.'

The butler knocked and entered. 'I'm sorry to disturb you, Madam, but the cook would like a word with you.'

'I trust the dinner isn't burned.'

'He didn't say, Madam.'

Roman shrugged. 'If it is, we can always eat in the hotel.' After Sonya left he commented. 'I thought you might have stayed longer when you last brought the girls to St Petersburg.'

'I can't explain why I feel the need to be here in Hughesovka, only that I do.' Alexei walked to the window although it was too dark to see anything outside. 'I know it doesn't make much sense but I feel as though Ruth is here.'

'It makes perfect sense. You were married for twenty years.'

'I knew that if I stayed in St Petersburg my long face would end up making everyone there as miserable as I was.'

'You're not miserable here?' Roman asked.

'Oddly enough, no. It feels right to be here, as if the shades of my dead are with me.'

'You have living family as well as dead, Alexei,' Roman reminded him gently.

'Perhaps it's because I'm not quite ready to let my dead go yet. It's so easy to remember the times when Ruth, Catherine and my mother were with me here.'

'It probably sounds odd but every time I visit their graves I could swear that they are close by, watching me.'

'That doesn't sound odd, but then I often talk to my father – sometimes I even hear him answer. So, you'll be moving into your half of Catherine's house and sharing it with Anna Parry.'

'Hardly sharing,' Alexei demurred. 'It was built as two separate units by my great grandfather one for him and my great grandmother, and one for Catherine should she need it after her marriage.'

'It's a fine house, or should I say two houses. I lived there with John Hughes when he arrived in Hughesovka and rented a wing from Catherine.'

'So, you did, I'd forgotten that.'

'How do you get on with Anna?'

'I like and admire her. I dine with her occasionally and we've discussed my moving in. We agreed that we won't be living in one another's pockets, but we've decided that we'll occasionally share meals but only after lengthy negotiations have taken place between Lada and Lyudmila. Make no mistake those two will run our establishments not us.'

'So, you intend to move the girls into your grandmother's house as soon as they return.'

'Yes. I'd like to talk to you about your plans to live in St Petersburg and Yalta. Richard and I have discussed expanding our interests and spending more time in the capital and less in Hughesovka.'

'Catherine left you her house in St Petersburg, as well didn't she?'

'To me and Kira, yes, she did,' Alexei confirmed.

'It's a fine house in a perfect spot and large enough to be divided into two establishments. You've had twenty years of hard work, Alexei, but you and Richard have succeeded in realising your dream. It's time both of took time to relax, sit back and enjoy taking your ease with your children.'

'That's good advice. But . . . '

291

'You regret waiting for "the right time" to retire from business and not doing it sooner when Ruth was alive.'

'How do you know?'

'Because it's exactly what I did with Sonya and the boys before the bullet in my back made me rethink the way I was living and my future. I was busy making money and plans for some nebulous future when I'd have all the time in the world to make up for the hours I'd spent in business meetings away from Sonya and the children. I've heard about Beletsky and Parry, and if rumour is halfway correct, it seems to me that you – and Richard - have amassed more money than either of you, or your children could spend in one or two lifetimes.'

'Add what Catherine left me, probably ten lifetimes,' Alexei corrected.

'Then enjoy it. Come and spend the summer with Sonya and I in Yalta so the children can have fun together.'

'And us?' Alexei turned dark, haunted eyes to Roman.

'We'll sit on the terrace, two old grumpy men sharing a bottle of well-aged cognac, watching the young having fun with a disapproving eye.'

'Disapproving eye?' Sonya returned in time to catch the end of their conversation. 'More likely egg the boys into more mischief.'

'I was trying to persuade Alexei to join us in Yalta for the summer.'

'With Richard and Sarah, Glyn and Praskovia and their children. Brilliant idea. We have plenty of room in our house.'

'Or Richard, Glyn and I could rent one. Who knows, if we like the resort we could even buy a house there.'

'And Anna?' Sonya asked.

'If anyone can prise her away from the hospital it will be Richard and Sarah.'

'I'll call and see her tomorrow when you visit the accountant in the New Russia Company,' Sonya said to Roman. 'But it will be odd to visit my aunt's house without her being there.'

'No, it won't, Anna has turned the house into a shrine to her memory,' Alexei said.

'She loved Catherine as much if not more than us,' Sonya murmured.

'Why more?' Roman asked,

'Because she stayed here with her, which is more than I did.'

CHAPTER TWENTY-SEVEN

Ignatova House Hughesovka July 1892

'You will come with us, won't you, Auntie Anna?' Kitty pleaded as Alexei's footman cleared their dessert plates.

'It will be such fun to have you there,' Olga coaxed. 'Andrei says the sun always shines longer in the day and later in the year in Yalta than anywhere else in Russia, so the weather will be warm enough for swimming, even when summer has ended here. Some of our friends' parents will be berthing their yachts in the Crimea so we can have sailing and fishing parties . . . '

'It is time for bed, you two,' Alexei broke in.

'But Auntie Anna hasn't said she'll come with us yet.'

'It's bad enough that I have your Uncle Richard and Aunt Sarah nagging me without you two joining in. I've said I'll think about it,' Anna said with a smile to lessen the sting of her words. 'And I meant it. But first I have to make sure that the hospital has enough surgically trained nurses. If it does then I'll ask Dr Kharber if he can do without me for a week or two.'

'A week or two is no good, Auntie Anna,' Kitty cried. 'Uncle Roman and Aunt Sonya are planning to stay for at least three months and . . . '

'And you'll be going nowhere if you don't go to bed now,' Alexei ordered doing his utmost to play the stern father. 'You're so exhausted from travelling you're both sleeping on your feet, and you're supposed to be spending the day with Pavlo, Tom and Ted tomorrow. They've missed you.'

'Yes, Papa,' Olga said with a sudden meekness that gave rise to a frown on Alexei's face.

The twins kissed Alexei goodnight, then Anna.

'Those two will give me grey hairs,' Alexei complained after they'd left the dining room.

'You already have one or two,' Anna teased.

'Shall we take our coffee and cherry brandy outside?'

'Please. I could do with some fresh air after spending all day in the hospital. Either I've brought the stench of disinfectant and chloroform with me or they've taken root in my lungs.'

'I've been breathing in smoke from the works all afternoon. This air seems intoxicatingly clean after the smuts I've inhaled today.'

'So, you're glad you moved out here?' Anna asked.

'It's safer and healthier for the girls and Ruth.'

'And you?'

'And me,' he conceded. He signalled to the footman who piled the coffee pot, sugar basin, glasses, and cherry brandy on to a tray and carried it through the French doors.

Anna stepped out on to the terrace that encircled both wings of the Ignatova mansion. 'Was it Roman and Sonya, Richard or the twins who persuaded you to holiday in Yalta?'

'A combination of all of them, but the twins have been the most vociferous since they returned from St Petersburg. Richard and I spent today checking the accounts of Beletsky and Parry collieries along with our managers' records to make sure that we could afford to spare the time to take a long holiday. When we discovered we could, we persuaded Glyn and Praskovia to join us.'

'I'm so glad you did, Praskovia could do with a rest.' Anna walked to the paved area that led to the winter garden.

'More than Glyn?'

'The truth is all of you need a holiday. It's been a long winter.'

'For you too, Anna.'

'I said I'll try and make time.'

'No one is indispensable. After looking at our books today, Richard and I decided that Roman Nadolny is right. If you've trained your subordinates well, you can afford to take time off, and you owe it to your family to do just that.

'You've spent the best part of the last two years training your nursing replacements.'

'The problem with training nurses is you need a good supply of different diseases and injuries they can practice one. Just when I think there's nothing more I can teach them a patient turns up with a rare operable condition that requires research into new treatments we haven't tried before.'

'So, you want people in Hughesovka to contract more rare diseases?'

'That wasn't what I said,' she laughed.

The footman set the tray he'd brought out of the dining room on to a metal table, while Alexei pulled out a chair for Anna.

'Thank you,' Alexei dismissed the footman and sat opposite Anna. 'I'm surprised Boris and Lyudmila allowed you to join the girls and I for dinner us this evening at such short notice.'

'I insist Boris takes two evenings a week off. Thursday is one of them, and for once Lyudmila didn't take much persuading.'

'I've never thought to ask Boris how old he is. To my shame I've never even thought about it, but he has to be in his seventies.'

'Seventy-one according to Lyudmila. Apparently, he came here as boot boy when your grandfather married your grandmother.'

Alexei pulled the cork on the cherry brandy while she poured coffee into their cups. He sniffed the air theatrically. 'The scent out here is heavenly.'

'It's the roses, Catherine confessed that she scoured her friends' gardens for the ones with the strongest fragrance and stole clippings.'

'I grew up so accustomed to the beauty of this house I took it for granted when I was younger,' Alexei said.

'That's only natural when it was a home you frequently visited. I would have loved to have had a family who owned something like this.'

295

'You did, you had Catherine.'

'I meant when I was a child. I had no idea people lived in such comfort and luxury.'

'Your house was small?' he asked curiously.

'We rented a damp windowless single roomed basement in Merthyr with a sleeping shelf close to the ceiling. All but the last foot of wall was below ground level so water seeped in, summer and winter. When Richard and I came here and moved into Glyn's house we thought we'd reached heaven.'

'That house was Catherine's too before she sold it to Glyn. It's sad to think I didn't really appreciate what she created here until she died.'

'It's middle age,' Anna smiled. 'When we're young we're too busy rushing around to appreciate anything.'

'You're probably right,' he murmured absently and Anna realised he wasn't listening.

'I've been remiss in not thanking you.'

'For what?' she asked.

'Watching over baby Ruth, befriending the girls when they needed a woman to guide them, for welcoming me here . . .'

'Into your own house?' she questioned. 'It's I who should be thanking you, it's good to have a neighbour I can talk to.'

He looked at her. She turned away. Despite their friendship, and his correct, courteous behaviour towards her she still found it difficult to meet his eye when he looked at her the way he did at that moment.

'So, will you come to Yalta with Richard, Glyn and their families and me and my girls, Anna? It's all arranged. We'll drive to Kharkov in our carriages, leaving our grooms to return them here, and take the train down to the Crimea. Roman's already found us a house or rather summer palace to rent that's big enough to accommodate us all. It has fifteen bedrooms so you will be guaranteed your own room as far away from the noisy young people as we can place it.

'I know Richard has invited you, but it would mean so much to my girls to have you there.'

'I can only tell you what I told the twins.'

'It hasn't satisfied them – or me.' He finished his coffee before reaching for the cherry brandy.

'Will you stop badgering me if I promise you that you'll be the first to know my decision?'

'You leave me no choice but to agree.' He filled two liqueur glasses and handed her one. 'Will you really carry on living here and running this estate after you've trained enough surgical nurses to satisfy Dr Kharber?'

'I haven't thought that far ahead. I enjoy living here and have done since the day Catherine invited me to move in with her, but it was different when I travelled to the hospital every day. Apart from when we had emergencies and I stayed in the hospital, sometimes for days at a time. But . . . ' she fell silent.

'But?' he prompted.

'Idyllic as this place is, I feel a little cut off here.'

'That's because you are cut off from the town,' he pointed out logically.

'It's home, but it's also still Catherine's place more than mine.'

'Richard mentioned that he's considering returning to Britain.'

'He and Sarah are thinking of the children. Ted wants to study engineering and Maryanna wants to become a teacher. Given that they speak English at home and go to chapel every Sunday, much as they love this country and are grateful for the opportunities it's given them, they are still more Welsh than Russian.'

'Do you intend to go back with them?'

'They have asked me to join them, but Richard and Sarah haven't set a date or even a year when they might leave as yet.'

He shifted uneasily on his chair, turning so he could look at the town's buildings outlined on the skyline. The flat landscape meant they were visible for miles. Thick smoke belching from the works' chimneys had settled in a dense pall over the roofs of the highest buildings, smudging the horizon. 'It's sad isn't it.'

'What?' she asked.

'That the city that John Hughes dreamed of that began life with so much promise has become such an unpleasant place. Although with hindsight it was inevitable. We couldn't stop people coming here to look for work, even when there were twenty men applying for every job, no more than we could regulate the amount of filth spewed out by the manufacturing process. As a result, we've ended up with a polluted town populated by desperate men, some out of work, with starving families to support, who are forced to live in foul filthy conditions in holes in the ground because of a lack of housing.'

'John Hughes did what he could,' Anna felt duty bound to defend the man, who more than any anyone else had changed her life and that of so many others.

'I'm the first to admit he did more than any other industrialist in Russia to improve the lot of the common working man. The fact that so many people flooded into Hughesovka from all over Russia and Europe to look for work and a better life says everything that anyone needs to know about him.'

'What about you, Alexei? Will you stay here if Richard returns to Britain?' she questioned.

'I don't know. Like you, I'd rather not think about the future. But I am Russian to the bone, so I can't imagine living in another country. As you know, Roman and Sonya are selling their house here, so they can split their time between St Petersburg, Yalta, and travelling around Europe. It sounds like a pleasant prospect.'

'So why not join Roman and Sonya? They'd love to have your company.'

'Maybe they would and maybe they'd soon be bored with me if I trailed behind them. The truth is I'm not a wanderer by nature like Roman. I've made a fortune and inherited another thanks to my grandparents' foresight, which is wonderful for me and the girls. But unlike Roman when I do travel I'm content to stay in the best hotel a city has to offer instead of building a mansion as a legacy for future generations.'

'Richard said when we first met you in Taganrog, you took him on a drive around the town and told him that when you made enough money you would build a mansion in St Petersburg.'

'So, I did.' he agreed. 'I'm amazed he remembered. We were both such solemn young men. I recall asking him to go into business with me that night. I was so impressed when he said he'd worked in a mine. But then I was already in love with the romance of modern industry . . . '

'Romance!' she mocked.

'That was before I'd seen the damage modern collieries and ironworks can inflict on this earth,'

'After living in Merthyr you'll have to forgive me if the romance of industry has escaped my notice.'

'At least the fallout from the furnaces doesn't reach this estate.' He thought for a moment. 'Catherine did make provision for the upkeep of this place, didn't she? She said she was going to, but if ever you need money for this house or anything . . . '

'I have more than enough, between my savings and the generous annuity Catherine arranged,' she assured him.

'I heard that you've been helping Father Grigor's charities with donations as well as caring for the sick and elderly who live on the estate.'

'I've done no more than Catherine would have. She kept meticulous accounts, and don't forget she bequeathed Mr Dmitri and his law firm to me as well.'

'I talked to Catherine about my moving to St Petersburg with the girls, at least for part of the year, before she died. She said she'd left the estate in good hands and she has.'

'It sounds as though you've made up your mind to move there?'

'Moving to St Petersburg, if only for the season, makes sense for the sake of the twins. I'd like nothing better than to see them settled and married well.'

'For love?' she smiled.

'Of course, for love.' He returned her smile. 'Ruth and I used to talk about it, hardly surprising given the plotting and secrecy that went into our courtship.'

'Olga and Kitty have certainly fallen in love with St Petersburg. They're already talking about next winter's season.'

'All they can think about is balls and parties . . . '

'Those are just a means to find love.'

'You think so?'

'The twins grew up with a grandstand view of the perfect marriage, yours and Ruth's.' She stacked their coffee cups and glasses on to the tray. 'It's hardly surprising that they want the same for themselves.'

'They've talked about marriage with you?'

'Of course.'

'I can't help thinking that you know my daughters better than I do.'

'I'm just an interfering godmother living the youth I would have liked to have had through them.' She looked up at the sky. 'This sunset is glorious. It tells me night is about to fall and it's high time I went home.'

'Must you?'

'I promised Father Grigor I'd deliver all the vegetables Lyudmila can spare to the soup kitchen early tomorrow morning.'

'As we share the kitchen garden I can't contribute but I can give you some money.'

'That too is always welcome.'

'Will you be free for lunch in the hotel? I hate eating alone,' he added when she hesitated.

'I have to go from the soup kitchen to the hospital. Noah has scheduled a full day's surgery for the TB cases in the isolation ward. He wants to try deflating some of the worse affected lungs not only as a treatment but a means of extending the life of those afflicted with the disease. But you and the girls could dine with me tomorrow evening if you'd like to give Lada a rest.'

'If you're sure Lyudmila won't mind.'

'I'm sure, in fact it might be as well to talk it over with her and Lada and organise it so we eat together every evening. Less work for them.'

'I'll talk to Lada now.' He set his glasses on the tray. After she followed suit he caught her hand and kissed her fingertips.

A simple gesture, but she wondered it made her feel uneasy.

CHAPTER TWENTY-EIGHT

Rented Palace Yalta August 1892

Anna spent the morning on the beach with Ruth and Olena. After lunch, Olena took Ruth up to the nursery for her afternoon nap. When Anna looked in on them five minutes later both were fast asleep. Anna checked that the window that overlooked the garden was open so she would hear Ruth if she cried, then went down to the terrace.

The row of empty steamer chairs looked inviting as did the refreshments laid out on the tables between them. She poured herself a glass of cherry juice from one of the covered iced pitchers and stretched out on a chair. The view over the gardens to the sea was hand-coloured, picture postcard perfect.

The crests of the waves sparkled with silver and gold gems of reflected sunlight. The sprinkling of yachts berthed around the pier had thinned considerably from her arrival two weeks ago, but those holiday makers who could afford to linger in Yalta were doing their best to enjoy the last days of summer. Snatches of music drifted up from the hotel that overlooked the sands. A group of young women dressed in white organza were playing a variation of tennis on the beach that allowed for a dozen to bat a ball back and for. A throw's distance to their right a raucous crowd of young men kicked and fought over a football in between preening their muscles for the benefit of the girls.

'You didn't go to the Duchess's garden party with the others?' Alexei dropped into the chair alongside her, and reached for the pitcher and a clean glass.

'Neither did you,' she commented.

'I've spent more time exchanging empty pleasantries here in two weeks, than I've done in the last two years in Hughesovka. I have absolutely no complimentary remarks left, not a one. Only rude ill-mannered ones, so I thought it best to stay away. What's your excuse?'

'After spending the morning on the beach. I pleaded a need to rest before returning to Hughesovka tomorrow. I have no idea why travelling should be so tiring when all you do is sit in a carriage of one sort or another but it is.'

'The Duchess will never forgive you. She wears your nursing credentials as a testament to her socialism. "Look at me, I may be a Duchess but I know a woman who works for a living".' He gave a credible impression of the Duchess's ear drum shattering, high pitched voice, and Anna burst out laughing.

'If she ever overhears you mocking her, you'll be forever excluded from her circle.'

'Do you think so?' he raised an eyebrow. 'That would be a blessing. I must remember to do just that the next time I find myself marooned in her company.' He placed his glass on the side table and scooped up a fistful of salted almonds. 'Did the children go to the Duchess's garden party.'

'None of them would thank you for calling them children, Alexei,' she rebuked. 'And no, they didn't. Andrei and Spartak have organised a picnic and bonfire for them and their friends on Roman's private beach.'

'Bonfire in this heat?' He picked up a magazine and waved it, in front of his face, stirring the warm air.

'There was mention of roasting potatoes, sausages and any fish they caught.'

'The boys, catch fish?' Alexei mocked. 'None of them have the patience to sit still longer than a minute.'

'I dare say they'll have enough to eat without fish. Pavlo and Andrei appointed themselves chief cooks.'

'I hope they cook the sausages thoroughly or I'll have two sick girls on my hands.'

'I believe the sausages were supplied by Richard's cook . . . '

'Good, wise woman that she is, she will have roasted them first.'

'So, the worst we can expect is charcoal poisoning when the boys burn them.' Anna lay back and closed her eyes against the sun. 'The twins said you had an unusually early breakfast this morning. Where have you been until now?'

'Riding. I took out one of Roman's horses.'

'It's beautiful country around here.'

'It is. I needed some "alone time" to think. Much as I love your brother and Glyn and their families . . . '

'So many people in one house means you have no time to listen to your own thoughts.' She opened her eyes and glanced at him. To her consternation she realised he was staring at her.

'Exactly.'

She turned back to the view of the beach and sea but she could still sense him gazing at her.

'Must you really leave this slice of heaven for Hughesovka and the hospital tomorrow?' he asked.

'Yes.'

'Although the house is booked until the end of next month and the rest of us are staying for at least another five weeks?'

'I trust you to enjoy it for me.' She steeled herself to meet his steady gaze again.

'Why won't you stay?'

'Too much of anything – even heaven is decadent.'

'Says who?'

'All religion teaches it.'

'Ah religion. Every priest I've ever met, no matter which creed they follow seem to see it as their purpose in life to prevent their adherents having fun.'

'That is blasphemous,' she protested, lightly. Lightly because it was the sort of tongue in cheek remark he used to make when Ruth was alive, with the intention of shocking her. Sometimes she wondered if Ruth's conversion to Russian Orthodoxy had been solely down to her love for Alexei and had nothing to do with any personal religious beliefs.

'It probably is,' Alexei agreed, 'but Father Grigor laughed when I suggested it. At the risk of shocking you further, I confess that my twins, Roman and your brother have converted me to the idea of decadence. I could bring myself to spend every summer here in this heaven.'

'And every winter season in St Petersburg?'

'I won't commit to an entire season but certainly a few weeks.' He fell serious. 'Must you leave?' he reiterated.

'I must, but I've already promised to return next year, and I'll be home when you return with the girls.'

'I'll miss you.'

'I'll miss you and the girls.'

He reached for the pitcher and refilled both their glasses. 'I've been thinking . . . '

'So, you said. Having nothing to do all day except, eat, sleep, sit in the sun and ride gives you time to do that.'

'It does and I've been thinking about what Roman said.'

'About leaving Hughesovka to winter in St Petersburg and summer here?'

'About living while we have the chance to live.' He swung his legs to the floor, sat sideways on his steamer chair and looked into her eyes again as he reached for her hand.

She was so unnerved she allowed him to take it.

'Marry me, Anna.'

She swallowed hard.

'Please,' he added.

'Alexei, you know who and what I am. You know why I'll never marry . . . '

'Listen, please. Just for a few minutes. I swear by all that's holy I'll never make any demands of you. You've said often enough that you'd like to have children, be a mother, a part of a family. I have three daughters including a baby who desperately need a mother . . . '

'I can't just walk into your family. I could never take Ruth's place . . . '

'Nor would the twins and I want you to, Anna,' he broke in. 'Like Ruth you are your own person and all three of us love you for it. But there is no escaping the fact that my youngest daughter recognises you more than me and you are far better at handling her than I am.'

'That will change as she grows older.'

'The twins adore you . . . '

'As I do them,' she interrupted, 'but I am their godmother and it is a godmother's job to spoil her godchildren.'

'And care for them should anything happen to the parents,' he reminded her. 'Ruth choose wisely.'

'Alexei, I will never marry . . . '

'I wouldn't have asked you if I believed that.'

'You have time to fall in love . . . '

'Time?' He raised an eyebrow. 'The one thing none of us can be sure of is that we have time. Ruth's death proved that. As for falling in love, after Ruth that would be impossible. I will never love anyone again the way I loved her and you as her closest friend know that.' He tightened his grip on her fingers. 'But we could be a family, you, I and the girls. A family that shares mutual love based on respect.'

She was very conscious of the pressure of his fingers closing over hers but whereas she would have pulled it away at one time she didn't even try.

'We could be comfortable together you, I and the girls,' he pleaded. 'Stay here with me for another week, and we'll travel back to Hughesovka together. I'll ask Father Grigor to marry us and you can bring up Ruth's baby.

307

'There is no one I trust more to tell her about her mother or see the twins grow into womanhood. There's no need for you to move into my wing of the house in Hughesovka. When we winter in St Petersburg, you can take your pick of whichever bedroom you want in Catherine's house. The only change in your life would be in the amount of time you spend with me and the girls please, Anna . . . '

She began to paint a picture of the future he promised her. It would be so easy. So, simple to agree. Her brother and his family were already close to Alexei, and if she did marry him she would probably see even more of Richard, Sarah and their children. She would move into Catherine's St Petersburg home, as much mistress there, as she already was of the Ignatova mansion in Hughesovka. After the success of the two weeks she had just spent in Yalta, and what Alexei had said, there would undoubtedly be a house here in the near future, possibly even this palace which she knew was up for sale . . .

The future she painted in her mind's eye grew clearer, more elaborate and beguiling until she remembered the premise it was based on. 'No!' she pulled her hand back from his.

'Anna . . . '

'No,' she repeated more softly that time. 'You are good and kind and there is no one I admire more, but no, Alexei. I have seen what a perfect marriage can be. Yours and Ruth's, Roman and Sonya's, Richard and Sarah's; and although not a marriage Glyn and Praskovia's. I would want nothing less for myself or my husband. If I couldn't be a real wife to him and he a husband to me, I wouldn't want to marry.

'You'd rather remain in lonely spinsterhood?'

'A nurse will never be lonely.'

'Until she is too old to nurse.'

'I could never be a real wife to you, Alexei, and I refuse to allow any husband of mine to settle for less.'

A thin wail of a baby's cry drifted from the upstairs window.

'That's Ruth.' Anna climbed out of her chair.

'Isn't Olena with her?' Alexei asked.

'Yes.'

He said the most brutal thing he could think of. 'Then, as you insist on leaving tomorrow, it's time Ruth became accustomed to your absence,' before running into the house ahead of her. She lay back on her chair and listened as his footsteps echoed over the marble stairs and up on to the wooden galleried landing. She closed her eyes against the sunlight, but her tears escaped, trickling down her cheeks, splashing salt and wet, on her lips.

Rented House Yalta August 1892

The night was warm, the air still. Unable to sleep Anna threw back the bedclothes and stared up at the ceiling. It was light enough for her to make out a spider's web that hung over a moulding in the corner of the ceiling.

She heard the clock strike in the hall and tensed. Four strikes for four o'clock. Richard had ordered the carriage for six o'clock to take to her the rail terminus at Feodosia which would take her on the first leg of her train journey to Kharkov.

Restless unable to sleep and too distressed to think about Alexei's offer of marriage she left her bed and opened the drapes. Dawn was breaking, gilding the horizon over the sea with a soft red gold glow. She went into the small bathroom pulled off her nightgown and stepped into the small tub one of the maids had filled with water the night before. The water was as warm as the air. By five o'clock she had washed, dressed and finished the last of her packing. She closed and locked her trunk and Gladstone bag, and left them in pride of place in the middle of her room for one of the footmen to carry down.

She glanced around the room as much to fix it in her memory as check she hadn't left anything. She had been happy here. But would she be again? And would Alexei forgive her for refusing his proposal?

The clock struck five, she picked up her leather travel satchel and walked down the stairs.

The bell pull rang, and the doorman opened the door to a telegraph boy as a maid and footman emerged from the servants' quarters.

'A telegram, for you, Miss Parry.'

Anna took it from the old man and opened it.

'Bad news?' Richard appeared on the stairs above her, in his nightshirt and dressing gown.

She looked up at him. 'It's from Nathan Kharber. Cholera's broken out in the town again.'

'He's sent for you?' Alexei joined Richard on the landing. His shirt was unbuttoned over an expanse of bare chest. His trousers were buttoned and he was wearing one sock and holding the other.

'Yes.'

'Then the situation is serious. I'll go with you, Anna.'

'Don't be ridiculous, Alexei, you can't take the girls back to Hughesovka when cholera's raging through the town,' Anna protested.

'I won't. They can stay here with Sarah and Praskovia. The peasants and Cossacks have always looked to my family for guidance. With Catherine gone, that's me.'

'Misha is there to command the troops,' Richard said, 'he can deal with any situation . . . '

'Even riots. Like he did last time?' Alexei asked.

Richard didn't answer him. None of them needed reminding that the last time cholera had struck the Donbass, the people had turned violent and not only in Hughesovka. Desperate to blame someone – anyone - for the rising death toll they had looked for scapegoats, settling on the traditional bogeymen of Russian fairy tales, the Jews, along with any and every official who represented authority.

'You can't travel there any faster than you'd already planned to,' Richard pointed out.

'Will you look after the girls for me, Richard . . . '

'Of course, Alexei but . . . '

Alexei was already shouting to his valet to pack his things. The man ran to Alexei's room.

'I suggest you and the others stay here until the weather changes then travel directly to St Petersburg, Richard,' Alexei said. 'That way you shouldn't come into contact with the cholera. I'll telegraph instructions to the butler so he can prepare Catherine's St Petersburg House for you, Glyn and your families. As soon as Anna and I arrive at Hughesovka I'll wire you as to the conditions there.'

'And after you've telegraphed us?' Richard asked.

'Then, we'll do whatever we can to help restore order and health to the town.' Alexei looked to Anna who was re-reading Nathan's telegram.

She looked up at him. 'You're determined to go to Hughesovka, Alexei?'

'I am.'

'If I had more time, I'd argue with you, but I don't.'

CHAPTER TWENTY-NINE

Train heading through the Donbas July 1892

'Your Excellency,' the railway official bowed and touched his cap. 'Our trains reach the most remote corners of all the Russias, and wherever they travel, the story is the same. Deadly cholera is being spread by the ungodly heathens. And where there is cholera, riots follow. There is fighting in every town and village between here, Moscow and St Petersburg, Siberia and the Urals and the violence is not confined to the towns. It has spread over the countryside to the smallest hamlet. People are crazed. They are behaving worse than animals. Men - women - children – the young – the old – the crippled – no one is sacred. The troublemakers are out for blood and are only happy when they see it running crimson in the gutters. They do not care who they kill or who they maim. Innocent Russian or guilty Jew, they paint the streets with their gore . . . '

'Kill?' Alexei interrupted the steward when he paused to draw breath.

The railway official glanced over his shoulder through the door that led into the corridor. 'Kill, Your Excellency,' he reiterated with a dramatic flourish. 'I myself, have seen the bodies of innocents lying in the streets.' Conscious of the importance of the news he was imparting, he drew himself upright and puffed out his chest as though he were on a parade ground.

'Have you heard what's happening in Hughesovka?' Anna asked.

'Only that it's as bad there as it is everywhere else. People rampaging, smashing everything they can get hold off, including the heads of the living. And what they can't smash they take an axe or a torch to. I spoke to a driver who left there only yesterday afternoon.

'He swore by all that's holy that he saw flames shooting out of the windows of the shops in the main street as he pulled out of the station. The porters told him that the Jewish doctors in the hospital kill every cholera patient as soon as they are carried over the threshold. But that's Jewish doctors and nurses for you. It's less work for them to kill people than try to save them . . . '

'That's nonsense . . . Doctors and nurses are trained to help . . . ' Anna fell silent when Alexei gave her hand a warning squeeze.

'The trains *are* running to Hughesovka?' Alexei asked.

'They were when I talked to the driver yesterday.'

'There've been no problems?'

'He said fires had been set on some lengths of the track but they burned themselves out. There was nothing serious enough to stop the engines running on time.'

'So, we should reach Hughesovka late this afternoon?' Alexei pressed.

'There's nothing to prevent you that I know anything about, Your Excellency.'

'No rioters with torches or axes . . . '

'Not on our tracks.' Realising from Alexei's tone that he didn't entirely believe the tales he'd been spinning, the official backed towards the door. 'We will reach the next station in half an hour. As you instructed, Your Excellency, this carriage will be disconnected and pushed it into sidings until the Hughesovka train pulls in. Then it will be added on to the end. There may be time for your and Madame to eat at the hotel.'

'We're needed urgently in Hughesovka so we'll stay on board,' Anna broke in.

'You arrive there by sunset then you can see the situation in the town for yourselves and decide whether or not I was speaking the truth.' The man leered slyly at Anna before moving into the corridor and down the carriage.

'Unpleasant creature, taking delight in painting grisly pictures and revelling in people's misery. Do you think-'

Alexei silenced Anna by placing his finger over his lips. He left his seat and closed the door before answering her. 'I think we'll find out what's happening when we reach Hughesovka. Not before.'

He rose to his feet and lifted down her Gladstone bag along with his own from the rack above their head. She folded her jacket and placed it next to her satchel on the seat beside her.

'If you don't want to leave the carriage I could send out to the hotel for food,' he suggested.

'I couldn't eat a thing.'

'You do realise that man wanted to shock us? He took us for gullible fools.'

'Yes, but I can't help worrying . . . '

'Don't.' He sat next to her and laced his fingers into hers.

'I was going to add every time I think about Nathan's telegram.'

'That guard is a lying idiot.' He forced what he hoped was a reassuring smile. But he knew it wouldn't fool her. He could dismiss the guard's gruesome tales, but like Anna, he couldn't discount Nathan's plea for her help.

Hughesovka July 1892

The acrid stench of burning wafted down the corridor as the train dropped speed on the approach to Hughesovka station. Alexei closed the corridor windows against a tide of black smuts. The sun had set an hour ago and eye-stinging smoke hung heavy and static in filthy dark clouds, blotting out the night sky.

Alexei picked up his own and Anna's Gladstone bags and moved out of their carriage to the door. As the floor of the platform loomed into sight below the lamps on the station walls they heard the sound. A dense low roaring, like thunder or a waterfall but louder, more discordant than anything in nature. Through the open entrance they saw flames shooting above the rooftops.

'Christ be with us! The town is on fire!' Alexei exclaimed as the train juddered to a halt. He gave her an apologetic look. 'That was a prayer not blasphemy.' He opened the door, stepped down on to the platform and into an ankle-deep layer of ash.

Anna followed him, crunching over the debris. The station was deserted. 'Where is everyone?'

'I've a feeling we're about to find out. Stay close.' In the absence of a porter, Alexei picked up both their bags and led the way to the entrance.

'There are no porters to get our trunks off the train . . . '

'They're safer where they are.' Alexei walked into the street and looked around.

Anna turned instinctively towards the hospital. Stunned, she dropped her coat. It fell into the sea of cinders that plastered everything in sight.

Too shocked to cry, she covered her mouth with her hands.

A bonfire of broken furniture and smashed window frames leaned against what had been a living tree to the right of the door of the hospital. The flames crackled and blazed, leaping high above the roof, illuminating the façade. The tree to the left of the door bore two figures. They'd been hung from the highest branches. Both swung gently like clock pendulums in the blasts of hot air emanating from the inferno. One was painfully thin, clad in black trousers and jacket worn beneath a white doctor's coat. The second was dressed in the blue workman's trousers and shirt that was the uniform of the porters.

Mesmerized, Anna didn't see the mob standing in front of the bonfire, or the line of mounted Cossack troops bearing down on them. She clutched Alexei's sleeve.

'We have to cut them down.'

Alexei realised they would be caught between opposing sides in seconds. He dropped their bags, closed his fist around her arm and shouted, 'Run!'

Alexei's grip tightened like a steel band around Anna's wrist as he dragged her back inside the station. Once they left the light radiating from the fire, darkness closed around them like a suffocating blanket.

Breathless, choking from the smoke, Anna coughed so hard she stumbled. Alexei made no allowances for her weakness and continued to haul her behind him. She fell. She managed to hold on to her satchel but lost her shoes. He heaved her to her feet and pulled her towards the end of the long platform.

The thunderous noise grew in strength and intensity behind them. Angry shouts and screams of, 'Kill the Jews!' accompanied by cries of 'Kill the Welsh!' in Russian and Ukrainian rang out behind them, accompanied by the discordant drumbeat thud of footsteps, the ring of hoof beats and the clash of steel blades.

'Jump.'

She heard rather than saw Alexei land on the tracks. When she didn't follow, his grip tightened on her wrist and he heaved her down towards him. She crumpled at his feet, stifling a cry when both her knees collided painfully with a metal rail.

Alexei lifted her into his arms and ran. The footsteps and shouts faded as the darkness thickened around them but whether imagined or real she could still hear a chorus of "Kill the Jews!" interspersed with "Kill the Welsh!"

The darkness lightened from black to dismal shades of grey when Alexei moved out from under the partial cover of station roof but the smoke still hung, stifling and suffocating around them.

Alexei lifted his arms high and pressed her against his chest as he continued to run. She bit her lips and closed her eyes against the pain in her knees. When she opened them again, the darkness was intense and total. As black as when she had worked the air traps in the tunnel mine in Merthyr as a four-year-old.

She gripped Alexei's shoulders as he continued to lurch forward.

———

She sensed they were under cover in a tunnel but the darkness around them was unrelenting, devoid even of shadows.

She blinked hard. Was it her imagination or could she glimpse a sliver of sky ahead? She leaned close and whispered. 'Set me down. I can walk.'

Alexei flung her high in the air. She landed on an unyielding rocky surface. She reached out scraped the skin on her hands and smelled coal dust.

A darker shape loomed over her. Alexei whispered, 'Where are you?'

'Here.'

'Hold out your hand.'

She did so and Alexei gripped it. 'If I land on you squeeze hard. Don't cry out. They may be close behind. I can't see a thing.'

She heard the sound of leather boot soles scraping on metal. Alexei lowered himself and stretched out beside her.

She felt his hands move upwards from her face to her hair. When he brushed it back with his fingers she realised she must have lost her hat

'Where are we?'

'Ssh! Feel my ear and whisper close to it.' He moved her hand to his ear lobe. 'We're in one of the trucks in the tunnel that leads to Beletsky and Parry's colliery loading bay,' he murmured. 'I heard a man's voice further down the track. Others could be hiding here. We must stay quiet and hope that the rioters will eventually exhaust themselves.'

She closed her eyes and an image of Nathan's body swinging high overhead filled her mind. Alexei must have sensed her grief because she felt his fingers brush tears from her cheek. He fumbled in his clothing, extricated his arm and pressed a handkerchief into her hand.

'Try not to think about Nathan.' He pulled her head down on to his shoulder, wrapped his arms around her and held her close.

317

She stared into the darkness trying to make out Alexei's profile but it was too dark to even decipher shapes. The image of Nathan's body, his hands bound behind his back, his ankles tied together above the tops of his boots had seared into her mind. She shuddered uncontrollably.

Alexei rubbed her arms. His touch was comforting, reminding her that she wasn't alone. She had the oddest sensation that the silence was buzzing around them. It was so quiet she felt as though she could hear the blood pumping in her arteries. Although it was too dark to see anything she kept her eyes open, in an effort to block the horrific image of Nathan from her consciousness.

'You awake?'

Alexei's whisper startled her, deafening because it was unexpected.

'Yes.'

He moved again and she felt a heavy weight fall across her body. 'Tarpaulin, we keep them at the bottom of the trucks to pull across the coal to stop petty thieving.' He leaned forward and arranged it over both of them. 'It won't fool anyone close up, but as we're in a line of hundred or so trucks, hopefully anyone searching for us will be too idle to poke into every one.' He drew closer to her. 'Are you all right after that fall?'

Her knees hurt but when she tried, she managed to move her legs. 'Yes. Alexei . . . ' Make love to me please?'

'Anna . . . '

The words tumbled out faster than she could give thought to what she was saying. 'I can't bear the thought of being murdered like Nathan and never knowing any man except the Paskeys. So please . . . ' She tugged at her blouse. The sound of fabric tearing filled the air as she ripped the pearl buttons from their loops.

He grabbed both her hands and held them still. 'You don't make love violently.'

'I thought men did.'

318

'Rapists might. Men who want to make physical love to a woman they care about don't.'

His fingers moved lightly tenderly over her face and neck. He stroked the sensitive skin below her ear and kissed her there. The touch of his lips on her skin was so gentle it felt like the brush of butterfly wings.

He continued to caress her as his lips sought hers again and again. He explored her neck, her arms, her breasts beneath the whale bones that stiffened her corset with his fingertips. She was barely aware of him removing her clothes, yet somehow, both of them were suddenly naked, their discarded clothes cushioning them against the sharp edges of the coal.

'I've dreamed of this many times during the last year, but when I did we were always in a feather bed in a bedroom in Ignatova House, not a coal tram outside Beletsky and Parry's colliery.' He buried both his hands in her hair, pulling it free from the remaining pins.

'We are,' she whispered as his hands closed over her breasts teasing her nipples. She gasped as he moved his hand between her thighs.

'Do you want me to stop . . . '

'No, Alexei. Please don't. Not now . . . ' she tensed herself for pain. But there was only exquisite pleasure as he moved his body over hers and entered her.

She was jerked awake abruptly by a resounding thud of something metallic hitting concrete. She opened her eyes and looked up at a roof of corrugated metal sheeting. Voices sounded in the distance. Slowly her memory returned and with it the horror of the day before.

She sat up and hit her head on the side of the truck.

'Careful,' Alexei whispered beside her. He reached out and cradled her head.

She rubbed her eyes and opened them wider. The darkness had lightened to a dull grey. Daylight shone through the open far end of the tunnel and she could see a slice of blue sky in the distance.

319

Alexei clambered awkwardly to his knees as he tried to disentangle himself from the tarpaulin without uncovering Anna. He found their clothes in a bundle at their feet. After sorting his from Anna's he handed hers over.

'Alexei?'

'Vlad?' Alexei peered over the top of the rail cart as the head porter appeared at the side of their open railway car. 'The rioters . . . '

'The ones that haven't disappeared into their lairs have been taken into custody by Misha. I've just come from the hospital. Misha's garrisoning the town with troops and organising patrols. It's safe. I came to fetch the others.'

'Others?' Alexei asked.

Vlad moved back and Alexei saw men, women, children, ward maids, porters and nurses climbing out of the cars alongside them. He recognised Miriam and Yulia among them.

Alexei pulled on his shirt, and scrabbled for his trousers. He climbed into them, buttoned his flies, braced himself on the side of the truck and vaulted down before climbing back up on a wheel and offering Anna his hand. She finished fastening her skirt and tucked the hem of her blouse into the waistband, folding it to conceal the tears around the buttonholes. When she tried to balance on the surface of the coal she lost her foothold. Alexei reached in, clamped his hands around her waist and lifted her bodily out on to the tracks.

Anna turned to Vlad. 'Nathan Kharber?'

'Dr Vries cut him and Boris down at dawn. Vasya Kharber has taken her husband's body to the Goldbergs' house in the shtetl. The Jews have closed ranks and armed themselves. Misha Razin has soldiers out hunting for Dr Kharber's and Boris's killers.'

'The porter they killed was Boris?' Alexei asked.

Vlad nodded. 'Misha has declared a curfew and telegraphed for extra soldiers. Anyone caught armed on the street is liable to be shot before being questioned.'

'The cholera?' Anna asked.

'The hospital was full before it was attacked by the rioters, but Dr de Vries thought we'd seen the worse. Dr Kharber disagreed, which is why he sent for you. I think Dr de Vries was right. We had only two new cases in yesterday.'

'I'll go and help.'

'Shouldn't you wash first and get out of those filthy clothes?' Alexei suggested.

Anna looked down at herself.

'Come on I'll take you to Glyn's house. Yelena will have kept the bath house fires burning.'

CHAPTER THIRTY

Hughesovka Hospital July 1892

Alexei and Anna stood in front of the hospital and stared at the devastation wrought by the riot. Alexei's wooden house was a scattering of burned ashes. An armed soldier stood in front of them in the ruin of what had been Alexei's garden. Glyn and Praskovia's front garden had been devastated, plants and trees uprooted and the front windows of the house smashed in. The outer door hung at an angle, suspended by a single hinge. But the inner door had held firm.

Yelena saw them and came out to meet them, leaving by the back door. She hugged first Alexei then Anna.

'Praskovia?'

'She, Glyn, Pytor and the boys are fine. They will shortly be leaving Yalta for St Petersburg. Praskovia will write to you.'

'Good! This place is finished. I'll pack the little that remains here and go and join them.' Without another word, she turned and went back into the house.

Anna looked across the road to the hospital.

'We could go to the Ignatova Estate,' Alexei suggested.

If Anna heard him she didn't say anything. She walked past the porters who were clearing the remains of the bonfire that had been built around the tree. Noah was standing in the shell of the office. The windows had been smashed in, the furniture dragged out to feed the bonfire. He stepped out of the shattered wall to meet her.

'You came.'

'As you see.' Anna found it hard to hold back her tears as she looked at him.

'I begged Nathan not to send that telegram because I knew you'd come.'

'You wanted me to stay away?'

322

'Yes, because things were turning ugly even before he sent the porter to the telegraph office, but I couldn't talk him out of it. He said you'd helped Sarah fight the first cholera epidemic here and well as the three since . . . '

'I did, and people died in every one of them. If there's a cure for cholera I have no idea what it is, but I can understand him sending for me.'

'You can?'

'Nathan and I fought many epidemics in this town together. Not just cholera but smallpox, typhoid, diphtheria . . . '

Noah turned and looked at the hospital. 'The fight that needs winning now, is the one to repair and rebuild the hospital. The company has already sent some carpenters and work has begun.'

'We can help.' She looked around for Alexei and saw him talking to Misha in front of the ashes of his house.

Misha nodded to her. 'I wish you could have had a less eventful welcome home, Matron Parry.'

'So, do I Colonel Razin.'

'You and Alexei look as though you've just crawled out of a coal bunker.'

'We have.' Alexei joined her and shook Dr De Vries' hand. 'It's good to see you unscathed.'

'You made the right decision to run back into the station after you arrived last night,' Noah said. 'Take a doctor's advice. Go home, wash and rest.'

'Not when there's so much to be done,' Anna protested. 'I can't speak for Alexei but I'm fine . . . '

'You're exhausted, Anna,' Noah contradicted firmly. 'Besides I've closed the doors of the hospital. We won't be taking in any more patients while there's a risk of more riots threatening the lives of the remaining staff. Go to Ignatova House. It might be full . . . '

'Full?' Alexei repeated in surprise.

Vlad walked over to them. 'I sent all the women and children who had escaped the cholera, there yesterday as trouble was starting. Lev and Lada took them in.'

323

'What about the cholera victims who are still in the hospital?' Anna asked.

'We have staff enough to deal with them without your help, Anna.' Noah said. 'Take my carriage, Vlad, and drive Matron Parry and Mr Beletsky to Ignatova.'

'We're filthy,' Anna warned Noah.'

'Vlad, take a sheet from the stores for Matron Parry and Mr Beletsky to sit on. My charity doesn't extend to making work for my orderly.'

Alexei and Vlad spread the sheet, before Alexei helped Anna into the back of the troika and sat alongside her. Vlad flicked the reins and they set off.

Alexei reached for Anna's hand. 'So, we go home scrub ourselves and sleep before we get married.

'Married!' she exclaimed.

'Did I dream last night?'

She blushed. 'If you did, I did too.'

'Then we find Father Grigor. I'm a widower with three daughters, I can't afford to behave in an immoral fashion.'

'Maybe just once more.' She stroked his cheek, trailing black finger marks on the few patches of clean skin that remained. 'Now I know what you can do in a coal truck. I can't wait to see what you'll do in a feather bed.'

EPILOGUE

Owen Parry's ironworkers' cottage Broadway, Treforest, Pontypridd 1956

1892 - Hughesovka was decimated by cholera and violence yet that year marked the onset of the happiest days of my life.

I turn the page of the family album my sister-in-law Sarah had so lovingly kept and find the wedding photograph I am looking for. It had been taken by Noah after a small and quiet ceremony. Noah, Lyudmila, Lev, and Lada were our only witnesses. To look at it you'd never guess that the town was under military curfew, or that Alexei had just spent the best of two hours "persuading" Father Grigor to forgo the banns on the grounds that we could all be murdered any minute.

Alexei – my Alexei – was dressed in a dark wool business suit, unsuitable for a wedding and the time of year. The photograph was monochrome but I didn't need to see the tint to be reminded of the deep cerulean blue of his eyes or the exact shade of his blond hair. I stood beside him in the doorway of Ignatova Russian Orthodox church, Father Grigor towering behind us in his tall hat, beaming like a benign parent. I in a gold lace gown I'd bought for the twins' christening, chosen because it was the best in my wardrobe and too old fashioned to take to smart Yalta.

Our clothes might not have been perfect for a wedding, but the look on our faces was. It was the beginning of a lifelong love affair for both of us. The fairy tale ending "and they lived happily ever after." I re-read the letter Catherine had left for me many times, dwelling on the line,

"I have a dream for you, Anna, one in which you find the happiness you so richly deserve."

Our happiness was gilded when our son Alexei Glyn John Beletsky was born in November 1894, the brother Alexei's girls had longed for. But how long is "ever after"? In our case it lasted twenty-five magical years. A drop in the ocean of the time, but more days than many are given. For me it wasn't enough. It was hard lesson to accept that it had to be.

Hindsight is a wonderful thing. Now, I realise Mr Hughes's death marked the end of life in Hughesovka as we had known it. He'd brought us together. When he was no longer with us, we began to scatter. Roman and Sonya, Glyn and Praskovia, Richard and Sarah and Alexei and I spent a few winter seasons in St Petersburg and summers in Yalta, where Alexei bought us a fine house.

We even occasionally visited Hughesovka because neither Glyn, Alexei nor I, could bring ourselves to sell our houses there, but we rarely stayed longer than a few days. The shadows cast by the riots were too bloody, too recent and too long.

In 1895 Richard, Sarah and Ted returned to Britain. Richard and Sarah to retire to Wales, Ted to take up a position as a lecturer in engineering in a London Technical Institute. With them went Ted's bride, Kitty Beletskaya, with Alexei's and my blessing. Roman, Sonya, Andrei and Spartak, sailed to New York in 1896 as Roman wanted to open an office there to represent his business interests. Newly married to Andrei, Maryanna sailed with them. They were young but their fathers had been forced to give their reluctant consent after relentless nagging, and advice from their respective wives. But I – and Sarah believed that women are destined to remember the powerful force love can wield more than men.

Glyn celebrated his sixty first birthday in 1898 by unveiling the New Russia Company Bessemer Steel Plant in Hughesovka. He watched the first production roll off the line, then retired.

Roman died in New York in April in 1914. By then Andrei was administering the Nadolny American empire from a New York Office, and Spartak the London office. Roman had built his business well, spreading his interests far and wide. They say a Russian can never live happily anywhere except Russia. Sonya proved the old adage when she returned to St Petersburg with Tatiana in July 1914, and tried to pick up the threads of her life. Alexei and I were glad to see her, but it was as though she'd been reduced to an empty shell of a lamp that no longer held a flame.

It took days for the news of the outbreak of war to percolate to Hughesovka and when it did, many of the men from Hughesovka's British community left to join the British army, Glyn's son Tom and our son Alexei among them. Ruth and Tatiana went with the men, both had trained as nurses. How could they not with Sarah and I as their godmothers?

Glyn died shortly after Christmas 1914 at the age of 77. We accompanied Praskovia, Pytor and Pavlov to Hughesovka and buried Glyn next to his brother Peter who had died in the first cholera epidemic to decimate the town in 1870. Praskovia, Pytor and Pavlov never returned to St Petersburg.

Alexei, Sonya, Tatiana and I hoped the war would be short lived. None of us, or our friends or even the government anticipated the abdication of the Tsar in 1917 or the advent of the revolution.

In 1918 with the country in turmoil we booked tickets on a train to Yalta in the hope of finding a boat to take us to England. Groups of marauding Bolshevik cavalry were everywhere on the steppe. We stopped at Hughesovka hoping to persuade Praskovia, Pavlov and Pytor to come with us. Praskovia refused, reminding us that she had been born in Hughesovka and planned to die there.

Pavlov, his wife and children and Pytor stayed with her, but Noah de Vries Yulia and Miriam decided to leave with us.

We waited four days for a train, but it was a short-lived journey. An hour out of Hughesovka we were halted by a barricade.

A brigade of Bolsheviks appeared at dusk and hauled everyone off the train. Despite our attempts to disguise ourselves and dress as peasants, their leader recognised Alexei, and Sonya, hardly surprising as Grisha was the captain and he'd appointed Nathan's foster sons Ifim and Naum as his lieutenants.

Grisha had just singled out Alexei and Sonya when Misha appeared with cohort of the White army. In all the confusion and fighting that followed I remember Alexei holding my hand and saying, "I love you. Tell the children and take care of them.'

Sometime during the darkness, the fighting stopped and the train moved out, armed Bolsheviks stood in the open doors of the carriages preventing anyone from climbing in. There was no question of leaving the steppe, or joining the victors or vanquished for me. All I knew was that Alexei was no longer by side. He and Sonya had been torn away during the night.

When dawn broke the steppe was littered with the dead and the dying, Bolshevik and White Cossack alike. For once I left the injured to the ministrations of others. People appeared, warning us that other parties of Bolsheviks were roaming the area they took us to shelter in their "hole houses".

There was no food, the children were crying and I was glad to leave at dusk to join the search for Sonya and Alexei with Noah. When we didn't find their bodies among the dead we rode out on some of the abandoned horses. Two miles from the track we fell in with the survivors of Misha's Cossacks.

They were digging the steppe. Noah and I joined them, shovelling the earth away with our bare hands. By the light of an oil lamp we uncovered Misha and Alexei. They lay, side by side, face muscles contorted, limbs in spasm. From the marks on their hands and the dirt packed into their airways we knew they had been buried alive.

Even now, thirty-eight years later I relive Alexei's last minutes over and over again in my nightmares. I fight with him for breath, see the thoughts as they whirl through his mind, taste the bitterness of the certainty that he will never see his beloved children or me again. They say we take love with us when we die. Did he take the love we bore one another and the love he bore for Mother Russia – a country so battered, bruised and torn it had produced a people complicit in the murder even of its patriots.

I wanted to take his body and bury it in the Ignatova churchyard with Catherine, his mother, sisters and Ruth. It seemed right that I return him to her in death. Noah and the soldiers, and perhaps even more than them, the endless panorama of the steppe itself dissuaded me.

I laid out Alexei and Misha's bodies, and washed them as best I could with the contents of a soldier's canteen. The lieutenant in charge of the soldiers recited as much as he could remember of the Russian Orthodox Burial Service before ordering his men to refill the grave.

The soldiers and Noah looked for Sonya while I said my final goodbye. The hardest thing I ever did in my life was leave Alexei in that ground. I turned back to take a last look before walking away, trying to fix the spot in my mind so in the unlikely event I returned I could find it again.

At that moment, the sun moved out from behind a cloud and shone directly on the bare earth that covered Alexei. I had enough faith then, and retain it now, to believe that was the only way open to Alexei to comfort me.

We sheltered in the hole houses for two months all the while asking every traveller sympathetic to the "Whites" who passed if they had seen Sonya. Another train eventually arrived and we continued our journey. We reached a Yalta packed with refugees, aristocrats and distant members of the Romanoff family – and miraculously Andrei and Spartak who were looking for their mother. They had a yacht and a letter from my brother Richard addressed to Alexei and me begging us to return to Wales, reminding us that Alexei had investments in Richard's business ventures. Incapable of making my own decisions I was glad to have advice to follow.

My son Alexei survived the war and married in 1919, Ruth married a doctor in 1920, both settled in Britain. I moved in with Richard and Sarah. Sarah died in 1921 at the age of 80. Richard lived for another ten years, but like Sonya after Roman's death it was as though the heart had been torn from him and not even his children and grandchildren could give him reason enough to cling to life.

Richard's house was too large for me to manage. My brother Owen had lost his wife and retired to one of a terrace of cottages he had bought outside Pontypridd in Treforest to provide him with an income in old age. I rented the one next door to him.

I continued to write to Praskovia until her death in 1937 and afterwards sent money to Pavlov, enough to help not only him but the friends who'd survived the war and revolution. Harriet disappeared a few years after Misha's death, as did Glyn's wife Betty Edwards and Grisha and his wife Alice. No one volunteered any information as to their fate but Post revolution Russia wasn't a place to ask questions.

I never stopped making enquiries or looking for Sonya, Not even after another world war. Neither did Tatiana, Andrei and Spartak. Those who searched on our behalf uncovered dreadful stories.

Of those labelled "former people" who'd held positions under the Tsarist Regime, being denied papers and ration cards to starve to death. Of the forced "socialisation" of young girls in the barracks of the Red Army where they were passed from private to private, in some cases until they died from what was being done to them. Of writers, poets, philosophers and poets being incarcerated in psychiatric wards and forcibly drugged until they did eventually succumb to insanity.

When I read those reports I was glad that my Alexei did to not live to see the new Soviet Socialist Russia, with its cruelty, shortages and gross inhumanity that wove a drab greyness through every facet of existence, sucking all joy from life.

Now – I have my family - Kitty and Ted live a few miles from me and one or the other calls in to see me every day. Her and Ted's grandson –a fourth generation Alexei is the mirror image of his great grandfather. He will soon begin to study Engineering in London. My Alexei would have been – and perhaps is - so proud.

I look down at the documents and files waiting to be carried to the archives. My work is done. I still have my past and it's true to say that you never really lose your dead. Soon I will join them but the part of me that I have documented will remain for those who are interested in one man's dreams and the legacy he left. The ironworks he built is still in production, the collieries mine coal. Governments and ideologies come and go, but people – I have faith that the best of humanity will survive.

A shaft of light pierces the darkness. The door opens. My eyes remain closed but I sense him stealing in, wary of disturbing me. It's too dark for me to see his face but I don't need the light. His features are imprinted on my memory. They are those of his great grandfather, alive again. I only have to close my eyes to conjure them.

He moves to the bed, removes the photograph album from my hands and lays his fingers gently on my forehead.

His touch is soft, cool, like the whisper of the spring wind brushing over a mound of earth on the Russian Steppe.

HISTORICAL NOTES AND TIMELINE

As of April 2014, Hughesovka – Stalino – Donestk - (to give the city all its names) - has been part of the "Donetsk People's Republic" – a self-proclaimed separatist entity, backed by Russia, which is embroiled in a civil war.

The Ukrainian Parliament endorsed a resolution to open a national John Hughes museum in the industrial city of Donetsk, originally called Hughesovka, as well as issue a commemorative stamp to mark the 200th anniversary of his birth in 2015.

After the fall of Communism, a statue of John Hughes was erected in Donetsk (Hughesovka) near the Scientific Library of Donetsk Technical University.

There are no statues or monuments commemorating John Hughes's achievements in Wales, however in 2014, an instrumental on the Welsh band Manic Street Preachers' album Futurology paid homage to him, referring to Donetsk by its former name.

The best and most special days are the ones when I hear from a reader. I would like to thank everyone who has written or e-mailed me to tell me that they have enjoyed reading my books, especially the direct descendant of John Hughes's eldest son, who telephoned me to talk about John Hughes and her family. A conversation I cherish. I hope she will enjoy this last book in the series.
Catrin Collier January 2018

TIMELINE

1903 - Questions were asked in the Duma about the high incidence of accidents in the New Russia Company's works and collieries. 8 men were injured on average every day.

1905 – Hughesovka's population was counted at 50,000 inhabitants, 4,500 men and women were miners and 5,000 were factory workers.

1906 – The French manager of the processing plant of the New Russia Company was shot and the British Foreign Office advised managers to leave.

1909 - A statue to the "Reforming Tsar Alexander II was unveiled in Moscow to commemorate his decree to end serfdom. Officially ostracised in 1917 it was removed in 1937 and replaced with anew monument in 2005.

1914 – John Hughes's heirs sold their last interest in the New Russia Company to a French consortium, before the outbreak of the First World War.

1917 - 2000 workers in Hughesovka met to hear reports on the workers' revolution

- February – the revolution began with strikes, demonstrations, and mutinies in Petrograd

March 2 - Czar Nicholas II abdicated on his own and his son's behalf. Nicholas' brother, Mikhail announced his refusal to accept the throne. The Provisional Government was formed

April 3 – Lenin returned from exile and arrived in Petrograd via a sealed train   July 3-7 – After the Bolsheviks unsuccessfully tried to direct public protests against the Provisional Government into a coup Lenin was forced into hiding

July 11 - Alexander Kerensky was appointed Prime Minister of the Provisional Government

August 22-27 - General Lavr Kornilov, commander of the Russian Army led a failed coup.

October 25 - The October Revolution - the Bolsheviks took Petrograd

October 26 – The Winter Palace, the last holdout of the Provisional Government, was taken by the Bolsheviks; the Council of People's Commissars (abbreviated as Sovnarkom), with Lenin at its head was in control of Russia

January 4th - the New Russia Company was formerly nationalised

March 3rd – The Treaty of Brest Litovsk between Germany and Russia, was signed formerly ending Russia's participation in World War 1.

March 8th - The Bolshevik Party changed its name to the Communist Party

March 11 - The capital of Russia was changed from St. Petersburg to Moscow

June – The beginning of the Russian civil war

July 17th - Czar Nicholas II and his family were executed

August 30 - An assassination attempt left Lenin seriously wounded

1920 - November – end of the Russian Civil war.

1922 - April 3rd - Stalin was appointed General Secretary

December 15th - Lenin suffered a second stroke and retired from politics

December 30th - The Union of Soviet Socialist Republics (U.S.S.R.) was established

1924 - January 21st - Lenin died. Stalin succeeded him.

HEARTS OF GOLD

CATRIN COLLIER

Chapter One

'Bethan! Bethan!' Elizabeth Powell rapped hard on the door of the bedroom that her daughters' shared.

'Coming, Mam,' Bethan murmured sleepily. She listened as her mother retreated back to her own bedroom then, keeping her eyes firmly closed, she reluctantly forced her hand out of the warm cocoon of sheets and blankets to test the air. It was icy after the warm snugness of the bed, and she quickly pulled her arm back beneath the bedclothes for a few seconds more of blissful warmth.

Once again Elizabeth's voice cut stridently through the frosty air.

'I'm up, Mam,' Bethan lied.

'I hardly think so.' Elizabeth opened the door and pushed the switch down on the round black box. Bethan screwed her eyes against the sudden glare of yellow light. It wasn't enough. Eyelids burning, she burrowed into the bed and pulled the blanket over her head.

'Breakfast in ten minutes, Bethan,' her mother's voice intruded into the darkness.

'Yes, Mam.'

She waited until she heard the fierce click of the iron latch falling on the bar. The third stair from the top creaked, then the seventh as her mother descended to the ground floor. Keeping her nose hidden beneath the blankets, she opened her eyes and peered sleepily at the room around her.

Apart from a change of wallpaper, it hadn't altered since her grandmother had left it fourteen years before. The thick red plush curtains that had been hers hung, faded but well brushed and straight, at the windows. The old fashioned Victorian mahogany bedroom furniture Caterina had inherited as a bride gleamed darkly against the heavily patterned red and gold walls.

Her favourite Rossetti prints hung on the wall next to the wardrobe, and the pink glass ring holder, candlesticks' and hair tidy that had been a present from her sons stood on the dressing table. The room might now belong to Bethan and her sister Maud, but it was also an encapsulation of Bethan's earliest childhood memories.

She had toddled in here when she was barely high enough to reach the washstand. Crouching behind the bed, she had watched her grandmother wash and dress and afterwards sit on the stool in front of the dressing-table mirror to brush out her hair. Rich, black, it was scarcely touched with grey on the day she'd died.

Once Caterina had finished, she'd turn and smile. A warm, welcoming, special smile that Bethan knew she kept just for her. And then came the excitement of *the tin*. The old Huntley and Palmer biscuit tin in which Caterina kept her prized collection of foreign coins.

Bethan had spent hours as a child, sitting on the cold, oilcloth-covered floor at Caterina's feet; playing with them, grouping them into armies fighting strange and wondrous battles that she'd heard the grown-ups talking about. Mons – Amiens - the Somme . . .

Not only Bethan's but also her sister's and brothers' happiest childhood memories stemmed from the time when Mam Powell had lived with them.

Evan Powell's' mother, Caterina, had been a large, warm-hearted, old-fashioned Welsh widow who'd spent her life working, caring, cuddling (or cwtching as they say in Wales) her family. True happiness for her had ended along with her husband's life; contentment vanished the day Evan, brought his bride into the family home. She tried valiantly to conceal her dislike of Elizabeth, but everyone who knew Caterina also knew that she'd never taken to her eldest son's choice of wife.

In her shrewd, common-sense way Caterina had summed Elizabeth Powell nee Bull up as a cold, arrogant, snobbish woman but, concerned only for Evan's happiness she could have forgiven Evan's love any failing other than hard-heartedness.

Fearing for the emotional well-being of her unborn grandchildren it was she who persuaded Evan to set up home with Elizabeth in the parlour and front bedroom of the house that her collier husband had bought for less than two hundred pounds in the "good times" before strikes and the depression hit Pontypridd and the Rhondda mining valleys. And she did it in full knowledge that Elizabeth would destroy the peace and harmony that reigned in the household.

Elizabeth fought hard against Evan's suggestion of setting up home with her mother-and brother-in-law, but Evan remained firm. Quite aside from his mother's wishes finances dictated compromise. Not a man to shirk his responsibilities, he accepted that it was his duty as eldest son to support his mother and his wife, and the easiest way he could think of fulfilling both obligations was by installing them under the same roof. Besides, in his acknowledged biased opinion, his mother's house was amongst the best on the Graig.

Certainly the bay windowed, double-fronted house in Graig Avenue had more than enough room for all the Powell's – three good-sized bedrooms, a box room, two front parlours and a comfortable back kitchen complete with a range that held bread and baking ovens as well as a hinge-topped water boiler with a brass tap from which hot water could be drawn. Doors from the kitchen led into a walk-in, stone-slabbed pantry and a lean-to washhouse.

The washhouse opened into the yard that housed the coal house and outside WC (all its own, not shared). It was a palace compared to the back-to-back, two-up one-downs at the foot of the Graig hill.

What Evan didn't discuss with Elizabeth or his mother, was the full extent of the mortgage on the house. He'd been fourteen and his brother William twelve when their father had collapsed and fallen in front of a tram at the Maritime pit.

Jim Owen, the pit manager, sent Caterina Powell ten pounds to cover the funeral expenses. It was good of him. She knew full well that as the accident was her husband's fault she was entitled to nothing. The Maritime's Colliers organised a whip round amongst themselves and raised another fifteen pounds.

It was the largest sum ever collected after a pit death, and a fine testimonial to Evan Powell senior's popularity, but it wasn't enough to buy his widow, or his sons, security.

Evan and William left school the day of the funeral, and Jim Owen took them on as boy colliers out of respect for their father.

So they began their working lives where Evan Powell senior had ended his and without giving the matter a thought, also assumed his obligations, paying his bills, his mortgage and providing their mother with housekeeping, the only money she ever handled.

And she, too grief-stricken to realise what was happening, allowed her eldest son to assume the responsibilities of the man of the house, responsibilities he shouldered with a maturity far beyond his years.

Time passed, Caterina's grief healed after a fashion - and then came Elizabeth.

The major alterations to the domestic life of the Graig Avenue household after Evan and Elizabeth's marriage came in the shape of the additions they were blessed with. Bethan was born seven months after their wedding day. Haydn less than a year later, Eddie on their fourth anniversary and Maud on Bethan's sixth birthday.

Caterina and Elizabeth were soon too busy to quarrel, and the initial resentment Elizabeth felt towards her mother-in-law for keeping hold of the domestic reins of the household faded with the birth of Haydn.

The babies generated enough work to keep a dozen pairs of hands occupied, let alone two. And although neither woman learned to like, let alone love the other, seven years under the same roof did teach them a wary kind of tolerance.

The thunder of Haydn and Eddie's feet hammering down the stairs shook Bethan out of her reverie. It would be wonderful to lie here for another two or three hours, staring at the walls, thinking of nothing in particular, but duty and her mother called.

Maud stirred next to her in the bed. Pulling the blankets close about her ears, her sister burrowed deeper into the feather mattress, making small, self-satisfied grunting noises as she curled complacently back into her dreams.

Bethan looked enviously at the mop of blonde curls; all that could be seen of Maud above the blankets. What it was to be thirteen years old and still at school. If Maud got up two hours from now she'd still make it to her class in Maesycoed Seniors by nine, but there was little point in wishing herself any younger.

Grabbing the ugly grey woollen dressing gown that her mother had cut and sewn from a surplus army blankets three Christmases ago, she sat up and swung her legs out of the tangle of flannelette sheets and blankets. Five o'clock on any morning was a disgusting hour to leave a warm, comfortable bed. On a cold, dismal January morning it was worse than disgusting. It was brutal.

For all of her five feet eight inches, her feet dangled several inches above the floor. Mam Powell's bed was higher than any hospital bed. Easy to make, but painful to climb out of when there was ice in the air.

341

Sliding forward she perched precariously on the edge of the mattress and ran the tips of her toes over the freezing floor in search of her pressed felt slippers. She found one, then standing on her left leg, the other. As she shuffled across the room she thought wistfully of the last film she'd seen in the White Palace.

Claudette Colbert had floated elegantly around a vast, dazzlingly pale, beautifully furnished bedroom in a creamy lace and satin gown that she'd casually referred to as a "negligee". The actress would probably sooner have died than don a grey woollen dressing gown and flat tartan slippers with red pom-poms. But then, Claudette Colbert looked as though she'd never had to trek out to a back yard first thing in the morning either.

If the newsreels and Hollywood stories in the Sunday papers were to be believed, film stars had luxurious bathrooms with bubble-filled baths the size of the paddling pool in Ponty Park. And they could afford to keep fires burning in their bedrooms all night without giving a thought to the twenty-two shillings a load of coal cost a miner on short time and rations.

She twitched aside the curtains and tried to peer through the coating of frost on the window pane. Breathing on the glass, she rubbed hard with the edge of her hand and made a peephole.

The street lamps burned alongside the houses in the Avenue in a straight line, golden beacons radiating a glow that dispelled the navy-blue darkness and lit up the high garden wall of Danygraig House opposite. Dawn was still hours away. She studied the unmade ground of the street beneath her. It was covered with a fine layer of white, but there were dark shadows alongside the stones. Too thin to be snow.

342

Frost and that meant a cold and slippery walk down the Graig hill to the hospital. She left the window and heaved on the bottom drawer of the dressing table. It jerked out sluggishly, with the stickiness of furniture kept too long in a cold, damp house. Rummaging impatiently through the tangle of clothes, she searched for an extra pair of back woollen stockings. Nurses, especially trainee nurses were only supposed to wear one pair, but her legs had been almost blue with cold when she'd left her ward at the end of yesterday's shift, and there hadn't been frost on the ground then.

She found the stockings and tossed them on to the pile of underclothes and uniform that she'd laid out on the stool the night before. Warm legs were worth the risk of an official reprimand, even from Sister Church.

Heaving the drawer shut with her foot as well as her hands, she went to the washstand. She picked up the unwieldy old fashioned yellow jug decorated with transfers of sepia country scenes and tried to pour its contents into the washbowl.

Nothing happened. Shivering as the chill atmosphere permeated her dressing gown she brushed her dark hair away from her face and looked down into the jug. Pushing her fingers into the neck, she confirmed her suspicions. A thick frozen crust capped the water.

Even if she succeeded in breaking through it without cracking the jug, the thought of washing in chunks of ice didn't appeal to her. Pulling the collar of her dressing gown as high as it would go she tightened the belt and left the bedroom, stepping down on to the top stair.

Unlike the bedroom, the stairs were carpeted with jute, held in place by three cornered oak rods. She trod lightly on the third and fourth stair from the top. Their rods were fragile – broken when her brothers, Haydn and Eddie, had purloined them to use as swords after watching a Douglas Fairbanks' film.

343

The rods had survived the fencing match, but neither had survived the beating her mother had inflicted on the boys with them when she'd found out what they'd done.

The light was burning in the downstairs passage as she made her way to the back kitchen. Her father, mother and eldest brother were up and dressed, breakfasting at the massive dark oak table that, together with the open-shelved dresser, dominated the room.

'Good morning, Bethan,' her mother offered frigidly with a scarcely perceptible nod towards the corner where their lodger Alun Jones was lacing his collier's boots.

Alun looked up and for all of his thirty-five years turned a bright shade of beetroot.

Irritated, Bethan tied her dressing gown even closer around her shivering body.

'Good morning,' she mumbled in reply to her mother's greeting. 'The water in the jug is frozen, so I came down for some warm,' she added, trying to excuse her state of undress.

In middle age, Elizabeth Powell was a tall, thin, spare woman. Spare in flesh and spare in spirit. Bethan, like her brothers and Maud, was afraid not so much of her mother but of the atmosphere she exuded which was guaranteed to dampen the liveliest spirit. Elizabeth certainly had an outstanding ability to make herself and everyone around her feel miserable and uncomfortable.

But she hadn't always possessed that trait. She'd acquired and honed it to perfection during twenty-one years of silent, suffering marriage to Evan Powell.

Her silence. His suffering.

At the time none of the Powells' friends or acquaintances could fathom exactly why Evan Powell, a strapping, tall, dark (and curly haired with it) handsome young miner of twenty-three had suddenly decided to pay court to a thin, dour schoolmistress ten years older than himself. But court her he had, and the courtship had culminated a few weeks later in a full chapel wedding attended by both families.

Elizabeth's relatives had been both bemused and upset by the match. In their opinion Elizabeth hadn't so much, stepped down in the world, as slid. True, she had little to recommend her as a wife. Thirty three years old, like most women of her generation she was terrified of being left on the shelf.

She certainly had no pretensions to beauty. Even then, her hair could have been more accurately described as colourless rather than fair. Her eyes were of a blue more faded than vibrant, and her face thin-nosed, thin-lipped, thin-browed, tended to look disapprovingly down on the world in general, and Pontypridd and the working-class area of the Graig where Evan Powell lived in particular.

She was tall for a woman. Five feet nine inches and Evan's younger brother, William, rather unkindly commented that the one good thing that could be said about her was she looked well on his brother's arm from the rear.

Before her marriage Elizabeth had possessed a good figure, and she'd known how to dress. But when marriage put an end to her career as an assistant school mistress in Maesycoed junior school, it also put an end to the generous dress allowance that had been her one extravagance. Not that she came to marriage empty-handed. She'd saved a little money of her own to add to the small nest egg her mother had left her, and Evan, generous and self-sacrificing to the last, had urged her to spend that money or at least the interest it accumulated, on herself.

However, her Baptist minister father had fostered a spirit of sanctity towards savings within the confines of her flat breast that was matched only by the feeling of absolute superiority to the mining classes that he'd engendered in her narrow mind. She would have as soon pawned the family bible as used her deposit account to buy smart or fashionable clothes.

The marriage, begun as an anomaly, continued in silence.

Evan never discussed his feelings with anyone, least of all his wife and Elizabeth, disgusted with herself for falling prey to what she privately considered a lapse into "bestial passion" never divulged what had attracted her to Evan.

Evan was extremely good-looking, even by Pontypridd standards where well set up strongly built colliers were the rule rather than the exception. Six feet three inches in his stocking feet, with an exotic swarthy complexion that he'd inherited from his maternal Spanish grandfather, he was just the type to excite John Joseph Bull's suspicions.

John Joseph was Elizabeth's uncle, the brother of her dead father. A Baptist minister too, he knew, or thought he knew, everything there was to know about lust, as those who heard his sermons soon found out.

"A devil sent demon to lead the weak and ungodly into a foul world of naked, hairy limbs, lewdness and lechery."

Small children sat bemused as he railed against both sexes for their fragile, miserable morals.

Unlike some of his colleagues he realised that women could fall prey to the temptations of that particular cardinal sin as well as men. As an active revivalist, evangelist and minister of God, his knowledge was not based on experience but on years of watching and noting the depths to which the people who lived within the boundaries of his chapel's sphere could sink.

He ascribed his interest in the human condition to charitable motives. Evan who was considered remarkably well read even for a miner, called it by another name. Voyeurism.

John Joseph's wife Hetty, a small, quiet, mousy woman some twenty years younger than he, had a sense of duty that extended into every aspect of their joyless married life, from the kitchen to the bedroom and the Sunday night ritual during which, after lengthy and suitable prayer, John Joseph lifted her nightdress - the only night of the week he allowed himself to do so.

Hetty was a paragon but John Joseph saw enough miners' daughters and wives to know that other kinds existed.

Some were even brazen enough to eye men when they sat in his chapel pews. He'd caught sight of them after the service, walking off shamelessly, arm in arm with their paramours into the secluded areas of Ynysangharad War Memorial Park, or up Pit Road where they disappeared into the woods around Shoni's pond.

The thought of his niece and Evan Powell following either route incensed and disgusted him. But Elizabeth Bull was way past the age when she needed a guardian's blessing to marry. He could do nothing except voice his disapproval. Which he did long, loud and vociferously, both before and after the ceremony.

He'd refused to give Elizabeth away on the grounds that he wouldn't be an active party to her social demise. But his contempt for Evan and the mining classes didn't prevent him from officiating as minister over the proceedings. It also gave him the opportunity to speak at the small reception that his wife Hetty had dutifully arranged in the vestry.

He saw himself as a plain speaking man, but even Hetty, who was used to his harsh, God-fearing ways, cringed when he pointed a long thin finger at Elizabeth, glowered at her darkly and bellowed that he was glad, really glad, that his dead brother and sister-in-law were not alive to see their daughter sink so low.

Elizabeth recalled his words every day of her married life. They came to here even now as she looked around her kitchen and saw her daughter in a state of undress, the unhealthy colour rising in the lodger's cheeks as he surreptitiously ogled the curves outlined beneath the thin cloth of Bethan's dressing gown, her son and husband sitting at the table, boots off, not even wearing collars with their shirts.

347

She felt that not only herself but her children had sunk to the lowest level of the working class life she'd been forced to live and had learned to despise with every fibre of her being.

'I'll draw the water for you, Beth.' Haydn smiled cheerfully at his sister as he pushed the last piece of bread and jam from his plate into his mouth.

'Thank you.' Bethan walked past the pantry and unlatched the planked door that led into the wash house. Switching on the light she sidestepped between the huge, round gas wash boiler and massive stone sink that served the only tap in the house. Opening the outside door, she caught her breath in the face of the cold wind that greeted her, placed her foot in the yard and slid precariously across the four feet of iced paving stones that separated the house and garden ways, grazing her hands painfully in the process.

She gripped the wall desperately trying to maintain her balanced while she regained her breath. The drains had obviously overflowed before the frost had struck, and the whole of the back yard was covered by a sheet of black ice.

'Sorry, Sis, I would have warned you, but you came out a bit fast.'

She squinted into the darkness, and saw her youngest brother Eddie brushing his boots on the steps that led to the shed and the square of fenced in dirt where her father kept his lurcher.

'I bet you would have,' she replied caustically. Rubbing the sting out of her hands she inched her way along the wall until she reached the narrow alley in the back right hand corner of the yard that led to the ty bach or "little house" that hid the WC.

Protected from the weather on three sides by the house, high garden wall and the communal outhouse wall they shared with next door, it wasn't quite as cold as the yard and thanks to the rags that her father had wrapped around the pipes and high cistern, the plumbing worked in spite of the frost.

The heat blasted welcomingly into her stiff and frozen face when she returned to the kitchen. Haydn was sitting on the kerb of the hearth filling her mother's enamel kitchen jug from the brass tap of the boiler set into the range.

'Mind you top that water level up before you go.' Elizabeth carped at Haydn. 'I've no time to do it, and if the level falls low the boiler will blow.

'I'll do it now:' Haydn winked at Bethan as he handed the steaming jug across the table. Six feet tall with blond hair and deep blue eyes that could melt the most granite-like heart, Haydn was the family charmer. His looks contributed only in part to that charm. His regular features were set attractively in his long face, and his full mouth was frequently curved into a beguiling smile, but it was his manner that won him most friends. At nineteen, he possessed a tact, diplomacy and an apparent sincerity that was the envy of every clergyman, Baptist as well as Anglican, on the Graig.

'You won't be topping up anything unless you hurry,' Elizabeth complained sourly. 'It's a quarter-past five now.'

'The wagons won't be leaving the brewery yard until seven. I've plenty of time to get there, persuade the foreman to give me a morning's work, and load up before they roll,' Haydn said evenly carrying his plate into the washhouse.

'It'll take you a good half an hour to get down the hill in this weather.'

'Don't look for trouble where there is none, Mam.' Haydn returned with a jug of cold water, and pinched Elizabeth's wrinkled cheek gently as he passed. He was the only one of her children who would have dared take the liberty. 'I'll be in Leyshon's yard before I know it, with all that ice to slide down.'

'Taking the backside out of your trousers like you did when you were a boy. Well I've no money to give you for new ones.'

'I don't expect you to keep me, Mam.' Haydn dodged past her and walked over to the hearth.

Not content with the sight of Haydn doing what she'd asked, Elizabeth turned on Bethan. 'And you, Miss,' she said sharply. 'You'll have to get a move on if you're to be on your ward at half-past six.'

'I'm going upstairs now, Mam.' Despite what she'd said, Bethan still hovered uneasily next to Haydn. 'I'll just get a dry towel.' She unhooked the rope that hoisted the airer to the ceiling.

'And you' can leave that alone when you like. I put a clean towel upstairs for you and Maud yesterday.'

'Thank you, Mam. I didn't notice,' Bethan said meekly. She had achieved what she wanted.

Her father and Alun Jones had pulled on their coal-encrusted coats and caps, picked up their knapsacks, and were heading out through the door. If she succeeded in lingering in the kitchen for another minute or two she wouldn't have to embarrass Alun, or herself, again by waking past him in her dressing gown.

'Good luck, snookems,' her father said with a tenderness that her mother never voiced. 'Not that you need it.'

"Snookems." It had been a long time since he had called her that. On impulse she replaced the jug on the tiled hearth, reached out and hugged him.

His working clothes reeked of the acrid odours of coal and male sweat, but neither that nor the coal dust that rubbed off on her face stopped her from planting a hearty kiss on his bristly cheek.

'Thanks for remembering, Dad,' she murmured. 'I need all the luck I can get today.'

'Not you,' Haydn commented firmly, picking up the rag-filled lisle stocking that served as a pot holder. 'You've done enough studying in the last three years to carry you to doctor level, let alone nurse.'

Bethan moved out of the way as he lifted the lid on the boiler. Clouds of steam filled the air accompanied by a hissing, sizzling sound as water splashed over the hotplates' as well as into the boiler.

'That's right, make a mess of it,' Elizabeth moaned. 'Just after I've black leaded the top.'

'Looks like I have. Sorry, Mam,' Haydn apologised cheerfully. 'If you leave it, I'll clean it off this afternoon.'

'As if I'd leave it.'

'We're off then, Elizabeth,' Evan said softly, pushing the tin box that held his food and the bottle that held his cold tea into his blackened knapsack.

'About time,' she said harshly, angry at being interrupted.

'See you tonight, Bethan,' Evan murmured as he and Alun left the kitchen.

As soon as Bethan heard the front door slamming behind them she grabbed the jug, and ran down the passage and up the stairs before her mother could find anything else to complain about.

When she reached her bedroom she found the door closed and the room in darkness. She switched on the light and carried the steaming jug over to the washstand.

'I thought you'd gone,' Maud mumbled sleepily from the depths of the bed. 'I had to get up to turn off the light.'

'Sorry. Go back to sleep.' Bethan tipped the hot water into the bowl and took the soap and flannel from the dish. The marble surface of the washstand was cold, the flannel encrusted with ice.

Shivering, she stooped to look in the mirror when she washed, wishing herself shorter and more graceful, like Maud or her best friend and fellow trainee nurse, Laura Ronconi.

She was huge. Big and clumsy, she decided disparagingly, as she sponged the goose pimples on her exposed skin. Life was completely unfair. She was the eldest, why hadn't she been blessed with Maud's looks?

Her younger sister was a fragile five feet four inches, with the same angelic blue eyes and blonde hair as Haydn.

Not yet fourteen, she had the quiet grace of a girl on the brink of attractive, elegant womanhood. While she had a dark, drab complexion, and the height of a maypole.

She finished washing, tipped the water into the slop jar beneath the stand, and began to dress.

Her hair wasn't *too* bad, she decided critically, studying the cropped black glossy waves, which Maud had coaxed into a style that wouldn't have disgraced an aspiring Hollywood starlet. And her eyes, large, brown and thickly fringed with lashes, were passable. Her mouth and nose were *all right,* taken in isolation, the problem came when the whole was put together. Particularly her enormous shoulders.

Wide shoulders looked good on her father, Eddie and Haydn, but they looked dreadful on a woman. Life would be so different if she'd been born pretty. If not small, fragile and blonde like Maud, then at least petite, vivacious and dark like Laura.

The chill damp of the bedroom penetrated her bones. Turning her back on the wardrobe mirror she pulled on her clothes as fast as she could. Chemise, liberty bodice, vest, long petticoat, fleecy -lined drawers, two more petticoats, one pair of stockings.

She picked up the second pair and noticed a hole. Unrolling one of the stockings from her leg she reversed them, donning the one with the hole first, trying valiantly but vainly to manipulate the hole to the sole of her foot.

Uniform dress, belt with plain buckle; she tried - and failed to suppress an image of herself wearing the coveted silver buckle of the qualified nurse - apron, cuffs, collar and finally the veil that covered her one good feature, her hair. Marginally warmer, she stood in front of the oval mirror on the wardrobe door and tried to see the back of her heels. There was a noticeable and definite light patch on her right heel. She debated whether to remove the extra pair of stockings, but the cold decided for her. If she was lucky Sister Church would be too busy, or too cold herself, to spend time checking the uniform of her final year trainees.

'Could be your last day as a student nurse.'

Bethan looked from her reflection towards the bed. Maud's eyes were open.

'You're tempting fate,' she retorted.

'You're more superstitious than Mam Powell ever was. I'm tempting nothing,' Maud said grumpily. 'If you don't pass, no one will.'

'Well, I'll find out soon enough.' Bethan hung her dressing gown in the wardrobe, and folded her nightdress before stuffing it under the pillow on her side of the bed. 'See you tonight?'

'If Mam will let me, I'll bake a celebration cake.'

'Don't you dare.' Bethan switched off the light and left the room. Running down the stairs, she lifted her cloak from the peg behind the front door and returned to the kitchen.

'You're not leaving yourself much time to eat your breakfast,' Elizabeth complained when she walked through the door.

'I'm not that hungry.' Bethan pulled a chair out from under the table.

353

The kitchen was hot and steamy after the bedroom. Oppressively so. She cut a piece of bread from the half-loaf that stood, cut side down, on the scarred and chipped wooden breadboard that had been a part of the table furniture for as long as she could remember. The farmer's butter that had been bought on Pontypridd market was warm and greasy in its nest on the range, and the blackberry jam she had helped her mother make last autumn was freezing cold from the pantry.

'I suppose you'll get your results today,' her mother observed as she poured our two cups of tea.

'I hope to.' Bethan pushed her chair closer to the range so she could make the most of its warmth while she ate.

The boiler and fires in the hospital were banked low with second-grade coal that smouldered rather than burned, barely warming the radiators and covering the yards with smut-laden black smog.

She cut her bread and jam into small squares and began to eat. Elizabeth sat opposite her, sipping her tea with no apparent enjoyment. Bethan didn't attempt to talk. She'd never been close to her mother and didn't miss intimate conversations with her because they'd never had one. Her father had always tried to help with her problems.

He'd given her all the childhood hugs, kisses and treats that she'd received at home, and if she needed a woman to talk to now, she went to Laura or her Aunt Megan.

A month after Evan and Elizabeth's marriage, Evan's younger brother William began courting Megan Davies. Megan was the antithesis of Elizabeth. To use Caterina Powell's terms she was "a nice, warm-hearted Welsh girl, who knew where she came from". (A reference to Elizabeth's refusal to acknowledge her own mother's working-class roots). The daughter and sister of policemen, Megan Davies was smaller, prettier and stronger willed than Elizabeth, and she point-blank refused to move into the Graig Avenue household.

She wouldn't have minded sharing a home with Caterina, in fact she probably would have welcomed the opportunity, as her own mother had died when she was twelve, leaving her with a father and six brothers to look after, but as she put it baldly to William, 'I would as soon move into the workhouse as into the same house as Elizabeth.'

It was left to Evan to solve the problem. Unbeknown to Elizabeth, he took a morning off work, saw the bank manager, and extended the mortgage on the house so he could buy out his brother's share. Elizabeth was furious when she discovered what he'd done and, martyr to the last, took every penny of her hitherto untouched savings and paid off as much of the debt as she could.

A lot more than Evan's pride was damaged by her gesture, but tight-lipped he said nothing and complained to no one.

Blissfully ignorant of Evan's pain, Megan and William were ecstatic. They put down a payment on a small, flat-fronted, terraced house in Leyshon Street. Its front door opened directly on to the pavement. A long thin passage (when she saw it Megan cried, "God help if you're fat") led past the tiny, square front parlour to the back kitchen. A lean to washhouse, two skimpy bedrooms, a box room and a back garden big enough to accommodate the coalhouse, outside WC, washing line, and precious little else comprised the rest of the house. But Megan and William were over the moon. Three streets down the hill from Graig Avenue, they were close enough to visit William's mother and brother when they wished, and far enough away to avoid Elizabeth - most of the time.

Elizabeth disliked Megan from the first, and not just because she had rich brown hair and eyes, a clear, glowing complexion and a slim petite figure that looked well in the discounted clothes that she bought from the shop where she worked.

355

Pregnancy took a heavy toll on Elizabeth's health and looks and by the time William and Megan fixed a date for their wedding she was on her second. Stubbornly refusing Evan's offer of a Provident cheque to buy a new outfit on the grounds that they couldn't afford the shilling in the pound a week repayment, she went to the wedding in a baggy old maternity dress that she knew full well he hated.

Elizabeth's uncle John Joseph, who did the honours for William and Megan as he'd done for her and Evan, publicly pitied Elizabeth, telling her how ill she looked in a booming voice that carried to every corner of the chapel. Satisfied with her sacrificial gesture, she refused to enter the Graig Hotel where the reception was being held, and returned to the house with her baby, secure in the knowledge that she had ruined the day for Evan and upset Caterina. But the wedding was only the first of many irritants that Megan introduced into Elizabeth's life.

Although Megan had come from Bonvilston Road, which was across town and as alien to the people of the Graig as distant places like Cardiff, she was instantly accepted into the community. Elizabeth felt the slight keenly. Despite the fact that she'd lived most of her life in and around Pontypridd, everyone on the Graig referred to her as "the young Mrs Powell" to differentiate between her and Caterina. In a village where first name terms were the rule rather than the exception the title was an insult, particularly when Megan was "Megan" from the outset. As popular, well-liked and accepted as Caterina, Evan and William.

Elizabeth burned at the injustice of it all. In the early days of her marriage she'd desperately tried to please her neighbours. She'd joined several of the committees of her uncle's chapel. She'd visited the sick, cleaned the vestry, organised Sunday school outings and even offered to coach backward children with their school work. But in doing all of that she'd failed to realise the potency of her neighbours' pride.

Rough, untutored self-educated, they earned their weekly wage the hard way, and held their heads high. Taught from birth to scorn charity, they mistrusted the motives that lay behind her overtures. And she, schooled by her father and uncle in "charitable deeds", was incapable of helping people from a sense of fellowship or kindness simply because she'd never possessed either of those qualities.

It never crossed her mind to blame her own short comings for her isolation from the community. Uncultured and uneducated as her neighbours were, they could sniff out those who condescended and patronised a mile off, and she continued to condescend and patronize without even realising she was doing so.

Outwardly she and Evan were no different from anyone else. They had no money to spare or "swank" with. In fact between the demands of her children, the mortgage, and what Evan gave his mother most weeks she was hard put to stretch Evan's wages until his next pay day. But close acquaintance with poverty did nothing to diminish her sense of superiority. If anything it entrenched it, along with her long suffering air of martyrdom.

A year or two passed and she gave up trying to make friends of her neighbours. She decided she didn't need them. After all, they were hardly the type of person she'd associated with in Training College or during her teaching days. Instead she concentrated on domestic chores, filling her days with the drudgery of washing, cooking, cleaning, mending and scrubbing. Making herself a slave to the physical needs of her family, and keeping herself and them strictly within the bounds of what she termed "decency". But in the daily struggle whatever warmth had once existed between her and Evan was irretrievably lost.

When war broke out and flamed across Europe in 1914 it affected even Pontypridd.

In the early days before conscription, some men, including miners volunteered, sincerely believing they were marching to glorious battle and an heroic personal future that would return them to their locals by Christmas. (With luck, covered with enough medals to earn them a few free pints)

Evan knew better. So did William – when he was sober. William and Megan celebrated their fourth wedding anniversary in 1915. Caterina looked after baby William, and William, excited by his and Megan's' first night out together in a long time, went to town. They started the evening at six o'clock in the Graig Hotel then gradually worked their way down the Graig hill, via every pub, until they reached the Half Moon opposite Pontypridd Junction station, and just the other side of the railway bridge that marked the border between the Graig hill and town.

Concerned about the state William was getting himself into, Megan stuck to shandy, and even then, she sat out a couple of rounds. There were over a dozen pubs either on or just off the Graig hill, and William had a pint in every one. Before he'd married Megan he'd been capable of drinking almost any man in Pontypridd under the table and walking a straight line home afterwards.

What he hadn't taken into account was his lack of practice at sinking pints since his marriage. When money was tight, the man's beer was generally the first thing to go, and Evan had warned him, 'The price of getting a woman into your bed is every coin in your pocket.'

William was an inch or two shorter than Evan, but he was still a big man, and worried about getting him home Megan suggested that they catch the second house in the New Theatre – there at least he wouldn't be able to drink any more.

As it turned out, William didn't need much persuading. He was having difficulty standing upright, let alone walking, and he loved the music hall.

In his genial, euphoric state he treated himself and Megan to one shilling and three penny seats in the stalls. It was an unprecedented extravagance that changed his life.

If he'd bought his usual sixpenny gallery seats he wouldn't have been able to reach the stage as easily as he did.

The musical acts were good - very good. There was a ventriloquist, an American Jazz band, and an extremely attractive blonde soprano who burst into rousing choruses of patriotic songs.

Unfortunately for William, and a good ten per cent of the men in the audience, she was joined on stage by a recruiting sergeant, who beckoned them forward. Mesmerised by the blonde, and singing at the top of his voice, William took up the invitation. Happy, drunk and on stage for the first time in his life, he signed the paper that the recruiting sergeant thrust under his nose and found himself an unwilling conscript in Kitchener's New Army.

Megan cried, but her tears softened nothing but her cheeks. William was shipped out that same night. She received a couple of abject, apologetic letters then a postcard emblazoned with a beautiful embroidered bluebird, holding an improbably coloured flower in its beak and a banner proclaiming "A Kiss from France".

A week later an official War Office telegram was delivered to her door in Leyshon Street. *Regret to Inform you· Pte William Powell killed in action.*

His commanding officer wrote to her, a nice enough note that told her little about William's life in the army or the manner of his death. Six lonely, miserable months later she gave birth to William's daughter. She named her Diana after a character in one of Marie Corelli's novels that she'd borrowed from Pontypridd Lending Library.

Megan wasn't one to break under grief. She had two children and a war widow's pension that wouldn't even cover the cost of the mortgage. Ever practical, she asked for, and got, a job scrubbing out the local pub in the early morning.

But even that wasn't enough, so she put two beds in the front parlour, and took in lodgers.

It wasn't easy to work even part-time with little ones to care for and Caterina used Megan's plight as an excuse to leave Graig Avenue and move into Leyshon Street.

Evan paid another visit to the bank manager. He took out a third mortgage on the house, this time for the maximum that the manager wood allow and insisted on giving his mother every pound that he'd raised.

Elizabeth was devastated and not only financially. Not realising how much she'd come to rely on her mother-in-law's assistance with her children, she'd barely tolerated Caterina's presence whilst they'd lived together, but after Caterina left, she felt her loss keenly. That, coupled with the crippling increase in the mortgage repayments, gave her yet another reason to feel rejected and ill used by Evan's family.

Bethan was six, Haydn five, Eddie two and Maud a baby when their grandmother moved into their Aunt Megan's house. They missed her warmth, her love and her cuddles, but fortunately Megan's house was within easy walking distance even for small legs, and for once in his life Evan stood up to Elizabeth, overrode all her objections and actively encouraged his children to visit his mother and sister-in-law.

Much to Elizabeth's chagrin Evan also developed the habit of dropping into Megan's whenever he walked the Graig hill. The neighbours began to fall silent when Elizabeth passed. She sensed fingers pointing at her behind her back, whispers following her when she left the local shops. She didn't need her Uncle John Joseph to tell her that, in Graig terms,

"Evan had pushed his feet under Megan's table".

As jealousy took its insidious hold, Elizabeth reacted in typical martyred fashion. She became colder and at the same time, a more efficient housewife. Whatever else was being said she made certain that no one could cast a critical eye at her house or her children.

———

Everything and everyone within the confines of her terraced walls shone and sparkled as only daily rubbing and scrubbing could make them.

In time the inevitable happened, the gossip mongers tired of talking about Megan and Evan, and turned their attention to other things. But Megan, young, attractive, footloose and fancy free, was never out of the limelight for long. Interest in Evan was superseded by interest in Megan's lodgers particularity one Sam Brown, an American sailor turned collier who'd made his way to Pontypridd via Bute Street, Cardiff, and the first black man to live on the Graig.

Caterina's presence in Leyshon Street kept Megan just the right side of respectability - just - because other gentlemen callers beside Evan and Megan's brother Huw found their way to her door.

The most frequent visitor was Harry Griffiths, a corner shop keeper. By Pontypridd standards Harry was comfortably off; by Graig standards he was a millionaire. Popular and well loved by his customers because he and his father had almost bankrupted themselves by financing the grocery credit accounts of the miners during the crippling hungry strikes of the twenties. He could do no wrong in the eyes of his neighbours. Megan couldn't have picked a better, "gentleman friend" if she'd tried. He was married, but the gossip had long since discovered that it was a marriage in name only as his wife refused to give him "his rights".

They lived above his shop which was housed in a large square building that dominated the corner of the Graig hill and Factory Lane.

Old Mrs Evans, who lived in rooms above the fish and chip shop opposite, saw him pulling the curtains of the box room less than a week after his wedding, and it wasn't long before everyone on the Graig became acquainted with the Griffiths' sleeping habits.

Mrs Evans continued her reports at regular intervals. The old iron single bedstead in the box room acquired a fresh coat of paint and a blue spread. Harry's clothes were hung on hooks behind the door, and a rag rug laid over the bare floorboards.

Mrs Evans was obliged to adjust her hours, and change to a later bedtime when Harry took to eating supper every evening with Megan in Leyshon Street, but then, as she whispered to Annie Jones who worked in the fish shop, "A man's entitled to a bit of comfort, and if he can't get it at home, who can blame him for straying".

Certainly not the women whose credit was stretched by Harry when their husbands fell sick or were put on "short time" by the pit owners.

Megan had steeled herself to face worse. Fingers were pointed, but not unkindly. Only Elizabeth gave her the cold shoulder, but the relationship between her and Elizabeth was already so strained, Megan barely noticed the difference.

The war widows on the Graig generally fell into one of two categories. There were those who became embittered, afraid to love anyone, man, woman or child, lest they suffer loss again, and there were those like Megan who were prepared to reach out to anyone who needed them, hoping that in so doing so they would, in some small way assuage their grief.

Megan found enough love and understanding for everyone she came into contact with. Her children, her mother-and brother-in-law, her nieces and nephews, her lodgers, her friends, her neighbours - her generosity became a byword on the Graig and an object of Elizabeth's scorn.

When Caterina died after contracting pneumonia Elizabeth expected her children to stop visiting Leyshon Street, but if anything their visits became more frequent. It was as if Caterina's death drew the children, Evan and Megan closer, and shut out Elizabeth all the more.

Caterina had always been the one to contact Elizabeth, and invite her to all the family births, deaths, marriages and celebrations. After she died Megan never climbed the hill as far as Elizabeth's house again, although she cleaned the Graig Hotel, which was practicality on the corner of Graig Avenue, six mornings a week, including, much to Elizabeth's disgust - Sunday mornings.

Bethan, like her brothers and sister learned early in life that if she wanted anything other than plain food and carbolic soap and water she would get it in Leyshon Street, not at home.

After Caterina's death Megan assumed the role of family confidante that had been Caterina's. And it was Megan who presented Bethan with her first lipstick and pair of real silk stockings, on her all-important fourteenth birthday. Thrilled, Bethan had rushed home to show them off. Tight-lipped, Elizabeth took them from Bethan's trembling hands and threw them into the kitchen stove.

Bethan retreated sobbing to the bedroom she shared with Maud, and later, when Evan came home from work, he wormed what had happened out of her.

He said nothing to either his wife or his daughter, but on pay day Elizabeth's housekeeping was short by the amount he'd taken to replace Megan's gifts. Elizabeth learned her lesson. From that day forward she confined her disapproval of Megan and her presents to verbal lashings, nothing more.

Whenever Bethan, Maud or the boys returned from Megan's with something in their hands, Elizabeth would enquire coldly if it had "been bought with Harry Griffiths' money".

The children too learned their lesson. They hid the presents Megan gave them and ceased speaking about their aunt, their cousins and the visits they made to Leyshon Street in their mother's presence.

So Bethan and her brothers and sister grew up, unwilling participants in a conspiracy of silence. Bethan learned about subterfuge before she even went to school. Whenever she did anything she knew her mother would disapprove of she ran to Caterina and later to Megan who would make it come right. She knew she could count on her aunt and grandmother to mend her torn dresses or replace the pennies she lost on the way to the shops. They wiped her tears, and slipped her a few coins for treats and school outings when Elizabeth wouldn't, and until Bethan left home at fourteen years and three months old to work as a skivvy in Llwynypia Hospital she never questioned how her Aunt Megan, a widow with two children of her own could afford to be so generous to her nieces and nephews.

And even when she was old enough to look at Harry Griffiths and see the answer in his frequent visits, she couldn't find it in her heart to condemn her aunt.

She loved Megan far too much to do that.

Catrin Collier was born and brought up in Pontypridd. She lives in Swansea with her husband, three cats and whichever of her children choose to visit.
Visit her website at www.catrincollier.co.uk.

HISTORICAL
Glyndwr - Book 1 the Foretold Son

Hearts of Gold
One Blue Moon
A Silver Lining
All That Glitters
Such Sweet Sorrow
Past Remembering
Broken Rainbows
Spoils of War
Magda's Daughter
Bobby's Girl

Swansea Girls
Swansea Summer
Homecoming

Beggars & Choosers
Winners & Losers
Sinners & Shadows
Finders & Keepers
Tiger Bay Blues
Tiger Ragtime

One Last Summer

Long Road to Baghdad
Winds of Eden

Scorpion Sunset

The Tsar's Dragons
Princes and Peasants
A Dragon's Legacy

CRIME (as Katherine John)
Trevor Joseph series
Without Trace
Midnight Murders
Murder of a Dead Man
Black Daffodil
A Well Deserved Murder
Destruction of Evidence
The Vanished

By Any Other Name
The Amber Knight
The Defeated Aristocrat

MODERN FICTION (as Caro French)
The Farcreek Trilogy
Lady Luck
Lady Lay
Lady Chance

Quick Reads
Black eyed Devils - Catrin Collier
The Corpse's Tale - Katherine John

Short Stories as Catrin Collier
Poppies at the Well
Christmas Eve at the Workhouse
Not Quite Leningrad